EVEN THE WEAKEST WOMAN WAS DANGEROUS

Faro narrowed his eyes against the glare of sun-on-sand, and quickly scanned the arena, focusing immediately on the girl who was his target.

It looked as if she were trying to hide behind her long, golden hair. The effect made her seem curiously vulnerable. He paused a moment, assessing her, and saw nothing to change his original ideas about her. She was helpless.

She was his.

He stifled an abortive feeling of pity, and strode out onto the sand. He gave her a moment to stare at him, make her own assessment, and contemplate the smile of hate on his face. He wanted her to be afraid.

He glanced around the arena, to make sure that there were no other threats. Then he charged. He knew better than to give her time to organize her power of conjuration, or to plan a defense. Even the weakest woman was dangerous, because of her magic. First he had to knock her down and out. Then pluck her eyes out. Then break her arms. Only then could he afford to start playing with her. To give the Queen her show.

He closed on the prey. She stared at him, frightened. She gestured. And in a single instant, the ever-fickle fates turned the tables on him . . . .

She had, after all, come to fight.

If I Pay Thee Not In Gold

Piers Anthony
Mercedes Lackey

BAEN

• Chapter 1

Xylina ignored the hum of whispered conversation that followed her as she wound her way through the crowded bodies in the bazaar. She kept her head high, pretending there was nothing more on her mind than the perfectly ordinary purchase of food. But her muscles were knotted with tension and she really would rather have been back in her home.

This task was ordinary for her, anyway, though odd or eccentric for any other woman. She sometimes wondered if she was the only Mazonite in the city who did not have at least one male slave to tend to the domestic chores. The bazaar thronged with male slaves, sent on the same errand she was performing herself. They were draped in the loose, soft, pastel tunics of household servants. The few freedmen who had permission to be in the marketplace at this hour were in black, and barefoot so that in theory they could not run very fast if they committed some crime.

The women in Xylina's immediate vicinity were leather-clad fighters in suede body-wrappings and trews, bearing combat-scars and the marks of armor and weaponry. Others were the heads of households, in their severe linen or samite tunics and breeches, the uniform of the workaday world for those who had property. For those who did not, dress was whatever the woman could conjure; in Xylina's case, a simple drape of soft mage-cloth. She had intended dark blue, but it had come out a soft sapphire. Whatever the color, it marked her as poverty-stricken; no female of substance wore mage-cloth.

1

Then again, there was no disgrace in being poor. That was not what the others were whispering about. She knew what they were saying, those scarred and hardened warriors who murmured to each other like gossiping kitchen-slaves; she'd heard it all before.

... coward ... fool ...

... soft ... weakling ...

... cursed ...

"Mama!" cried out a child; by the shrill voice, a very young one, too young to know better than to shout in public. "Mama! Look! She has hair like a *man!*"

Snickers and sly, sideways looks followed that innocent exclamation—and muffled laughter from those male slaves in the bazaar who were not in the company of their mistresses. Xylina continued to hold her chin up, despite the flush she felt spreading from her ears to her cheeks until her whole face burned. There was nothing else she could do; she did have hair like some pampered male leisure-companion, long and luxuriant and well-cared-for, cascading from her head to her waist in a curtain of gold silk. It represented a tiny defiance, another mark of her difference from the rest of them. Most Mazonites cut their hair short, or even shaved their heads. A banner such as hers was an invitation to an enemy, a weapon he could use against the wearer. Only one or two Mazonites Xylina had ever seen wore their hair longer than to the shoulders, and they had been warriors of such surpassing excellence that they flaunted their skill in this manner. Let he who dared, try to touch those tresses!

One of those had been her mother, Elibet ... and that was why Xylina wore her own hair this way.

She bent over a cart full of fresh vegetables, glad of a chance to hide her blushes. Someone nearby spoke, with an audible sniff of contempt.

"Dresses like a pretty little dancing-boy, too. You'd think she'd have the decency to bind those breasts." It made no difference that binding her embarrassingly full bosom made it hurt, and that nothing could be done about her slender waist and round hips. *She* was at fault for the way she looked, as if she had deliberately conjured up her appearance. Everything was held against her. "Girl's a disgrace," the harsh voice continued. "Gives the freedmen ideas."

Xylina's blush deepened, then faded. What was the point? It wasn't as if this were the first time.

"Well," drawled another, a voice Xylina recognized as Panterra. She dared a glance aside, and saw that Panterra wore the uniform of the Queen's army, with the insignia of an officer. She'd bullied the younger girls of the neighborhood for years, and now was presumably bullying them in the Queen's army. "At least we won't have to put up with her little airs and graces for much longer. She goes to the arena tomorrow. Xantippe's scheduled it." There was a snicker. "Should be quite a show."

Xylina felt her blood turning to ice, and her muscles knotted even tighter. She was perfectly well aware of both the date and hour of her woman-trial, for she had scheduled it herself. But to hear about it on the street only reminded her, harshly, of what it meant.

"It's about damned time!" the first woman said acidly. "The little bitch's been flouncing around the city for three years now, putting it off, while decent girls her age did their trials and began acting like responsible citizens!"

The two of them moved off deeper into the bazaar, and if Panterra made any reply, it was lost in the general crowd noise. Xylina made her meager choices, ignoring the avid—and perhaps, slyly gloating—interest of the slave minding the cart. Her stomach knotted; her depression deepened. Especially after seeing how little her coins would buy. A tiny summer squash, a handful of insect-scarred damson plums; that was all she could afford.

She moved on, grateful that the only other purchase she needed to make was a small goat-cheese and a loaf of bread. No point in lingering to look at anything; she would spend her last coin on the bread. That, and the growing threat that she would be exiled as a coward if she didn't undergo the rite, had prompted her to finally schedule her woman-trial.

She had sustained herself as long as she could, but the past year—in fact, the past several years—had not been the life of ease Panterra's friend seemed to think it was. Oh, her ability to conjure was a lot more formidable than anyone guessed, and she could produce evanescent luxuries enough to sate anyone, but they were fleeting things, vanishing within a day, and conjured food nourished no one. It was, however, one reason why she was so slim— eking out her limited resources with conjurations.

She wondered why she had bothered. Mostly, it was habit, she supposed; the habits of the day overpowering the wish to end it all when the sun went down and the gloom of night added to her own gloom. Then, one dark gray morning several months ago, she had awakened to the realization that she had just turned sixteen, and very soon now the Queen's officers would be enforcing the law against avoiding the woman-trial. Her time was running out. Within weeks she would have to fight for her life, or be exiled for cowardice.

There was nothing left to sell but the tiny house itself, her bed, and a few household items. Not even clothing or utensils, tools or furniture; all that she conjured when she woke, and in the evening it was all gone, and she had to conjure it again. The possessions her mother had left her had long since been worn out, used up, or sold a little at a time.

The buzz of conversation around her increased, as she bought her cheese and bread, and the covert stares became open. Although the afternoon was hot, Xylina's skin felt chilled by all the hostile glances. And she was no little bewildered, holding back tears, which would have been unwomanly.

She didn't know more than a tenth of these people, if that, she thought. She tried to keep her eyes fixed in some vague middle-distance, with a lump in her throat, and her heart sinking to the soles of her sandals. Why were they all staring at her? Why did they all hate her? She hadn't done anything to them—

But she knew the answer. If she hadn't done anything, her mother surely had, simply by being obstinate enough to bear her child in defiance of the curse.

Never mind that the curse—if indeed, there really *was* a curse—was more a matter of myth and hearsay than recorded fact. Xylina's mother had gone to the Queen's own library of chronicles, and had been unable to find anything but a vague hint about it. Something about a barbarian shaman who immolated himself in the midst of his articles of power, rather than endure capture by Xylina's great-great-grandmother, and had hurled his curse at her from the heart of the fire. The chronicler of the time had not thought much of this "curse" except as a kind of joke, proving the superstitious nature of the barbarian men. Everyone knew curses had no strength against a Mazonite. Her very ability to wield the magics of conjuration granted the Mazonite immunity from such petty nonsense as "curses."

Xylina's mother, when she first realized she was with child, had scoffed at such superstitious drivel as a curse, and had refused to give the thing any credence. And while she lived, she had sheltered Xylina even from the knowledge that it existed.

But when Xylina's mother had been crushed by a fall of stone during an earthquake—and when the family fortunes had taken an abrupt turn for the worse, as the earthquake turned what had been productive farmland into an arid desert by turning the course of a river and stopping up a spring—and when a plague had killed most of the slaves in the month following—that was when the whispers of "curse" had surfaced again, and not even Marcus, her faithful steward and protector, could keep her from hearing them.

" . . . curse . . . "

The word rang out amid the babble, as Xylina turned towards home again; as did the reply, spoken loudly enough that she could not avoid hearing it.

"We'd better hope the curse takes *only* her!" said an age-harshened voice. "Or hadn't you heard the whole of it?"

"Only the part about 'child of the fifth generation, ill-luck touches all who touch her,'" replied the original speaker.

"Not just those who touch her—" the second said, grimly.

Xylina forgot about politeness, and simply shoved her way through the crowd to escape the hateful words. But she could not erase them from her memory, where they repeated in a pitiless refrain. She remembered the first time she had seen the words—on a sheet of paper pinned to her door one morning, paper that proved its conjured origin by dissolving into mist by noon.

I send you doom in your own seed, twisted monster of depravity. I send you a child of the fifth generation. Ill-luck touches all who touch her; those who dare to love her see their doom in her eyes. Child of the tempest, child of the whirlwind, destined for the teeth of the dragon; fate casts his dice at her feet. As death follows the child, upheaval follows in the woman's wake, and nothing is the same where she has passed.

She blinked stinging eyes, determined not to show the tiniest bit of emotion. If ever there was a reason to think she was the cause of every bit of the troubles that had dogged her heels all her life, there was the confirmation of it. Her mother had ignored the warning.

And she died, said the insidious little voice in her mind. *So did Marcus. So will anyone else who cares about you. You're better off dead, you know.*

She reached the sanctuary of her home—a stone building of two rooms in the poorest quarter of town, with a tiny paved court in the rear and a high wall around the whole.

That wall, and the pump and trough in the courtyard, showed what it had originally been: the stable attached to her mother's larger townhouse, where they had kept her mother's horse and her own pony. Originally, the "rooms" had been two large box-stalls. Her mother's horse had been a nasty gelding, inclined to bite; hence the partitioning of the stable into two rooms with a wall between them. Later the doorway had been cut in the wall, when she and Marcus had moved into the building.

Now the townhouse lay on the other side of two walls: the original wall that had hidden the sight and smell of horses from those in the garden, and a wall that had been put in place three years ago, when the freedmen had been given permission to expand their quarter.

Xylina's mother had been dead for several years at that point, and there had been no one left but herself, Marcus, and two other slaves she'd had to sell. She had wanted to free them—but she had no choice. The value of property in this part of town plummeted as soon as house-owners learned what direction the expansion would take. Xylina had been planning to sell her mother's house anyway, but suddenly she found she would be getting much less for it than she had hoped. What had been a valuable townhouse had dropped to a tenth of its original price.

She had sold it, nevertheless. She and Marcus had needed the money from the sale of it and the other two house-slaves because Marcus had been terribly ill, the wasting disease that would take his life when she was thirteen. A consortium of freedmen had bought the house, and once they had bought all of the property they could afford, the Queen ordered the new wall erected to seal off their quarter from the rest of the town. The new wall, to confine the freedmen within their own place after curfew, then rose a full arms'-length above the rear section of the old, head-high wall that had surrounded the little stable-yard.

She and Marcus had taken what was left of their belongings to the stable. Then she had encountered unexpected

kindness from a source she would never have believed. The
wall was built by the freedmen themselves—and some of
them, it seemed, knew Marcus. On the very day they were
to move out of the townhouse, a round dozen of them had
appeared from the quarter, scrubbed the stable down to
the stone inside and out, contrived a little outdoor kitchen
in the courtyard, and cut the doorway between the two
rooms. All that was left was for the two of them to move in.
The freedmen had worked in haste and silence, as if afraid
they might be caught in their charity, and would not stay for
thanks. Xylina had been too young to feel anything but
gratitude.

For that reason, when from time to time the sound of
coarse revelry drifted over the wall, Xylina chose to ignore
it. This afternoon was one of those times. Hoarse male
voices shouted at one another, slurred with drink. Utensils
clattered, and the savory smell of rich foods wafted in on
the breeze.

She winced at the clamor, but there was no point in getting upset about it. There was nothing she could do. Had
she been wealthy and powerful she could have sent her
own slaves into the quarter to enforce the rules of silence,
or demand that the Queen do so. She was neither wealthy,
nor powerful; she had more rights than a slave, but no way
to enforce them.

And besides, some of those men might be the ones who
had helped her.

Instead of wasting her energy in anger, she used it in
conjuration. If this was to be her last night—if she died in
her trial-by-combat—she was determined to enjoy it to the
best of her ability.

Half the bread and cheese went into the tight wooden
box that served as a pantry, to be saved for breakfast. The
rest, with what was left of her barley and the squash she had
bought, would be her supper.

But not alone . . .

She gathered her concentration and her power, and

began to conjure. Magic flowed from her hands, visible and glowing in the dusk like a misty rainbow. It swirled and danced, sparkled with a joy she could not feel, until it finally solidified into whatever her will directed. As one object materialized, she moved it aside, and went on to the next. While she was conjuring, she would not, could not, think or feel. She could not *feel* and concentrate at the same time.

When she was done, the sliced squash had been joined by rare mushrooms, crisp baby carrots and peas, a lump of fine beef, garlic, ripe olives, and little heaps of expensive herbs, including saffron. The barley had been augmented by superb olive oil in a simple (non-conjured) pot. The best honey and creamiest butter had been conjured up into two more little pots, to spread on her bread with the damsons. The cheese had been joined by two more kinds, both costing far more than the original goat-cheese at the marketplace. By tomorrow night, these delicacies would be gone, of course—but by then, her trial would be over.

And she would probably be dead. . . .

And in any case, she was getting her nourishment from what she had purchased; the conjurations were only to give her a fleeting illusion of lost luxury.

She put the vegetables and meat to cook above her fire of conjured charcoal, set the bread on a grid of conjured wire to warm, and turned her attention to her rooms.

She would make these two rooms into a tiny palace for one night, testing her ability to conjure right up to its limit, something she had never dared do before. Why, she didn't know; perhaps because it would have reminded her too much of Elibet, who had been able to conjure almost anything. Perhaps because the Panterras of the city would have condemned her for flaunting such conjurations.

Before the sun set, scent filled the air—from the conjured oil burning in her lamps. She still had no furniture, but rather than conjure anything that required construction, she magicked up great swaths of colorful silks, and soft, puffy nondescript shapes to lounge upon. Streams of brilliant sparks and plumes of luminescent mist followed her hands as she directed her conjuration across the ceiling and down the walls. Draping the entire outer room in festoons of red and orange and yellow, she worked until the place resembled the inside of a luxurious tent, then conjured up pads of velvety mage-cloth as thick as her thumb to serve as carpeting.

She turned her attention briefly to her food, but it was cooking nicely, so she completed her conjurations in her sleeping-room. This she draped in blues, from sapphire to midnight, and created a huge puff of material, as soft as a cloud, to sleep on. It took up most of the room.

As she completed the last of her conjurations, she felt the last of her power run out, as if it were water and she a jug. For a moment, she was exhilarated. No one she knew had this much power! What she had just done would have taxed the conjuration of anyone but the Queen herself! She had mostly limited herself to creating a length of material to drape around her soft body for clothing, a pallet to sleep on, something to augment her plain, dull food, and wood or charcoal to burn in the winter. She had, infrequently, decorated and lit her sleeping-room and had of course practiced creating small objects of many kinds. Yet she'd had no idea she could conjure this much at once! Her power had grown.

But immediately depression set in again. What did it matter, anyway? Conjured material wasn't *good* for anything permanent. By this time tomorrow it would be gone. Assuming she was still alive to care.

In this subdued state, she ate her dinner—carefully, to make each bite last—and gathered her courage for the difficult task that lay ahead of her.

For when the sun set, she had an appointment with Xantippe, the slave-keeper of the arena, to select her opponent for the fight tomorrow.

"I suppose you know you left it too long," Xantippe said

rudely, as she let Xylina in through a set of double-locked doors set in the yellow stone wall of the arena itself. Xylina had swathed herself in a wrapping of dark cloth, and the dusk itself had hid her from curious eyes as she slipped from shadow to shadow. She had not wanted anyone to see her. The encounter in the bazaar had been bad enough.

Xantíppe brought her down a set of torch-lit stairs, across several corridors, and finally into the slave-quarters. The arena-slaves were kept confined beneath the arena itself, in cells holding one man each. The grizzled, battle-hardened veteran of hundreds of arena-fights glanced at Xylina, who carefully controlled her expression, even though her palms were damp with nervous sweat and her stomach knotted around her illusory meal. She swallowed, hoping she wouldn't vomit with fear. "If you'd come here earlier in the year, like the other girls did, you'd have had a better choice in opponents."

Easier, Xantippe meant. While the men confined here for the women's-trials were never inferior or diseased specimens, there was a certain amount of choice insofar as size or agility went—or rather, there was at New Year's and at Midsummer, the days when Xantippe combed the slave-markets for new stock. Now—the men left were the ones even the bravest girls feared to face, and for good reason.

Most were battle-captives, which meant that they already knew how to fight. And even though they would be facing their opponents bare-handed, that gave them a distinct advantage. They had learned how to kill; had experience in killing. For all their training, the Mazonite girls making their trials-by-combat had never had that experience.

The rest were simply formidable. Damnably formidable.

Forbidden by their keeper to speak, they sat or stood in their cells, staring back at Xylina as she paced the cold, torch-lit stone hall, examining them.

There were around a dozen of them. Fully half of them leaned against the back walls of their cells, staring sullenly at her, despising or hating her, but unwilling to chance punishment for displaying that hatred aggressively. Most of the rest sat on their bunks and stared somewhere over her head, faces blank, eyes unfocused. One or two looked away, carefully, as Xantippe glared at them.

One, however, did not stand at the back of his cell. Instead, he posed defiantly right behind the bars confining him, massive, muscular legs braced apart, fists on his hips, chin up, glaring directly at both of them. Xylina in particular.

She glanced at him, feeling a kind of electric spark leap between them—not of attraction, but of recognition. Here, perhaps, was someone who loathed her as much as she loathed herself.

Hatred struck her like a palpable force, and she stopped, forced almost against her will to return his stare.

He was huge, perhaps the largest man she had ever seen. The top of his shaggy, ill-kempt head loomed high above hers. His shoulders were broader than a prize bull's, his chest as deep and as heavily muscled. Eyes the color of storm-clouds glowered at her from beneath coarse black hair and heavy black brows. Sweat gleamed from the curves of sharply defined muscles in his shoulders, chest, and arms. His blocky face could have been carved from granite, and the scowl-lines seemed permanently graven there. No racing-stallion possessed more powerful legs. His hands, by contrast, were not the hard, heavily calloused implements of labor she had expected, but were manicured, clean, and scrupulously cared for.

Xylina stared back at him, wondering what he saw. Certainly she didn't look like much of an opponent. Small, slim, with full breasts and long, slender legs—wheat-gold hair down to her waist—surely there was nothing in her to inspire such a look of virulent, poisonous malevolence.

And yet she could have been as hardened a warrior as Xantippe, for there was no softening in his expression. If anything, his expression grew crueler as a shadow of a smile crossed his lips.

It was not a pleasant smile—it had no sense of good humor about it. But it did promise horrors if he ever got hold of her. She could well imagine what he had in mind. Rape would be the easiest, simplest thing that he would do to her. She returned his vicious, rage-filled gaze, transfixed, hypnotized by what she saw there.

He wanted to get his hands on her. He lusted not merely for her body, but for the vengeance he would have once he got her. And no one would stop him, if it happened in the arena. In fact, he would be freed and set loose on the border of Mazonia. This was the only time a man had a free hand to strike back without penalty at the women who enslaved him. In this case, at the person of a single girl, not yet officially a woman.

For a girl of the Mazonites had to meet a man in single combat, no holds barred, in the arena. And she had to do so after she began her courses, but before her seventeenth birthday—or face exile. *He* was trained to fight from the moment he was selected for the arena. *She* must prove that not only could she conjure, she could do so under pressure.

Xylina would be allowed to use her formidable ability at conjuration as her chief weapon. She would be permitted to conjure anything she pleased to use as armor or as weaponry. But she had to do whatever she intended before her opponent reached her, and she must use whatever she conjured effectively. If she was to survive.

Her reward would be possession of the man she had conquered, if she didn't kill him, and full citizenship.

It was no secret that many girls were killed in these rites of passage. That was as the Mazonites preferred; there was no place in Mazonia for weaklings. Every woman must be prepared to protect herself, for there would be no one who would protect her, ever, unless and until she grew wealthy enough to buy bodyguards. A weak woman was a liability— even a danger—to the nation.

The fewer women there were who made the passage

from girlhood to womanhood, the fewer there were to share the power and the privilege of citizenship. And the fewer to challenge the Queen to trial-by-conjuration for the right to lead.

Xylina tore her eyes away from the slave's by force of will. Xantippe was watching her with a sardonic smile on her face. Xylina tried not to show how shaken she was, but her stomach fluttered and her knees trembled.

"Like that brute, do you?" the slave-keeper said, with heavy irony. "Sound of wind and limb, I can tell you that much for sure. Would you believe his mistress had him trained as a *scribe?*"

Xylina blinked in surprise, thrown off-guard by the revelation, but said nothing. Xantippe took that as an invitation to continue.

She tapped the bars of the man's cell with the end of her whip; the man inside didn't flinch, or even appear to notice. "Little Faro here used to belong to Euterpe until a few months ago. She had him educated; he was supposed to be her scribe and private secretary." Xantippe grinned maliciously. "She sent him off to the training center. Then he had the poor taste to start growing, and pretty soon he was getting a little too big for his desk. The scribe-teacher got the wind up and sent for her. Euterpe got one look at him, and just about dropped a litter of cats. She called the auctioneers, and they agreed to take him."

She laughed. "Then he got wind of the news that she was going to sell him off, as a common laborer."

She tapped the bars again, sharply this time, to get Faro's attention. He transferred his glare briefly to her.

"Poor Faro. Didn't like the notion of getting those pretty hands all calloused up in the fields, did you? Didn't care for the idea that you weren't going to that soft life after all?"

His lips writhed in a silent snarl, but he said nothing. Xantippe crowed with laughter.

"That was when he went crazy—broke up some furniture and a few heads. Euterpe couldn't get rid of him fast enough." She chuckled and shook her head. "I pity the wench who has to face *him*. A rabbit would have about as much chance against a wolverine, even an experienced arena-fighter."

Xylina felt a moment of pity for the man—small wonder he hated the Mazonites! As a scribe, he would have known that eventually he would probably win his freedom. It was the custom among the Mazonites to free one slave every seven years, and the ones freed were usually those of the artisan ranks. Faro would have been able to sell his services to those who could not afford their own scribe-slaves, to his fellow freedmen, and to the demons who traded with the Mazonites and the freedmen impartially, and who conducted most of the trade that passed the borders of Mazonia.

And there was no reason—other than Euterpe's fear—to demote him from such a position purely on the basis of his size. In fact, before Marcus' illness left him wasted and racked with coughing and pain, he had been as heavily muscled as any arena slave, and he had served Xylina's mother well as scribe and steward. This Faro had been deprived at a single woman's whim of a life of interest and relative ease, and assigned to a much shorter life of back-breaking labor with no prospect for eventual freedom, and all for no fault of his own.

Poor man—she thought, fleetingly. She would hate Mazonites too.

"Well, girl, time is wasting," Xantippe said, interrupting her thoughts. "Which one of these beauties are you going to pick?"

Her sardonic smile said it all—she didn't expect Xylina to survive against any of these slaves. In fact, she expected Xylina to beg for an extension until after Midsummer, when there might be better choices.

Or she expected Xylina to prove herself to be the coward that everyone thought her, and choose exile over the trial. Xantippe had been no friend of Xylina's mother; she would be equally happy to see the daughter go down to either disgrace or death.

If the choice was no choice—

Then Xylina would make it in style, and confound everyone who had branded her a coward. Live or die, it didn't matter. She would show that she was her mother's true daughter, and as brave as any Mazonite alive.

"Him," she said, pointing, and doing her best to keep her hand from trembling. "The one you call 'Faro.' "

And with that, lest she lose control over herself, she turned and left.

She walked back to her tiny home in something of a daze, but as soon as she crossed the threshold, she collapsed across her bed, trembling.

Why had she done that? she wondered. Why?

The lamps burned out in the outer room, leaving her in darkness. The revelry on the other side of the wall had finally given way to exhaustion—either that, or someone with more power than she had sent someone to deal with it. That left her alone in the darkness, with her thoughts, which were as dark and heavy as the night air. As alone and forsaken as if she were the only inhabitant in the city. But then, she had been alone and forsaken for three years. Now there was no one who cared if she lived, and several who would be just as pleased to see that she died.

First her mother—Xylina hadn't been more than six when her mother died, but she remembered Elibet distinctly. A woman who laughed a great deal, with lovely flaxen hair, and whose ability at conjuring was second to no one's but the Queen's. But more than that, a loving presence when darkness brought nightmares, a steadying hand at the right moment. Readier with a smile than a frown, and with a kiss of reward than with a whipping. A golden light that colored every day, and drove away the shadows at night.

Then, all in one horrid day, when the earth itself trembled and shook, all that brightness was gone, forever.

Then Marcus—

He had promised he'd help her train, when her powers came, she remembered bleakly. He had promised he'd make sure she was the best in the arena—that her trial would be the talk of Mazonia.

But he left her too.

Everyone left her.

She killed everything she cared for.

Perhaps that was the reason why she had chosen Faro—because she was better off dead.

What did she have to look forward to, anyway? The last of her money was gone. She'd spent it today, in the bazaar. She might persuade some woman to hire her as a companion and teacher for *her* daughters, but that would be a meager living at best. Other than that, she had no abilities that a well-trained slave could not duplicate.

So why bother to go on? Wouldn't it be better to die? At least—

At least if she were dead, she wouldn't be lonely any more.

She'd thought about killing herself any number of times before this, and for the most part, it had been only accident that had stopped her. There were no bodies of water in the city that were large enough to drown herself in that were not terribly public—which meant she would likely be stopped. There was nothing tall enough to leap from except the towers of the Queen's hall. The idea of hanging herself gave her the horrors; it must be a quick death, and not a slow one.

Not like Marcus, strangling slowly, fighting for each breath ...

She had no money to purchase poison, and didn't think she knew enough about poison to try conjuring it. She could have conjured a knife—and had, a dozen times—but someone always came along before she could use it. In fact, it was as if the same curse that took everyone she loved had conspired to keep her alive against her will.

That, and pride. She couldn't bear to be thought a coward, to disgrace her mother's name. That would be—a betrayal.

But Faro was not likely to be "kind" enough to kill her immediately. She shivered, thinking of his eyes, and all the pent-up venom in his gaze. No, if she simply went through the motions, he would probably do terrible things to her before he killed her. . . .

She had to do more than pretend to fight him, she decided bleakly. She had to humiliate him; make him so angry he forgot what he wanted to do to her, until all he wanted was to kill her. She had to shatter whatever self-control he had until he wasn't thinking anymore.

That wasn't going to be easy; if Euterpe had planned on having him become her scribe, he had to be very intelligent. She would have to keep that in mind.

Odd: for a moment there, in the cells, she had felt something more than his hate. For a moment, she had thought she felt a kind of shock of recognition.

Maybe she did feel something. In a strange way, it was almost as if they were each other's fate, as if something worked to push them at each other. Each of them betrayed, in a way . . . both of them alone. What did he fear? she wondered. She didn't think it was death.

She fell asleep in the midst of those strange speculations, exhausted by the emotional turmoil of the day, and she did not wake until the Queen's guard came to take her to the arena.

• Chapter 2

Faro had not really believed that the slim young girl would choose him as her opponent. When Xantippe paraded the latest contender in front of the cells he had hoped it would happen, of course, but he had not believed. She would have been the ideal opponent: a lamb to his lion. The slender girl with the banner of golden hair was too fragile to even think of coming up against him.

But he could show his hatred and contempt of her, of all her kind, and he had done that much. Xantippe had not punished him for his small defiance, which meant mostly that she didn't care for the girl either. Otherwise she'd have used that whip of hers, for his insolence.

No, he had been certain she wouldn't be *that* foolish. Rape and death was certain for a pampered, frail thing like her. So he simply poured all the bitter rage within his heart into his glare. Yet even as he did so, there had been something that mitigated his emotion. Of course he hated her, as he hated them all, but—

Then the girl had picked him.

To say he was stunned would have been an understatement. He stared after her, wondering what the fickle fates had in store for him this time. Freedom—it was *almost* his! A moment or two in the arena, and he would be free forever! Elation warred with the ever-present rage, and for a moment, won.

But soon it evaporated. As Xantippe went off to lock up behind the girl, he frowned, suddenly wondering just what trickery was behind all this. It couldn't be this easy. The bitches were going to raise his hopes and destroy them

19

again for their amusement. The girl couldn't be as helpless as she looked. Her winsome beauty had to be a trap. For all he knew, she could conjure better than the Queen—or else she was some kind of specially trained fighter. He had heard of those from the other arena-slaves: women (or men, in the outer lands) who looked ordinary, even weak, but could kill with a single hand. Hustlers, sent in to enhance the entertainment of the regal class by humiliating foolishly confident men. Such examples also served to warn *all* men of their place, in case any should be tempted to rebel. Maybe she would take a false fall, pretend to be terrified, weakened, helpless. Then, just as he thought to reap his reward with her luscious little body, zap! and he would find himself a eunuch, as the crowd laughed. Then a slow death as she did all the things to him he had hoped to do to her.

But he knew the answer to that ruse. Steel himself against her insidious, childlike attraction, attack with caution, and pursue without mercy. Make sure she was blind and paralyzed before going between her legs, and never try to kiss her at all. Then break her neck.

Yet when Xantippe returned, she was frowning, and there was nothing in the way she behaved to indicate that kind of trickery.

She looked at him and shook her head, as if she believed it no more than he.

"Crazy," the slave-keeper said, finally. "Crazier than her mother. Or else that curse has addled her brain."

The statement distracted him a little. *Curse?* What would a curse have to do with the girl's woman-trial?

Xantippe regarded him with brooding eyes, not speaking for a long time. He stared right back at her, doing his best to betray nothing of his own thoughts or confusion.

"You, boy," she said, finally. "Barring intervention by a god, you're going to have your freedom out of this. You have to know that."

He nodded, once, slightly. Barely acknowledging that he

had heard her, and that—if he assumed she was telling the truth—she had confirmed his first reaction.

"Fine," she said shortly, almost as if she had not even noticed his nod. "Now listen up. This girl is nothing; she had no training to speak of. This probably looks like it's going to be easy for you, and you're right."

He concealed his surprise, but he finally met Xantippe's eyes. She did not look as if she was trying to fool him in any way, and over the past several weeks, he thought he had learned to read her fairly well. There was none of the slyness that meant she was lying or trying to deceive him. "I don't care how easy it is; I want you to work at this. You're going to have to earn your freedom. The people coming here want a spectacle; the Queen wants a show. Draw it out, you hear me? Make it last, however easy it is, don't let it look easy. Do you understand what I'm saying?"

Once again, he nodded, this time with satisfaction. He would be only too happy to give them their "spectacle." This was his one chance to take his revenge on the entire Mazonite culture, and the girl would not die an easy death.

Perhaps he would break her back first, then—

Lost in his contemplation of a catalog of things he could do to her, he didn't even notice when the slave-keeper left him alone. When he came out of his reverie, and saw that she was no longer standing before his cell, he left his own place before the bars and lay down on his pallet.

Only then did he allow himself to realize that he almost wished that this particular girl hadn't chosen him. She just didn't seem like a typical Mazonite. Suppose she *weren't* a hustler? He would still have to kill her, because if he didn't put on a good show, Xantippe would have him killed anyway. Freeing victors was custom, not law. Where would his vengeance be if he killed an innocent girl the Mazonites didn't like anyway?

Sleep would not come—nor did he particularly want it to. There were too many possibilities for the day ahead.

And what difference could a little lost sleep make? He would have all the days of his free life to make up for it.

Time and time again, he found himself coming back to the same question, a question that obscurely bothered him, although he could not have told why it did.

Why had she chosen *him?*

What had she seen in him that had driven her to pick him? Was she so incredibly self-confident that she could not conceive of her own defeat?

At first, that was a very satisfying notion. Self-confidence to the point of arrogance would explain why her fellow Mazonites seemed set against her, why the slave-keeper clearly wanted her to fail her trial. That kind of attitude made enemies, not friends. And would make his own victory that much more gratifying.

But he was a logical man, and something so very unlikely could not satisfy him for long. And besides, arrogance and self-confidence was not what he had read in those pale blue eyes. A kind of shock, blankness, carefully cloaked fear— he was not certain what he *had* seen there, but it had not been self-confidence.

Whatever it was—it had been as bleak and hopeless as he had felt the day that he learned he was to be turned into a beast at the whim of a stupid woman who could not even write her own name.

Could it possibly be that she had deliberately chosen him, not out of self-confidence, but in the confidence that he represented her certain death?

And what could have led her to do that?

And what evil would he be forced to do, if that were really the way of it? Faro did not hate all women, just the arrogant mistresses. That distinction had not seemed significant, until now.

He stared up at the stone ceiling, wakeful, until dawn.

The Queen settled back in her seat, acknowledging the cheers of her subjects with a slight bow as she took her place in her private box along with her guests. It was somewhat unusual for the Queen to appear at a woman-trial, but so far as she was concerned, this was no ordinary trial.

This girl's mother, Elibet, had come near to challenging the Queen for her right to rule—and only that providential earthquake had prevented a trial-by-combat to determine which of them had that right.

For years she had cherished her hatred of Elibet, but she had been unable to touch the woman's child because of the constant vigilance of Elibet's slave, Marcus. But when the girl turned thirteen, Adria had known that her vengeance would not be delayed much longer. Once Xylina came to take her trials, the Queen could arrange things so that only a miracle would enable her to win. The girl herself had given no indication that Elibet's talent had been inherited.

But that, after all, was what this trial was all about.

Somewhat disappointingly, Xylina had shown no emotion, even though she must be sure that she had no chance—no shock, no dismay. A pity, in a way.

Still, the important thing was what would happen here. The Queen only hoped that the spectacle to come would not be as disappointing as the girl's lack of reaction. Xantippe had assured her that the slave the girl had chosen understood what he must do.

A hush of anticipation suddenly settled over the crowd, and the Queen leaned forward, her attention riveted on the entrance to the arena below her.

Xylina stepped forward, without fanfare, with no words. In accordance with the strictest rules of the trials, she was unclothed and there was nothing about her that could be used as a weapon. Not even a tie to hold back her long hair, which she had arranged to partially cover her breasts. From the flush spreading over the girl's face and neck, she found her nude state profoundly shaming. To that extent her judgment was accurate; the arena seldom saw as uselessly curvaceous a creature as this.

Queen Adria smiled. That flush was encouraging. It said that the girl would probably be foolish enough to first conjure clothing. A potentially fatal mistake.

Across the sands of the arena, a second door opened, and the slave Faro strode through it. Oh yes, he was a fittingly savage specimen!

Faro narrowed his eyes against the glare of sun-on-sand, and quickly scanned the arena, focusing immediately on the girl who was his target.

It looked as if she were trying to hide behind her long, golden hair. The effect made her seem curiously vulnerable. He paused a moment, assessing her, and saw nothing to change his original ideas about her. She was helpless.

She was his.

He stifled an abortive feeling of pity, and strode out onto the sand. He gave her a moment to stare at him, make her own assessment, and contemplate the smile of hate on his face. He wanted her to be afraid.

He glanced quickly around the arena, to make sure that there were no other threats. Then he charged. He knew better than to give her time to organize her power of conjuration, or to plan a defense. Even the weakest woman was dangerous, because of her magic. First he had to knock her down and out. Then pluck out her eyes. Then break her arms. Only then could he afford to start playing with her. To give the Queen her show.

He closed on the prey. She stared at him, frightened. She gestured. And in a single instant, the ever-fickle fates turned the tables on him.

Queen Adria leaned forward in her private box, smiling with anticipation, ignoring the guests on either side. She was waiting for the girl to make her first mistake. Xantippe leaned forward with her, but her other guest, the demon called "Ware," leaned back, his saturnine face enigmatic.

But the eager smile on her face was wiped out in an instant. Instead of making the fatal error of wasting time by conjuring something to cover her nakedness, Xylina fought back—in the best and cleverest way possible.

She conjured lengths of metal, like rods or blunted spears, about as long as her own forearm. They appeared in her hands so quickly that the Queen literally could not see the process of conjuration; they leapt into her grip, and were thrown just as quickly. The girl began hurling them at her opponent before the man had taken more than two steps, somehow producing them and throwing them so rapidly that one was still in the air as another formed in her hands. Her physical expertise was surprising, considering her lack of muscle; she must have trained for this. She had, after all, come to fight. Of course it would take more than lightly thrown rods to save her. Much more. Still, this was not a good sign. The girl was starting to resemble her mother. But no; that had to be a fluke. Her one desperate effort, doomed to failure as the man discovered that it was all she had.

The slave was not prepared for the rain of missiles. He was not even prepared for Xylina to fight. Several of her weapons actually struck his body with dull, meaty thuds, before he realized what was going on and protected his head and face with his arms. But he continued his charge, obviously well aware that the only way to end the potentially deadly hailstorm was to reach the girl and get his hands on her.

He never got the chance.

Xylina changed her target the moment he protected his head, and began hurling her metal bars at the slave's legs. One of them scored as he reached the middle of the arena, tripping him and sending him heavily to the ground. One of the bars made a lucky strike to his lowered head.

He lay there for a moment, half stunned by the blow; moving, but not to any purpose.

At that moment, the huge, dangerous man was completely at Xylina's mercy.

The Queen scowled, taken as much by surprise by the girl's conjurations as her opponent was. She had been incredibly swift and precise, both in her choice of weaponry and in her ability to use it. There had been no warning of anything like this in Xylina's past—

—except that she was Elibet's daughter.

Then, as the slave shook his head and dragged himself to his feet, the girl abolished her conjurations. To the Queen's amazement, she stood waiting for him, seemingly helpless. As if she were refusing to act on her momentary advantage.

What could she be thinking of? Now the slave was angry. He would certainly kill Xylina. The girl had been terminally foolish, failing to finish it when she had her one lucky chance. Was it sheer idiocy—or lack of will? Either was enough to destroy her. This was after all no playground.

Or was it foolish confidence? Well, the slave would quickly test it, and put her down brutally.

If he could. If *she* didn't have something else planned. Adria was no longer willing to bet that the girl was as helpless as she looked.

The Queen bit her lip in vexation. The prudent course would have been to kill the slave before he recovered. Surely the girl couldn't possibly be planning to tame this brute, could she? Admittedly, he was a valuable commodity, and if she made him surrender, he could be worth a nice sum to the impoverished girl. But how could she dare even think of it?

Events were proceeding faster than Adria's thoughts. The slave did not waste any time, once he got to his feet. Again he charged, this time obliquely, and with an eye out for more metal projectiles.

But Xylina did nothing either he or the Queen expected. Instead, she drew her hands through the air, where they filled swiftly with a kind of metal mesh. She cast this net of metallic fibers over him as he rushed her, stepping aside in the manner of a bull-dancer and throwing it at the last possible minute, as if wanting to be certain she hit her target.

She did indeed; as the audience of mixed warriors and their attendant slaves roared with either approval or disbelief, Faro was completely entangled in the netting, staggering away, unbalanced. Xylina dashed in to gather up the edges and jerk the net, throwing her own weight fearlessly backwards as Faro's feet flew out from underneath him. As he fell, she ran to the opposite side of the arena, as far away from him as she could get. And once again abolished her conjuration.

The audience screamed, as at least half of the watchers leapt to their feet. The Queen watched in complete bewilderment, clutching the arms of her chair. What was the girl up to? Was she suicidally soft-hearted? Surely she knew that the man would kill her in a heartbeat now that she had shamed him twice before others. No one could afford this kind of bravado in the arena, not even an experienced fighter!

For the second time, Faro rose, turned, and charged her.

Xylina held out her hands. A torrent of thick, opaque mist rose from the sand. He blundered into it—and she stepped in too. Both of them vanished in the expanding fog. The cloud of conjured smoke filled the center of the arena, too thick to see into.

The crowd fell silent, waiting.

The Queen held her breath. That *must* have been an act of desperation. Xylina's powers must have been running out. She could not hide in there forever. Sooner or later Faro would find her and—

Faro staggered out of the fog.

With Xylina on his back.

The crowd went insane.

There was something in Xylina's hands—something that kept the man from trying to claw her from his shoulders. After a moment, the Queen saw what it was—a loop of fine wire that Xylina had cast around his neck. If he made a single move that she did not like, Xylina could choke him to

death in a breath, or even, if she got the right leverage, slice
his throat. He was as helpless as if she had him bound hand
and foot at her feet.

He staggered to the center of the arena, and stopped
there. Once again, the crowd fell silent—so quiet that Adria
clearly heard the cries of birds above the arena, the barking
of dogs in the streets outside.

Then, slowly, Faro fell to his knees, bowed his head, and
raised his arms in the posture of complete surrender.

Xylina had won. She had tamed the brute man. He had
acknowledged her as his mistress.

But she was not yet finished. She dismounted carefully,
abolished the wire, and faced the audience, her back to
Faro.

Once more, hope surged into Adria's heart. There was
no honor in the arena; the arena-slaves were the dregs of
society. Faro could still kill her and earn his freedom.

But he did nothing.

Now Xylina conjured a simple drape of bright fabric and
wrapped it gracefully around her nude body. As the girl
looked up at the Queen, Adria was startled by her expression—totally blank, as if she were as astonished by this
victory as Adria herself was.

Then Xylina shook her hair forward to hide her face, and
walked slowly to the victor's exit, ignoring the screams of
the crowd, the cowed slave, the flowers and coins that
showered down onto the sand. She walked past Faro, into
the darkness of the doorway.

Faro swallowed experimentally, breathing heavily, and
was a little surprised that there was so little soreness. Xylina
had a delicate touch, it seemed. Her body had been marvelously light, almost childlike—no, light but definitely not
childlike!—yet her touch on the wire about his neck had
been persuasively sure. She certainly could have hurt him,
had she chosen to.

When she dismounted as if he were some strange breed

of horse, and turned away from him, he was well aware that he could still attack and kill her. Surrender was not an absolute, and there was nothing that would say he had violated any code of honor if he struck her down.

But he had his own honor, his own integrity—even if none of these women believed that a slave could have honor.

Besides, he thought with a touch of irony, there was no guarantee that Xylina could not counter a fourth attempt to kill her. Or a fifth, sixth, seventh. She had spared his life—and he was suddenly aware how much he wanted to live, a revelation that had come in the brief moment when she had cut off his breathing and before he had stopped struggling.

Yet she had not really hurt him in any way. She could readily have given him any number of injuries—nothing that would seriously impair his value, but which could have kept him in crippling pain for days or weeks. Just to make her point.

There could be worse mistresses. In fact, he'd had one. This one at least knew the meaning of mercy. That might seem like a weakness, but now he realized that he could live with it. That he *wanted* to live with it.

So when she passed him, silently, her face a blank mask, he acknowledged his indenture to her by rising and following her. He saw the arena keepers already coming out to clean up the ground for the next event. This particular show was over.

As a former arena-slave, he was well aware that he was in a very special case. He was not eligible for freedom within this society, except by special dispensation of the Queen, and his life was tied to Xylina's. If she died, he would be executed. If he wished to live, he must now defend her as savagely as he had fought her.

"Well." Xantippe leaned back in her seat, and gave Adria a long and significant look. "That was certainly—impressive."

"There is no question as to her ability or her nerve," the demon Ware observed, his heavy-lidded eyes betraying nothing. "I do not know when I last saw a more decisive woman-trial." He lounged indolently in his seat, long and elegant fingers toying with the stem of a glass goblet of conjured wine.

The Queen glanced sharply at him, but he did not seem to be exercising his formidable and sharp wit at her expense; he was simply making an observation. Without a doubt, he had seen any number of woman-trials during his life in the city.

She wondered what he was thinking. Demons were tolerated in the city, and in the Mazonite culture as a whole, provided they qualified. They qualified only if they took binding oaths to do no harm, to do nothing to change the existing order, and to serve the Queen personally, bowing to whatever her whim might be. Many demons seemed to find these oaths humiliating, and so shunned Mazonia as a whole. But not Ware.

The Queen found his wit and ironic sense of humor amusing, so long as they were not exercised against her, and he was often her guest. Some of her subjects found his presence unpleasant, even disturbing, but she was not one of them, and she had found his talents useful in the past. She was not certain how old he was—several hundred years, at least. And he was as ornamental as he was witty: graceful as a cat, pale-skinned, dark of hair, with a thin, sculptured face. Only his eyes gave him away for what he was; there was no mistaking the eyes of a demon for anything else. They were a peculiar color: an odd dark red, with golden flecks, like gold-dust floating in rich, unwatered wine—and the human looking into them suddenly felt the weight of every year of his many centuries.

In fact, a human looking into them too long stood a chance of becoming mesmerized by them. That was one of the many powers that demons possessed, powers they were sworn not to use against the women of Mazonia, although they were perfectly free to exercise them at the expense of the freedmen. The demons who swore their oaths to the Queen had a great deal of commerce among the freedmen. They often acted as the Queen's agents in trading outside the borders.

The demons were useful in other ways, such as supplying lifelike female surrogates: a kind of conjured, animated doll, as an outlet for men's primitive urges. Adria had a shrewd idea that a great many of these surrogates bore her face and the faces of other prominent Mazonites. It didn't matter. Whatever the freedmen got into within the walls of their private quarter made no difference to her rule. So long as no one actually dared bring such indiscretions to her attention, she could afford to ignore them. It made the freedmen content with the illusion that they were beyond her control.

Ware had never been anything but a pleasant guest with her, never alluding to any commerce he might have with the freedmen, never being the least insolent to her. Yet, despite the fact that he was as comely as any of the men in her companion-quarters, the Queen felt no attraction for him. Coupling with a demon was forbidden, anathema, the depth of depravity; the very idea made her nauseous. Adria would sooner have coupled with her prize stallion.

"What are you thinking, you monster?" she asked him lightly. "What schemes are running through that ancient head of yours?"

He steepled his hands in front of his chin. "That this is one who bids fair to follow in the footsteps of her so-talented mother," he replied, just as lightly. But the look he sent her was one of warning. "Elibet was a formidable warrior and magician, and she had her supporters, in her day."

Adria felt a cold finger of fear touch her. So Ware knew whom Xylina's mother was! Well, perhaps she should have expected that. He had served her predecessor, and the Queen before her as well. But was he warning her obliquely that Xylina might well challenge Adria's right to rule, as Elibet had been about to do? His advice, when he tendered it, had always been good in the past.

If so, she should take heed of the warning, and do something to eliminate the girl before she got a good idea of her own power, and where it could lead her.

One of the arena-attendants intercepted Xylina as she headed blindly for the street. "My lady—" he said urgently. "You must take this—" He thrust a small leather bag at her, one that jingled dully.

"This" proved to be a small bag of mixed coins, mostly copper, but more money than Xylina had possessed for some time. But where had it come from? She hesitated to take it, looking at him with some confusion. What would it mean if she accepted it? Could she get into some kind of trouble?

Once again, she longed with a feeling indistinguishable from pain for Marcus. Marcus would have known what to do. He would have been able to advise her.

A deep, musical voice behind her gave her the answer she needed. "Those are gifts from the watchers," the unknown man said, with careful neutrality. "This is a kind of reward for a good and entertaining match. Your supporters and admirers tossed coins out along with the flowers. Most of them are probably real; it would be in very poor taste to throw conjured coin. I'm sure there are a few bits of conjured metal in there, thrown by those who lost money in betting against you, but they will have no city stamp upon them; they will simply be blank disks."

Xylina started, and turned to see who had spoken.

It was the slave she had fought, the one called Faro, who was now her property. In her shock, she had forgotten that by defeating him and making him surrender to her, she had claimed him for her own. As, it appeared, she could claim these coins.

"Ah—thank you," she said, taking them from the arena

attendant, who scuttled off, relieved. She looked back at Faro, wondering who had tossed this money—and if they could afford such gifts.

He seemed to read her mind. "Those who showered coins upon you were those who had bet for you to win," he said, with no expression whatsoever. "Considering the odds, they profited well on your performance."

She had heard some of the banter before the fight. Considering the odds, her benefactors could well have afforded a small fortune!

She looked up and down the stone corridor, but the attendant slave had taken himself out of sight, and there seemed to be no one else here at the moment. She looked back at Faro, who stood behind her as impassively as any statue.

Obscurely, she wanted to apologize; she wanted to explain that she hadn't *intended* to win, that all she had wanted was to make him angry enough to kill her quickly. But something had happened out there in the arena; suddenly, some deeper instinct had taken over and made her fight to live instead. Before she quite knew what had happened, she had won.

But no words came out; they couldn't. And he would never have understood. No Mazonite would apologize to a man for defeating him. No Mazonite would apologize to a man for anything.

So, after a moment of frozen indecision, she turned again, and headed for the street, with Faro following along obediently. She took the shortest way home, in a kind of daze, hardly noticing where she went until she found herself on her own shabby street, approaching the front gate to her house.

When they reached her little home, she felt another moment of shame. This was not a place she cared to bring even a slave—but she had no real choice in the matter. It was, after all, the only thing she owned. They had to sleep somewhere.

She opened the gate in the wall and let him in, but instead of immediately following her inside, her new acquisition stood in the tiny forecourt for a moment, fists on his hips, looking at the building. She flushed, embarrassed. He must have been used to much, much better.

Again he spoke, startling her. "If I were in your place, honored lady, I would make a loan, and buy a better house. I would sell this one, if I could, for earnest money, but it would be very important now that many people knew my face—if I were you—to act upon that notoriety and present a prosperous front."

"I'm not sure I understand," she said, carefully. "Would you explain why I should do this?"

She thought she saw him smile slightly, and his mien definitely softened. He stopped looking beyond her and looked directly into her eyes.

"It's not just for comfort," he told her. "Gracious lady, you are a woman now; you have the right to engage in business and make contracts. Selling my services, for instance; I assure you that I have been completely educated in everything a scribe should know. But no one with any money will come *here*. You have to have a house in a decent part of town; you have to look prosperous. In order to make money, you have to look as if you already have it and do not necessarily need it."

She nodded, slowly. That made sense, in an odd kind of way. And speaking of money—

She took the pouch of coins the attendant had given her, and counted out enough to buy both of them food for a good evening meal. "Go to the market, and buy us bread, cheese—a little fruit, and some vegetables," she said, then added, softly, "I'm sorry to use you this way, but—well, you can see—"

"You don't have any other slaves." He looked at her as if her half-apology surprised him, then slowly, almost reluctantly, a faint smile really did appear. It softened his grim features. "That's quite all right, little mistress," he said, and his voice was gentle. "Going to the market is not exactly a hardship. Because I am a scribe I also know how to handle money, and no one will cheat you."

Then, before she could respond to that, he took the coins and headed out on his errand.

She wondered, fleetingly, if he could cook.

Faro awoke in the middle of the night, all his senses alert. Something was wrong.

When he had returned from the marketplace, with far more food than Xylina had expected (having shamelessly used his size and forbidding aspect to frighten vendors into bargain prices), she had astonished him by cooking for both of them. That was just as well, since that was not one of his skills, and he had expected to eat everything raw. In his absence she had conjured a comfortable bed for him, which surprised him yet again.

She was treating him with far more courtesy than he ever remembered being extended to a slave, and he wondered why. He had not always been as suspicious as he was now— and there did not seem to be any guile in this young woman. Perhaps—perhaps he could trust her.

To trust his mistress . . . that was something he had not expected. To be trusted by his mistress—that was something a slave could anticipate. It was the last step before being freed. A trusted slave was one who received responsibility and one who could expect reward for handling it well. But to trust a woman again, when the one who should have rewarded his diligence had betrayed him—no, that was so far from his mind that the idea had never occurred to him until now.

Food had made him sleepy, and the poor district in which the house resided was a quiet one, at least. They had both been exhausted by their mutual ordeal in the arena, and as soon as the sun had set, Xylina had gone to sleep. After making certain that the gate to the street outside was locked, he did the same, setting his bed across the doorway so that no one would be able to get by him. There was something about this situation that felt wrong, and he was taking no chances that she might come to harm.

After all, no matter what his feelings in the matter were, if she died, he would be executed. That would have been tolerable if he hated her; he could have been less than diligent in her defense, and in that devious manner taken her with him. But it was not tolerable now, for a reason he was unable to quite fathom.

He was not certain what had awakened him, until he glanced through the door into the other room, and saw that Xylina's bed was empty. He almost went back to sleep then, assuming that she had left it for the obvious reason, but his feeling of *something wrong* would not leave him. So, instead, he left his own bed and walked softly into the back court, where the little pump and the outdoor kitchen were. He moved quietly, with great care, not certain why, but somehow knowing he should make no noise. The hard-pounded dirt of the courtyard was still warm from the sun beneath his toughened soles, and he reflected that the sun would be unbearably hot in high summer, without a single tree to shade all this stone and bare dirt. Yet another good reason to move.

He eased around the corner of the building, sure that he had heard something odd.

There, he froze in shock.

Xylina was in the middle of the courtyard—kneeling on the hard dirt, as hard as stone. Her long hair covered her face, falling loose about her shoulders.

Weeping.

And in her hands, a knife-blade glittered; from the way she held it, Faro had no doubt that she intended to use it on herself.

The realization that had eluded him before abruptly burst into awareness. Not only did he not hate his new mistress, he cared for her. Not as a man for a woman, of course; that was beyond his aspiration as a slave. But as a family member. As he might care for a child. She was so—so innocent. So much in need of protection. He had to serve and protect her, of course; it was his oath and his duty. But now he realized that he also *wanted* to. That put a significant new perspective on it. He was prepared to die in her defense, as any slave was for his mistress. But now he was prepared to do more than that. He had to keep her alive—which was not the same thing.

His mind swam. What was he to do? If he surprised her, she might plunge the blade into her breast—if he left her alone, she would almost certainly do that anyway. If she died, he died—

And *why*—

She looked up, and saw him, a dark shadow against the white stone. She gasped and froze, like a frightened doe. She had probably forgotten that he was with her now, and took him for an intruder.

That gave him the chance he needed, and he took it. Moving quickly, he leapt to her side and took the blade from her hands. He cast it across the yard, where it hit the wall with a clatter and dropped into the shadows. She remained where she was, paralyzed, looking up at him. She looked dazed, as if she had been sleepwalking—or sleepweeping. He had clearly startled her so much that she was not able to think clearly.

"What in demons-fire did you think you were doing?" he snarled, as if she were another slave and not his mistress.

"I—" she began, then folded in on herself, her shoulders shaking with sobs.

Those sobs cut straight to his heart, cut through all the layers of indifference and self-protection he had built about himself. He forgot himself, his position and hers. She was only a frightened, damaged child—and he responded to that.

He didn't even stop to calculate what he was doing; he just picked her up as if she were a child who had hurt herself, and he smoothed her hair, murmuring comforting things to her, until her weeping subsided into exhaustion. She dropped all of her masks, dazed with her shock and her grief, and the words spilled that explained everything.

Her mother's death—the plague—the constant eroding of her fortunes, and the pain of loss after loss, until even trusted Marcus had died and she was left alone, with no one to advise her and no one to confide in.

Where were her relatives? Surely her mother could not have been without sisters, cousins at least. Or had they been persuaded to leave the child to struggle, completely on her own but for the single slave? And if they had been so persuaded, who had done so?

His suspicious nature was aroused on her behalf. He did not have answers yet—but he would. A slave saw a great deal, and heard more.

He realized that she had stopped talking. She was looking askance at him. She was beginning to realize how far the two of them had transgressed the bounds of mistress/slave association. He couldn't afford to let her do that, right now while she was so vulnerable, because she might try to kill herself again. Yet how could he stop her?

"Faro," she said, and he knew it was coming. "I shouldn't have tried to kill myself. I know why you stopped me."

"You have no good reason to kill yourself now," he said quickly. "You won, today! You became a full Mazonite citizen, and you gained a useful slave. Your lot is already improving, and I will help improve it more. This I swear."

"Yes, that too," she agreed. "I was being hopelessly foolish. Maybe the excitement—I just wasn't thinking it through. But what I meant was that I shouldn't do it while you're here, because then you'll be executed. Tomorrow I'll take you to the border and free you. Then you'll be safe. I— I apologize for not thinking of that before."

"Don't apologize to a slave!" he protested, though that was not his real concern.

Now she gazed at him with a certain wistful insight. "I

think I stopped thinking of you as a slave when you started talking like a scribe. I'm sorry I embarrassed you."

"You're doing it again! Never say you're sorry for a slave's feelings. They don't matter."

She shook her head. "I know you're right, according to our custom. But somehow—"

"I swear never to tell," he said. "I must protect your reputation as I do your person."

"It won't matter, after I free you."

"Don't free me!" he said, anguished.

"But I must, because—"

"I don't want to be freed," he said carefully. "I can not be a freedman in Mazonia, and I would have a worse life elsewhere than I would as your slave. You are a compassionate mistress, and I want to remain with you."

"You don't have to say that, Faro," she said. "I saw your hate for me when I chose you to fight. I thought you would kill me. I—"

"I think I never had a chance. Your powers of conjuration—I've never seen such strength of magic before."

"Oh, surely the Queen—"

"Maybe the Queen," he agreed. "But no lesser person. You are destined for greatness."

"Not with my curse," she said wanly. "But that's not the point. I don't hate you, Faro, and I don't want to humiliate you, or doom you with my fate. So it's best that I free you."

"I don't hate you," he said. "I never hated you. I hated the society. I thought you represented it, but now I know you don't."

She seemed surprised. "Please, Faro, I'm trying to do the right thing. Please tell me the truth."

"Don't ask me, *tell* me!" he snapped.

She smiled, faintly. "Tell me the truth about your feelings, Faro."

So he started talking, unmasking himself as she had unmasked herself. "When you chose me to fight, I knew I had to kill you, or be killed by you. I hated you as the representative of Mazonia, and the barrier to my freedom. But there was a faint doubt. Then we met in the arena, and you beat me—but you didn't kill me. I was ready to die, but you gave me the alternative I had not planned on. My hate had nowhere to go—except the opposite way. I had no neutral setting."

"I don't understand."

He smiled. "I hardly understand it myself. But I think if I can't hate you, I must love you."

"Love me!" she said, startled.

"As a servant," he said quickly. "I would never—"

"Oh. Of course. So you really don't want to go?"

"I really don't. I want to serve you and help you to be the great lady you can be."

She gazed at him. Then her eyes overflowed again. "Oh, Faro, thank you."

"Don't thank a slave!" he said, but this time not harshly. She was incorrigible in this respect.

"Then just hold me, Faro," she said. She smiled briefly through her tears. "I won't tell if you don't."

He held her, not speaking further. What else was there to do?

Eventually, she fell asleep in his arms. He suspected that she had somehow confused him with that long-dead confidant of hers called "Marcus," for he was quite sure she would never have wanted him to know the things she had poured out to him in her bewilderment and long-pent grief. The loss of her mother—the deaths of everyone she knew—the gradual wearing down of her spirit by everincreasing poverty. The incredible nonsense of the curse—and behind it all, something that he was fairly sure she had not recognized. The signs of a steady conspiracy of harassment, meant to break her further.

They had that in common too, then, for surely all the world was ranged against him, and had been from the moment he grew too large for the comfort of his mistress.

Once again, his world realigned. Now it was two against the world—himself, and this battered but still-valiant child.

He rose, took her back into her tiny house, and put her to bed as tenderly as if she were his own child, then took himself back out into the night to stare up at the stars and think. He sat on the warm earth of the courtyard, put his back against the stone wall, and stared at the bright points in the sky.

Small wonder that she had wanted to die. How not, when all the world seemed ranged against her?

He hoped that he had done something concrete about that particular desire; in her exhaustion and near to sleep, still confusing him with Marcus, she had begged him to promise not to leave her again. He had promised— extracting from her the promise not to court death again. She had seemed willing enough to give that pledge, but then had begun to realize what had happened, forcing him to respond more personally. He had done so—and now was glad of it. For himself as well as for her.

He leaned his weight against the wall of the house and contemplated the stars above, wondering now at himself, and not so much about her. He, who had sworn to hate all Mazonites, suddenly found his loyalty bound to one small woman. Was it her amazing mercy in the arena, as he had told her, or was there more? He still wasn't sure. Was it pity? Perhaps in part—and he chuckled a little as he recognized the irony of a slave pitying his mistress. But how could he not pity someone who had suffered such a crushing burden of loneliness for so long?

But it was partly admiration as well. Under that soft exterior, there was a soul of tempered steel. She had *not* broken under all her misfortune; she had adapted and survived. He could admire that. She was smart, and capable, and possessed of phenomenal magic. With a little help, mostly information that she simply did not have, she could become a formidable power in her land.

She could even aspire to the throne, he realized after a moment. And suddenly his thoughts took a whole new turn.

After all, their prosperity was linked. The more wealth she acquired, the more comfort he would enjoy. And if he could somehow get her to take his careful advice, he might be able to guide her to more than just prosperity. Dared he make an arrow of her, aimed at the Queen? Her ability to conjure was certainly formidable enough. That would be no bad thing—to be chief counselor to the Queen. . . .

Few slaves ever had the opportunities that had just presented themselves to him.

In fact, this might just be preferable to freedom, even for one who had not suffered a conversion of emotion. He had been cursing his fates—but now, he wondered. If he had been set free, it would have been to eke out his way as best he could in the lands outside the borders of Mazonia. Was there any need for scribes outside the lands he knew? He had no idea. He might well have wound up scratching out a brutal sort of existence like a barbarian, hunting and scavenging his food, fighting to stay alive. He had spoken from the passion of the moment when he asked her not to free him, but the matter stood up to more dispassionate scrutiny.

Now—he had fallen into the hands of someone who treated her slaves with courtesy and consideration, who listened to his advice and would probably act on it. Someone who valued his training and his intelligence.

In short, Xylina was perhaps the only woman in all of Mazonia who would treat him as a person, and not as a possession; the only one he could serve with a whole soul.

He pondered that for a while, before the demands of his weary body drove him back to his bed, still marveling at how his life had changed.

• Chapter 3

Xylina woke late the next morning, with sun beaming down onto the pale brown, hard-packed dirt of the court outside her room. She felt curiously at peace for the first time since Marcus had died. And why not, after all?

Stretching her arms over her head and enjoying the cool, silken softness of her conjured bed-coverings against her skin, she felt as if some huge burden had been lifted from her shoulders. Or as if she had been ill for a long time, and suddenly woke up healed.

This morning could not possibly have been more different from yesterday morning. She had passed her woman-trial: she was a full woman, and a full citizen. She had a pouch full of coins, she had a slave of her own.

Faro was a good man; that was what was so unbelievable, like something out of a fable. Another like Marcus—someone she could trust to advise her. They had begun as enemies, the deadliest of enemies, but within the course of a day and a night, they had somehow become allies, even friends.

Last night, when she had come so close to finally ending her miserable life, he had convinced her that her life was only beginning. He was the first person ever to show any concern for her since Marcus had died; the first to show her that she had a future. Granted—as an arena-slave, his life was tied to hers, and he had a vested interest in keeping her from killing herself. But there was something more there—a concern that had surprised her, for she had not thought anyone would ever care whether she lived or died again. She had offered to free him, and he had refused: that was a key test. This was the kind of empathy, the kind of friendship, she had with Marcus.

And he had convinced her, with hours of careful conversation and persuasion, that Marcus had not "left" her. Her friend had not abandoned her—not of his own will, at any rate. He pulled out of her memory many recollections of her friend and slave's despair at knowing his days were numbered—and recollections of how he had tried to prepare her for a life alone. Things she had totally forgotten, lost as she was in her own loneliness. Things she was ashamed that she had forgotten.

Where he had gotten this talent for counseling, she had no idea. Perhaps the schooling for scribes included advice on managing difficult mistresses. She was not going to argue about the source, not when it gave her so much more interest in life.

She finally rose, conjured herself a new chiton to pin about herself, then, feeling more interested in how she looked than she had in months, conjured a hot bath for herself. She heard Faro walking about in the courtyard, but the sound was more soothing than disturbing.

Once bathed, she banished her conjuration, which vanished without leaving even a damp spot. A distinct advantage over real water and soap, she thought with a faint smile.

She pinned her newly-conjured length of fabric at her shoulders, and tied it at her waist with another, narrower band, both in shades of blue. Then she stepped out into the courtyard, to see what Faro was up to.

Somewhat to her surprise, she found him examining her yard in minute detail, even pushing one of the two wooden crates she used as a chair up to the shorter wall and peering over it.

"Have you eaten?" she asked, concerned that he had been waiting all this time for her to appear. "I did give you permission to take care of your own meals, didn't I?"

He jumped down from the crate and dusted his hands.

"Yes, mistress, you did, and I have," he replied. It seemed to her, in the aftermath of last night's purging, that his face seemed much more relaxed and open. Probably a good night's sleep had done him as much good as it had her.

So he had eaten. Well, that was a relief. She went to the cupboard-box and extracted the end of a loaf and some cheese for her own meal, then took a cup to pump out some water. Faro intercepted her, taking the cup, pumping the water, and giving her the cup back, full. She took it, with a brief nod of thanks—it had been a very long time since she'd had a slave; having things done for her felt rather odd.

"What were you doing?" she asked, curiously.

"I was examining your property, mistress," he told her, as she seated herself on the other crate and began nibbling her food.

"Do you have any idea of what it might be worth?" she asked. "You did suggest that I should sell it."

"I am not an expert," he replied, standing between her and the sun, so that he was haloed by it. She realized that he was doing that to keep the slanting sunbeams out of her eyes: another little slave service. Probably he didn't realize how the light enhanced him.

"Well, I know that, but you are a trained scribe," she said, with gentle logic. "A scribe has to do many things, at least, that's what I remember. Surely you can give me a general idea."

To her pleased surprise, he chuckled a little. "That is true," he admitted. "And I do have some ideas."

She leaned forward with interest and began to question him closely, and as what he told her gave her some ideas of her own, she asked his advice on them as well. She couldn't help but notice how her interest and enthusiasm pleased and intrigued him. Was she that different a mistress from what he had expected? She was only trying to emulate how she recalled her mother talking with Marcus, who had been her most trusted advisor.

When they had formed a plan about how to dispose of

the house, she began asking his advice on other matters in which she was ignorant—for a trained scribe was much more than simply a secretary for his mistress. He often handled household accounts and management, and he was frequently privy to many of her political and personal secrets. She distinctly remembered Marcus filling those functions for her mother. And now, in the person of Faro, she had someone who could fill them for her.

She shook her head, still bemused by it all. "Oh, Faro, I'm glad I chose you to fight in the arena. If, as you say, I was fated to win, you were the best possible prize I could have won. I was incredibly lucky—because I wasn't thinking of life after the match. I thought there wouldn't be any. What would I have done with one of those other brutes?"

Faro nodded. "I suspect my fortune matches yours. I, too, was not thinking of a life such as this. You are better than I deserve."

She decided not to debate that. Who ever heard of a mistress exchanging compliments with her slave? "I hope it is a sign that my family's curse is over, or was false. I never really believed in it, yet somehow I couldn't quite disbelieve either."

He looked oddly doubtful. "There are curses, and there are curses," he said. "Be careful, mistress."

Later, she sent him out to the bazaar for food for the evening's meal and for breakfast on the morrow, and she felt rather ashamed of having to entrust that to him. "This is below you," she confessed, looking up at his eyes, acutely aware how tiny she was next to him. So strange; hard to believe that she had defeated him, and yet she had. "I wish I had someone else to send to do this."

"You will," he said, firmly. "And in the meantime, I am pleased to serve you this way."

And with that, he took the pouch of coins, and left her alone for the first time this day.

She surveyed her tiny home with new eyes, trying to think of it, not as a home, but as something else. While most of the quarter's inhabitants seemed content to go all the way to the bazaar for what they needed, she had the feeling that they might well welcome something like a small shop here, with foodstuffs—or a bakery. Or perhaps a tavern? That had a great deal of potential, for the last tavern in this quarter had closed when the freedmen expanded their quarter, and bought the building that had housed it.

By the time Faro returned, the bed-clothing that she had conjured the night before had vanished, but she had already produced replacements. They shared a companionable meal, and continued their plotting until after moon-rise, and Xylina went to bed well contented. For the first time in a long while, she slept peacefully and without distressing dreams.

The next day was spent in looking for a new home—and it took the entire day, even after eliminating the poorer and wealthier quarters. She and Faro ate sausage-rolls in the bazaar, without ever going home, until it grew too dark to look any more. They returned home, footsore but content. She conjured new bed-clothing and a foot-bath for each of them, and they both retired to bed. She was so weary she hardly remembered her head touching the pillow. She realized that she felt safe now, because of Faro's presence, and that was another unexpected blessing. It meant that she could sleep relaxed instead of nervous.

In the morning, she bathed and dressed herself with especial care. She could not conceal the fact that she had conjured her clothing, but she *could* conjure something that was as much like what her mother had worn as she could remember. She even dressed her hair in the single, long braid her mother had favored. Thus dressed, as carefully as if she were once again going into combat, she left the house with Faro and headed into the more prosperous quarters of the city.

Then she smiled to herself. Dressing for combat? She had fought naked! Nevertheless, she liked the notion. She was no longer facing arena combat, but the purchase of a house was likely to entail combat-like negotiations.

Acting on Faro's advice, Xylina went to an information-monger at the bazaar and for a tiny coin bought information on property brokers. As the info-monger recited the kind of property they handled and who their latest clients were, she watched Faro out of the corner of her eye. He shook his head, very subtly, when a broker was not what they were looking for.

At length though, he nodded. She memorized that broker's address, and the process continued.

They ended up with three brokers who seemed likely, and since one was very close to the bazaar, Xylina decided to visit her that moment. With Faro following behind, at the proper, respectful distance, she sought out the address.

As a house, she and Faro had decided that her property was not worth much—but as the site for a small business, say a shop selling staples like flour and salt, or a bakery, or even a tiny tavern, in a neighborhood which had none of these things, it might be worth more. The fact that it had its own pump and well made it much more valuable as a commercial property. The outer room and the forecourt could be made into the shop or tavern, and the rear into living quarters for a woman and two or three slaves. Or, even more likely, it could be run completely by slaves, and the woman who owned them and the property need not set foot there except to collect the profits.

She would not have the connections in the court to gain permission to change her house from a living-place to a residence and commercial establishment. Someone else might. If she found the right broker, she might even be able to trade the value of the place as initial payment on a better home without actually having to sell it. That was what Faro thought, and it seemed worth the trial. What could they lose? The worst that could happen would be that the broker wasn't interested in such a proposal. The best, that she would want it immediately. And it wasn't as if they had a great deal to move. In fact, there wasn't anything that Faro couldn't carry to a new establishment in one trip. All else was conjuration.

The broker, one Antione Sibelle, recognized her immediately, as soon as she entered the woman's office. That was something she had not expected.

"By the stars, it's Xylina, isn't it? The young woman who bested that monster in the arena a few days ago?" The middle-aged broker rose from behind her desk to give Xylina the handclasp of full citizens, as her secretary remained impassively at his own desk in an unobtrusive corner. Xylina envied her the smooth linen tunic and breeches she wore, the same blue as her own outfit, but obviously not conjured. Other than that, the broker was past her prime, but still fit; her neat, short hair about half gray and half brown, and the hand that took Xylina's was the hand of a worker, not soft, but strong.

The office was a very pleasant place. It was paved with blue and white tiles, and with plastered walls that had been painted with murals of girls exercising and playing games in a garden. It was well-ventilated by a window which took up nearly the entire wall that looked out onto a garden. It was cool, and comfortable, and faintly scented with flowers from the garden. It held the broker's desk, a case holding rolled documents behind that desk, a chair for the broker and one for her desk, and a smaller desk and chair in the corner for the broker's slave-scribe.

One day, perhaps, Xylina would have an office like this, and Faro would have a comfortable desk of his own from which to oversee her business.

"A thousand congratulations, Xylina—" she continued effusively. Her clasp was firm and dry; it felt honest, at least. "My goodness, people are still talking about you! And you are Elibet Harmonia's daughter, aren't you?" At Xylina's nod, she smiled. "Ah, I thought so! Tragic, that earthquake—your mother wasn't the only loss, though she was sorely missed. You have her look about you, the hair especially, but I'm sure you know that."

Xylina tried not to show her feeling of sudden disorientation, but it was a difficult task. She hadn't expected this total stranger to be privy to her own past—or at least, part of it. Antione spoke of her mother as if she had known her personally. That was more than Xylina could say, in many ways. She had only observed her mother as a child; this woman had known her as one adult knows another.

"Here, come, take a seat—" the broker said, directing her to the armless chair before the simple wooden desk. "Now, what can I do for you?"

"I'd like to sell my house and purchase something in either the Moonflower or the Blue Lantern quarters," she said carefully. She and Faro had paced the entire city yesterday after all, she with an eye to the property itself, and he talking to the household slaves and getting a feel for what the relative prices were in the area. It was in those two quarters—one old and currently out of fashion, one that was brand-new, built to hold the people who had been displaced by those whose houses had been bought by the freedmen, and who had not yet gained a fashionable status—they found properties that seemed to match their requirements.

"As it happens, I am handling homes in both those districts," Antione replied, her brown eyes shrewd and knowing. "You have a good eye for value, Xylina; I consider both those quarters to be undervalued at the moment. Now, what have you to offer me?"

Now came the moment of truth. How persuasive could she be? She would not admit that her home had once been a stable; it no longer looked as if it had housed horses. "At the moment," she admitted, "my property is very modest. I have my own house—which is at the edge of the Wall, in the Glass Fountain quarter. It is not a very big house, but it does have some potential, I think."

Here she outlined what she and Faro had discussed: how

it could be converted to a variety of businesses, and which businesses the quarter lacked. Antione pursed her lips thoughtfully and nodded, her graying curls bobbing over her broad forehead, as she followed Xylina's arguments.

"If one put in any kind of commercial establishment one would have to get the permission of the Queen or her council first," Antione pointed out. "But—that is really a small matter, and I suspect it could be done at the level of the privy secretary. It seems to me that it wouldn't be a handicap. I could manage such permission, for instance."

Xylina smiled, for this was just exactly what Faro had told her. Already his advice had proved apt.

Then she added the idea that had come to her as they walked here this morning. It was an elaboration on something she and Faro had discussed, but she felt rather proud of it. "If it were my investment, I would put in a tavern," she concluded. "The advantage would be twofold. A woman who was only a fair magician could sell conjured wine and beer, for there is no one in that quarter who is able to conjure any such thing. That is one way that one could actually sell conjurations legally, I think."

"And one can become just as drunk on a conjuration," Antione said, with a chuckle. "Indeed, I am told that the hangover is not so bad! There are several taverns selling only conjured products in the city."

"There was another notion that I had. Perhaps if someone with court connections could obtain permission from the Queen to cut a door in the wall at the back, she could also sell her conjurations to the freedmen," Xylina said, feeling a bit audacious. "Perhaps I am wrong, but it seems to me that this would actually be safer than the current policy of allowing the demons to sell them real liquor, for if they became drunk and threatened to cause trouble, the woman in question could simply banish her own conjuration—"

"Rendering them instantly sober!" Antione applauded her forethought. "You are correct, this does make your property potentially far more valuable than it would appear." She scratched her temple, and seemed to be thinking. "Were you actually willing to trade the property outright for a portion of the price of a new residence?"

Xylina nodded, wondering if she dared hope—

"Well, as it happens, I personally have a small house in Moonflower Quarter which I own and have been renting." She made a face of distaste. "I have not been as successful at getting the kind of tenants as I had hoped for. It has been vacant for three months now; it might be smaller than you had wanted, but the advantage is that it is already furnished."

Xylina caught her breath, then schooled her face in an expression of simple interest. Furnished? That meant that she would never have to conjure furnishings again. That daily chore might have sharpened her conjuration facility, but she would be glad to let it go. For furnishings, she would be willing to sacrifice a fair amount of space.

"Now as it happens, my own daughter has about the level of conjuration such a venture as your tavern would require," Antione continued, her eyes bright with speculation. "She has been working for me, but to be frank, her talents do not extend to managing property."

"This would be easy," Xylina ventured. "She could install one of her slaves there to run the tavern—or perhaps two slaves—she could conjure the liquor, and need only oversee the slaves. I think she could do well, and I am sure you have all the court connections you would need to get permission for both the tavern and the door to be cut in the wall behind it." She tilted her head a little to one side, thinking aloud. "In fact, the front room faces on the forecourt, and the rear on the rear court and the Wall. The freedmen and the women of Glass Fountain need never even see each other; each could be served from a different room."

Antione nodded, her eyes showing her surprise, as if she had not expected that Xylina would be so shrewd. "If you would be willing to trade your property for a third of the value of my little house, I think you could move in today."

Careful, Xylina warned herself. *Be careful. Don't act too quickly—* Yet she was excited; she wanted to jump up and shout her agreement. This was everything she had wanted, and more than she had dared hope for.

"I would like to see it first, of course," she said, as if a little reluctant.

"Well, of course!" Antione signaled to her slave, who brought her a wrought-iron key from a rack of many such keys on the side of his desk. "I'll take you there myself, this instant. I would like to put this all in motion as soon as possible, if you are in agreement."

Xylina hardly noticed the walk, so eager was she to see the house. She already wanted it, no matter how shabby it was, for it certainly could not be poorer than the place where she lived now.

Antione led her to a wrought-iron gate in a high stone wall, a gate that had spikes built into the top to prevent anyone from climbing it. She opened the gate with a flourish, and Xylina and Faro followed her inside, finding them in the forecourt of the little house. The house was, indeed, smaller than most of the others in Moonflower—in fact, a woman with any sizable household would not have been comfortable there.

The forecourt was cool and lovely, however, shaded by two enormous plane-trees, and paved with blue slate. The single door, built into the blank wall, led into the house proper.

The first room was the public or common room; it was furnished with two couches and two chairs, with small tables beside each. It was lit from a skylight, since no one would have any windows looking out on the gate and the street beyond. There was a small room just off this common room that had been fitted up as an office. Then came the sleeping quarters, coming off a hall that led from the common room to the kitchen at the rear. It only had one real bedroom, with quarters for three slaves, or a combination of children and slaves. The kitchen and the bathing room were at the rear, and then came a door that led out into the rear court and the gardens there.

But it did have that lovely little forecourt that boasted a tiny fountain. The kitchen-garden in the rear court, although overgrown and weedy, had an apple tree and a fishpond and, unlike her old place, was supplied with water from the aqueducts, which meant no more pumping, or wondering if the well had been contaminated.

The bathing room was a *real* bathing room with running water from the city aqueducts, a luxury Xylina had not enjoyed in years. This meant that if she wanted a real bath, with real water, she could have one—and Faro could bathe without her having to conjure a bath for him, if ever she was too busy to do so.

The furniture was of very plain, heavy wood—much scarred by ill-use, and a little chewed upon. It would need new cushions, eventually, but she could live with the ones there now, once they had been cleaned and beaten free of the dust and hair that was thick upon them.

"The previous tenant kept dogs," Antione said, distastefully. "Very large dogs. The neighbors complained about the barking until I had to ask her to leave."

Xylina nodded wisely, and pointed out the defects in the place: that the hypocaust, and the stove that heated its air, would need a thorough cleaning; that the fishpond had been allowed to go dry and would need restocking; that the dogs had made a mess of the kitchen-garden, not to mention the furniture.

But she was in love with the little place, and it didn't take much persuasion on Antione's part to get her to agree to the bargain.

They returned to her office, and the slave was sent to the Office of Records to obtain both deeds. After that, it was simply a matter of signatures, and it was accomplished.

Faro had followed her everywhere, of course, and she had done her best to ignore his presence as Antione had ignored the presence of her own slaves. But once the gate was closed behind the two of them, Xylina dropped her pretense.

"Well?" she demanded, eagerly. "What do you think? Did we do well?"

He didn't answer immediately, but then, he never did. He had the habit of thinking over everything he was going to say before he said it, and she had gotten used to that. He examined the forecourt carefully, with the same attention he had given to her old home.

"There were some other defects you didn't catch," he said, finally. "I think the stove in the kitchen will need repairing before it can be used, and there's some settling in the foundation that has caused some cracks in the wall in the kitchen. But on the whole—this was a good choice. There's only one thing I truly don't like."

"What is that?" she asked, puzzled.

"This place—it's not defensible," he replied, with a frown. "It's terribly open. There are no bars on the windows in the rear, and only the front gate locks. I can see no way to put a lock or a bar upon the front door without making it look like the door to a prison. If I'm to guard you effectively, I will have to sleep in your chamber, across your threshold."

She dismissed that with a shrug. "I can't imagine who would want to break in here," she said. "It isn't as if we have any real valuables to steal. And what profit would there be in attacking me?"

He looked at her strangely, as if he could very readily think of a reason someone would want to attack her, but he didn't share it. "Very well then, little mistress," he said. "Would you like me to get your belongings, then go to the market for you?"

"Please," she said, gratefully. "I know you've said many times that you don't mind doing such a lowly task, but I feel I should keep thanking you. You really are above a task like that, and as soon as I can afford a kitchen-slave, you can stop doing this."

As she said this, she couldn't help feeling a heady sense of exhilaration at the very thought. As soon as she could afford a kitchen-slave. Not "if," but "when." She never could have dreamed of that before.

He smiled: one of his rare, slow smiles. "Think nothing of it, little mistress," he said. "After all, you are undertaking the lowly task of cooking, which I would dread to attempt."

"I don't mind," she replied earnestly. "I did it for myself and Marcus; I don't mind doing it for both of us."

But Faro frowned, as if he were determined that she should not have to cook much longer. "I am also going to see while I'm there if I can't find someone in need of a scribe—a freedman, perhaps. There is no sense in wasting time in getting employment for my skills. I am valuable, little mistress; I would be remiss if I did not begin to augment your income at once."

This man was incredible; he seemed to take more care of her than she did of herself. She smiled and shook her head. "You amaze me, Faro. Sometimes—sometimes I wonder how it is that our fates crossed. Whether it really was luck. You know, I wondered before I fell asleep last night if it was Marcus who somehow sent you to me."

"Sometimes I wonder myself, little mistress," he replied, in complete seriousness, "and the same thought occurred to me last night. Who knows? No one knows at all what is on the other side of death. Perhaps the dead can influence the living, or the fates of the living." And with those surprising words, he turned to go. She had given him the charge of most of their money on the second day of their association, saying that she saw no need to issue it to him in driblets as if he couldn't be trusted with it. He had been touched; she had seen it in his eyes.

Then, just before he left her alone, he turned back. "Please lock the gate after me, little mistress," he said, and there was real worry darkening his eyes. "I would feel better."

"All right," she said. "If you insist."

She followed him to the gate and locked it after him. She watched him until he was out of sight, then turned and surveyed her new home.

She wanted to sing or dance. She could hardly believe the way her life had turned.

But rather than celebrating, she had better get herself to work. She did not have the slaves another woman might have to clean this place. She must do as much of it as she could by herself, until Faro returned to help her.

The first and easiest thing was to scrub the walls and floor of the three rooms they would be using first: the kitchen, the bathing-room, and the mistress's bedroom.

This task would be the easiest, because she would be using conjured soap, sponges, and water. There would be no need to carry and mop up water, rinse sponges, or deal with the same sloppy mess that a slave would need to. In place of mops, she would tie conjured sponges to the ends of sticks, with no worry about whether they wore out. It didn't matter; she could always conjure more.

It was amazing, the amount of filth that came pouring off the walls as she conjured soapy water to cover them and scrubbed with her impromptu mops. When she banished the water and soap, the dirt remained on the floor, in the form of dry dust, easy to sweep away. She dealt with the filthy floors the same way, except that she swept most of the dirty water out the door before banishing it.

It was hard work, but no harder than she was used to. She thought wryly as she scrubbed the walls and floor, putting good effort and muscle into the work, that such chores could serve as adjuncts to training. Certainly after a few days of this, her back, shoulders and arms would have had a thorough workout. Her efforts to clean her prior residence had improved her physical vigor; she had thought that to be an incidental benefit, until she started throwing rods in the arena.

But these activities were, of course, for men. Even though there were plenty of women too poor to afford more than one slave for chores, none of them would ever admit it. It was not fitting for a woman to perform menial chores, publicly. Xylina could not afford to be seen doing so, and therefore the courtyard would have to wait until Faro had time to deal with it. Dirt went out into the back gardens, where no eye would see her doing the work of a slave.

An amazing amount of time passed before she realized it. Faro still had not returned by mid-afternoon, so she gleaned the last wild vegetables from the garden and made a kind of meal of them. While she ate, she gave thought to how best she could lease out Faro's services, for although her old home had paid for part of this new one, there was still a debt of real gold to be discharged, and at the moment Faro's size and skill were all she had to earn that gold.

The surest, quickest way to discharge that debt would be to send him right back to the arena, but she had considered that idea and discarded it without a second thought. He had saved her life; she would not gamble his.

So, one way to capitalize on their new—and probably short-lived—notoriety would be to trade on the obvious and the invisible. The obvious was Faro's size and strength; the invisible, his skills. There would probably be any number of women who would pay to see the hulking brute write a letter. It would, in fact, be a considerable novelty, like a talking horse.

At least it would for a while. Long enough, she hoped, to be able to buy seed for the garden, food for their meals, and to make small payments on her debt.

And then what?

Well, she might let him pursue that idea of hiring his services to the men of the quarter. Or—perhaps there might be more gold in novelty. Perhaps other, wealthier women would pay to have Faro discourse with them at parties and the like. Would he be willing to do recitations? She had no doubt he could memorize any kind of poetry or prose, and he was probably familiar with the works of some of the philosophers. The question was, would he be willing to play the role of the educated freak? This plan would need his cooperation; it would come to nothing if he sat in a sullen silence and would not perform.

And speaking of performing—what of the theater? Could she, perhaps, put on some kind of extravaganza for paid ticket holders? Could she have him make a recitation while hoisting weights above his head or something of the sort? A silly idea, perhaps, but sillier ideas had succeeded in the past.

She finally tired by late afternoon, and banished the last of her cleaning conjurations. She wandered through the rooms of her house, admiring the work she had done, noting how much more still needed to be done. Her path brought her out eventually to the outer court and the gate.

She had not been paying a great deal of attention to anything other than the things she knew needed repairing, calculating how much could be done by Faro under her direction, and how much each repair would cost. The westering sun cast long, dark shadows across the court; the overshadowing walls on either side made it very dark. She was considering conjuring lights for the evening when a hint of movement where there should not have been any made her freeze.

It was that which saved her life. She glanced down, and a rush of mingled fear and horror galvanized her, knotting her stomach and sending a thrill of cold up her spine. The adder, coiled and waiting almost at her feet, poised to strike, hesitated.

Xylina did not.

Reacting quickly, she conjured a waist-high plate of metal between her and the serpent. The adder struck at the same instant, and hit the metal plate.

Xylina pushed the plate over onto the snake in the moment when it lay stretched out and vulnerable. Then, powered by hysterical energy, she conjured another massive weight of material right on top of it, flattening the creature against the ground. This was definitely not the time to charitably abolish her conjurations.

She sat down abruptly on the broken masonry surrounding one of the half-dead trees, her energy leaving her. She gasped for breath, as if she had been running. Her knees were weak and her stomach had turned to water. She was grateful now for the setting sun, the heavy shadows in the courtyard, that hid her from anyone looking in.

Her mind was completely blank, and she simply sat where she was, shaking, until full dusk. Then she banished her conjurations, and stared at the flattened remains of the deadly adder.

There were no snakes in the city. Not even in the temple of the Oracle, whose symbol was a serpent. A small army of vermin-catcher slaves, accompanied by their terriers and ferrets, kept the city free of rats, snakes, and even helped keep the mouse population within bounds. There *were no* snakes in the city; there had been no snake-holes anywhere in the courtyard.

Someone must have brought it here and set it loose.

Someone wanted her dead.

But who? And almost as importantly, *why?*

• Chapter 4

Xylina gazed at the wreck of her garden. The sun, directly overhead, illuminated the damage pitilessly. Healthy young plants, carefully nurtured from seed and watered by hand, had been uprooted and scattered across their beds. Young vegetables had been partially devoured. Something—or someone—had gotten into it while she and Faro had been out, and had destroyed all the tender young plants, leaving them to wilt in the sun. By the time the two of them had returned, it was too late to save any of them. They would have to be planted over again from seedlings rather than seed, or else they wouldn't mature before the first frost. It had been almost too late when they planted the seeds, though luck had been with them, and the plants had grown quickly.

Replacing the plants would cost money; money they could ill-afford. Not replacing them meant that they would have to buy all of their food, instead of only staples and meat.

"Guinea-fowl," Faro grunted, straightening from his examination of the ruined beds. "Look, you can see the scratch-marks, and the places where they pecked the seedlings apart. Somebody turned a whole flock of guinea-fowl loose here. Too bad there aren't still some birds here; you could have conjured a net over them, and they're tasty eating."

Xylina shook her head, feeling doom descend upon her, a heavy weight settling on her heart.

"What's the matter, little mistress?" Faro asked, evidently reading her sinking spirit from her expression.

61

"It's the curse," she blurted, without thinking. "I'm cursed, nothing I do is going to turn out right! I'm going to destroy anyone who is with me!"

Faro turned to give her a reproving look from under his black brows. He left the ruined garden and came to stand at her side, blocking her view of the withered plants. "That's rot," he said shortly. "I don't believe in magic curses, and neither should you. I *do* believe in accursed people: people who send snakes through gates and toss guinea-hens over a wall. Someone wants to ruin you, but that doesn't mean you're under some kind of a mythical influence."

Xylina shook her head again, wishing she could believe him. But why else would snakes appear where there were none, or guinea-hens mysteriously turn up, destroy only *her* garden, and vanish again? Surely if anyone else had seen the fowls, or had their gardens destroyed, the neighborhood would be buzzing with indignant homeowners.

Faro seemed to be reading her mind. "Guinea-fowl can fly," he reminded her. "And you don't know what they did in other yards; just because the neighbors aren't out in the street complaining, doesn't mean they didn't have problems. *They* have garden-slaves to chase off the pests; you don't. The birds might still *be* here, in someone else's garden. For that matter, they might have been some fool's idea of watch-fowl or garden-birds, and they might have gone home again. You don't know that you were the only one with a garden the birds invaded."

But she knew he was wrong, deep in her heart. She knew that if she asked—which she would not—she would learn that no one else's property had been touched, that no one had a flock of guinea-hens, and that no one had seen or heard anything. She knew this, because no one else's gate had been smeared by paint-wielding vandals, no one else had rotting garbage appear overnight in their forecourt, and no one else had to fortify her doors and windows against intruders when she left. She had asked her neighbors if they had been disturbed, or had even seen or heard anything, after the first two incidents, and had been rewarded with odd looks and denials of trouble.

"This is such a quiet neighborhood," said one woman. "We've never had any incidents before."

Before you moved here . . . That was what had been implied. After that, she had stopped asking.

The protection against intruders, at least, had been relatively easy. She simply conjured massive metal plates in front of all of the portals whenever she and Faro left, and banished them when she returned. But the first time it had happened, she and Faro had come home to find all their food ruined, the cushions on the furniture slashed, and the walls smeared with filth. It had taken them several days to clean up the mess, and both of them had been forced to take up needle and thread to mend the slashes. At least she was buying this place and not leasing it. She would not have to account to the owner for the damage done.

Once again, Faro seemed to be able to read her mind, understand her doubts and fears without any word from her. "People did all these things, Xylina," he said gently. "Not curses, not gods, not some invisible hand. People. Someone does not want you to succeed, and that is the simple truth. You have an enemy—it might even be an enemy you 'inherited' from your mother, a feud you did not even know about. It would suit that person for you to believe in this curse, for that would make you despair and look no further for your persecutor. I think this has been going on for years; that was my concern when I first joined you. Your misfortunes seemed too patterned. But I didn't want to alarm you with a foolish conjecture. Now it no longer seems foolish."

That made sense—and as his words sank in, they made Xylina angry. She raised her chin defiantly, taking heart from Faro's inexorable logic. "You're right, Faro," she replied, letting her anger burn away her despair. "You're right. I don't know who or what is behind this—but—but

I'll be *damned* if I give in to her! No one is going to break me!"

Faro nodded approvingly, and his expression lightened just a little.

She surveyed the ruined garden with renewed determination. "Well, we'll just have to get seedlings somewhere," she said. "We can't just give up the garden; we need the food we can grow ourselves." She thought for a moment. "Don't farmers thin out their plants now and again?" she asked her slave. "Wouldn't seedlings be cheaper from them rather than from a nursery?"

"I'd have to go outside the city, but I think you are correct, little mistress," he replied, his eyes warming. "We would have to take a chance that the roots had been damaged, but if I speak with another slave, we might be able to persuade him to take some care in the thinning and in his selections. It would probably take several days, one day for each kind of seedling we need—"

"Why would you have to go outside the city?" she asked. "Couldn't you make an arrangement with the farmers' slaves in the city market? I've often seen slaves there rather than the farmers themselves. Couldn't you ask them to bring in seedlings with the vegetables, perhaps pay them some in advance?"

Faro smiled slowly. "I could indeed," he said, dusting off his hands on his tunic and nodding. "I think that would be the best plan. And one slave will often do something for another that he would not for his mistress. If I make it clear that my own future dinners depend on this garden, it may make a distinct difference."

"Then, once we have replanted, I can conjure a metal net to protect the whole garden—yes, and the forecourt too," she told him with grim determination. "That will let the sun in and keep birds—and anyone else—out. And perhaps I had best conjure some kind of barrier at the front gate as well. Then the only damage they will be able to do will be to the exterior wall."

"Good." Faro nodded approval of all her remedies. "We have an appointment tonight, do we not?" he asked, abruptly changing the subject, as was his habit when he felt the subject had been exhausted.

Xylina grimaced; in the ruin of her garden, she had forgotten that. Though they had gone to the marketplace every day to post Faro's services for hire, the men of the quarter had been as yet unwilling to use him as a scribe, and the women were not sufficiently intrigued by his novelty value to become steady customers. She had finally interested one of those wealthy women in her idea of using Faro as a kind of entertainment; he would "perform" at a party held by the noted merchant Klyta Stylina tonight. Faro had not particularly liked the idea, but he had to admit it was a faster way of making their payments on this new dwelling than hiring himself out as a market-scribe. At a copper-bit for every letter and tally, it would take a long time before the house was paid for—and the plan he and Xylina had formulated together depended on being able to buy more slaves and educate them, so that she could supply a cadre of trained scribes to anyone who might need them. Merchants just setting up a new business for instance, or someone whose trusted scribe had become ill or had died. He was convinced there was a need for such a cadre; she was inclined to agree with him.

But none of this would take place while they were struggling simply to make ends meet.

"What are you going to do?" she asked. "I need to know if I'm going to act properly as a foil for your performance. You know, I am sorry to be asking you to perform like some kind of trained dog—and that is exactly what they will think of you. I'm not very comfortable seeing you in that role, and I wish I didn't have to do this."

"I know," Faro replied, and his smile turned feral. "I honor you for that, little mistress. Well, since they are expecting a trained dog, I think we should give them a trained wolf instead. It will give them a feeling of threat—

that if you were not there to restrain me, I would tear them to pieces."

The unbidden thought occurred to her, *As he would, if he had the chance.* The smile alone said it all. Xylina was under no illusions; Faro hated the Mazonites for what they had done to him. He honored only her, for seeing him as an intelligent being, for treating him as one. And perhaps for being a friend. She sensed, beneath his words, as they spoke of many things in the hours between dusk and bed-time, that he had been as lonely as she in his own way. He was just too different from the other men to have taken pleasure in the gossip and harem-politics, in the trifles of dress and status in the household. His mind ranged as far as the stars; confining it to the narrow rooms of the harem was as wrong as clipping a falcon's wings and making an orna-ment of him. If he had been a woman, she had no doubt that he would have been Queen by now.

He did not fit; neither did she. Perhaps that was why they were friends as well as mistress and slave. She could not see a slave without seeing the man beneath the livery, the human being. And she was only one step above slavery herself, having endured poverty for so long. Indeed, most slaves were better off than she had been, in the last year before her woman-trial.

In this, she knew that she was following in her mother's footsteps, for her mother had been Marcus' friend as well as his owner, and had not been wealthy or even moderately secure.

"I shall recite some of Arimis' *History of the Slave Revolt,* unless you choose otherwise," he continued. "That will titil-late them with my boldness. Then I shall lift some weights, until I have alarmed them. Then I shall complete the per-formance by lifting some large weight, with you perched atop it all."

She nodded. "What if I conjured the weight for you?" she asked, tilting her head to one side. "If there are to be performing creatures here, we might as well both perform." She hoped that this offer would ease the bitter feelings he must be experiencing, but to her surprise he saw something more in the idea.

"That is an excellent thought, little mistress," he exclaimed. "Think of all the powerful women who will be at this affair—and you will demonstrate your ability at conjuration before them all, in the guise of an entertainment! They will be impressed, and when they have time to think about it, they will also wonder just how good you truly are, and wonder why they have heard and seen nothing of you except for the arena-trial."

That gave her pause. "But what if one of them is this unknown enemy?" she ventured. "Would this not make her angrier, and inclined to make further attempts to destroy us?"

"We learned one thing in our training as gladiators," he told her, his eyes darkening with unpleasant memories. "The one who loses his temper loses the fight. You saw for yourself how that was true, for if I had not lost my temper, I think I might have won even against you." He paused. "It is my habit to review my experiences, and I think that if I had grabbed one of your rods from the air and hurled it instantly back at you, I might have scored. You must see that no other opponent ever has the chance to use your conjurations against you; you must be ready to abolish them the moment they leave your hands." He paused again, and she nodded, appreciating the advice. Then he continued. "If this enemy of yours is among these women, I think it would be a good thing to goad her into losing her temper, for it will make her rash and inclined to act before she plans. Thus, she will expose herself, and we can take steps to rid our path of her."

Xylina tucked a strand of hair behind her ear, and looked up at him, thoughtfully. "Are you really sorry you did not win?" she asked quietly.

He took a deep breath, and his expression stilled for a moment. She knew she should not have asked; he had, after all, tacitly reassured her on that point. Yet reassurance seemed to be something she could never quite completely accept, so she had to verify it, and re-verify it.

"At the time—yes," he said, after a moment of silence. "But now—" He shook his head. "I cannot say. If it had been anyone but you, I think I would rather have died. No, I would have died. I would have kept attacking until she was forced to kill me. You—were so different, I did not know how to react. Often I still don't. When you leaped onto my back, naked, and I felt your breasts and thighs on my body, my will to fight faded, even before you conjured the wire at my neck." He gave her a crooked smile. "So now you know the great secret, little mistress."

So he had been aware of her body. She had not thought of that at the time. Her femininity had been a weapon! There was more, much more, unsaid between them. But she would not force him to say those things aloud.

"We should go back to the marketplace before the farm-slaves return to their mistresses," she said instead. "Then we can get something done about new seedlings before we need to prepare for this exhibition. Should I conjure you a costume, do you think?"

"Yes to both," he replied, going to hold open the door to the house for her. "And we should discuss the costume on the way to the marketplace."

The evening was an unqualified success, at least insofar as Xylina was concerned. Faro had given a performance that pleased both of them, and had caused a sensation for their hostess, who obviously had not expected that the slave would be nearly so erudite. The guests had gasped at the demonstration of weight-lifting, which had ended with Faro hoisting an incredible pile of "stone" pieces, with Xylina enthroned atop them in a slab-sided "chair" of her own conjuration. Perhaps they suspected that Xylina had conjured a very light form of stone; it didn't matter. The women had expressed their enjoyment to the wealthy merchant at being entertained in such a surprising way. And the hostess had, in her turn, expressed her pleasure in the form of an addition to the agreed-upon fee.

The entertainment had been held in a spacious and luxurious room just off an inner garden of the villa. The perfumes of night-blossoming flowers mingled with the subtle odors of incense and the exotic fruits and wines that the merchant served her guests. The guests half-reclined on scarlet upholstered couches, and were served by discreet slaves, who saw to it that the cups remained full and the bowls of fruit at their sides remained cool and attractive. Perfumed lanterns lit the room, giving them plenty of light to perform by, yet preserving a warm intimacy. There were about a dozen guests, all of them dressed in rich fabrics and heavy gold jewelry. Some of it might have been conjured, but Xylina doubted it. She didn't recognize any of them, but she hadn't really expected to—the women who had attended her mother's entertainments were not generally found among the merchants, but among the artists and warriors.

Faro had somehow managed to keep the proper balance between "dangerous" and "under control." Xylina had no idea how he had managed, for she had seen the signs of anger on him many times during the evening. But then, she had trod a fine line herself as she was drawn into the conversation. She had tried to convey the impression that she was much more aware of city gossip and the current tales among the wealthy Mazonites than she actually was. Her conjurations had at least impressed many of the merchants and wealthy women at the party; she had caught more than one of them regarding her with an appraising look when they thought her attention was elsewhere.

But there was no indication that any of these women were her mysterious enemy, or even if indeed such an enemy existed.

Both she and Faro were as tired at the end of the entertainment as if they had been putting in a day of heavy manual labor. Conjuration took a great deal out of a woman in terms of concentration, if nothing else. And Faro had been lifting huge weights until his bare torso, minimally decorated with "gold" chains, ran with sweat.

Her attention was not always on the conversation; when it drifted away from her, she found herself coming back to the mysterious enemy, and the threat she posed. At least the house was secured against intruders; it would take an entire crew of workers with a winch and levers to remove the conjured stone blocking the front gate, and another crew with metal-saws to cut through the conjured mesh she had created between the top of the outer walls and the house itself. The good thing about protecting her property with conjurations was that she could, quite literally, create something that had no entrance. Where there was no way to get in naturally, an intruder would have to create one at a huge cost in terms of time and effort.

Faro continued to amuse the women reclining on their couches around him with his audacious replies to their questions for more than an hour after their performance was over and the hostess had paid Xylina. But as the night lengthened and the party showed no signs of breaking up, she gave Faro the signal that they should take their leave, and whispered as much to the hostess.

"I'm certain you have things to discuss that you would rather outsiders did not hear, great ladies," Xylina said into a momentary lull in the conversation. "I am, after all, only a very young woman, and by no means could I have anything to contribute to your wise counsels. So with your permission, we will take our leave."

A few of the Mazonites looked as if they would rather have enjoyed Faro's rather caustic wit for a while longer, but as Xylina had expected, they did not object. No "party" was ever held strictly for entertainment; she recalled that quite clearly from her childhood. At some point in the evening, the slaves would be sent away and the women would get down to some serious discussions of politics and business. Often, they were one and the same, and when that was the case, the discussions continued until dawn.

So when she and Faro ventured out into the lamp-lit street outside Klyta Stylina's villa, she was not surprised to look up and see from the stars that it was well past midnight. She pulled her conjured "cloak" a little closer around her shoulders; the air was chill and rather damp, and she shivered as she covered a yawn. She hated to think about getting up at dawn to go down to the market to get the promised seedlings, and to post Faro's services for hire, but one good fee did not make up for possible lost revenue. In fact, she would need every copper-bit of the added gratuity to help ease the financial burden those new seedlings were going to place on their resources.

Strange: here she was worrying about seedlings, gardens—but a short time ago she was ready to die. Sometimes the changes in her life made her feel as if she were astride a runaway horse, being carried on to some unknown destination, whatever her wishes in the matter might be.

There was no one in the street at this hour to see them, so Faro fell in beside her, rather than taking the proper position of a slave, three paces behind his mistress.

"You were excellent, Faro," Xylina told him, warmly and honestly, as they walked slowly to the cross-street that led most directly to their quarter of the city. "I don't know how you managed to keep your temper when some of them asked you about the arena and our fight."

The street was bordered by the walls surrounding the forecourts and front gardens of the expensive villas of this section of the city. Walls of limestone, of granite, of glazed tile and of semi-polished marble loomed high over their heads on either side of the wide, brick-paved street. Those walls were broken from time to time by massive doors, or iron or brass gates; on either side of these portals were lanterns or torches that would burn all night. The tops of the walls would be set with flint-shards, potsherds, broken glass or revolving spikes to ensure the privacy and security of the wealthy owners.

By day, those portals would stand open, allowing the passerby a brief glimpse of luxury, but at night they were closed firmly against those who haunted the night. Mostly those were simply the poor, who prowled the streets at night looking for usable discards. Xylina had done so herself, in the past, finding just enough to make it worth the shame of possibly being seen. But there were thieves, and vandals; there were also the gangs of slaves commanded by renegade women who would do anything for a price. More than one Mazonite had hired such gangs to work as much damage as possible to an enemy or rival. Xylina had seen one or two of those gangs on her own nocturnal expeditions, and had hidden herself in the shadows with her heart in her mouth, waiting for them to pass. She could have defended herself with conjurations, of course, but the shame of being discovered on the street at that time would have haunted her.

And in between such commissions, they took on other "work"; robbing anyone who happened to cross their path. Usually they only robbed any women they encountered, for the penalties for a man to harm a Mazonite in any way—even if he had been commanded to do so by his mistress—were far too high for any of them to take the risk of identification and reprisal. But male slaves, sent out on late errands, were beaten without mercy, and often killed.

The lanterns and torches made puddles of light between the huge stretches of shadow; shadows that could hide almost anything. From over the walls drifted sounds: laughter and talk from the party behind them, then soft music, then another flurry of women's voices in talk and song, then the melody only fountains and falling water could produce. Occasional scents wafted over the walls as well: savory food, incense, the heady perfumes of night-blooming flowers.

The sounds and scents coming over the walls evoked an aura of calm, but the huge blots of shadow evoked the very opposite.

"It was—difficult to remain calm, little mistress," Faro said, long after Xylina had stopped expecting any kind of reply. "One of those women was my former owner."

Xylina noted that he did not say, "former *mistress.*" She did not think that this distinction was an accident. Faro would acknowledge no Mazonite as his mistress except Xylina—that much she was certain of. To call a woman his mistress implied that she had a right to rule him; he would no longer give any Mazonite but her that right.

"I didn't know that," she said, after a long, awkward moment. "If I had, I do not think I would have asked you to perform that way."

To her surprise, he chuckled. "Oh, little mistress, believe me when I tell you that it was much better this way. I think I terrified her all over again. She heard my threats, when they took me away to the arena, of the things I would do to her. She expected me to lunge for her and make those threats good every moment that we were there. I suspect she will insist that all her slaves guard her every step on the way home, and will post more guards around her very bed tonight and every night for some time, certain that I will escape you and come for her." He chuckled again. "All things considered, this is a much better revenge than I could ever have hoped for."

She giggled a little. "Was that the scrawny woman in the gold-tissue, with too many earrings?"

"The same," Faro confirmed.

"She did look as if she expected you to leap on her like a tiger." Xylina had to smile. "I suppose she thought my control of you far from adequate. Because she was failing completely to assign any possibility of self-control to you."

"Exactly," Faro agreed. "And there you have it. Everything I do—or do not do—will be credited to your control of me."

"Such illusion!"

"No illusion, mistress."

He did not seem to be joking. Xylina shook her head as they turned the corner and headed towards their home. "Perhaps Mother was different—perhaps I am simply remembering things wrongly—but I don't remember her ever treating her slaves that way. Certainly she and Marcus talked all the time about everything under the sun, and she listened to his opinions and often followed his advice."

"What happens in private and what happens in public are two different things, little mistress," Faro cautioned. "I am certain that your mother must have acted in the same arrogant fashion as any other Mazonite in public. And you must do the same, if you are going to impress other women with your control, your strength and—"

Whatever else he was about to say was lost, as a hint of movement in the shadows of the street ahead of them made them both stop dead in their tracks.

The lanterns and torches were fewer and farther between here; the blotches of shadow larger and deeper. And there was something in the third pool of shadow from where they now stood.

They remained right where they were, beside one of the lanterns, in the full light. That made it difficult for them to see into the shadows, but impossible for anyone to sneak up on them.

The only sounds were the ones coming over the walls; distant reminders of a different kind of life. Xylina felt her stomach knot, her spine tingle with a premonition of danger. A moment later, the danger manifested.

Impatient for their prey to come to them, the ambushers moved out of concealment and into the lit portion of the street.

There were five men and one woman. The woman hung back, remaining at the edge of the shadow, only the outline of her form revealing that she *was* a woman. The men were all large, roguish-looking, with cruel, hard eyes and the scars of those who had fought others before.

But they were not as big or as muscular as Faro—and none of them had that "arena look," a look as if they longed for death and did not care whether the death was their own or someone else's. They carried no weapons; that was a death-penalty crime for any man without a special permit, even if the weapons weren't used.

They said nothing, nor did they need to. It was obvious that their chosen targets were Faro and his mistress. What they could not have guessed was that the two might oppose their attackers as a team.

For an ordinary man to be armed within the city was death—but a man might carry a stave or a staff, and although the law said that it must be of light, hollow material, easily broken, who was to say what that staff might truly be made of? Especially if it had been conjured and could be banished long before the City Guard arrived at the scene.

No sooner thought than done; Xylina gathered her power from deep within, spread her hands palms up, and conjured a staff as tall as Faro, but made of metal. She staggered a little as it dropped into her hands, but tossed it quickly to the slave.

He took it immediately, casting her a feral grin, and went into a "guard" position with it.

She dropped behind him a step, her heart pounding and her mouth dry, as the ruffians rushed them.

She used the strategy that had been so successful against Faro: conjuring metal rods and hurling them at the legs of their attackers. One went down in mid-charge; two more stumbled but recovered.

The two who had not been stopped hurled themselves at Faro; the other two came for Xylina.

She conjured a metal net and threw it at them, dancing backwards and hoping there were no more of the ruffians behind her. The net ensnared the first of the attackers neatly; the second continued to charge.

Out of the corner of her eye, she saw Faro snap up the tip of his staff, taking the first man to reach him under the chin. The man's head jerked back as the tip connected with a meaty *crack*. He fell over backwards, landing in a limp heap in the street, and did not move.

Now Xylina's second attacker was within arm's-length of her; she changed her tactics and conjured something different: a double-handful of grit that she tossed directly into his face before ducking under his groping arms and getting behind him.

He cried out with pain and his hands flew to his face—but he still had the momentum of his charge, and now Xylina was in a position to add to that.

She did, with a kick to his back that sent him into the wall. He landed heavily against it, hitting it with his head and shoulder. She conjured another heavy rod the length of her forearm, and while he was still dazed, she clubbed him across the back of his skull.

The impact jarred her hand and made her let go of the rod, but it no longer mattered. The man dropped to the bricks like a felled ox, his scalp split open and bleeding.

She heard a sound behind her and ducked, dropping to the ground and tumbling out of the way. Just in time, for the man she had tripped with her rods had recovered—and had one of the rods in his hand. He swung—

Just as she banished her conjuration. How apt Faro's warning about that had been!

The sudden loss of his improvised club startled him—giving her a chance to repeat her trick with the grit. She hit both his eyes with the stuff, and he yelled and stumbled back—right into range of Faro's staff.

Faro dispatched him with careless ease and a blow to the side of the head, and turned his attention back to his other opponent before the clubbed man hit the pavement.

This was when the woman in the shadows made her move.

She left, abandoning her slaves.

Xylina could hardly believe it when the woman whirled and took to her heels, running off into the shadows and leaving her men to fend for themselves and extract themselves as well as they could. But she had no time to congratulate herself on her luck, for the third man came at her, and she was fairly certain that he would not be taken by either the rods or the net, nor would he leave his eyes vulnerable to a handful of grit.

He was fast, charging her like a sprinter, and there was nowhere for her to run.

So she conjured a patch of the most slippery oil she could think of right under his running feet, then dodged to one side as he hit it.

His feet went right out from underneath him and flew up; his head hit the bricks of the street with a sickening *crack*.

He did not get up.

Faro used the moment of distraction as she took out her third opponent to eliminate his second. He drove the tip of the staff into the ruffian's stomach, then brought the other end down on his head. The man went down with a muffled cry.

And the street was suddenly silent.

Quickly Xylina banished her conjurations. The woman *might* come back with the City Guard, and accusations of an armed slave. Faro stared at his empty hands for an eyeblink, then quickly dusted them on his tunic.

"Are you all right?" he asked Xylina carefully, as if he were having trouble forming words. She could understand that; she trembled from head to toe with reaction, and she was not certain she would be able to talk coherently for several moments yet. She simply nodded, and walked cautiously over to one of their felled opponents. Felled? No—she realized as she touched the first one that she and Faro had done their work too well. There would be no one to question, for they had killed all five.

As she had half-expected, there were no badges or livery, or anything else to identify the woman who was their mistress. Their tunics were plain, coarse linen. There were no brands of ownership on them, either. Even the slave-rings about their necks were cheap iron bands with no writing on them.

She straightened from her examination to see that Faro was doing the same thing—checking the dead men for anything that could identify them.

Or was he?

She took a closer look—to see that he was rifling the bodies!

"What are you *doing?*" she blurted in astonishment.

He calmly pocketed the pouch of coins the man had worn about his neck, and went on to the next victim. "I am doing to them what they were going to do to us," he said with calm logic. "The pickings seem to be meager, but every copper-bit we take from them is one we didn't have before."

She stared at him for a moment with open mouth— then, as the logic behind his statement sank in, she closed her mouth with a snap, and bent again to do the same to the man at her feet.

After all, these men might have been hired by her unknown enemy. And if that was the case—

Well, it was poetic justice to have the one who had destroyed her precious garden in the first place help to pay for the new plants.

• Chapter 5

Walking quickly, they reached their home without further incident—which was just as well, since Xylina did not think she had the energy to defend herself twice in one night. Her magic was strong; stronger than she had ever guessed, but her resources were not infinite. It took strength of character and purpose and all her concentration to banish her conjurations, and she was so grateful to see her bed that she could have kissed the pillow. Right now, she did not want to think about the attack, what it meant, what it would mean for the future. All she wanted to do right now was to sleep.

But first—she had been rolling around on the street and sweating like a horse; she needed a wash of some kind. The water in the reservoir above the bathing-room would still be warm from the sun, and there would be water enough for both of them if she was careful. Faro had been sleeping in the chamber just outside hers, but as she made a sketchy sort of bath to rid herself of the dirt and sweat of their fight, she heard him dragging his thick pallet out of his own chamber and into hers.

For a moment she was surprised, then as she bent to brush the street-dust out of her long hair, she chided herself. His action seemed more than sensible on second thought, and she was surprised she hadn't thought of it for herself. When she appeared at the door of her chamber, he was just arranging his pallet where anyone trying to get in would have to fall over him to get to her. Now she was rather grateful that her bed-chamber had no windows, only ventilation slits less than a thumb-breadth with metal mesh over them to keep out vermin. The only real way to get into the bedroom was via the door.

He glanced up, and she thought perhaps he looked a little guilty. Or possibly embarrassed, worried that he might have something other than protection on his mind. She wasn't concerned; he could do nothing to her that she did not want, and she truly did not think that he considered her in a sexual context—any more than Marcus had. "Little mistress," he began, "I thought—"

"We've both been rather stupid," she said, interrupting him and twisting her long hair into a braid. "When these attacks began, I should have asked you to sleep in my chamber—and even after that woman set her slaves on us, I *still* didn't think of it. I'm just glad that you did. There's water enough for a warm bath for you, too."

He gave her a wry smile. "I fear I need one, little mistress." He bent back to his task of arranging both pallet and an improvised club beside it. She thought she had seen a flash of relief at her quick understanding before his expression resumed its usual stoicism. She watched him for a moment, trying to think of something else she could do for their defense. Her strength really lay in her ability to conjure and her quick thinking. If she were startled out of sleep, it would take a few moments for her to gather her wits. He would bear the brunt of their defense for those moments.

But the sight of the club reminded her of something; it was illegal for a man to be armed within the city streets, but *not* inside a Mazonite's home and on her property. In fact, many wealthy Mazonites kept small armies to protect their property and govern the rest of their slaves. There was no reason why she could not arm him now. She turned and went back to the kitchen, and found the heavy butcher knife she used to cut up meat and tough fowl, locating it on the kitchen-counter by feeling carefully along the wall until her hand encountered metal. She no longer felt as if she had the energy to conjure a light. She found the wooden

handle and brought the knife back with her, and handed it
to him hilt first as she edged past his pallet to get to her own
bed.

"Here," she said as he took it, "and remind me to get you
a better knife tomorrow. That one doesn't keep an edge
worth a conjured coin, and it doesn't really have a point. I
wish I could afford to buy you a sword, but a good, big knife
will be much cheaper." They really couldn't afford the
knife, either, but she had a certain squeamishness about
using the same tool to cut up food that Faro might use to
kill someone with. And really, Faro needed a bigger knife
than this one. "A sword wouldn't really be useful in close
confines, would it?" she finished, hopefully.

"No, little mistress," he said, taking the knife with a smile
of gratitude. "Perhaps later, but a sword would not be useful to me now. But a good knife—yes, I could use that here
and now. And when we go out, conjure me another one of
those staffs, only make it look like wood, if you can. I can
use that as well; with a staff in my hand, I can take on as
many as four men."

She well imagined that he could, although she wondered
where he had gotten the training to use swords and knives
and staffs. That sort of training wasn't in a scribe's usual
repertoire, even one built as powerfully as Faro.

Then the answer came to her fatigue-fogged mind. *The
arena, of course,* she chided herself, as she slid into bed and
extinguished the lamp beside it. Faro had already taken his
place on his pallet, and she felt comforted by his silent
presence. She hated to think about it, though. They must
have done awful things to him, trying to break his spirit.
And when they couldn't, they must have been training him
for the exhibition-fights, where they set the slaves to hack at
each other until one of them died. Someone like him would
have given them a lot of entertainment before he died.
Faro could never do anything poorly; he would have set
himself to learn to fight with the same single-mindedness
that he had when he learned his skills as a scribe. She was

certain of that. Faro could never be less than his best—even when it came to killing.

She wondered if it troubled him that he had helped her to kill five men tonight whose only offense was that they had obeyed the orders of a woman. She was under no illusions; he had hated all women, and now he hated all but one. She had seen that carefully veiled hate in his eyes, heard it in his caustic wit, just one short step from insolence. Was he lying on his back, on that pallet, wondering if he should have spared their lives? Or did he simply feel that as tools of the woman who had owned them, they were as corrupt as she must be?

She knew how she felt about it: no one had forced that Mazonite to attack her, and there were laws governing the behavior of slaves. Any slave attacking a woman—regardless of whether that was something he had been ordered to do, or something he had decided to do on his own—would be put to death, instantly. Only in the arena, at either a woman-trial, or the rarer fighter's-challenge, could a slave do his best to kill a woman with no reprisals. They would have killed her; she had no compunction about killing them. After all, she had been trained by Marcus to know that one day, she would have to fight at least one man, and the odds were even that it would have been to the death. Every Mazonite knew that; those that entered the army spent their lives killing.

Those men had not really been men to her; they had been things. They were not like Marcus or Faro. If they had run, as their mistress had run, she would have let them live. They had not; she had not.

Why didn't she feel anything? she asked herself, as she stared at the darkness of the ceiling. Was it that she was simply too tired? There was nothing inside her, no energy, no feeling, not even anger.

Perhaps that was it. Perhaps it was simply that she had nothing left to feel with tonight.

Or perhaps it was just that she was in a kind of shock. She

certainly felt stunned. It was one thing to believe that someone wanted to frighten her; it was another to know that someone wanted to kill her.

She hated to think about it, and hated to remember that Faro was a trained killer. It was not how she cared to think about him, but it was a good thing for her that he had learned those things. If he hadn't—

She fell asleep before she could finish the thought.

They replaced the plants; they fortified the house when they were gone. The cost of the plants and the arms she obtained for Faro ate into their money, but she could not grudge the expense. They saved every copper-bit they could, and they continued to be very wary.

It was just as well, for within six days they were attacked again.

This time it was by a band of eight, a larger group than the one that had attacked them before.

Once again they were on their way home, but this time from a more modest encounter. And this time it was in broad daylight.

The circumstances were odd, too. A woman who often booked public entertainments had thought that other Mazonites might be willing to pay to see Xylina's woman-trial restaged. Xylina was dubious, and Faro ominously silent, but she decided that the woman was too important to offend by an outright "no." They went to hear her out, but in the end, Xylina felt she could not put Faro through that kind of humiliation a second time. Bad enough that she had once ridden him like a broken horse. It would be worse for him to recreate his moment of defeat twice a day for however long audiences continued to come. And they might not come at all; that, too, was a possibility. Or they might come in such small numbers that their share would not be worth the loss of other, more "respectable" income. And what about being naked? Xylina had not liked that at all, though she understood the need in the arena. The men could be clothed, because they were under the control of the trainers and never had any weapons to conceal, but the women had to prove they brought nothing in with them. Not only did Xylina not want to parade naked again, she didn't want to press her thighs and breasts against Faro's body again. Not now that she realized how he had reacted. Not in public and not in private.

She declined, however, on the grounds that such a show might anger the Queen, being a blatant display of her own ability to conjure. That reason had taken some quick thinking on her part, for the woman could not possibly take offense at such an excuse. She pointed out that such re-creations could be viewed as a challenge.

It was a pity; the woman lived in a lovely home and had at least fifty or sixty slaves, and it was obvious from her prosperity that the spectacles she staged were generally very popular. The room they had been received in was all of the finest marble, with comfortable, suede-covered couches for Xylina and her hostess, and a leather-covered stool for Faro. The entrepreneur herself wore fine silk breeches and a tunic dyed in expensive scarlet, and Xylina was served a generous selection of expensive cheeses, savory breads, thin-sliced meat and succulent fruit, with the leavings going straight to Faro. The rest of the house was like this part of it: cool and luxurious, though not as sumptuous as the villa. This woman evidently had a high degree of success in judging what others might well pay to see. But Faro's set expression and the smoldering embers of his eyes told Xylina that this would be too much. She could not offend him this way, by ordering him to do this. Not after all he had done for her.

"Truly," she said to her hostess, trying to appear modest and thoughtful, "I wish that I could. But I have no intention of even making it *appear* that I was challenging the Queen's power. Now I'm sure you understand that I have no ambitions for the throne; I would not know how to govern, and I would make a very bad ruler, I fear. Yet our Queen is suspicious, and has reason to be—and even if I proclaimed my lack of ambition from the rooftops, she would still suspect a challenge."

Their hostess frowned, but nodded. "You have a point, and a good one," she replied grudgingly. "What you say is very likely. Our good Queen has challenged others on the basis of things much less suspicious."

"And only think how it would look to the Queen that *you* had been the sponsor of such a display!" Xylina added, as if in afterthought. She clapped her hand to her mouth as if dismayed. "Demon-spawn! She would think that *you* had ambitions to be the power behind the new monarch! She might well decide that you had posed a challenge through me!"

"Holy mothers, you're right!" the Mazonite exclaimed, her brown eyes going wide with alarm, jerking her head up so that her sandy curls bobbed with agitation. "Perhaps I had not thought this out completely."

Now was the time to soothe her, before she decided to turn around and report this to the Queen's agents. "I promise you, if you can think of a way for Faro to perform that will be successful without appearing to challenge the Queen, I shall be most pleased to enter into such a venture," Xylina told her calmly, rationally. "I think that would be a most successful spectacle. Perhaps something involving his strength—not a fight with another gladiator, for that would be too much like the combats that the Queen sponsors—but perhaps he could undertake to fight a wild boar, or lift heavy objects, or break a wild horse—"

"I shall think on it," their hostess said, her anxious expression betraying her mixed emotions—greed for the money she could earn from the original idea, warring with real fear of the Queen. And not without reason; the Queen had right-of-challenge too, just as any of her subjects did if they wished to try for the throne. If she felt an unspoken challenge had been issued against her, she could issue a challenge of her own, and the challenges *she* made were invariably to the death. Only self-exile could save the Mazonite so challenged from the inevitable end.

After a moment of struggle, the fear won, and the woman escorted them to the street, promising to keep in touch.

It was hard to walk through the cool marble hall, past the front garden with its lovely waterfall and artistically shaped trees, knowing that the wherewithal from just a few successful "re-enactments" could have made *her* house look like this one. But she had not had a friend for so long—no, she could not betray him in that way. Not for something as stupid as gold.

Their hostess left them at the front door, leaving a slave to see them to the gate to the street. The gate shut behind them with a *click* that sounded very final to Xylina. "Well, at least we got a meal out of this," Xylina said philosophically, looking back over her shoulder to talk to Faro as they made their way down the street. Walls in this part of town were all the same, with the only variations being in the gates set into them. The paved street was hemmed in on either side by stucco walls of a pale beige. It was almost sunset, but there was plenty of deep gold-tinged light. The streets were bare of traffic. The entrepreneur had specifically invited Xylina to share supper, probably hoping to get her into a more conciliatory mood with food and drink, and Xylina had made certain to eat heartily; the other inhabitants of the city were within their own doors and gates, enjoying their own evening meal right now.

Faro's expression lightened considerably, once they were out of those walls. "You should do something about my costume, if we get many more invitations like this one," he replied from behind her. "I could have filched enough fruit, bread, and cheese for all of tomorrow's meals, if I'd had somewhere to hide it. As it was, I only purloined two of those wax-covered cheeses."

Xylina turned to look at him, wondering if he was joking.

She saw no sign of anything hidden in his tunic. And certainly their hostess had given her no sign that she had seen Faro taking and concealing anything. "You didn't—" she said, her eyes wide.

"I did," he grinned, and displayed the two red balls of cheese like a conjurer, making them appear and vanish again into the breast of his tunic. And once there, although she had seen them disappear, she could not see where he had hidden them.

She smothered a fit of giggles. Faro, a sneak-thief? Who would ever have believed it? "How did you do that? Where did you learn such a thing?" she demanded.

"From one of the boys at the scribe school, when I was about nine, and was still small," he replied, "I was hungry all the time, and the boy claimed my growling stomach kept him awake at night. They never gave us enough time to eat our fill, and they never let us carry food away from the table. One of the other boys was the son of an entertainer, a dancer and conjurer; he taught us all how to filch and conceal food, and what foods were best for the purpose." His tone was light, and she caught a real smile lurking around the corners of his eyes and mouth. He obviously found her surprise quite amusing.

"Is there anything you *don't* know?" she asked, wondering yet again at the twist of fate that had brought them together, and led her to keep him after she had won him. For all of the horrible things that had happened to her, this—not only the ownership, but the *friend*ship—made up for them. Next to Marcus, he was possibly the most wonderful person she had ever known. She would die if she had to do without him, she thought, suddenly. Die—or if they were right, and she had a terrible enemy, she would be killed.

"There are many, many things I can't do. I can't cook," he pointed out wryly. "As you well know, given the number of meals I have near-ruined. I can't sew. I can't clean unless someone shows me what to do. I am not particularly good at supervising others, although I believe I could learn. And as you are well aware, I know very little about gardening other than that seedlings come from farms and that they must be tended—you have had to teach me all of that. When you come to own a horse, you will have to find someone else to buy to deal with it, for you have seen for yourself how horses hate me."

"Not all horses," she said, stifling another giggle, for he was referring to a most unfortunate encounter with the dun mare that pulled the vegetable cart that serviced their neighborhood. Faro and the mare had confronted one another one morning a few days ago. For no reason that Xylina could fathom, the mare had decided that Faro looked like an enemy. She had gone for him, and had tried to bite him every time she saw him. The first time she had attacked him, Faro had not been aware of how fast she could strike nor what her range was. She had connected with his right buttock. And a horse's teeth, as Xylina had learned after treating the wound, made very large and painful bruises. The worst part was that the same mare adored Xylina and would beg for caresses whenever Xylina walked by, turning in the next instant to attack Faro.

"The only horse I have ever seen hates me," he replied. "And she loves you. I can only conclude either that all horses hate me, or that she is a Mazonite to the core, and believes men should be beneath her hooves, making the pavement soft for her to walk upon."

Xylina could no longer contain her laughter. She stifled it behind her hand, as Faro grinned ruefully, and they turned the corner with her wiping tears out of her eyes.

It was at that moment that Faro grabbed her arm and flung her into the wall; she hit the surface with both hands, softening her impact.

As she landed, she caught sight of a large stone sailing through the air where her head had been. It was an attack; it could be nothing else.

She quickly turned, using the impact with the wall to

give herself extra speed, and looked for the danger. The first thing she saw was Faro, standing between her and harm, his back toward her. He was already using his staff against a pack of men, fending them off, gradually driving them away from her and the wall until they all stood in the middle of the wide street. It looked for all the world like a mastiff being worried by a pack of terriers, for he stood a head higher than any of the others.

But terriers could be effective. One of them, a man with a raw, broken branch with bark still upon it for a cudgel, succeeded in getting past the staff to smash his club against the side of Faro's head. Xylina winced at the sickening *crack,* but was too busy calling up her power to do anything to fend the attack off.

The blow missed the temple, but the club laid open the scalp, and Faro staggered a little, stumbling forward two steps before regaining his balance.

There was no time to waste; she had to act quickly before they took advantage of Faro's injury. She did not exactly think; she assessed the situation and acted, exactly as she had in the arena.

The worst thing that could happen to these men would be that they should get into each other's way. That would mean that Faro could use his own blows effectively, and they would not be able to get at him.

Yet anything she conjured to hamper them might also hamper him: oil on the street, or a rain of slippery stones, or flinging things at their legs or heads.

If he only had a corner to stand in—

That thought was all that she needed. She conjured him one. Power surged through her like an upwelling spring, and it did not even manifest from her hands this time, nor create a ghost-object before the full conjuration appeared. Instead, it simply flashed instantly into what she desired, creating two slabs of stone behind him that met in a "V" at his back.

The immediate effect of the conjuration was to shove the

men who had been standing there out of the way, as the stones sprang into being before their eyes and partially within the space they had occupied. Those men were knocked to the ground, taking them temporarily out of action. And now the rest of the ruffians could come at him only from the front.

That evened the odds considerably. Now she was free to deal with the men between her and that newly-conjured stone. With the stone standing high between herself and Faro, she need not worry about hurting him with what she did.

There were three of them, one kneeling, one still on his behind, and one staggering to his feet, all reacting to the sudden appearance of walls of stone in front of them. They stared at the stone, and not at her. That was a mistake. Before they could recover, she acted.

The easiest thing for her to conjure was fabric—so she conjured that, yards and yards of it, dropping it over them and muffling them in its hampering folds. It dropped down right out of the air above them, again without a mist-shape presaging the actual conjuration, and without the conjuration actually touching her hands. Cries of surprise and rage came from beneath the fabric, and the folds churned and bounced as they pushed at it. Then she conjured a torrent of water that fell out of the empty air, like a sudden downpour of rain, soaking the fabric and turning it heavy and clinging, handicapping them further. She had made certain that it was icy water too, not hot—shocking them with the cold and giving her a chance to conjure up her next weapon.

This was almost fun. While they floundered, she moved in. She felt no fear during the action, merely determination to get the job done.

She conjured herself a length of metal; it came to her hands, heavy and cold and smooth beneath her hands. And very satisfying. She made the few steps to the trapped men and clubbed every lump that moved under that fabric.

Crunches and cries of pain came from beneath the cloth. The dark fabric was stained darker in places, but she ignored all of it. Anger gave her strength, and outrage guided her aim; she clubbed the forms beneath the cloth until nothing moved.

By the time she was finished, so was Faro. She came around her conjured stone wall, club at the ready, just in time to see Faro drive his staff across the temple of the last man still facing him; it hit the man's head with a distinct and uncomfortably familiar wet *crack*, and she saw the bone cave in before he dropped to the ground. As she looked around for more ruffians, she saw that two more men had taken to their heels, and even as that final attacker fell, they were disappearing around a corner.

Faro grounded his staff, and leaned against it heavily. Xylina banished all her conjurations but his staff, revealing the six bodies strewn across the street. None of those bodies showed any sign of life. Once again, they had defended themselves too well to leave anyone to question.

"Good thinking, little mistress—" Faro managed, around his pain. His eye was swelling, and the cut on his scalp bled down the side of his head and stained the breast of his tunic. He looked as if he might collapse into the street at any moment. She found herself with a length of conjured gauze in her hand to use as a bandage, and she hurried to bind his wound quickly before it bled any further.

"Don't talk," she urged him, adding her strength to that of his staff, helping to keep him upright. Finally, only now after all the noise of fighting had ceased, she heard a gate creak behind her and turned to see a slave peering around the edge of the gateway with round, frightened eyes. Cowards! she thought angrily. *Now* they came look to see who was being attacked, after it was all over!

"Get your mistress," she ordered him peremptorily. "Let us in; my faithful slave has been wounded and I do not care to stand here in the street while he bleeds! Then go fetch someone from the Guard. We have been attacked by a gang of thieves, and this must be reported to the authorities."

She pushed Faro around and towards the open gate before the slave inside could object, and interposed her body so that the slave would not dare close it. In a moment she had Faro inside the enclosure. She looked around quickly, assessing the surroundings, looking for the best place to get Faro off his feet. This front garden, like her own, was not large, but it had a tree with a bench beneath it, and a tiny fishpond. She sat Faro down on the bench beside the pond before the slave could object, and began cleaning his scalp-cut with conjured water and cloth. The slave stared at them for a moment before fleeing into the house—presumably to get his mistress, as Xylina had ordered.

And when she showed up—and the City Guard—Xylina hoped she could get something other than words out of them.

But words was all she did get, and vague promises; no kind of help at all.

When they finally reached their own gates, it was well past sunset; Xylina had been torn between assisting Faro and letting him totter behind her as was proper for a slave, even an injured one. Since it was still possible that people might see them, she elected to be the proper mistress and ignore her slave's condition, but she was not happy, and she kept apologizing to Faro for her behavior. One small bright spot: during all that fighting, the cheeses Faro had purloined had remained unharmed. As they left the garden of their reluctant hostess, he showed them to her with a pain-filled smile.

Although the three members of the Guard who had been summoned by the frightened slave had questioned her closely, there had been no suggestion that they did not believe Xylina's story of "ambush by a pack of ruffians." That was where their agreement ended, for Xylina attempted to persuade them that being attacked twice by rogues was beyond coincidence. The Guards, however, were insistent on a claim that their attackers had been "wild" men; escaped slaves, or criminals being sheltered within the Men's Quarter. They would not even entertain the notion that a fellow citizen could be responsible. After all, she was told, Xylina was hardly important enough to have anyone feuding with her—and not rich enough to attract the attention of one of the notorious female criminals with bands of slaves obeying her orders to attack and rob.

"We've had some trouble with packs like this in the past," the senior Guard had said casually, poking one of the bodies with her sheathed sword. "They're freedmen who haven't learned their place, or think because some mistress was soft enough to free them that they're as good as a woman. One of those brutes gets the idea he's going to pay back women for what they did to him—forgetting the women who fed and clothed and took care of him before he got uppity. Then he gets a gang of runaways to go along with his craziness, and the next thing you know, there's trouble. First time they've attacked to kill like this, though, that I know of. Mostly they're happy just to knock you down and make off with your goods."

"Sounds like it's about time for a purge, if you ask me," the householder had said darkly. She had not appreciated being interrupted in the middle of her meal to deal with an altercation on her doorstep. She had offered Xylina no help, and had tried her best to ignore Faro's existence altogether. She had not even asked Xylina's name. "It's about time the Queen sent the Guard through the quarter and checked every house against the roster. That'll take care of these 'wild' men. When the tame ones see a purge coming, they'll turn the bad ones over fast enough."

The Queen ordered purges of the walled Freedmen's Quarter periodically, although the last one had occurred before Xylina's mother had died. She would order all the gates sealed, and conjure the same kind of metal mesh barrier over the walls that Xylina had protecting her house from invasion from above, thus effectively sealing off all routes of escape. Then the Guard would move in, and make a house-to-house search, checking the inhabitants against the roster of those who were *supposed* to be living there, looking for hidden rooms and secret passages. Any house with men living there that were not on the roster had better have exception-papers for them, or every inhabitant in the house would be taken for the arena. And the owner of any house with secret rooms or passages would find himself bound for the arena as well. There was no point in trying to hide from such a purge, for the entire Guard would be involved in making certain that no one escaped.

As Xylina's unwilling hostess had indicated, the mere announcement of a purge was generally enough to make the inhabitants of the Men's Quarter turn over most, if not all, illegal dwellers. And it was enough to make thieves from the quarter confine their activities to their own kind for a while.

But despite what the senior Guard thought, Xylina was fairly certain that this was no attempt at mere theft, nor were these men acting on their own. Even though she had seen no indication of a woman directing them this time, she felt that the mind behind this attack and the previous one was the same. The attacks were much too similar, too close together, and too well coordinated.

And the hand she fancied she saw behind both of them was that of her unknown enemy—who just might be powerful enough to have some influence in the Guard itself. How else could you explain the complete absence of a patrol within shouting distance on not one but *both* nights they had been attacked? And how to explain the boldness of an attack when it was still daylight?

That notion was confirmed when a fourth Guard came with a message for the others, just as they were completing their questions. The four conferred for a moment in a little huddle, then the senior Guard turned back to Xylina, who still sat beside Faro on the bench beside the pond.

"We've gotten all we need from you—thank you, lady. You can go now," the Guard said briskly—no, brusquely—then turned to the homeowner. "There'll be a collector around for the bodies in a bit. Meanwhile, just stay inside. I doubt anyone is going to come back, but why take chances? You'll be safe with your slaves on guard. We've been called back to the barracks."

While the homeowner remonstrated fruitlessly, railing about "protection" and "security," and most of all, about "her rights as a citizen," the senior Guard joined the others, totally ignoring the homeowner. Before the Mazonite could do anything to prevent them from leaving, the four of them pushed open the gate, and left at a trot. Xylina exchanged a meaningful glance with Faro, and nudged him to his feet.

The homeowner, stubborn, or genuinely fearful, was following the Guards, still complaining about the lack of protection and what she was entitled to as a full, tax-paying citizen. Xylina figured now was a good time to get out of there, before the woman decided to turn her complaints against them, or find a way to make some kind of claim on them.

"No offer of escort," Faro grunted from beneath his bandage, as they made their way hastily back towards their home. It hadn't escaped Xylina's attention that the four Guards had gone in the opposite direction.

"I noticed," Xylina replied grimly; although she could not help Faro, she refused to let him walk behind her. "Aren't I entitled to escort, after something like this?"

"Technically," Faro said. He limped a good deal, but she was fairly certain that nothing was broken. She was mostly worried about that blow to the head. "Although—you're poor, and they did point that out, none-too-discreetly; the poor get short-shrift often enough. Still."

"Still," she agreed. "Let's get home before something else happens."

There were no further incidents on their way home, but it was a nervous several blocks, nevertheless. Now, if ever, would be the ideal time for another attack. Faro was incapacitated, and she was hampered by needing to protect him. Several times she thought she saw someone lurking before or behind them. But if it was anything other than shadows and her imagination, the lurker had vanished the next time she looked.

She was wearily grateful to see the gate of her home, at last; once inside, she felt as if she could let her guard down a little. And once inside, she could order him to let her help him, adding her support to that of his staff.

By then, Faro was reacting to the blow to his head with complaints of a headache and a certain amount of dizziness and sleepiness. That worried her further, for it seemed to her that she remembered that these were symptoms of something serious. She was not certain whether she should let him sleep, but she thought she recalled that Marcus had kept a similarly injured slave from falling asleep for a good several hours after the injury.

So she got him into the bathing-room and made certain he had a good, hot, soaking bath for all of his aches and bruises. Then she tended him more thoroughly, rebandaged his wounds with real and not conjured material, and took him into the kitchen at the rear of the house to keep him sitting up at the table. He looked at her blearily as she chattered at him, making a cup of headache-tea and forcing it into his hands.

Finally, he spoke. "Why are you torturing me like this?" he asked, his eyes glazing over with pain.

"Because I think I remember that people with a head injury are not supposed to sleep at first," she told him. "I'm sorry Faro, but I think you really must stay awake."

"Little mistress, if you were not my friend—" He sighed. "I hate to admit this, but I think I may recall hearing the same thing." He touched his bandaged head gingerly. "I shall be of no use in the morning."

"Nor shall I," she reminded him. "If you must remain awake, it is I who must keep you awake." Perhaps if she got his mind on something else, it might help him with his pain. "Faro, do you think that my enemy is someone important?"

"I cannot say," he admitted. "The Guard could have been called away, perhaps to deal with more such gangs as attacked us; and the senior Guard could have been completely right. In fact, if there was more than one gang active tonight, they could not have been spared to escort us. And you are of little or no importance; it will harm no one to slight you by denying you the escort that is your right. But I do not like it, that they hurried away so quickly, after the fourth woman arrived."

"I don't like it eith—" She suddenly sniffed, as the acrid odor of smoke came to her nostrils. She glanced sharply at the kitchen fireplace behind her, but she had extinguished her blaze as soon as the tea was done brewing.

"Faro, do you smell—" she began.

That was when the closed door into the next room burst into flames.

The next few moments were a blur; they flung open the door into the kitchen garden just in time, as the fire roared into the kitchen right on their heels. She looked back only once, to see that her entire house was aflame; then she somehow found the energy to conjure a pile of blocks to take them over the wall and into their neighbor's garden, where they both collapsed.

There she sat, in the middle of a broken patch of pungent onions, as the neighbor's slaves and family boiled out of the house, the night rang with shouts and alarm-bells, and the sky turned as red as blood. And all she could see was the end of everything.

The end of all her hopes, all her ambitions.

The return of the curse . . .

• Chapter 6

In the morning, things were no better.

She stood just inside the gates of her house, and stared at the ruins. Smoke still rose in places, little wisps of it rising into the still morning air. The blackened remains of the walls, crumbling even as she watched, enclosed only ashes. The was no sign of anything that had stood inside, not even the interior walls. Just gray and black ashes. The fire had burned so hot that even metal must have melted.

The house and all she owned was gone. For the second time, the garden had been destroyed, this time by the heat of the fire. Nothing had been spared.

By the time she had recovered enough from her shock to conjure water above the fire, it was too late. The water seemed to do nothing, other than to keep the fire from spreading to the neighboring homes. She had been picked up in the garden by her rearward neighbor, Lycia, who seemed not at all worried about her onions, but only concerned that Xylina and her slave were unhurt. Her neighbor, who proved to be a retired member of the Guard, had not even bothered to ask what Xylina wanted as soon as she realized who she was and what had happened; she took charge of the situation immediately. Like an old war-horse, she responded to the emergency with the energy of a woman half her years.

Lycia Tigeran sent Faro off to her tiny slave quarters in the hands of her own personal attendant and manservant, a man who had been with her since he was a child. She told Xylina that he had been trained in field-medicine, as were many of the slaves of Guards, and he served her as a rough physician during her entire service. She swore he had plenty of experience in tending injury, and certainly, from the competent way in which he took charge of Faro, Xylina was inclined to believe her.

Lycia herself had coaxed Xylina first into a hot bath, ordered another slave to give her a soothing massage, and then she had gotten Xylina into a bed. "I remember your mother, darling," Lycia had said, plying her with tea. "She was a wonderful, brilliant woman, and this city needed her badly. If I'd known her daughter was still alive after the plague, I'd have adopted you myself. Marriage can be a nuisance, because a man can act so hurt when he gets dumped, but adoption is another matter." Lycia had continued to speak quietly about nothing, distracting and actually relaxing her. Only when Xylina found herself falling asleep despite more than enough troubles to keep anyone awake for a week, did she think she might have been drugged.

She fell asleep, fighting it to no avail, and slept until the sun was well up. But in the morning, no amount of coaxing by the mistress of the house or her manservant could make her remain in Lycia's home. The slave brought her clothes, newly cleaned, but Lycia extracted a promise to return. Not that Xylina had a choice; Faro was still there, being tended for his wounds from the day before. The older slave had assured her that he was not in any danger, but he did have a serious head injury, and his skull might even have been cracked. She left the house to make the long walk around the block to her own, determined to know the worst.

And discovered it as soon as she entered her gates. There was nothing left; even the walls had crumbled and collapsed under the intense heat. Xylina felt like collapsing, herself. There was nothing but a blackened husk where her house had been—

A house for which she still owed more than three-quarters of the price in gold, a debt for which she was still responsible. With no place to live, and no way to earn the rest of the price. Now that it had been destroyed, the original owner would surely demand the rest of the price immediately. And where would she live? She could not remain a guest in Lycia's home forever, no matter what the woman said.

She returned to Lycia's home in a daze, hardly knowing what guided her feet. The slaves met her at the door, saw her face, and immediately fetched Lycia. Lycia seemed to realize exactly how she was feeling, and the older woman wisely refrained from offering her any empty words of consolation. Instead, she took Xylina into the rear of the house, sat Xylina down in the garden, gave her a cup of watered wine, and left her alone.

She stared at the wine, trying to comprehend the magnitude of her disaster. And the cause. Surely no fire that burned that completely could have been natural or set by the hand of humans. *The curse.* That was all she could think. Only the curse could have so destroyed everything she had built up. *Surely* no human agency had created a fire like that; no human could. The fire had spread so quickly—as if it had a will and a life of its own. It had reacted as if the water she had poured down upon it were oil, feeding the flames. And yet it had not spread beyond her walls. Granted, her neighbors had soaked down their walls and roofs, but it still seemed uncanny, supernatural. And what was more supernatural than that curse?

And if the curse was, indeed, in operation, what chance had she of recovering from this? None. None. Anything she did would turn to a disaster, and anyone who was associated with her would be caught up in that disaster.

Despair came down upon her, smothering her in dark, heavy clouds. The sun lost its warmth, and the bright garden seemed as desolate as a desert. Her heart ached, her mind went numb. There was no reason to go on, no reason to try. She was doomed, anything she tried was doomed. What worse could happen to her now?

"Xylina—"

She looked up from her despairing thoughts to see her hostess standing in the doorway, a frown on her lean face, and a stranger beside her. The stranger stood very stiffly, and she did not look at all friendly. Her square face was tight, her lips pursed.

"Xylina," Lycia said, and there was a note of anger in her voice, "I didn't want to bring you more bad news, and I'm certain that there must have been a horrible mistake, but this—person—insists on seeing you. She says that she has official business that you must deal with right now."

The person was a middle-aged woman with a hard, disagreeable face, wearing the livery of the Queen. "Are you the owner of the house on the other side of that wall?" the woman demanded, arrogantly. She pointed at the back wall of the garden, where wisps of smoke still rose into the air.

"What's left of it, yes," Xylina replied dully. "A few bricks and a ruined garden. Why?"

"Then you owe sales tax of twenty percent of its value," the woman said, a smirk of indecent satisfaction on her face. "Due immediately. This is the law, and you must obey it, or suffer the consequences."

Xylina stared at her, unable to believe what she had just heard. Sales tax? But the house had not been sold, it had burned! She had not realized any profit on it! How could she be taxed for a sale that had not happened? Was the woman stupid? Did she not understand what had occurred? Finally she blinked once, and said, as if to a very simple-minded person, "I'm afraid you've made a mistake. The house wasn't sold, it *burned.* There was no sale. There was no profit. In fact, it is a loss—"

One she had no way of making up, much less paying a tax on! She continued to stare at the official, but the woman did not drop her eyes. In fact, she looked pleased, if such a disagreeable face could assume such an expression. Xylina could not help thinking that this official looked like a frog, with her wide, down-turned mouth and eyes that bulged ever so slightly. Her complexion was even an odd olive-green.

"Are you living in the house?" the woman asked, as if Xylina were the simple-minded one. Her bulging eyes narrowed, and her mouth quirked up, just a little, as if she were anticipating something.

Like a nice juicy fly? But perhaps the fly was Xylina. . . .

"No," Xylina replied testily. "Obviously not. It burned to the ground. I told you that."

"Can you live in the house?" she continued, ignoring Xylina's sarcasm. Her mouth quirked again. Xylina's heart sank. There was no mistake.

But she still had to try to make this woman see sense. "Of course not," Xylina snapped, her temper and her voice both cracking. "There *is* no house. It's *gone*. It is no longer there to be lived in!"

"Then if you are not living in it and cannot live in it, and no longer have the use of it, it is sold," the tax collector said, her tone triumphant as she displayed her "logic." "There are no exceptions. You owe the Queen her sales tax. It is due immediately."

"I think not," Lycia said icily. "It is the law that *no* tax is due immediately."

"But in view of the situation," the woman amended smoothly, "you may have until the end of the moon to pay it."

She turned on her heel and left, with Xylina and Lycia dumbfounded in her wake. Xylina had thought nothing else could go wrong; now she knew better. Lycia was the first to recover.

Lycia's reaction was a continuance of her outrage. *She* was not cowed by that officious official.

Then again, she was not threatened with yet another debt she could not pay. And what would the consequences of not paying be?

"I simply can not believe this," Lycia said angrily. "That is the most ridiculous piece of bureaucratic nonsense I have ever heard! *Sales* tax on a house that has been destroyed? There *must* be a mistake somewhere!"

Lycia's gray hair was standing out all over her head from the way she kept running an agitated hand through it. Xylina could only sit and shake her head in despair. There was no way out. Punishment probably would be banishment—and that could be worse than death. She could be caught by enemies of the Mazonites, be tortured, be made into a slave herself. Death would be preferable.

Maybe she should just kill herself and get it over with, she thought savagely. The more she thought about it, the more it seemed that was the only solution, although she did not voice her conclusion to Lycia. She should never even have tried all this. It was useless from the start. Useless, hopeless. She never had a chance. No one would ever miss her. No one would care—

But even as she thought that, she realized, with a sob that she choked back, that she no longer had the freedom to escape by killing herself. If she died, Faro died. His life was tied to hers, by the same law that had sent him to the arena in the first place. An ordinary slave would simply be taken as partial payment for the debt, but an ex-arena-slave would die when his mistress died. He did not deserve death. How could she do that to him? And she knew that she could not take him to the border and free him; he would not accept his freedom. Even if he changed his mind, she would not be able to get to the border, because debtors were not allowed to leave Mazonia, and they would assume she was trying to flee.

Another sob rose in her throat, and this one escaped. Then another, and another. She tried to hold them back, but they fought past her will, and burning, painful tears followed them. As the hot, shameful tears came of their own will into her eyes and trickled slowly down her cheeks, scalding her like acid, Lycia clutched at her short hair, wearing an oddly helpless expression herself. She didn't know what to say or do—and Xylina could not help herself.

"Don't—" Lycia said, finally, awkwardly. "Please, dear—I know some people, let me go talk to them—"

And she fled, leaving Xylina alone in the garden, free to cry into the wine-cup, turning the sweet wine bitter with her tears.

As Xylina had expected, Lycia's efforts came to nothing; she returned that evening and confessed her defeat at the hands of a legion of bureaucrats who quoted rule after senseless rule until Lycia had thrown up her hands in despair. Xylina could not offer her anything other than a murmur of thanks for trying.

"I don't understand it," Lycia muttered over a supper that Xylina could not eat. "I just don't understand it. This is all so senseless—"

Xylina toyed with a bit of bread, ignoring the coaxing of Lycia's manservant. Her stomach was in knots, and her head ached; her eyes were dry and hot, and swollen after more than one bout of weeping. She understood Lycia's lack of success only too well, for when she went to talk with Faro, a talk that was more a case of her saying whatever came into her head out loud than anything else, she came to a terrible conclusion.

The curse *had* a human agent; it was the woman who had set the vandals on her, and the gangs of ruffians, and might have somehow engineered the burning of her house. She said to Faro that the fire had burned as if someone had poured oil on it—and it would have been simple enough for a good conjuror to create a pool of oil on the roof to begin the fire, then continue to conjure oil to feed it. Small wonder that she had not been able to douse it with water in that case—and small wonder that everything within the walls had been reduced to ash.

It had to be someone in authority—in *high* authority; perhaps a Mazonite answerable only to the Queen herself. For only someone that important could conceal her tracks, and engineer this final disaster. That would make sense in terms of a powerful conjuror, too, since the best magicians ended up in the Queen's service, sooner or later. The motive was not obvious to Xylina, but Faro had managed to suggest a number of possibilities. One, was that the Mazonite in question viewed Xylina as a rival; certainly someone with Xylina's ability at conjuration would soon be asked to join the Queen's staff as soon as another conflict with the lands beyond Mazonia arose. In war, every skilled conjuror would be needed, and someone like Xylina could rise in rank very rapidly.

Another was that it was an old rival of Xylina's mother; this person too could have risen high in the ranks of the Queen's service by now.

Either seemed possible. Both meant doom.

Faro was not at his best—but he was coherent enough (and knew her well enough) to have already divined what her thoughts in the garden had been. And before she left, he seized both her wrists in his hands and forced her to look into his eyes. His expression was open, for the first time in their acquaintance; she saw in it fear for her, pain for her, and a will to do anything to aid her.

"Little Mistress Xylina," he had said, as forcefully as he could manage, though his face was lined with pain, "you must *not* think of ending your life. I know you have thought of this; I can't blame you, for your troubles must seem endless. But you are not alone. I will help you. We will find some way around these troubles. I do not know what it is—but we *will*. We need only time. If you must do anything, find a way to delay them, little mistress. Give us the time to think. That is all we need, for we *are* more clever than they are. Believe me in this. We can and will find our way through."

She shook her head, dumbly, and he swallowed and closed his eyes. "I will even gladly suffer you to defeat me publicly, three times a day, for a year and a day or longer if need be. I will do it in an arena before thousands of *them*, if it will extricate you from this. And I will be glad to do this for you."

She cried then, as unashamed to do so before this man who was her friend as she had been ashamed to weep before Lycia. She knew what it cost him to offer that—and it was the greatest gift that anyone had ever offered her. He had given her back her life twice now—and had offered up his own as well. More than that, had offered his spirit, his pride, his dignity. What he had not given to any Mazonite under the most extreme punishment, he had given her out of friendship. She could not have ordered that from him—would not have asked it of him—and he had given it to her of his own will.

She wept, and so did he—and when they were both finished, she somehow knew that he was right. Somehow, they would find an answer.

But when she emerged and saw Lycia, the answer seemed very far away.

"Xylina—"

Xylina looked up; Lycia patted her hand. "Don't give up, girl," the old woman said roughly. "I'm not finished yet. I don't have the money to get you out of this, but I think I know some women who may—either others who knew and admired your mother, and there are more of them than you may think, or even someone who saw your woman-trial and is willing to give you a hand. Let me go out and do some talking tomorrow, all right?"

"Why are you doing this?" Xylina asked, bewildered.

"Partly because I admire you—and partly because I don't like what's being done *to* you, and I don't like what it implies for the rest of us," Lycia replied forthrightly. "What's happening to you is rather of a piece with some other disturbing things around here lately. Ah, never mind. Here—"

She held out another cup; this time it was clearly one with some kind of potion in it. Xylina raised an eyebrow at it and sniffed it delicately. It smelled of herbs.

"Are you going to drug me again?" she asked.

Lycia snorted. "Damned right I am," she said. "If I

don't, you won't be getting any sleep at all. If you don't get any sleep, you won't be able to think. If you can't think, what good are you going to be to yourself or anyone else?"

Xylina knew when to concede defeat. She drank the potion, and went straight to bed.

Adria leaned back into the leather cushions of her throne, and regarded Ware from beneath half-closed lids. The demon had appeared at her orders to discuss the actions of last night, and their continued actions. There were no witnesses, not even slaves, for what Adria was doing was not even remotely legal.

And Ware seemed to harbor a fair number of doubts about this. "Are you quite certain you know what you are doing, my Queen?" The demon Ware looked directly and challengingly at Adria with his many-colored eyes, all the colors of which had darkened with some kind of indefinable emotions. Certainly Adria would not try to define them; who could fathom the thoughts of a demon?

Bad enough that she was worried about someone discovering what she had done; she did not need a conscience-stricken demon to plague her about it too. "Of course I am certain!" Adria snapped, straightening in her seat to conceal her weariness. Last night's exertions had taken their toll on her; she had not dared entrust *this* job to one of her underlings.

It was easy enough to find a renegade with a gang of ruffian-slaves, and under the cover of a disguise, hire her to attack Xylina in the streets. Or rather, it *had been* easy.

After two efforts had left two piles of bodies in the street, the city underground no longer held anyone willing to attack this "easy" target. Adria had been forced to change her tactics, and had opted to go after Xylina personally.

But not directly; she decided to let the "curse" manifest itself in fire.

As a result, she was exhausted. Once Ware had set the

fire in Xylina's home, it had been up to her to make certain that it kept blazing, and that the girl was unable to put it out. She had not conjured that much of *anything* in so short a period since the last war. By the time the flames had engulfed most of Xylina's house, Adria's powers were beginning to ebb, and she had fallen back against the cushions of her litter as wearily as if she had fought a dozen men hand-to-hand.

She toyed with the ends of her golden sash, as she watched Ware carefully, trying to divine his thoughts. He could not betray her—but if he chose to vanish from the city, she would be able to do nothing to stop him, and she would lose his services. How far dared she push him? She needed to be rid of Xylina, and to do so, she might still need Ware's abilities.

When Xylina had escaped the first ambush, she had been amazed. Even though Xylina had done well in the arena, that had been under controlled circumstances, and when she had time to prepare herself mentally for the event. Adria had no idea that the girl was such a quick thinker in an emergency—nor that the slave would fight *with* her, rather than standing passively on the side, or giving only a half-hearted attempt at defending her.

That had been what had made the difference, and it had made no sense whatsoever. The slave had no real reason to defend his mistress, after all; she had humiliated him in front of hundreds of women and their slaves. He should have been of limited reliability in an ambush.

But not only had he defended her, they had worked as a team, or so the woman who had lost her entire gang of ruffians had said. Adria saw no reason to disbelieve her, for the evidence was clear enough. They had dispatched all the men sent against them, even though they had been grossly outnumbered. That had been the first pile of bodies, left for the Guard to find. Xylina had reported the attack the next day, and had apparently accepted the Guard's assurance that it was a gang of lawless freedmen that had attacked her.

If the slave had not defended the girl, she would have been overwhelmed.

Adria had not known what to think, at first. For a moment, she had even toyed with the notion that Xylina had some heretofore unknown power over her slave's mind. But after a moment of sober reflection, the reason for the slave's apparent loyalty was obvious enough. He was, after all, a former arena-slave, a condemned criminal. Even a dullard would be bright enough to know the law that applied in his case. His life was bound to his mistress's, and if she died, he would be executed. He had no choice but to defend her.

So the second time Adria hired an ambush to take them, she had made certain that the numbers were sufficient to get the job done. This renegade had almost double the number of slaves that the first had, and these men were bold enough to attack in broad daylight. It had taken Adria a great deal of time and effort to find this woman, and after the failure of the first gang, it had taken a great deal of gold to hire her for the task. The gang's first priority was to rid Xylina of her slave, or somehow separate the two. Kill the slave, Adria thought, and the girl would fall.

And yet, on the afternoon the attack was to occur, her first word of what had happened came from her own Guard.

It was the duty of the Guard-Captain to report all unusual occurrences directly to the Queen. On that afternoon, she had received a report from the Guard that told her that the numbers were *not* sufficient, that once again Xylina had won free of the attack.

Xylina had escaped the ambush unharmed, and had taken refuge with her slave in the garden of a nearby homeowner. All but two of the slaves who had attacked the girl and her slave had perished in the attempt.

Adria had sent word to the Guard to muster out all patrols, and search for the "gang of runaway slaves" that had made this attack. She had specifically ordered the

Guards who had responded to the incident back to the barracks to make a fuller, more detailed report, thus denying
Xylina a protective escort. She had hoped that a robber
would see them as they made their way home, and find
them an irresistible target. If the slave could only be killed,
Xylina would be vulnerable. But nothing happened, and
they reached home safely. Adria's spies reported back to
her as soon as the pair entered their own gates.

That was when Adria had sent for Ware, determined to
at least ruin this potential rival to the point of bankruptcy
and exile, if nothing else. She conceived a plan; to wait until
Xylina had been in her home for a few hours and thought
herself safe, then to set a fire at the front of the house.
Hopefully the fire would cut off escape; and she would
make certain that it was a fire that would be fierce and hot
enough to burn everything in its path.

For that, she needed a demon. She could not conjure
fire; no woman could, any more than she could call a wind
or a storm. A woman's magic created only inanimate things.
Fire, though not alive, was a process rather than a thing.
But Ware, like any demon, could call fire—and Ware could
insinuate his power past locked gates and closed doors to
do so, setting it on the roof to burn downward.

With Xylina and her injured slave asleep, there would be
ample opportunity for the fire to take hold. Then once the
fire had been set and had burned a hole in the roof, she
could conjure enough oil and pitch to soak everything in
the room below. That would keep the fire burning with an
intensity that would destroy everything in its path, and
make it spread as quickly as a thought.

So she and Ware had gone to the street outside Xylina's
home, and the plan had been made reality. She had come in
a plain, unornamented litter, carried by four mute slaves
who could neither read nor write. He had walked beside
the litter, wrapped in a cloak, looking like nothing more
than a shadow.

She had hoped that Xylina had gone to bed; it would

really have been best if the girl had been asleep. Then she would have gone up with house and slave, since Ware had set the fire directly over the master bed-chamber.

But somehow they escaped; Adria knew that as soon as another hand began conjuring torrents of water in an attempt to douse the flames.

That was why she had determined to feed the fire with oil. Oil floated upon water; oil would not yield to water. And Adria knew that if she stoked the fire until it burned even the paint from the walls, the flames would turn the water to harmless steam before there was any chance of the water accomplishing anything. So Adria stretched her abilities to the limit, conjuring as much or more oil than Xylina could conjure water. She had kept the flames fed and sent them higher and higher.

Finally the girl must have given up, no matter where she was; water ceased to pour into the blazing building and the fire roared on, no longer opposed. That had been enough; no matter what else happened, Xylina was financially ruined.

Adria knew she could stop at that point. She fell back upon the cushions of her litter, drew the curtains, and directed her slaves to bear her back to the palace. The demon disappeared somewhere; she never saw him go. In fact, she really didn't remember him being there once she had begun her own conjurations. Perhaps he had gone as soon as he had set the fire at her direction. It did not matter, particularly; he had done his work, and done it well.

She returned home, to the palace, coming in by a side entrance, and dismissing her litter and the slaves. The palace had been silent, for she had sent everyone to their quarters except for her own personal guards—all slaves, and as mute as the litter-bearers. This was not the first time she had undertaken something that her fellow Mazonites would not have approved of, and it probably would not be the last. Mute guards could be trusted not to reveal what they had seen.

Once she entered the palace, she returned openly to her bed-chamber, secure in the fact that no one who saw her would even think to question her whereabouts, or reveal her absence to others who might. She longed, desperately, for sleep. She had not felt this worn out in many long years. Not since the last challenge, in fact.

Yet there would be no sleep for her yet, not while there was work to be done.

Once she reached her bed-chamber, she cast a longing look at her bed, but sat down instead at a small desk in the corner of the room. She drew up instructions for the tax-collector, called another slave, and had the directive sent to the tax-collector's office in the palace. In the morning, when the woman arrived at her office, she would find them waiting for her with the Queen's seal upon them. The rationale for the change in the law was a simple one, and she congratulated herself for thinking of it.

There had been too many cases of arson in the city, when a property owner could not be rid of a house but wished to be relieved of paying the tax upon it, her edict stated. Therefore, unless it could be proved that a fire was completely accidental, when a house burned the owner must pay the same sales tax upon it that she would if she had sold it.

There would be no one who would connect this edict with Xylina—for how could Adria have known that Xylina's house had burned? And since it would be impossible to *prove* that the fire was accidental, Xylina's financial ruin would be assured.

For the first time since she had seen Xylina win her woman-trial, Adria felt peace descend on her soul. She undressed quickly, dropping the garments she had worn into the privy, and took a quick bath to remove the last traces of smoke. She then allowed herself to seek her bed and fall into a deep and dreamless sleep.

Morning came all too soon, and with it, the report of fire in the city. As she had seen for herself, Xylina's house was a total loss. She allowed herself a look of a concern; ascertained that there was no other damage, and expressed her pleasure at the girl's escape, then went on to other reports, as if Xylina was no more to her than any other young Mazonite woman.

Inside, however, she gloated. The girl must be frantic by now, trying to figure a way out of her predicament. Soon she would realize that there was no way out—except bankruptcy and exile. Would she kill herself, rather than suffer such a fate? Adria could hardly wait to hear what the tax-collector had to say.

But Ware arrived at the palace just before she received the report of her tax-collector. He presented himself as if it were just another day, as if he had no particular business in mind other than to amuse her. But his eyes were dark with secrets, and when she granted him audience and permitted him to listen to the reports of her various officials—including the tax-collector—he did so with an odd expression. His impassivity was gone; there was something else there in its place. Something about this situation evidently interested him, although he had seldom shown much interest in the doings of the Mazonites before this. Finally she dismissed her officials, and faced him alone.

That was when he dared to ask her if she knew what she was doing.

"I know exactly what I'm doing," she told him forcefully. "If I cannot remove her in one way, I must remove her in another. There has never been a conjurer to match me since I took the throne, and I do not intend to let anyone know that Xylina could be that match."

In sober truth—though she would never tell him that— she feared that the girl was already more than her match. If it came to a challenge today, Adria was afraid there was a very real possibility that she, and not Xylina, would lose.

Ware shook his darkly handsome head. "I fear that you have aroused more than you guess, my lady," he said, his melodious voice making pleasant the unpleasant words.

"This girl is no tamer than her mother was. If ever she finds out who is behind all this, you will have a challenge on your hands."

She looked into his eyes, and quickly looked away. One thing she definitely read there: he knew very well that she feared Xylina's youth and strength, and the powers of magic the girl commanded.

Unspoken, the thought hung between them: *That would be a challenge you might not survive.*

"Let me be the judge of that," the Queen replied waspishly. "You are only an inhuman thing; what can you know of human nature? This girl is nothing: naive, ignorant, easily fooled. She will have no notion that it is not a curse that moves against her, but my hand. How could she? How could she ever discover what has been behind her misfortune?"

"I do not speak only of this girl, but of your other subjects, my lady," Ware replied evenly. She flushed, then paled with mingled anger and dismay. He was right—and she hated him for being right. "What you do to her is against your own laws. You should either challenge her openly, or let her be. If your people discover what you are doing, they will call you to account for it."

"They will not," Adria said, with a carelessness she in no way felt. And a thin thread of chill rose along her backbone, for the demon had accurately predicted the actions of her people, if they learned what she had been doing. If ever the other Mazonites discovered how she had misused her power, they could not only call her to account for her actions, they could condemn her for them. They could force her exile, sending her off the throne, and into the wilds beyond the borders of Mazonia.

But they would not find out, for there was no one to tell them. The women she had hired to ambush Xylina were not aware that it had been the Queen who had hired them. She had gone in disguise, had never given her name, and had paid in common coin. She had found the women in the first place by roundabout means, and had met them in low taverns where no one knew what the Queen looked like. Only her litter-bearers knew what she had done last night, and they were mute slaves who could neither speak nor write. No one else, human or female, was aware of what she had done and where she had gone. Only Ware himself, who was bound to her service by the most terrible of oaths. *He* could not break those oaths to betray her. Only she could release him from them.

No, she should be safe enough.

"Within the week, the girl will either be dead or in such dire straits she will flee into exile on her own," Adria announced loftily. "You and I are the only ones who know the hand responsible for her misfortune. Gossip in the marketplace says that it is entirely the action of that curse which she dared to flaunt. I think we are safe enough.

"We," she said, to remind him that he was a party to this, and that if she suffered for it, so should he. There were ways to punish demons, to confine them forever. That was why they swore their oaths to the Queen for the freedom to walk the streets openly—to be free of those punishments. The Queen knew those magics, and if Ware betrayed her, she would use them on him.

"And if the girl finds a rescuer?" Ware asked, his eyes curiously bright, strange dreams dancing behind them. She kept glancing at those eyes, caught by the life and light in them. Ware had never looked this alert before in all the time he had served her. He had always seemed to be at one remove from the rest of the world—as if he walked in a waking dream. Now the dreamer seemed to be stirring. . . .

"She will not," the Queen replied, with a laugh. That was one thing she was certain of. While there were women who had more than enough wealth to come to Xylina's rescue with a gift or a loan, why would they bother? They had not achieved that wealth by giving it or lending it to foolish young girls. "No one would be so foolish as to make a loan on such little security as she possesses—one slave, who on *her* death must be put to death, unless she has sold or traded him before that date. No, I think not." Her eyes hardened. "And you would do well to recall that she is our enemy, and must be disposed of."

Suddenly the demon's eyes lost all their light, and became opaque and colorless. "Very well, my lady," Ware said, his tone curiously flat and without emphasis. "I seek only to protect your reputation, as the oaths I swore require me to do. If you will not act according to my advice, then the conditions of that oath have been satisfied."

She stared at him for a moment, then turned away and ignored him. She rang for her majordomo, and signaled for the first petitioner of the day to be allowed in to see her.

It turned out to be a very wealthy merchant, an important supporter, and Adria spent some time with the woman, untangling a complicated legal problem to their mutual satisfaction. When she looked around, Ware had absented himself.

Without asking her permission to do so.

She frowned, then shrugged. After all, he was a demon; she could not expect him to act like one of her own subjects. He often forgot or ignored the rules of protocol, and he was useful enough that she permitted him to do so. He was an unnatural creature; it was not reasonable to expect him to act naturally. And she had no further use for him today, at any rate. He had been extremely tedious, and if he was not in the mood to amuse her, she would rather that he stayed away altogether until she called him.

She signaled for the next petitioner, and put all thought of Ware out of her mind.

Lycia left the house early, before Xylina awakened from her drugged slumber. Despite the drugs, Xylina's sleep had not been restful; she had endured horrible nightmares all night long, struggling up out of one only to descend into another. Several times she had awakened in a cold sweat, with her heart pounding, and her mind paralyzed with reasonless fear.

She did not remember what her dreams had been, except for one. Only the last one remained with her, and that only because she fought off sleep after she awakened from it, lying in her bed and trying to clear the fog of fear from her mind. She had shivered as she lay there, staring up at the pale blue ceiling, telling herself that it had simply been a dream and nothing more.

Yet it had felt all too real at the time—so real, she had awakened shivering with bone-deep chill, and was a little surprised not to find herself beslimed with mire.

The dream had been a hideously simple one. She had found herself in a dark, cold swamp, in sticky mud and murky water that came up to her hips. She had been completely nude in the dream, and her conjuring ability had somehow deserted her. She could not even call up a simple length of cloth to wrap herself in. The sky had been overcast, and tall, dank weeds blocked out the view on all sides of her. She had no idea where she was; no idea how she had gotten there. And she was totally alone.

Then she had heard something—several somethings—howling in the distance, a hideous baying sound that had never come from the throats of dogs. And in the dream, she had known they were on her trail, that they would devour her if they caught her.

She had tried to run, but the mud and the cold water slowed her down, keeping her progress to a bare crawl. She fell, time and time again, once going completely under the water as she fell into what seemed to be a bottomless hole, and was barely able to flounder into shallower water. Sedges cut her, and thorns scratched her. Beneath the water, rocks cut her feet until they bled. There were huge snakes under the surface of the water, which rubbed up against her legs just often enough to let her know that they were there. Horror deepened within her soul, and a terrible fear. The fear increased every time she heard the howling. Her limbs ached with cold and strain, and her long golden hair was matted with mud.

She could not even tell if she was going somewhere or traveling in circles, for everything looked the same. And yet she had to try to escape; fear drove her ever onward. The howling had grown closer with every moment, and the mud grew deeper, stickier, harder to move through. She knew that when the howling things found her, it would be over—

Then just as the howls came from just beyond the screening reeds behind her, and she had been certain the horrible creatures that made them would break through at any moment, she woke up.

When she finally rid her mind of the last clinging tendrils of the nightmare, she arose. Lycia's manservant, attentive as always, had been waiting for some sounds of life from the bed-chamber; the moment he heard them, he was at her side, to ask what she wished. She licked dry lips and rubbed her cold arms. It seemed as if the cold of her dream-swamp had followed her right into the waking world.

"A hot bath, and clean clothing," she said absently. "And something to eat, please, while I am soaking. Is Lycia still here?"

She wanted to ask the older woman if her dream meant anything, or if it was simply a night-fear, a manifestation of her daytime troubles. The older Mazonite had a wealth of wisdom that Xylina instinctively trusted.

But Lycia had already gone out for the morning, the manservant said regretfully. "But she will return by noon," he added with eager helpfulness.

He led her to the bath and left her there to soak away the last of the cold that the nightmare had left in her mind. But when he returned with her breakfast, it was with a puzzled look on his face.

"Mistress Xylina, there is a manservant here to see you, sent from Lady Hypolyta Dianthre," he said. "This is not a lady of my mistress's acquaintance; indeed, I have never heard of her before."

"Neither have I," Xylina replied, after a moment to plumb the old memories of her mother's acquaintances, to see if this lady was among them. "Do you—"

She was about to ask him if he thought she should talk to this slave, but then she remembered that this man was not Faro. He would not feel free to advise her.

"Never mind," she told him. "I shall see this man in a moment."

She would have asked him if he knew what the slave's errand was, but if he had known, he surely would have told her. And she did not particularly want him to ask. If it was more bad news, she would rather Lycia's manservant was not privy to it just yet. He already knew more about her private affairs than she liked. Not that she didn't trust him—she had no reason to mistrust him, after all. But it was a truism that slaves gossiped, and what he knew, the marketplace would probably know before long.

There was no point in spreading the tale of her misfortunes any further than it had to go.

So she devoured the hot egg pastry that Lycia's manservant had brought her, drank down the watered wine in a single gulp, and arose dripping from the water while it still steamed. She dressed herself quickly, in the garments he had brought her: breeches and a tunic that were clearly Lycia's, since they were far too large for her and had to be belted in before they looked like anything other than sacks. She had put her long hair up in a knot for the bath; now, perversely, she let it down again, so that it fell in ripples to her waist. The manservant looked on, clearly not approving of such unseemly haste, then took himself off to inform the waiting slave that Xylina would see him.

She made her way to Lycia's reception chamber, half expecting it to be some other message from the tax collectors, and she was rather surprised to see that the slave waiting for her was not dressed in government livery.

She took a seat on a padded bench, wishing that Faro was able to take his usual place beside her. The slave remained standing, as was proper, and waited until she nodded tensely at him, granting him permission to speak.

"I am sent from Lady Hypolyta," he said, without pre-amble. His voice was very low, and musical. "She is not a personal acquaintance of the mistress of this house, nor of yours, nor of your mother Elibet—but she did see your performance at your woman-trials in the arena, and she wishes me to express her admiration, and the fact that she was greatly impressed by your courage and your resourcefulness."

Is that all? Xylina restrained her impatience, and nodded to the slave, indicating that she had heard and understood him, and that he was to go on. He was a most unusual looking man: very slim, and very graceful, with long dark hair that shone like black silk, and hung to below his shoulder-blades, and very curious, dark eyes. At least, she assumed they were dark, as she could see very little of them. He kept his eyes cast down as he spoke to her and she could only infer their color. But despite the fact that he kept his eyes lowered, he carried himself with a kind of unconscious pride, much like Faro. He was incredibly well-spoken, actually, and despite her current throng of worries, she found herself envying the woman who owned him. She must take great pleasure in him.

"My mistress sends me to tell you that she is a woman of substance, and she is prepared to make her admiration clear in material ways," he continued, apparently unaware of her scrutiny. "To make myself completely clear, she has heard of your current rash of troubles, and she would like to make you a loan sufficient to cover your current needs. This loan would be payable in installments, so as to keep the repayment from being too onerous."

Xylina could not keep her amazement from showing, and the slave did not—quite—smile.

"You need not fear that my mistress is either a mad-woman, or a lady who is likely to change her mind from one moment to the next," he said smoothly. "She simply recalls her younger days, when she encountered tribulations, and she wishes to help those deserving of help so that they need not fear the future. Would you care to meet with her?"

"Why—of course," she replied, trying not to stammer. "When would the lady wish to see me, and where?"

"This afternoon, if it pleases you," the slave said. "And in the lady's own home. I shall come to take you there, if you find that convenient."

A thousand possibilities ran through her mind—and one of them was the notion that this might be a trap by her unknown enemy. Faro was in no condition to go with her, and who knew where this odd manservant might take her?

On the other hand, what choice did she have?

"I shall be happy to meet with your mistress at that time," she said, hoping her hesitation didn't show. "And please convey to her my heartfelt thanks."

• Chapter 7

Hypolyta Dianthre was nothing like the woman Xylina
had imagined. She had expected someone like Lycia and
most of the other Mazonites of her acquaintance: a tough
old warrior, who could still pick up a blade and trounce men
(and women too, for that matter) half her age. Such a
woman would be broad-shouldered, tall, and muscular,
with the physique of any true veteran. Perhaps she would
bear the scars of many combats; she might even still wear
the leather of a Guard.

Xylina had also expected a house something like Lycia's
home, perhaps a little larger. The comfortable but not
extravagant dwelling of a Mazonite who had done well in
her life, a place with a room or two for guests, and perhaps a
half dozen slaves to serve her.

Such a woman, in such a house, would fit the description
of the friends of Elibet, Xylina's mother. That would be
where Xylina could expect to find her support. And such a
woman might well, with care and prudence, have amassed
enough wealth to be able to afford to loan it to so odd a
debtor as Xylina. Such a woman would not have felt the
need to squander her savings on ostentation or luxury, and
would feel well able to spare it.

Instead, she was conducted to a part of the city that
she had never seen before. She had thought that her
region was quiet, but here the walls were so high and the
gates so thick that the quarter might have been completely deserted. The distance between gates was
somewhat intimidating, too. Were the homes behind
them as huge as this implied? Just exactly who and what

was Hypolyta, and how had she made the fortune a villa like this must cost?

Several times she was certain that her would-be patroness could not possibly live in this quarter, that the manservant was only taking her through this section on the way to somewhere much more modest. But then he came to a halt before one of those gates, and opened it to display a lovely "wilderness garden" full of birds and the sound of falling water, bisected by a lane that led to an enormous villa. But strangely enough, as she neared it, and could see beyond it, she realized that it was positioned right against the wall around the Freedmen's Quarter. That seemed very odd, as normally only the poorest Mazonites lived anywhere near the Freedmen's Quarter.

There must be prosperous freedmen, men with villas and servants of their own. Perhaps the section of wall this villa abutted was backed by those islands of prosperity. In such a place, the danger of robbery from renegade men would be nonexistent, as would noise from over the wall. Most of the Freedmen's Quarter was poor, but Xylina had heard of men who had acquired wealth and position and even traded outside Mazonia. Such men were tolerated, provided they kept to their place, because the enormous taxes they paid to the Queen made toleration worthwhile.

The manservant was the only slave she saw as they walked up the heavily tree-shaded lane to the door. There was not even a gardener in sight, although the grounds were wondrously beautiful and it must have taken a small army of slaves to cultivate the impression of controlled wildness.

The entered the front door, which was standing open to let in a gentle breeze, and as Xylina stepped onto the polished marble floor it seemed to her that the villa was echoingly silent. Although it must have taken another small army of slaves to tend this dwelling, there was not a single sight nor sound of them. Either they had been trained to

work without a noise, and without being seen, or the place
was tended by magic!

Still, it was hardly empty. As she followed her guide past
the antechamber (a lovely jewel-box of a room, all marble
and glass mirrors), past the large reception chamber
(marble-floored and paneled in cream silk, full of comfortable chairs and couches upholstered in matching fabric),
down a wide marble hall and into a smaller parlor, she could
not help but notice the luxurious furnishings and appointments. There were huge ceramic pots containing generous
swaths of colorful dried grasses, enormous fans of exotic
feathers, or whole living trees. The lamps were all of delicate porcelain, thin enough for light to shine through.
Furniture was uniformly made of gracefully carved pale
woods, upholstered and padded in creamy leathers and
satins. Windows stood open to gentle breezes, revealing yet
more gardens outside. There was room enough and more
for a huge extended family, with slaves to tend to every
need, yet she saw no one.

It was all very strange.

By now, she was anticipating someone like the hostess of
that entertainment that she and Faro had graced. Someone
very wealthy, very powerful, and very much aware of both
those attributes. She could not imagine how such a woman
would have heard of her, much less actually seen her at her
woman-trial.

Yet the woman she met matched neither of the images
she had created in her mind.

The manservant ushered her into a small parlor, paneled
in fine, pale-golden wood, and furnished with comfortable,
casual couches covered in soft golden leather and beautiful
marble-topped tables. Her hostess awaited her, seated on
one of those couches, with a table beside her holding wine
and two cups.

The woman greeted Xylina in a soft, almost hesitant
voice. She looked like a plump and peace-loving
grandmother, not like the kind of woman ruthless enough

to have accumulated the wealth it would take to pay for a house like this one. Her short silver-gray hair clustered in tight curls about her head; her round face bore a curiously serene expression. She had a wide brow, round, very blue eyes, and a generous mouth that smiled a greeting to her guest.

Hypolyta wore breeches and a gracefully draped tunic of peacock-blue silk so heavy and lustrous that Xylina could not begin to guess how much it cost. Certainly more than the very expensive clothing she had seen at that party. Her round face was kind, with no scars or any other visible signs that she had ever been a warrior, and her voice was so low and so shy that Xylina had to lean forward to hear her properly. She patted the seat of the couch opposite hers, inviting Xylina to take her place there, and immediately poured the girl a cup of wine with her own hand.

"I greatly admired your performance in the arena, child," Hypolyta said, handing her the cool silver goblet. "It reminded me of my own, in a way—both in the fact that you spared your opponent's life, and in that you used cleverness to offset a situation that seemed doomed from the start. The simple-minded brute I picked as my opponent had no more brains than a day-old chick, poor dear. It was ridiculously easy to befuddle him with simple tricks, then run him until he fell down from exhaustion. *My* woman-trial was far less of an ordeal than yours, and so I admired you that much more for your accomplishment."

She paused to sip her wine and continued. "When I heard from my young cousin in the Guard that you were in dire straits, I thought it would be a great pity if no one rewarded your cleverness and tenacity. And I thought it would be even more of a pity if something as utterly ridiculous as the situation you find yourself in forced you into exile. Our land needs more young women like you, not fewer."

Xylina shook her head, deprecatingly. This woman completely befuddled her. That low, soft voice was very hypnotic; it made everything in her want to respond to anything Hypolyta wanted, and it was difficult to keep her instinct of caution to the fore. "I do not know what to tell you, Lady Hypolyta. There are many in this city who would say that all this misfortune comes about because of the curse on my family—and who would remind you that according to that curse, those who aid me are doomed to face ruin themselves." She shrugged. "Given the ill-luck that has pursued me, I would not blame you in the least if you had second thoughts about aiding me. There are many in the city who would think less of your intelligence for even asking me here and risking the curse."

Hypolyta laughed delicately, and put down her goblet on the table beside her. Water droplets ran down the side. Xylina continued to hold her own goblet, to keep her hands from betraying her nervousness. "Anyone who believes in curses is a fool," Hypolyta replied simply. "No Mazonite with any sense would give credence to such a tale. And I think of my offer more as a good investment than a silly indulgence. It was my good investments that brought me to the position where I am today. I think that you will, in time, repay my loan many times over. You will repay the loan itself, and you will become a good source to invest in, for you are clever, you have good sense, and your ability in magic is quite amazing."

"I have yet to think of a practical use for that ability," Xylina pointed out wryly. "Thus far, the only use has been in fighting off ruffians." She took a sip of her own wine; it was cool and slightly sweet, very light, suitable for the warm weather.

"In time, I think that you will," Hypolyta countered comfortably. "Certainly, when our Queen goes to war again, your magic will be of major importance." She leaned forward a little and her demeanor changed subtly. "Now, about this loan. I understand that your current debt is something on the order of fifty gold coronets?"

The coronet was the largest gold piece in circulation in

Mazonia. It was stamped with the image of the ruling Queen; the crown controlled the issuance of money. Xylina had tried not to think of the enormous sum, and now, faced with it, she could only nod. "Part of that is in payment for the house that I bought, and the rest is—"

Hypolyta waved a dismissive hand. "That absurd tax. Indeed. Now, if you had only that, you would really be no better off, you know."

That had not occurred to Xylina—she had not even thought past the huge sum of money she owed. It had stood in her mind like a wall she could not possibly climb or see past.

Hypolyta smiled when Xylina widened her eyes with surprise. "Oh, it is true. I have looked over the situation. You would then own a vacant lot, upon which you would still have to pay property tax—you would have nowhere to live—and the city might still levy yet another fine on you for not clearing the ruins of your house! If you tried to camp upon your own property, the city would fine you for not living in a proper dwelling, and if you managed to clear the property with the help of your slave, you would still have to build a dwelling on it that matched the city standards for that area."

Xylina felt the blood draining from her face, for that had not occurred to her, but Hypolyta was not finished. She truly had investigated Xylina's situation thoroughly!

"In addition, if you could actually sell the place, you would then have to pay *another* sales tax on it. You would lose money on it, as you could only sell it for the value of the land alone. That would not retire the debt, and in the end you would find yourself back in a two- or three-room hovel much like the one you moved out of." Hypolyta shook her head, and reached out her plump, oddly graceful hand to take up her wine-goblet. She took a sip, and Xylina followed suit, her mouth dry. "You would then be in no position to even begin to repay a loan. That would be a very bad investment on my part."

"But—" Xylina began. She did not know what she was going to say, but she got no chance to interrupt.

For all that her voice was soft and shy, when Hypolyta spoke of business, she was impossible to stop. She waved her hand and Xylina held her peace. Clearly, Hypolyta had some ideas of her own.

"If, however, I were to give you a loan of, say, one hundred coronets, you would be able to discharge your debt, have a new house built, and hire more slaves to protect yourself and to develop a proper estate of your own." Hypolyta smiled, a smile of maternal sweetness and pardonable pride. "I can recommend someone who will do the work cheaply and well. You will have a plain house, but it will be a good one. It will cost you much less to build on your own land than to buy another house, and you will be able to tailor it to the type of business you wish to pursue."

"Business?" Xylina said faintly.

"Oh, yes. You should capitalize on that magnificent slave of yours, but not by such paltry means as entertaining at gatherings!" She smiled, making the mild rebuke even milder. "Surely there are many things that boy could teach others, and you should make use of that while he is still notorious for defeating all those ruffians. And you should have your new home built to take care of that. For instance, if you intended to train fighters for the arena, you could have the back garden cleared and the area prepared instead as a training arena."

At Xylina's wince, which she could not quite conceal, Hypolyta added hastily, "I only offer that as a supposition. You could just as easily train slaves to become needleworkers, bakers, or laundry-handlers. Or—surely that slave could train others to repel attackers; with two attacks upon you in the last several days, many older women, no longer able to defend themselves, are becoming nervous about their security. The trade in trained slaves is a good one, and it is one in which I made my fortune."

Xylina looked askance at her. She could not imagine this

gentle woman training gladiators. "What did you train your slaves as?"

"Skilled gardeners," was the surprising reply. Or—in view of the way the grounds looked, perhaps she should have anticipated it. "It is more of an art than most realize—until they turn their expensive pleasure-gardens over to the hands of men who cannot tell a rare seedling from a weed. I supply all of the most highly trained gardeners in the country to the wealthy women of Mazonia. My slaves are experts and artists, and when they leave my hands, there is nothing they do not know about growing things."

Xylina smiled, relieved. She did not think she would have been able to accept a loan from a woman who had made the money supplying trained gladiators to the arena. It would have felt too much as if she were betraying Faro by accepting gold tainted with blood. Nor could she even guess how he would have reacted to the discovery.

The notion of training slaves as unarmed bodyguards was a good one, though, provided Faro could be coaxed to do something that would ultimately protect women he hated.

"What would the conditions of this loan be?" Xylina asked cautiously. "How soon would I be expected to repay it, and what kind of payments would they be? How much would the loan cost me?"

At once, Hypolyta became a cool, calculating businesswoman. The transformation was quite remarkable. She sat a little straighter, and while her voice was no less hypnotic, it was a little less warm. "Payment would be in equal amounts, over a four-year period," she replied. "The first payment would be due one year from now, and it would be in the sum of forty-five crowns."

Xylina sighed. That would mean that she would be paying an extra twenty crowns a year for the privilege of borrowing the money—and yet, what other choice did she have? There was no one else willing to loan it to her—certainly no one willing to *give* it to her. It was either this, or exile, or so it seemed to her.

On the whole, paying eighty crowns to save herself from exile was not a bad bargain.

Was there any other way she could borrow less and save herself some of that fee?

"That seems honorable and reasonable to me," she responded, after a long moment of weighing her options and coming up with no other plan that was even remotely as good. Hypolyta was right; without *more* money to help her replace what was gone, she would be no better off. She could not remain Lycia's guest forever.

"Very well," the older woman said, with another sweet and matronly smile. "I will call my manservant, and we will draw up the contract."

Lycia's reaction was elation, when Xylina returned with her gold. It was carried by the slave, armed to the teeth and with a special permit that allowed him to be so. Lycia's rugged face lit up when she saw the gold, and she congratulated Xylina on her good fortune, with no hint of ill-feeling. She had not had any luck at all in finding someone to loan Xylina the needed money to discharge her debt. Those of her friends who were sympathetic did not have nearly that much to simply loan away. Those women she knew who had that kind of capital were no more than acquaintances, and they were not at all inclined to loan gold to a strange child, particularly one who seemed to attract bad fortune. Her generous nature made her happy for her new young friend.

"I've never heard of Hypolyta directly, but I've heard of her slaves," she assured Xylina. "They're quite famous actually; I just never knew where they came from. Many of them are eventually freed, but continue to work for their former mistresses for a wage."

"I'm not certain what to do," Xylina said hesitantly. "Faro is not well enough to guard me if I were to take the money to the tax office—"

"Faro needn't do any such thing."

Lycia called for her own manservant and sent him out immediately to the tax-collector and the former owner of the house, with messages telling them to come collect their debts. "Let them come to you," she told Xylina, with a cynical smile. "Since you are doing them the favor of giving them money. Let *them* provide the guards for that money. Why should you? Why should you go to them?"

When she put it that way, Xylina realized that Lycia was right. And after all, both the government and the broker could afford guards. She could not.

The tax-collector arrived first, with no slave to guard her, clearly thinking that this was some kind of ruse. She showed up at the door, and was ushered into the reception chamber where Xylina and Lycia waited. "I hope this is not a waste of my time," she began. "My time is the Queen's time, after all—"

"I don't think it will be," Lycia said dryly, and Xylina laid out the coronets all in a row on the table.

The other woman stared, her frog-like face a blank.

"What?" she stammered.

Xylina said nothing, only gestured. The tax-collector was completely shocked and appalled when she realized that Xylina had delivered up the tax-money, and somewhat hysterically demanded that Xylina prove that it was not conjured coin.

Xylina had had enough of the officious creature, and threw the small sack that had held the coins on the table in front of the woman. "Look for yourself," she said, with barely-concealed fury. "These are *minted coins*. You know very well that no one can conjure minted coins, only blank disks! And even if I could do so, you have only to look at the coins themselves to see that they were minted in many eras! How would I accomplish that particular miracle?"

Her question was unanswerable, for she was entirely correct. Conjured gold *could* have been stamped with imprints taken from real coins, but where would Xylina have gotten so many different coins? And if she had them, why would she have needed to conjure coin?

Even so, all the tax-collector had to do was hold the coins overnight, in a special locked box. They could not last for longer than that if they had been conjured. Xylina would have gained nothing.

The tax-collector could only stare at the coins, her face a mask of panic, as Xylina scooped them all back in the sack and thrust it at her. Her hands grasped it nervelessly, then dropped it. The sack fell right between her feet. Xylina did not touch it. "Take it!" she demanded, as the woman continued to stare at the sack at her feet, speechless. "Take it, and begone with you and your foolish rules!"

Lycia took a hand, then, staring coldly at the woman, since she showed no signs of leaving or even picking up the sack. "Indeed," the old warrior said, taking an aggressive stance. "You trespass on my hospitality. You have gotten what you demanded, out of all reason or sense. Now sign this receipt and go! You have no more business here." She drew herself up to her full height, and Xylina saw more than a shadow of the old warrior.

It was the law of the city that a woman reigned supreme in her own house; no one other than the Guard on a mandate from the Queen herself could trespass where she was not wanted. It did not matter that this woman would be going out into the street carrying a small fortune, with nothing but her own skills and her bare hands to protect herself—unless she found a Guard or two on the way. She was not wanted in Lycia's home; her brief welcome was over, now she must leave.

After all, it was her own fault that she had not believed the message, that she had come out with no escort, without even her own sword. If she ran into trouble, it was on her head.

The miserable tax-collector was forced to put her signature to a receipt specifying that she had gotten the stipulated sum from Xylina's hands, gather up the sack and go.

She bent down and picked up the little sack with shaking hands. And she was clearly afraid, for she was no ex-warrior like Lycia. It could even be that she had passed her own woman-trial simply because she had been lucky enough to find a particularly vulnerable man. A sum of the size she carried would make her a target for ruffians of all types— and tax-collectors were not popular with anyone. If she ran into trouble, she could not count on help from ordinary citizens.

If she lost the money to robbers, she would be forced to replace it out of her own funds. She might even be forced to pay a fine for being so stupid as to risk collected tax-money by going out after it without a Guard. She could only hope that word of Xylina's sudden prosperity had not spread to the underground, and that no one knew, as yet, that she was in a position to pay all her debts.

Xylina did not trouble to hide a smile as the woman left, visibly trembling, with the pouch of gold shoved into the bosom of her tunic. Nor did Lycia; in fact, the older woman practically cackled with glee.

The tax collector scuttled down the street, everything about her saying that she was grossly unhappy and afraid. Xylina felt a surge of contempt. This toad was a full citizen, with an important job, while she, who had won her woman-trial fair and square against a formidable opponent, was the one who was in trouble!

The other woman, who actually had not yet come forward to demand payment in full though she was entitled to, was far wiser. She arrived with six strapping young armed slaves, and the permit for them to carry swords and daggers. And with her she also brought a bottle of a fine vintage wine.

Lycia warmed to her immediately. They were two of a kind. And Xylina was much happier to see her than she had thought she would be.

"My dear, I cannot tell you how glad I am that you have found a solution to your problem," the woman said warmly.

"I had not troubled you in the hopes that if I left you to think, you would find a patroness somewhere. A young woman as resourceful as you are could not help but find a solution if you were simply given a chance. You had such good ideas for the use of your old house—I thought that a moon or two to get your ideas together and get over the shock would be much better than pestering you at a time when you were confused and under stress."

Xylina was touched, both by the words and the feeling that the woman meant them. Lycia seemed to think that the woman meant them, too, for she warmed even further.

"Not that you wouldn't have come calling at the end of a moon or two," Lycia said, her voice heavy with a certain amount of friendly irony.

The woman shrugged. "And would I have had a choice?" she asked, quite reasonably. "The Queen would be demanding her taxes of me, too. I cannot afford to forgive a debt of that size any more than you could afford to take it on, Lycia, and you well know it. But whatever I could do, I intended to do. I was trying to think of some way that Xylina could work off the debt; perhaps she could have leased her slave to me—it wasn't my debt that I worried about, it was the tax. Tax-collectors have no heart."

Lycia shrugged, but she appeared to soften a little more. "The law has less heart than tax-collectors. At least you had the good taste not to come around here like the jackals at the battlefield, looking for bones," she admitted. "So thank you for that."

"Indeed, thank you very much," Xylina said softly, and smiled. "If I am ever in a position to pay that favor back, be sure that I will."

The woman blinked, as if she had not expected that from the girl, and somewhat sheepishly handed Xylina the bottle of wine. "This is by way of congratulations," she said. "I would like to toast your good fortune—if you would permit me."

"I would be honored," Xylina said honestly. She opened the wine and Lycia sent for goblets; it was a good vintage, not a stingy one.

And this time when their second visitor left, the smiles that followed her were cheerful and not full of malice.

Xylina sat on the side of Faro's cot. He looked better now than he had for some time, but there was no doubt that he still needed rest.

He had listened to her with a puzzled frown on his face, and Xylina did not blame him. Told baldly, the entire story sounded like something out of a tale. "I still do not understand this," Faro said, when Xylina finished her story. "This makes very little sense. We do not know this woman, you say that you do not think your mother knew her, and she is no friend of Lycia's who *was* a friend of your mother's. Why should she help you in this way?"

"I don't know," Xylina admitted. "I agree that it makes no sense at all. I wish that it did, that I could find some kind of explanation. It was not conjured gold, so it can't be a trap of that kind, at least."

Now that the debts had been retired, she had an even larger one—and now that she was away from Hypolyta's rather mesmerizing gentleness, very little about the woman's actions made sense to her. Lycia was inclined to take it all at face value, but the more Xylina thought about it, the more it seemed to be some kind of trap.

Evidently Faro felt the same. "Could this be the work of your enemy?" he asked. "Is this a trap of some kind? Was everything properly witnessed and sealed?"

"So far as I can tell," she said, handing him the contract. "It is all properly notarized, and she called in witnesses from outside as the law requires."

He looked it over carefully, frowning as he forced his watering eyes to focus properly.

"It seems absolutely correct to me," he admitted. "And I have made many such contracts in my time. But Xylina, can we retire such an enormous debt?"

She sighed. "We can only try, Faro." She looked past
him, at the blank wall, wishing that the future would reveal
itself on that wall. "We can only try."

Six months later, she had a new house and a thriving
business.

The house was small; smaller than the original had been.
There wasn't a garden any more, and not much of a front
area. There was one large room for her hired guards to
sleep in, a kitchen, a small reception-area, a bathing room
and her own bedroom. Faro still slept in her room, on a
pallet across the door.

The rest of the area had been devoted to a training
yard. True to his promise to do anything to help retire
their debt, Faro had (reluctantly) agreed to train young
slaves in unarmed fighting and staff fighting. Not that
there weren't other men perfectly capable of giving them
the same training—which Xylina was quick to point out—
but none of them had Faro's current notoriety for
trouncing ambushers.

That notoriety was considerable. As the story spread—
slowly, of course, since she was of no real importance, but it
did have some amusement value—the total number of ruffians he had killed grew, doubling and even tripling the
original number. Soon there were many Mazonites who
were interested in having him train their litter-bearers or
bodyguards. After all, it was a nuisance to have to get a permit for one's slaves to bear arms within the city; it was much
easier to give them staves and special training. Pressure
from women worried about the "gangs of runaways"
changed the law to permit slaves to bear staffs at any and all
times, though not swords.

Any man could learn to handle a staff, and one did not
have to worry quite as much about watching one's back as
when the slaves were armed with edged weapons. The very
idea of men with swords—even for a short period of time

and under the proper supervision of a female—made some Mazonites very nervous. That was all to the good so far as Xylina was concerned; it meant that she and Faro had more business.

That was the positive side of their situation. On the negative side, Xylina had been forced to hire six guards to watch over her property. There had already been two more attempts to set her house ablaze; both foiled because she or Faro had caught the fire before it began to spread. Xylina had practiced the conjuration of fire-stifling vapor, learning well from her mistake with water on oil. There had also been a number of attempts at ambushes. It would have been cheaper in the long run if she had been able to buy the slaves outright, but at the moment she could not afford that many trained men.

But she did not have time to think about her finances. There were training-contracts to arrange, a household to run, the training itself to oversee, and a hundred details to take care of. There never seemed to be any end to it. And she never had any time to really look into her financial state. She could only assume that since there was more money going into their account than leaving it, that everything was fine.

There was, however, one matter she realized she had to address. "Faro," she said one evening before sleep.

"Yes, mistress?" He had been about to lie down across her doorway, as usual.

"I think I don't know exactly how to say this," she said, aware of the awkwardness of the situation, but determined to get through it. "I don't want to offend you."

"I think you could not do that if you tried," he said with a low laugh.

"You have been a good slave and a good guard and a good friend. You have served me so much better than I had any right to expect. But I may not have treated you with the same consideration."

"I have no complaints, mistress."

"You are a man. You—surely have male needs. And I—"

"I think this is a dialogue we do not need to finish," he said gruffly.

He was misunderstanding the very way she had feared. "I want you to be—be satisfied—somewhere. As I understand other slaves are. So that your life will have some—some pleasure. But I don't know how it is accomplished."

"Oh. There are pleasure houses run by freedmen. Slaves go there when given leave, or in groups by appointment. Their mistresses give them coins to purchase the service, much in the manner of any other market."

"Take what coins you need," she said. "Go there when—when you need to."

"Mistress, I can't leave you. Someone would see me go, and know that you were not properly guarded."

This was every bit as difficult as she had feared it would be. "I am prepared to risk it. I want you to be—be taken care of, and I just can't—do this particular thing for you myself. Please go, Faro."

He was silent a moment. "Mistress, I thank you sincerely for your offer. But I could not enjoy myself anywhere if I knew you were left vulnerable. I must not leave your side. So I beg you, think no more of this matter."

"I can't put it aside," she said. "You have risked your life to protect mine, and you are making it possible for me to repay my debt of gold. I must give you some—"

"Mistress, I'm sure you don't want to walk with me to such a house," he said, laughing.

"Walk there with you," she said thoughtfully. "Yes, I could do that. Is it safe in their—their antechamber?"

"Certainly. They have women from other cultures, ones without magic, and they guard them well. But—"

"Tomorrow," she said. "Tomorrow we shall go there. There is one close by?"

"Such houses are everywhere. They do not advertise their presence, but all slaves know their location. There is one near."

"Tomorrow we go," she repeated with determination.

And the next day they did. The house turned out to be unpretentious. In fact it seemed to be a knickknack store, with slaves entering and departing fairly constantly. That was its cover. Its real business was in the several chambers in back. Faro showed her to a door that seemed to lead to a store room, but beyond it was a waiting room where several slaves sat. They sprang to attention the moment Xylina entered, looking alarmed. One was armed with a staff.

"Be at ease," Faro said quickly. "My mistress merely wishes to know the nature of the establishment I might visit. She has no concern about you."

A freedman appeared, readily identified by his costume and attitude. "I am Bulmer, the proprietor. Is there a problem?"

"My mistress feared I might be cheated or waylaid," Faro said smoothly. "So she came to see the establishment for herself, as is her right."

"Come into my office," Bulmer said.

They followed him to a small private chamber. The freedman turned to Xylina. "Is this a surprise inspection? I assure you we are in order."

Xylina decided to tell him the truth. "I depend on Faro for protection. There have been incidents. He is concerned that if he leaves the house, I will be vulnerable. So I came here, so that he need not be concerned about his absence. Are your premises safe?"

Recognition came. "You must be the Lady Xylina! And Faro is your trainer. The neighborhood knows of you, and respects you. This is the type of generosity you show."

"Yes. I want him to—to be able to visit here."

"But we can not have a lady such as yourself being seen at a place like this!" Bulmer protested. "Someone might misunderstand."

"Misunderstand?" she asked blankly.

"He means someone might take you for one of their women," Faro said. "He's right; you should not be here, mistress."

"But this problem is readily solved," Bulmer said. "We can send a woman to your estate. The cost would be more, but the convenience—"

Faro shook his head. "Cost is a concern. I do not wish to deplete my mistress's exchequer frivolously."

Bulmer considered. "It occurs to me that my guards could use the kind of training I understand you do. Suppose I send a woman with a guard, and you would train the guard, and the woman would remain until you had time to train her privately? I would consider this a fair exchange on an indefinite basis."

Faro looked at Xylina, surprised. "If my mistress agrees—"

"I agree," Xylina said, relieved. This would handle the matter without costing her precious coins.

"Then we shall give you your choice of women now," Bulmer said. "Sheel is free at the moment, but soon there will be others for your selection. Sheel is typical of my girls. She is from the Stripe culture, some distance from Mazonia, and all of them are known for discretion."

"I'm sure Sheel will do," Faro said.

Bulmer snapped his fingers. In a moment a woman appeared—such as Xylina had never seen before. She was human, and shapely, but her skin was striped black, white, and blue, vertically. The stripes carried from her hair down across her face and on through her neck to her bosom. It looked like paint, but Xylina suspected it wasn't.

"Show yourself, Sheel," Bulmer said.

The woman opened her robe, showing her bare torso beneath. The stripes carried all the way down to her feet.

"She will do," Faro said.

Bulmer snapped his fingers again. The slave with the staff appeared. "Sheel is making a house call," Bulmer told him. "You will guard her there, and bring her back when she is done. You will be trained there by this man." He indicated Faro. "The financial arrangements have been made. You will not speak of this matter elsewhere."

The slave nodded. Sheel closed her robe. Bulmer showed them out by another door. Just like that, they were on their way home.

Thereafter Sheel came regularly to the house, accompanied by one guard or another. Xylina gave word to the hired guards to ignore them. She did not inquire herself into the scheduling of the training sessions or pleasure sessions. She pretended to be unaware, and there was never any awkwardness. In fact she soon was oblivious to the arrival of the striped woman, because she was just one of many who came and went in the course of a typical day. Sheel normally wore man's clothing outside, with a brimmed hat that shaded her face. She looked like a youthful slave, and sometimes she carried a package. Thus it was easy to take her for a delivery boy. There was no embarrassment.

Except for the first night, when Faro laid his bed across Xylina's doorway. "Thank you, mistress," he said. For a reason she chose never to explore, that left her blushing in the darkness. But she knew she had done right.

One year after signing the contract with the Lady Hypolyta, she found out just how mistaken she had been in her optimism. Faro had finally had a chance to do the accounts, and the result was not good.

He brought Xylina the books, and the bad news. She stared at the page with dismay, as it lay on the desk in front of her. "I thought we were doing better than that," she said after a long moment. "We have so many contracts—"

"If we had not been forced to hire those additional guards, we would have had a substantial profit," Faro said wearily. "If the city hadn't found a way to tax everything we do here except eat, sleep, and breathe, we would still be all right. As it is, though, after we paid all the taxes the city found to levy on us and after we paid to hire those guards—this is what is left. You need forty-five coronets for your payment. We have thirty-five."

"If we had forty-four it would still not be enough," Xylina replied gloomily. "It must be the full payment or nothing. That is the stipulation in the contract. A partial payment is the same as a default." Her stomach knotted, and her temples began to throb.

Faro's expression hardened. "Perhaps if we sell something—"

"There is nothing to sell," she pointed out. "We must have the house to continue the training contracts we still have. The furniture is rented. I don't actually own anything except the house and land." She did not mention the fact that she owned Faro; selling him was not an option either. She put her hands over her temples as the pain of a terrible headache overcame her. "I can think of nothing—if only I had time—"

"I should have done the accounts sooner," Faro said, fists clenching. "If we'd known—"

"You did them just last week," she reminded him. "We were fine right up until the tax-collector came with that tax on private schools. We would have it, if it hadn't been for that. If only I had time to *think* of something!"

But there was no time. One of the hired guards came to the room with word that Hypolyta's manservant was at the gate. There could be doubt of what he wanted.

Xylina's options had abruptly run out.

• Chapter 8

It was, as she expected, the same manservant as before. She had him brought to her office, a tiny cubicle just off the kitchen. Windowless, it held only her desk and chair, and the storage chest for important documents. All three had been built by her own hands. While the construction was inelegant, she felt it hardly mattered. When she needed to impress someone, she covered them in rich swaths of her own conjured fabric. The chest then served as a bench-seat. But she did not want to impress this slave with her prosperity; she wanted to impress him with the fact that she was doing her very best to meet the debt and the deadline.

Faro ushered the manservant into her office, then stood beside the door. "Lady Xylina," the slave said, bowing. "If you would be so kind—I should like to speak with you about the matter of the first payment upon your debt." He looked significantly at Faro with his strange, dark eyes. "Alone," he added.

She glanced over at Faro, who shrugged minutely. It would make very little difference whether she spoke to this slave alone or in Faro's company. After all, she simply did not have the money to give him. However, he might well have some influence with his mistress, and if she acceded to his request, they might be able to get a precious week or two of time. There were funds coming in and going out constantly; her normal cash flow would enable her to make up the difference, given that leeway.

She nodded, and Faro took this as a sign to depart. He carefully closed the door behind him, leaving her alone with Lady Hypolyta's graceful slave.

143

Whose demeanor suddenly changed.

The change was subtle, but suddenly there was nothing subservient in his posture or his expression. Instead, he stood a bit straighter, looking directly into her eyes, a hint of smile on his sensuous lips suggesting that they were not slave and slave-owner, but equals. His clothing no longer seemed to be the typical livery of a slave, but a quaint costume he had chosen to assume, and could just as readily put off.

"I know that you are in no position to make the stipulated payment upon your loan," he said without preamble. And before she could protest, he shook his head. "Do not trouble yourself to deny this. I have many sources of information, who have given me detailed accounts which very likely exactly match the ones before you now." He nodded at the closed account book beneath Xylina's hand. The rough linen covers seemed suddenly harsh, and the book felt inexplicably warm as her throat tightened.

"You have exactly thirty-five coronets deposited with the bank of Lady Eccolo," he continued boldly, as she paled. "You cannot redeem yourself. You know this, and so do I."

She did not know why a slave should speak so boldly, but she did not have the strength at that moment to challenge him. For indeed, what he said was only too true.

She felt the blood draining from her face with his every word, but bravely drew herself up and looked him straight in the eyes. "I have been levied unexpected taxes. The training school is doing well, and we expect to begin training scribes as well as bodyguards soon. Faro's other abilities have been noticed, and the slaves he has trained are being very much admired. If I had a little more time—"

He shook his head, interrupting her. "All the time in the world will not help you. You have a very powerful enemy who will make certain that you *can not* redeem yourself. It is in her interest to be certain that you fail."

"Who is it?" she cried, half in fear, and half in hope. Finally someone confirmed what she and Faro had only suspected! She *did* have an enemy, it was not simply a paranoid fantasy. "You must tell me!"

"I can not tell you," he replied, and for a moment, anger rose in her. How dared a mere slave refuse to answer her question? A slave had no right to withhold anything from a a citizen!

Then the anger collapsed, for this was no ordinary slave; that much was clear. And he was not subject to her orders. If his mistress had told him not to reveal something, Xylina could not countermand those orders. "It would do you no good in any case to know who it is," he continued. "But— that is not why I am here."

"Yes?" she prompted, hope rising with the words. Was he about to offer a solution to her dilemma?

"I came to tell you that there is another way that you can repay this debt. Your enemy is certain that you will forfeit, and face exile or prison. This is another way. A certain service to me." His eyes glowed strangely, and she had to forcibly pull her gaze away. His burning glance was nearly hypnotic.

"A service to your mistress. Lady Hypolyta, you mean," Xylina said faintly. What on earth could the woman want of *her?* What could *she* possibly offer? Faro's services, perhaps? Could the lady want his potential as a sire? Was she not beyond the age for that? Perhaps not—perhaps she wanted him for her daughters. Certainly, as strong and clever as he was, he would breed strong and clever daughters, ideal Mazonites—*if* he would agree. How would she ever get him to agree? That sort of thing required cooperation!

"No," the man said boldly, destroying her train of thought and her growing embarrassment. "Not to the so-called Lady Hypolyta. To me. There is no Lady Hypolyta. She was and is a baker, hired by me to play a part, the part of your would-be benefactress. If you look upon those contracts, you will discover that the signature is not hers, but mine."

No Lady Hypolyta? Xylina had contracted with a *male?*

But that was not legally binding, and surely he must know that! Or did he think she was so ignorant she would not be aware of that? What was going on here?

"That's not possible," she said flatly. If he thought she was an unlearned young fool, he was about to learn otherwise. "No mere male can contract for anything outside the Freedman's Quarters, and his contracts can't be with a woman. No man can sign a contract that is legally binding on any Mazonite; he can only contract with his fellow freedmen. Everyone knows that."

"Ah," the man said, his mouth widening in a broad smile, showing strong white teeth. Vulpine teeth, she thought distractedly. They seemed—oddly sharp. "But you see," he continued delicately, "I am not a man."

At first Xylina could not understand what he had told her. Then she understood only too well. She shrank back a little in her chair, and stared at him, only now understanding the meaning of the strange eyes, the too-handsome face, the too-graceful body. And the sharp, sharp teeth. "You—you are a demon!" she gasped. "Monster!"

He bowed a little, a mocking parody of a slave's bow to his mistress. "Ware," he replied. "It is my name, Xylina. Things will be much more agreeable if you use it, rather than 'demon' or 'monster.' And I think if you will review the laws, you will find that a contract signed with a demon is quite as legally binding as any other between Mazonites. We are protected citizens, with most of the same rights that you enjoy. Save only that we may not challenge the Queen, nor disobey her wishes." He straightened, his smile mocking her. "We may hold property, for instance—the villa is mine, the slaves were mine, and this much was true, the money that bought the villa and slaves came from the sale of trained gardeners, who are also mine. We may contract with freedmen on behalf of Mazonite clients—how did you *think* commerce happened between your world and the Freedmen's Quarter? We supply certain comforts to the freedmen, for a price. We may make investments, and we may contract with Mazonites on our own behalf." He raised an eyebrow gracefully at her. "Surely you did not think that we lived on light and air and magic?"

She felt as if she were falling down a chasm; she could hardly move for the shock, and she could not think at all.

"What—what do you want of me?" she asked faintly.

He leaned back against the door of her office, crossed his arms over his chest, and surveyed her from half-closed eyes. "At the moment—your potential," he said lazily. "What you may become, in time. I have peculiar tastes among my kind. Or rather, let us say that I have *particular* tastes. My brothers and sisters are a little less discriminating in their choice of partners than I am. I do not much care for women who are thick-headed, broad-backed and broad-shouldered—who look and act more like drafthorses than I care to contemplate. My tastes run to females who are intelligent, graceful, lithe, as attractive physically in their way as I am in mine— women who are out of the ordinary. You are more than that, Xylina. You are extraordinary. Quite lovely, in fact, and the closest thing to a match for me that I have seen in centuries. Exactly the kind of woman I would choose to be my lover."

With every word, Xylina's shock deepened, but at his final sentence, her outrage overcame her shock. She leapt to her feet, so enraged she could hardly see.

How *dared* he! How dared he come to her with such a perverted proposition!

If he had been something other than a demon, she would have attacked him then and there, or challenged him for his slight to her honor. But caution forced her rage to cool a little—he *was* a demon, after all; his powers of magic were just as strong as hers, and they were utterly unknown. Demons were incredibly dangerous; that was all she knew. He could probably defend himself against her perfectly well.

In fact, from the way he was acting, he could probably not only defend himself, but do it with ridiculous ease.

She contented herself with glaring at him instead, putting every iota of her detestation into her gaze. "Give me a moon," she said, forcing the words out between clenched teeth. "You tricked me—you owe me at least that much, *incubus*. If you know anything of honor, you will give me a moon to make up for that."

Ware shrugged. "A week, a moon, what does it matter?" he said with indifference. "You still will not have the coronets. The proposition will be the same."

"A moon," she insisted. "I swear it." She shifted her stance, and unconsciously raised one hand, invoking the gods to witness her oath as she spoke in the formal words of binding. "If I pay thee not in gold, I will pay thee in silver!" Unspoken was the real import: she would never pay him in sex.

He blinked a little, as if taken aback by her vehemence; the formal words which made her pledge into a solemn oath, and the force of will with which she swore the oath. Then he smiled, lazily. "Very well, then," he agreed. "One moon. It will make your surrender all the more piquant for the wait. I have waited years to find a woman like you; I can wait a moon."

Before she could order him out, he winked, slowly, and vanished before her eyes. He was a demon, without doubt; both his magic and his arrogance attested to that.

Ware returned to his villa in the tiny section of the city that housed mostly demons and those few wealthy women who found the incubi and succubi to be quiet and agreeable neighbors. He was very pleased with himself, and well satisfied with his encounter with Xylina. It had been altogether successful as far as he was concerned. He had been generous—more than generous. In recompense for his tiny deception, he had given Xylina more time to raise the gold she needed to pay her debt. That was just; that was honorable. A tiny concession to make up for a tiny deception. Now she knew what her options were and that she had an enemy—and that, too, was honorable. The Queen had forced him to swear that he would not tell Xylina the identity of her enemy, or else he would have done just that. But now that she knew that she *had* a powerful enemy, he could skirt around the outside of the oath to give her more information. If *Xylina* guessed her foe was Adria, then Ware had not violated his oath. He was fairly certain she was bright enough to do just that, if not now, then in a moon, when he brought her more such information.

In human parlance, "all the cards were upon the table." There were no deceptions, there was only his ability and hers. A challenge of sorts, though a bit one-sided. She could not win, not with the Queen against her.

She was, he thought, a most incredible creature. Every day seemed to add to her beauty—the more she grew in wisdom and maturity, the more she ripened, rather than souring. Her courage in defying him was quite amazing. No few Mazonites in Adria's service had quailed and cowered when confronted with a demon—but not Xylina! She stood up to him, her magnificent eyes flashing, and demanded that extra time of him, demanded honorable recompense, as was her right. She was a far cry from the child in the arena, a child whose bleak eyes had told him that she was ready for death. Xylina would not consider death to be an option now; she would fight to the last breath in her body before admitting defeat.

This was good; he did not want a poor, shattered creature who longed for death. He wanted a spirited woman quite prepared to meet him on his own grounds. She was, he thought with a touch of longing, a fair match for Thesius. Now if only . . .

He let himself into the villa with a touch upon the gate, but instead of entering the building, he followed one of the paths leading off deep into the wilderness garden, to one of the many half-hidden alcoves the garden boasted.

He had not lied to her about this; one of the sources of his ordinary income came from his own training school, which supplied skilled gardener-slaves to most of Mazonia, and the ones who tended his own grounds were second to none.

Here, deep in the cool shadows beneath his trees, there was a quaint little half-cave beside a tiny, artificial waterfall. Although some suspected that his magic had a hand in creating this spot, it had been constructed entirely by his gardeners. The water fell down a graceful cascade of rocks into a pool containing three red-gold fish, who flashed among the smooth water-worn stones of their pool like shadowy living treasures hidden there by an eccentric miser. He flung himself down on the thick, deep emerald green moss carpeting the cave and the rocks surrounding the pool, staring at the waterfall without really seeing it, listening to its music without truly hearing it.

How beautiful she had been! And how graceful! With her golden hair flying like a battle-banner as she tossed her head and defied him, and her deep blue eyes flashing like precious sapphires, she had been incomparable. Indeed, she was everything he desired in a woman. Not like that black cow of a Queen, nor the dun cattle that were her subjects. No, it was no great sacrifice to give her the time she asked for; it would only increase his desire to wait a little longer.

In fact, the longer he waited, the more chance he had to work subtly upon the mind of the Queen, to try to make her see reason regarding this girl. Once he won her, he would have to keep the Queen from destroying her, and that could be difficult, given his oaths. And he could not chance the Queen discovering their relationship—for the foolish Mazonites considered demon-loving to be the height (or rather, depth) of perversion, and it would mean Xylina's exile. No, he must soften the Queen's resolve, make her realize that the girl truly had no ambitions for the throne, make her see that wasting her time in trying to destroy

Xylina was only taking energy and resources that could be much more profitably spent elsewhere.

So this moon could be spent defusing the Queen's malice; that would be a good thing. On reflection, this extra time would be no hardship, and might turn out to have been a wise choice. The Queen was a woman of reason; she was a decent ruler of her people—perhaps not as good as some had been in the past, but by no means the worst. She exceeded her legal powers when she felt threatened, but then, what creature did not strike back in such circumstance? Ware and the others of his kind prospered under her tolerance, and she had not made undue demands upon them. There were some who said that the Queen had gotten above herself, that she acted as if she had forgotten her own humble origins, but there would always be those who would say that of someone who had succeeded where they had not.

No, he would just as soon not see the Queen replaced by a girl with no more idea of how to govern properly than a goat. At the least, it would mean a period of terrible chaos, and no one would prosper then. At the worst, the freedmen would take her accession to the throne as a time of weakness, and revolt. Hundreds, thousands would die, property would be destroyed, and even though Xylina and her Mazonite troops would win, the country would be years in recovering.

He should point out this option of his to the Queen. It would be a way to negate Xylina without killing or exiling her. He did not think that Adria had realized this. Of course, given the revulsion with which most Mazonites regarded a liaison with one of his kind, perhaps the option had never even occurred to her.

He rose from his impromptu couch with his plans firmly made. He would go to the Queen and begin his attempt to influence her. Xylina would, of course, attempt to raise the rest of the payment. At the end of the moon, they would see who had succeeded.

Perhaps, he thought with a smile, they both would. Then she would have another year, during which she would struggle to raise the money, and the Queen would attempt to ruin her. The game would be prolonged. That would make his quest to win her all the more of a challenge. He loved such a challenge; the longer Xylina managed to win, the more desirable she would prove herself to be. He almost hoped she would manage to prevail against the Queen and raise the money in a moon. Certainly she would not endure to the end of the full term; the Queen would see to that.

Xylina sat at her desk, and gazed at the total in her account books with a sinking heart. Despite help from Lycia's friends, many of whom sent their slaves to be trained by Faro with *no* prospect of ever needing slaves that were trained as bodyguards, the total was the same.

Forty-one coronets, seven circlets, and two silver sheaves. Not forty-five coronets. Not even close.

She had lost her bet. Her only choices now were bankruptcy and exile, bankruptcy and debtor's prison, or—

Or the unthinkable.

She shuddered. That was no answer, for even if she swallowed her revulsion and gave in to that—creature—it would only delay the inevitable. As soon as anyone found out—if there were even mere rumors that she had taken a demon as a lover—she could face not only exile. It was possible that she would be stoned from the gates. Such things had happened in the past, although she could not recall anything of the sort in her lifetime. Still, if her enemy was that powerful, Xylina might find herself facing the full force of an antique law.

But the very notion of yielding—no. It was not possible.

She put her aching head down in her hands. Her throat was tight and her eyes burned, and yet she could not weep. She was acutely aware of everything around her: the distant voice of Faro as he shouted at his clumsy new pupils, the *crack* of wood on wood as he drilled them, the scent of fresh bread from the kitchen, the harsh texture of the wood under her elbows, the faint movement of air through the ventilation slits in her office.

So she knew the moment something changed; felt the *presence* of someone else beside her, before he even moved and closed the door.

She dropped her hands to her desk and glared, but she had known whom it was the moment he entered so silently, unheralded. Only one creature could simply appear in her office like that. Only one had any reason to.

The demon called Ware.

And it was, indeed, he.

Today he made no pretense at being anyone's slave. He wore garments of black silk, artfully draped, and richly embroidered black-on-black about the hem, clasped with a belt of chased silver in the shape of a serpent that held its tail in its mouth. Beautiful and deadly, and she wondered how it was that the Queen held such power over his kind that they obeyed her. She could not imagine anyone controlling him, even with his consent.

"Tomorrow," he said simply, once again leaning back against the door of her office with arms folded over his chest. He looked absurdly out of place, so elegant amid the crude furnishings. "And you do not have the payment."

He made it a statement, but she knew better than to try and bluff him. His sources of information had been completely accurate before, and she saw no reason why that should have changed. She simply nodded, and stared at him, mouth a thin line of tension, every muscle and nerve taut as harp-strings.

"The option is still open," he said, delicately. He did not have to say which option.

"I will pay you," she snapped, wondering if she could borrow a half-coronet from each of Lycia's circle of cronies—just enough to make this payment. They could spare that, and she could pay them back a half-coronet each week, agreeing in advance what the order would be of repayment. That might save her this time—

"There will be more payments," he said, as if he were reading her mind. "Three more, to be precise. If you borrow from others, you will only be increasing your debt, and decreasing the amount you can save toward the next payment. And you will not be able to make the next payment. This I know."

"I wouldn't be so certain of that!" she snapped. "Business is better than ever—"

"Only because it amuses your enemy to allow you to think that you succeed, just before she brings another blow down upon you," he interrupted severely, like a teacher chiding a student for not having an answer she should have known. "Have you not thought this through? Your enemy is still your enemy, and will continue to be so. You have prevented her from burning your dwelling down a second time; now she will go on to more subtle means of destroying you. You will find yourself levied with strange fines, odd taxes. At every turn you will face another regulation which you are violating, for which you will have to pay. For every coronet you bring in, you will lose half in fines alone. She will leave you enough to give you the illusion that you are prospering, but it will be as much of an illusion as conjured gold, and it will disappear as quickly when tested."

She stared at him, mouth agape. Such power—who in all of Mazonia had such power? To change the very laws themselves to work against one specific woman—

"That—that's ridiculous!" she stammered. "That's impossible! Why, to do all that, this enemy of mine would have to be the Quee—"

She paled as he nodded, smiling a little. This time he looked like the teacher whose student had finally given the correct answer.

"No—" she whispered, heart struck as still as a stone, stomach sinking, throat tight. If the Queen was against her, she was surely doomed! But why her? "No—that can't be. Not the Queen—"

"Adria was rivaled in power only by your mother," Ware told her, his strange eyes utterly still for once, and dark as a gathering storm. He recited this dispassionately, as if it were some kind of lesson from remote history. "She feared your mother, but seeming fate took Elibet out of her path for her. I promise you, if the earthquake had not killed your mother, Adria would have eventually found another way to rid herself of a dangerous rival. Adria permits no rivals, dangerous, or otherwise."

Xylina stared at him, wondering how he knew all this. The same sources of information that had so accurately reported her inability to pay her debt? Or something more than that? And his reference to her mother—

"How could the Queen summon an earthquake?" she asked disbelievingly. "No woman has magic like that!"

"No woman," he agreed.

Xylina was aghast. "The demons? They have magic like that?"

"Or the ability to make it seem so," he said. "A little selective physical violence and a lot of illusion. It was, as I understand it, a desperate measure. But the Queen truly feared Elibet. Now she fears you."

"She—she murdered my mother?" This was almost too much to believe, yet the horrible sense of it was appearing. To eliminate a rival without suspicion—Xylina herself had never questioned the reality of the earthquake. Now she realized that there had been odd aspects, things she had attributed to the vagaries of cruel nature. This explained those things. An imperfect illusion.

But he was continuing. "While you were a child, she ignored you, for you were of no consequence, and she does not waste thought or effort on inconsequentials. She permitted the story of a curse to spread throughout the city in order to keep anyone from aiding you, but she was content to leave it at that and take no active role."

So that was where the story of the curse came from! Maybe there really was a curse, but as Lycia said, no one with any sense believed in it—until the Queen began giving it credence, and then it became believable.

Ware paused for a moment, as if to gather his thoughts. He stared over her head, at a point on the wall, and continued. "As you grew older and did not succumb to poverty or illness, she worried a little. But then—then you came late to your woman-trial. Adria assumed it was because you had no strong talent for conjuration, and were afraid. She was pleased. When she heard how you had no real choice of opponents, she was elated. She came to witness the death of her rival Elibet's line for herself. This time she did not need to take direct action."

So that was why the Queen was at her woman-trial! She had wanted to see Xylina die!

Ware shook his head. "But then—oh then, Xylina, you proved that you were truly your mother's daughter. You proved that you had inherited your mother's power and more. You showed the entire city that you were powerful, *and* clever, and at that moment, the Queen knew you were very likely the one Mazonite who could take her throne away from her."

"But I never—" Xylina croaked, appalled. "But I haven't any such aspiration! I don't—"

"It does not matter," Ware said, pitilessly. Now he lowered his gaze to hers, as if he were endeavoring to make certain that she heard and believed him. "It does not matter what you want, what you intend. Adria is right. Your ability will ultimately lead you to challenge her. Even if you never develop the ambition on your own, there will be those who will persuade you that it must be done."

She must have made some signal that she found his notion unlikely, for he frowned. "Xylina, I have seen all this before," he said sternly. "What do you think your friend Lycia and her circle are doing, if not slowly encouraging you to think that Adria is not as good a ruler as she could be? Are they not reminding you of her abuses of power that have near-ruined you, and telling you of other such abuses?"

Shocked, she could only nod, for that was precisely what had been happening.

Ware smiled grimly. "You see. Soon it will go beyond simple complaining, and turn to suggestions of what might be done about Adria. And then all eyes will turn to you, for none of them have the power of conjuration in the strength that you have it. You would be the only logical choice for a challenger."

"But what if I left them—" she began. "If I stop going to their gatherings, and slowly sever the relationship—"

Ware laughed, softly. "If you leave them, after all they have done for you, you will feel you have been ungrateful, and will have to return," Ware replied, before she could finish the sentence. "You know that is true, as you know that they will come to *you* and make you feel ungrateful for spurning them. And indeed they will have reason, for they have treated you generously."

That was true. They had not only helped her in her time of despair, they had given her their time and friendship. She could not condemn them for that. Their course made sense: to promote a friend to be Queen, replacing the bad Queen. Yet this was folly for Xylina! There must be something she could do, she thought frantically, trying to come up with some plan. "Perhaps I can persuade them to another course—" she offered.

He shrugged. "I do not think you can. And if it is not Lycia and her friends, it will be someone else. Perhaps even your own good friend Faro. I am certain he harbors an ambition of his own, to be the silent advisor behind the throne. Who could blame him? It is the highest position to which any slave can aspire, better even than being freed! Do not doubt me, *he* will be primary among those who encourage you to challenge Adria—and the sooner he discovers that your enemy is the Queen, the sooner he will tell you to challenge her in order to defend yourself. His very hatred for Mazonites will make him urge you to it, even if he has no ambition for himself." He paused for breath, and regarded her with a solemn gaze. "You will find yourself wanting, eager, to challenge the Queen. Perhaps not this year, nor the next, but it will happen in due course."

Xylina could only shake her head a little. She felt as if someone had dropped a wall upon her, and she was too stunned even to breathe. This was all too much, too soon. She had expected an enemy, she had not expected this kind of an enemy. She felt like a mouse, looking up at a shadow, expecting to see a jay come to steal her corn, and seeing instead a hawk come to devour *her.*

"Adria sees all this, as she has seen the ambitions of others before you," Ware said gently. "She knows she must nullify you before you can come close to challenging her. That is how she remains Queen, and has done so for as long as she has. You are not the first child who has posed a challenge to her power, and you likely will not be the last. You are merely the most serious so far."

Xylina finally took a breath. She had assumed that her enemy was some woman in a high position; she had never once considered that it could have been the Queen! If it had been anyone else, she could have exercised her right as a citizen to petition the Queen for a hearing. She could have set her grievances before the Queen. She could have confronted her enemy and forced the issue, making it clear that she had no vendetta and wanted only to live in peace.

Wait. She could still do that. The fact that her enemy was the Queen in no way changed that.

"I must go to Queen Adria myself," she said, pushing her chair away from the desk. She shook her head, distractedly. "I must do it now—reassure her that I have no intentions or ambitions to—"

"Oh, Xylina!" To her surprise, he began laughing, softly. She settled back into her chair, staring at him. "Oh, poor, naive child! You truly have no idea how sure the Queen is that you are a threat! Adria is a realist, my dear. Yes, she will believe that you mean what you say *now*—I think you are innocent enough to convince even her of that. But she is well aware that you will not remain innocent forever."

"I don't understand," Xylina said, half pleading, half in protest. She had never imagined anything like this. She could not see herself becoming the woman that Ware described.

Yet if she thought Lycia and the others were in danger, and thought she had to protect herself—

Then they might persuade her.

Ware shrugged. "I have seen many of your years, and many young girls like you, Xylina. The Queen has also seen many of your kind come and go. In time, she knows that you will become hardened and ambitious. You will think about how she tried to destroy you, and how she *did* destroy your mother, and your anger will grow, your resentment burn in your heart, and your need for vengeance will fester. One day, you will look at her, and you will think, 'That old hag is no longer the woman she was. I can take her. I can make her feel all the misery she made *me* feel.' And you will do it, Xylina."

"No—" she mouthed, unable to picture herself as he painted her. Willing to act to protect herself and others, yes—but hard? Ambitious? Ruthless? Yet he was right about her mother; already the rage of that discovery was a spreading fire, tempering her will with its heat.

"Yes, Xylina. And Adria knows it." He stared at her as if to drive his words into her heart, past all doubting. "Adria was once as innocent and naive as you—now she is as she is. I saw it happen to her, saw her mature into the Adria who now rules Mazonia and shares her power with no one, disposing of all contenders." He seemed remotely saddened by it all. "The same will happen to you, for you are only human, and to be human is to change."

Xylina felt numb; she did not know what to say. Ware seemed to sense this; he finally sat down beside her on the document-chest, and sighed.

"Let me show you how deeply deception runs in her,

how she can and will do anything to preserve her power. *I* am an agent in her little drama; I set the fire that burned your house, under her orders, which as you know I can not disobey."

She had thought she was beyond shock, but she was not beyond surprise. No wonder they could not imagine how the fire began, she thought, staring at him. No wonder they thought it must have been by magic. It *was*—but not human magic.

Ware continued. "When you found friends, Lycia among them, who might have caused trouble in the Council on your behalf, I was told to deceive you into incurring a debt you could not repay. When you default, she will have the pretext she needs to exile you or confine you to prison. Your threat to her will have been eliminated. You will either be gone, or completely under her control."

He raised one eyebrow. "It was my suggestion that there was another way to eliminate you as a threat without exiling you. The laws against congress with such as I have been softened in the last several years. While taking a demon as a lover no longer is punished by exile, there still must be a price. And since your deities do not approve of such things, such intercourse does render one—hmm—sacramentally unclean. I entered that service clause into the contract, and told the Queen that I might persuade you to accept what I offered. I sought to save you from exile at least, Xylina, for you know that exile is simply a longer road to death."

Xylina finally saw the nature of the double trap she was in; she whispered, appalled, "But if I were to—what you wish—to pay the debt, then I would be unclean, and no Mazonite who is unclean can take the throne—"

Ware smiled, as if at a clever child. "Precisely. The Queen's onus against you would be forever abated."

"But my oath—" she protested. "I swore—"

"Oaths can be interpreted in many ways," he said smoothly. "I swore an oath not to tell you that the Queen was your enemy. In just those words. And I did not. I gave you the information you needed to infer Adria's name and rank; *you* came to the conclusion, I did not *tell* you. My oath was not violated, and yet I also treated you with honor."

She shook her head, and her hair fell across her eyes like a curtain to cover her shame and embarrassment. But she was learning the ways of the world only too quickly this afternoon, and she knew that there was no curtain thick enough to hide her from what already was. And yet—there was one thing that she did not understand, and that was Ware himself. He seemed to think kindly of her; he had concocted this scheme to save her from exile, which as he pointed out, would have meant death. Yet he what he wished of her was impossible, and he must know that! She knew very little of demons; the few stories she had heard painted them to be lust-driven monsters.

"Why are you telling me all this?" she asked, finally. "If you know anything about me, you must know that I will die rather than yield to your lust!"

But rather than react with anger as a human would, Ware merely smiled. "I know you would do *nearly* anything rather than 'yield to my lust,' as you put it," he said, "and I do not intend to put you in a position where you would be forced to die to avoid something you consider utterly repugnant. I do not desire your body alone, Xylina."

As she stared at him without comprehension, he sighed.

"Must I put it into simpler terms then?" he asked, and grimaced. "Very well then, although my nature revolts at saying these things so baldly. These feelings of yours are a part of what makes you so desirable, to me, at least. I know that you will never grant your body to me unless your heart and spirit have already been given. Unless and until you come to love me, Xylina. It is that *love,* that so-human, so-precious gift, that I truly desire."

She felt her chin dropping, and quickly snapped her mouth shut. For a moment, she thought she had gone mad. Then she thought he surely must be joking—or trying to trick her.

But one look at his face, so human, and yet so unhuman, convinced her that he was utterly serious.

"You have only to say that you will take my option, and the debt will be canceled, Xylina," he persisted. "I will not put pressure upon you to actually fulfill your promise. I have patience—" He paused to smile and chuckle. "I have all the patience of my kind. I can wait as long as it will take. I can wait for fifty years, if need be."

That complete absurdity, in the midst of all the rest of this, made her laugh a little hysterically. "Fifty years!" she exclaimed. "I'll be an ugly old woman by then!"

He merely smiled, as if he knew some kind of secret that she did not. The smile quelled her hysteria as effectively as a dousing of cold water.

"Very well; you will not accept my offer. In that case, I am still patient, and I can wait until you come to wish it of your own will." He shrugged, and she stared at him. "Until you come to care for me," he said carefully, as if he wished to be sure that she understood him completely, "it is obviously in my interest to help you to survive—and to keep your citizenship and reputation intact. Why should I wish you to be judged unclean and suffer the scorn of your fellow citizens? No, Xylina, I shall even give you a *gift* of my advice, now, with no conditions attached, because I believe that I can bring you to desire me as ardently as I desire you."

She simply blinked, and licked lips gone dry and hot with tension and anxiety. Things were moving too quickly for her. She was no longer in control of her own destiny. She could only hope to ride out this storm and see the end of it.

"Since I have not pledged the Queen that I would not help you, I shall advise you how to extract yourself from this situation," he said. "The Queen will not know what I have told you, if you do not yourself tell her. This is what I advise, and remember that I have known Adria for as long as she has been Queen, and that I watched her come to power."

She nodded. What did she have to lose? At the worst, his advice would be so poor it would be obvious.

"You must go to the Queen," he said, once again surprising her. "But you must not tell her that you know the identity of your enemy. It would be well if you did not even mention that you are aware that you *have* an enemy." He paused to make certain that she had heard and understood him. "You must tell her your difficulties; how they began with the fire, and how you contracted a debt only to discover that it was not to the honorable Mazonite woman that you thought, but to a demon. Tell her that I proposed you give yourself to me to have the debt canceled, and explain how utterly revolted you are by the prospect. Tell her of your oath, if you wish. Then beg that she find you some honorable way out of this dilemma."

In light of everything he had told her, this seemed the rankest of folly! Why would he tell her *not* to go to the Queen, then tell her now that she should?

"But the Queen will not help me!" she exclaimed, protesting. "You told me this yourself! She wants me to fail!"

But he merely half-closed his eyes in that peculiar, cat-like way of his, and smiled. "She wants you to be disqualified for the office of Queen," he corrected her, gently. "She has no personal animus against you. I have reminded her of that, over the past moon. I have reminded her that if you were *her* daughter, she would have been proud of all you have accomplished thus far, and she has in fact agreed with that. If you come to her not with a grievance, but with a plea for help, she will find it difficult to deny."

Xylina paused and sat in thought for a long time. Put that way, she realized that he was right. The Queen had no reason to persecute her, only what she represented. Slowly, dubiously, she nodded her agreement. The matter of her mother still burned in her soul, but she knew she had no proof and no way to get redress. At the moment her only choice was to survive.

"Remember," he cautioned. "You must not make any charge that you cannot document. If she asks you if you think you have an enemy, you may say that you do, in order to avoid a lie—but do not say that you know it to be her. You must not let her think that you have found her out, or she will destroy you to save herself. You might not like the solution she finds for you, but it will not be exile, prison, or being—'forced'—to accede to my wishes."

"Very well," Xylina said, still feeling as if there was something about all this that she was missing. "When do you suggest that I approach her?"

"Now," Ware replied firmly. "Ask for immediate audience. Your debt comes due tomorrow, and if you wait, she will suspect something. Take Faro with you, if you feel you need him at your back, but you must go—and now."

And once again, with a sinking heart, she realized that he was right.

For once again, she had no choice.

• Chapter 9

Xylina had not really expected to get an immediate audience, despite Ware's insistence that she go to the Queen right away. She presented herself to the majordomo and sat on one of the hardwood benches in the dark, polished-granite anteroom. She heard her name called, ahead of others who had been waiting there longer.

She was certain there was some mistake, or that she was going to be told to return in the morning. The majordomo was a high-ranking slave who had the duty of relaying the Queen's orders when it came to whom she would see and whom she would not. When new petitioners arrived, the majordomo would send a slave in with the new name to the Queen, and she would decide whether she wished to see a particular person that day. Xylina expected to be told to return later. That would be fine, since she would at least have the evidence that she had presented herself today to show that she felt her cause was urgent.

But the majordomo beckoned, then ushered her into the audience chamber without a single word. Light spilled out as he quietly opened one of the bronze doors just enough to let her inside, then closed it behind her.

The silence within the audience chamber was intimidating. Xylina looked around, and suddenly felt very small. She took a firm grip on herself and took a second look. The chamber had obviously been designed to achieve just that effect of intimidating the petitioner and making her feel insignificant. The great double door behind her was far larger than it needed to be. The white marble from which the chamber had been crafted made it difficult to judge exactly how large it was, as the walls and ceiling receded into a haze of light. Everything in the room seemed to be just the slightest bit oversized. The empty benches beside her, for instance, which would hold waiting groups while their spokeswoman approached the Queen, were all just a little too tall and too wide to fit the average Mazonite comfortably. The bronze oil-lamps riveted to the white marble wall were of the same shape and style that she had seen in many other homes, yet they, too, were larger than normal. She had the feeling that the walls were not exactly parallel, that they were slightly skewed. The chamber focused on the raised platform at the end, and the scarlet-draped throne placed in the middle of it, the only spot of real color in the whole room. There was a single armed Guard behind her, and the Guard's eyes were focused on some point high above Xylina's head. If not for the gentle movement of the Guard's chest and the occasional blinking of her eyes, she could have been a statue. Beside the throne was a small bronze gong.

As if to contrast with the white of the room and the scarlet of her throne, Adria wore starkly cut black silk, ornamented with gold embroidery at the shoulders and hems of her tunic and breeches, clasped with a belt made of gold and onyx plates. A simple, brushed-gold coronet adorned Adria's short gray-threaded black hair, and she sat relaxed and erect in her throne with an air of complete self-confidence.

She showed no sign that she recognized Xylina. As the girl approached, walking softly so that the sound of her footsteps would not echo in the enormous room, there was not even a flicker of recognition in the Queen's eyes.

But she reminded herself that Adria must have years of practice in maintaining control over her expression. The Queen was a consummate politician, of course, and it would be important that her enemies never be able to judge what she was thinking from her face. It would be just as important that Adria's own people never know what she was thinking.

She must remember this, Xylina told herself firmly. She must be as controlled as the Queen was. Adria must not know what Xylina was thinking, either. If the Queen knew, she could manipulate her; if she didn't, Xylina might control what the Queen thought of her, at least to some extent.

But how to accomplish this, when Xylina had no time to prepare herself, and was only a little less naive than she had been before today? She was not used to hiding her feelings—she was more accustomed to blurting out the truth than concealing it. And she still felt bewilderment and anger at Adria—both of which had to remain hidden.

Then she realized that she need not hide anything—she need only choose what to display. She could use one set of emotions to cover another. She would remember how she felt a moon ago, when Ware revealed his secret to her. That was hardly difficult; it was in fact far easier to call up that rage and fear—which was still with her—than it was to maintain the complex welter of emotions with which today's conversation had left her. The anger at Ware was closest to the surface and easiest to call upon. Despite what he had said to her, the way he had tried to help her, she was still full of that rage. After all, what he had said about her mother's death might not be true; it might be a ploy to set her against the Queen. And fear—that was easy to invoke as well. Who wouldn't be afraid, faced with exile?

She made up her mind all in an instant. This must be simple; she was calling upon the Queen for justice. The demon tricked her because he lusted after her. She did not know that Ware served the Queen; she did not know that the Queen had been trying to destroy her.

She approached the throne with her heart pounding loudly in her ears, her stomach quaking, but her head held high. She tried to keep those two things firmly in mind—her anger at Ware and his deception, and her fear of what might come. Adria's expression of bored tolerance did not change in the least. Xylina realized that she would not know if her plan was succeeding until Adria reacted—possibly when it was too late.

The majordomo had not told her what to do or given her any kind of instructions on protocol. But Xylina had always been taught that a Mazonite bowed to no one, not even the Queen. So she stopped two steps from the foot of the dais, and inclined her head, slightly. Then she stood stiffly erect, waiting.

This brought an ironic smile to Adria's lips. The expression did not move beyond her lips, nor did it warm her face to something less mask-like and more human. "So stiff," she murmured. "So proud. Well, Xylina Elibetas, what brings you before us that is so urgent it impressed even our majordomo?" She used the royal plural, but Xylina had expected that. What she had not expected was the quality of Adria's voice. Warm, dryly persuasive—Xylina found herself wanting to believe everything that voice told her. And she found herself wondering if Ware had lied to her.

Never mind. What she was about to do did not depend on the Queen's innocence or guilt, it depended on telling the truth. Not what she thought or guessed, not what Ware had said, but just the simple facts. In fact, if Adria was innocent of what Ware had accused her of, it would be all the better. The Queen would surely be inclined to give her aid, then.

"The need for justice is what brings me, Queen Adria," Xylina replied, letting her outrage creep into her voice. "Justice that only you can dispense. I have been driven to the danger of exile—or of worse—through no fault of my own, and I ask your aid."

Briefly, she explained her "misfortunes," making no accusations, acting (as best she could) as if she truly believed that everything that had happened to her had been just a long series of mischances. She reported everything, from the first vandalism through the series of attacks by ruffians. She concluded with the fire. Throughout her recitation, the Queen's expression had not changed.

Except—except that each time she detailed how an attack or "accident" had driven her further into debt, the Queen's eyes gleamed for a moment. Had she not seen it happen repeatedly, she might have dismissed it as a figment of her imagination.

"One might almost think you had some unseen enemy, Xylina," the Queen said casually. "Or perhaps that tale you told us of the curse is a true one."

Xylina hung her head for a moment to hide her shock, for she had not spoken of the curse, nor had she implied that she had thought of an enemy. Was the Queen baiting her?

"I can't imagine who would be my enemy, Queen Adria, unless it could be a device of the demon to put me into his debt," she said quietly. "And I was always told that no Mazonite could be touched by the curse of a mere male."

"Very proper," the Queen murmured.

Xylina looked up as soon as she thought she had her expression under control again. Her indignation grew, as she began to detect another subtle change in the Queen's expression—a growing smugness.

Adria thought Xylina a fool.

Then came the second realization. The Queen really had done all this. She really was her enemy.

The realization that Ware had been right, and that she must continue to play the fool, galled her. Yet there was no choice for her, when all was said and done. She must let Adria think that her head was as empty as a jug with a hole in the bottom, if she wanted to survive.

She recited the aftermath of the fire—the knowledge that she must now pay the whole of the sum she owed, and still have nowhere to live. Then she told of the shock when the tax-collector arrived. She did not accuse anyone, she only told of her bewilderment.

And the Queen's eyes lit with unmistakable enjoyment.

"We know it must seem unfair to you, but that law was instituted because there were Mazonites who could not pay their year-taxes, and chose to burn their own property so that they need not do so," the Queen said coolly. "You know that we cannot make an exception for anyone, lest those same women come flocking to us, looking for an exception for themselves."

"Of course, Queen Adria," Xylina said meekly.

Xylina had never heard any such thing, and neither had Lycia or any of her friends. That was utter nonsense; no one with any intelligence would ever believe it.

Finally she detailed the loan, how the manservant had come to her with the offer. She told the Queen that she had believed that Hypolyta had been nothing more than a generous and kind-hearted businesswoman, only to learn she had become indebted to a demon. "And he did not reveal himself to me until after the debt came due," she said, and she did not have to feign anger. Her voice shook when she related Ware's suggested "bargain," and when she told the Queen of her answer, she knew that she was hot with rage and shame.

Through it all, the Guard behind her looked completely indifferent to what she said. Xylina wondered for a moment, looking up at her, if there was anything that could make the Guard change her statue-like calm.

"Did this demon tell you his name?" Adria asked.

"He said that it was 'Ware,' Queen Adria," she replied softly. "I can't say if it was his true name. I did not even know he was a demon until he told me—I have never seen a demon before."

The Queen smiled, just a little, and she picked up an ebony stick that sat beside her and tapped the bronze gong set into the floor beside her throne with it. The majordomo appeared immediately.

"Is Ware in attendance with the court?" she asked. The majordomo bowed and answered in the affirmative. "Then summon him here, before us," she ordered. She turned to Xylina. "You can tell us if this is the demon who contracted with you."

The servant disappeared, and returned in a heartbeat or two, Ware pacing elegantly at his side. The demon bowed low before the Queen, and raised a long, tapered eyebrow at Xylina. He had already changed his costume; now he wore shirt and breeches of scarlet silk, and a tunic of crimson velvet. With them he wore belt, gorget, and rings of rubies and gold.

"Did you contract a debt with this young woman?" Adria demanded. "A debt that you knew she could not repay?"

Ware smiled. "It is within my rights, my Queen," he said pointedly. "Yes, I did. I have only exercised a right that every creature of my kind has, as granted by long tradition and the law. You can not deny me that right."

"We are not disputing that," Adria replied. "We only wish to know if you offered a more—physical way of discharging the debt, when this Mazonite could not make her payment. There are certain outgrowths of that proposition that we are not certain the young woman was aware of."

"That is also within my rights, Majesty," Ware reminded her. "It is not incumbent upon a demon to keep your subjects from disporting themselves with my kind. And my kind favor congress with yours, as you well know. If she should choose to exercise that option, the price is more than fair, considering the magnitude of her debt."

He would have said more, but the Queen cut him off with an imperious gesture. "Enough," she said, and turned to Xylina. Now she wore an expression of interest and amusement. "This is intolerable, of course," she said warmly. "But there is nothing we can do about the contract or the offer. Ware is right; there are no laws *against* what he offered. These creatures twist and turn their just rights about until they no longer resemble anything like the original intentions of our fore-mothers. However, we do not care for his presumption, and we feel that he has tricked you. You have certainly not had justice; something must be done here. Allow us a moment to think; this must be something that will not violate the law, nor make exceptions to it."

She appeared to think for a moment, then turned again to Ware. "You have entrapped this young woman, and that is certainly not to be permitted. We will guarantee the debt," she told him severely.

Ware only bowed, and said nothing. Xylina thought she saw his eyes glinting with amusement, but she could not be certain.

The Queen turned to Xylina, and explained, as if to a very small child, "This does not mean, Xylina, that you no longer owe this demon his agreed-upon sum. You contracted a debt, and it has not been discharged. You will still owe it to him, with interest—but with the guarantee of the Crown, no annual payment will be required. This means that you do not owe him anything at this time, nor next year, and so on, until the full term of the debt is over."

Xylina nodded, and blinked, trying to look innocent and not irritated at having all this explained to her. But she felt free to show her amazement at the Queen's action, as this gave her three more years to make good.

The Queen continued. "If the term of your debt—or you—expire without the debt being paid, the Crown will pay it off. That is what the guarantee means." She glanced at Ware, obliquely, and there was no doubt in Xylina's mind that something about this arrangement pleased her immensely. "Now, this also means that this demon must make every possible effort to see that you repay him; he must, therefore, forfeit his other interests and accompany you wherever you may go until the debt is paid. You must offer him lodging in your home, if he wishes it, or you may move into his if he prefers that. If you go somewhere, he must go with you."

Xylina paled as she realized what the Queen had just done. With the demon following her everywhere, there would be many opportunities for him to get what he wanted from her. In fact, only by being extremely careful to have witnesses about her at all times could she *avoid* the imputation that Ware had obtained congress with her. She was thankful only that Faro was so devoted to her; she must get him registered as able to serve as a witness, so that no one could contest his word. Ordinarily a slave could not be a legal witness, but it was possible to have one certified in advance so that he could provide signatures on a contract or testify in a court. She did not think that the Queen realized she knew this, and that was a chink in whatever plan Adria had in mind.

"Now, we cannot leave you destitute, and with no means of repaying this creature," the Queen continued smoothly, her eyes glinting with enjoyment. "Obviously, your efforts up until this moment have not been sufficient. And you must also repay the service that the Crown is doing you. We have a plan that will serve in both cases. In recompense for our generous action, we will require a little service of you."

Her tone left no doubt in Xylina's mind: Adria would not accept "no" for an answer. Xylina had agreed to this simply by asking the Queen for a solution. She was now bound to whatever the Queen asked.

Still, until she heard what this service was, she should not reject it out of hand—her only other choices were the ones she had before, and they were all impossible.

"If you complete this service successfully," the Queen continued, "we will be happy—very happy—to pay off the debt immediately. That is a Crown promise, Xylina, and we will contract to it if you choose. So, you see, this is a good solution for everyone."

As Adria leaned back in her throne, a pleased and smug smile now openly on her face, Xylina knew that this "little service" was going to be neither "little" nor easy. But what choice did she have?

If she refused, Adria would have every reason to simply cast her into prison or send her into exile at once. Xylina had in effect given the Queen license, so there would be no impropriety in such action.

"What is this service, Queen Adria?" she asked, stalling

for time to think. "Please, I would like to know what it is before I say anything."

"We need a stone—a jewel of a kind," the Queen replied, regarding Xylina from beneath long eyelashes. "It is quite unique and very valuable, one of the last of its kind in existence."

A stone—a gem. Probably it was hundreds of leagues away, and guarded by monsters.

The Queen appeared to be thinking, but Xylina had the impression that she was only pausing in order to savor Xylina's discomfiture. Her next words confirmed Xylina's fears. "It is actually a fragment of a crystal, rather than a jewel or a gem. It is only fair to warn you that it is in a very dangerous place, well outside our realm. Those who have it now will fight to retain possession."

Meaning they probably were monsters.

The Queen paused again, this time for what appeared to be a moment of genuine thought. There was a gleam in her eyes that Xylina did not immediately recognize until she looked at Ware out of the corner of her eye. He was regarding her with a certain peculiar expression that seemed compounded equally of greed and acquisitiveness. The Queen wore the same expression, talking about this stone. "Additionally, once you have it, there is another problem. The stone itself is treacherous. Stones like it have been known to turn upon their possessors."

As Xylina listened, she became aware that this really was the emotion that possessed the Queen whenever she contemplated the notion of this gem. It was an avariciousness that surprised her. Adria really *wanted* this stone, deeply, greedily—whatever, wherever it was. There was a different kind of gleam in Adria's eyes when she spoke of it, a gleam that had nothing to do with eliminating her putative rival.

"It is also fair to warn you that it is possible that you will die in this quest, child," the Queen continued, her tone replete with satisfaction. "Only a truly talented, resolute, and powerful woman will be able to accomplish what we are offering you as a quest. But you have already proved your ability in the arena—you are exceptional. If anyone can bring this stone back to us, it is you. We believe that you should do this, that you would be an ungrateful fool if you did not accept our offer."

There it was: her marching orders. And they *were* orders; there was no mistaking the iron under the silk of Adria's voice. Xylina felt her voice quavering, and she did not try to stop it. Let the Queen think that it was fear and not anger. "Am I to attempt this alone, Queen Adria? This hardly seems better than the choice I have without your quest! Is this not a kind of exile? Do I not face death equally if exiled from Mazonia or on your mission? Prison would be safer!" She did not mention acceding to Ware's desires.

The Queen laughed. Oddly, it did not sound as if she was gloating, but as if she were truly amused. "Alone? Hardly, child! You are one of our best and brightest subjects, and if you survive you will be invaluable to us in the wars of the future. It is not in our interest for you to fail, after all; we want this stone, and we can make use of your abilities when you bring it back. We will not force you into an impossible task; we will give you whatever assistance you might need. We will send you with an ample entourage: servants, guards, supplies, and whatever gold and silver you might require. It will be a military party, in fact, of which you will be the leader. We send you to a far and hostile land, but we will not send you alone or unprepared. You will represent Mazonia on this mission."

Xylina pondered the "solution"; certainly if she were killed, this would solve Adria's problem, with no guilt or censure being attached to the Queen afterward. But she was making the offer of help and supplies with Ware still present as a witness, and demons were acceptable as witnesses. Her promise of help was genuine. She truly wanted that stone; this was no ruse. Perhaps even more than she wanted Xylina dead or compromised.

"Do think," the Queen added, coaxingly. "You will be the

head of a military expedition. When you return, you will already have had experience commanding in the field. We would not be averse to granting you a high position in our Guard or our Council based on that experience. Ware will go with you, of course, but the presence of our guards should guarantee your safety with him. This is an excellent chance for you. There are many among my Guard who would be glad of such an opportunity."

Then why not offer it to them? Xylina thought wryly. She knew, of course, that it probably had been offered to Guards in the past—and that since the Queen still did not have the stone, they had in all probability died in the attempt to fetch it.

Xylina was not particularly sanguine about her own survival, as far as that went. Still—this would be better than being escorted to the edge of Mazonia and left there with only the clothes on her back. It was preferable to prison. And it was much preferable to giving in to the demon. She had been maneuvered into this commitment, but it did have its points.

"You are right, Queen Adria," she said, trying to sound naive and sincere. "This is a good solution to the entire situation. I must accept your offer with all gratitude. I would, indeed, be a fool if I did not."

"Excellent." The Queen applauded. She rang again for the majordomo, and directed him to bring her seal and paper. When he returned, she wrote out a note under her seal, guaranteeing the debt and specifying both the "service" and that the debt would be paid when Xylina returned with the stone. This she gave to Ware, who accepted it with a bow.

"It will take about a week to assemble the party and supplies," the Queen said, when she had finished. "If you can think of anything you might need, simply send word to my majordomo and he will arrange for it to be added to the expedition. We will send for you when the party is complete, to give you your final instructions and send you off."

"Thank you, Queen Adria," Xylina said.

The Queen smiled winningly. "We simply do our best for a loyal subject. Now remember, Ware must accompany you wherever you go, and this must begin from this moment."

Xylina had forgotten that, and it irked her, but she nodded her agreement. Ware, too, had maneuvered her rather more neatly than she liked.

The majordomo escorted them both out a side door. Ware looked about for observers, but there was no one in sight. Nevertheless, he waited until they were some distance from the walls before he said anything. "This is rather what I had expected her to do," he said, as Xylina wondered if he were more her foe than the Queen. "This is the most serious challenge that the Queen could have arranged for you, but I did not expect less from her."

"You might tell me something I could not have guessed for myself!" she snapped. "The likelihood is that I am going to be killed on this foolish quest!"

But Ware only smiled. "This is where she miscalculated. She still does not realize that I intend to help you. Without me, you would certainly die. But my desire for you is extraordinarily greater than incidental lust. With me, and with my help, you can complete this task. However, there are special precautions that you must take."

Once again, Xylina was taken aback by both how human and inhuman he was. And by how accurate his reading of the Queen was. Certainly, if Adria had thought that Ware intended to aid her rival, she would have done something to prevent him from going along, instead of the opposite. Now that she thought about it, she realized that Adria could have assumed the debt herself, buying it from Ware. Xylina would still have been forced to go on this quest, but without Ware's help. Surely the Queen assumed that the only action Ware might take would be to whisk her away from certain death, and take advantage of her. And in *that* case, Adria would not even have to assume the guilt for sending Xylina into a fatal situation.

"What must I do?" she asked quickly, but Ware only shook his head, and made a cautioning movement.

"It is too public here," he replied. "Let us wait until we are within your walls—and let us wait until you have Faro with you. He will likely play an important role in this; he should be fully informed."

She could hardly restrain her impatience, but Ware was right. Faro should be present, and not just to receive information. She held her tongue until they were within her gate and she had sent for Faro to come to her little office.

Faro knew only what had occurred up until this afternoon. He had no idea of what Ware had said and done since he had arrived in Xylina's office this day. The slave drew himself up protectively, glared angrily at Ware, and he said, threateningly, "I do not care what you are, demon, nor what your powers are. If you hurt my little mistress in any way, or dare to do anything she finds repugnant, I shall rend your limbs from your body, pull what passes for your heart from your chest, and stuff it into your deceitful mouth! You may have tricked her, but I am bound by no vows regarding you."

Xylina blinked, astonished by his protective vehemence, but Ware only nodded with approval. The demon seemed completely undisturbed by the threat. "Good," he said. "It is as I hoped, and as Adria does not guess." He turned to Xylina. "She thinks that this slave hates you, as he most likely hates all Mazonites, and will do nothing to protect you when he has no obvious responsibility, Xylina. That his performance in street fights will not be echoed when the threats are more subtle. We must not let her become aware that she is wrong."

Faro was clearly taken aback by Ware's casual acceptance of his threat. And a moment later, he was deeply absorbed in everything the demon had to say, as Ware explained all that had happened since he arrived in Xylina's office.

"Now you understand why your willingness to protect Xylina is so important," Ware concluded, speaking to Faro

as he would to an equal, which also surprised Xylina.
"Xylina can protect herself, but only while she is awake, and
not against overwhelming odds," Ware continued. "She
must sleep sometimes. I doubt that Adria will send any
females with her. The armed guards she sends will be all
male slaves, licensed to be armed outside of Mazonia, and
as the only female with a Mazonite expedition, she will be
the obvious target in an attack. Anyone who has faced
Mazonites before knows who the leaders are in any group,
and they will know that without Xylina, the slaves will be
free to run away. The guards that Adria sends may be half-
hearted in their defense because of that—but not if they
know that you, Faro, will beat them senseless, then remove
limbs, if she comes to grief."

Faro actually smiled, a feral, hungry stretching of the
lips. The smile of a man who had been trained for the arena.

"Are we all agreed, then?" Ware said. "Are we to work as
a team? Our purposes differ, but on this mission I believe
we have a common cause. We all want it to succeed. Faro, I
pledge you my word that I will do nothing with Xylina that
she does not herself approve. In fact, she will tell you what
she wishes in that respect."

"Agreed," Faro said positively, knowing Xylina's strength
of will in this matter. Xylina nodded.

Ware sat back, in a relaxed pose. "Now, let me tell you all
that I know about this stone that we are to retrieve. If you
have any questions, please ask them at any time. I do not
wish to leave anything out, and your questions may prompt
my memory." He grinned. "It is at times as fallible as any
mere human's."

Somehow, despite everything he had done to her,
directly or indirectly, Xylina found herself beginning to like
the demon. So far, except for what he wanted of her, and
that deception about the contract, he had been completely
honorable with her.

"This crystal—or rather, crystal shard—dates from a
time long forgotten by your people, Xylina." Ware's face

took on an absent and thoughtful expression, almost as if he was dreaming of something. His eyes swirled with many colors, an effect that Xylina had never before seen when she looked at him. His face changed as he spoke of the remote past, subtly, but unmistakably. At this moment, she knew he was truly unhuman; there was something about the angular shape of his face and that remote expression that made him appear truly alien. Now she wondered just how old Ware really was, how much he had seen.

"It is a lost fragment of a much larger crystal which was shattered long ago," he continued, his voice as remote as his eyes. "This original crystal polarizes all the magic of this realm—it makes the magic work in particular ways, along specific lines and following specific rules. Do you understand this so far?"

"I think so," Xylina replied. She had never before thought of magic as following rules, or being governed by anything. It just *was*. And she had certainly never had the notion that there was some relic of ancient times behind it all.

"Where is this crystal?" Faro asked. "Are we going to be trying to find it, too?"

"The main crystal is hidden in the heart of a fortress in the center of the realm. It is heavily guarded." Ware raised an eyebrow. "Although the Queen is not aware of it, the guards are descendants of the very first Mazonite Queen and a select number of her Guard. They are there, not to keep the crystal from being stolen, but to keep a new fragment from coming near it. Not surprising, since whenever a missing fragment is brought to it, its polarity changes— and that causes the magic of the entire realm to change."

"Change?" Xylina said, puzzled. How on earth could magic change? "What do you mean?"

Ware grimaced. "It is difficult to explain. The last addition brought about the present order, the one that you and all Mazonites believe that has been in place forever. Once, my dear, women were not the rulers. Men were not slaves.

Your order is not the 'natural' order, it is only one of many possibilities."

She blinked. Where did that leave the words of the historians, who recorded nothing but female superiority since time began? Where did that leave the priestesses, who told their followers that the Supreme Power was, of course, female?

"Since that addition," Ware continued, "magic has been that of conjuration, and is channeled only through women. And since I am sure that you are curious, yes, I do know what the previous order was like."

Xylina hung on his words, avid with curiosity.

"Before the moment of that addition, it was a kind of magic that could make events occur," Ware told them. "What I mean is that this magic would force things to happen that would not otherwise have occurred, and it was controlled not by women, but only by virgin children under the age of puberty. The next addition—" He shrugged. "Who knows what that will bring?"

"What do you think?" Faro asked shrewdly.

"Well—" Ware lowered his eyes for a moment. "Let us say that I do not yet have an opinion. Many of my kind believe that it will bring about a complete reversal of the current order, and that magic will then be channeled through men. I do not think I need to tell you what that will mean."

Faro's eyes gleamed, and Xylina held her breath. Really, the only thing keeping men subservient to women was the women's ability at conjuration. If that were lost—if, in fact, *men* got magic power of some kind, the entire world would change. And she had no doubt how it would change. . . .

"They would make us their slaves," she murmured, awed and horrified. "They would force us to serve them in every way, to wait upon them, bear them child after child, to serve their pleasures whenever, wherever they pleased—"

She shuddered. She knew that although she cared for and respected Faro, as she had Marcus, she could not live under a regime of that sort.

"I do not know that this will be true," Ware cautioned. "Just because such a reversal seems logical, it does not follow that it will be so. The last change did not follow such a logical reversal—the next may grant magic only to those who are blue-eyed, or those with golden hair, or to virgins, or those past bearing children. Or to those with a particular birthmark, or of a particular lineage! I can not say. This magic is not even remotely logical."

Xylina let out a sigh of relief, and Faro looked disappointed for a moment. Then, oddly, his face cleared. She thought she understood why. No matter what the change was, it would mean that power was no longer completely in the hands of women. That would be enough for him. . . .

"The new magic will also be more powerful, because the main crystal will be closer to being complete," Ware continued. "Just as the magic of Mazonite conjuration is more powerful than the magics that preceded it. The more of the crystal that is added, the stronger magic grows. When it is complete—perhaps *all* humans will have magic, and all forms of magic will be in effect. We do not know. Or perhaps—there will be no magic, and every human will have to rise or fall only on his or her own efforts."

Xylina tried to imagine a world without magic, and failed. But Faro nodded thoughtfully. Perhaps it was easier for him, magic-less, to imagine a world without it.

"We demons have known of this all along, of course," Ware said, matter-of-factly. "This is why so many of my kind are 'courting' the freedmen; frankly, we expect this change to take place within the next fifty years. And if magic goes to men, then the demons will be ready to remind them of all the favors we did them in the past."

"Favors?" Xylina said, doubtfully, distracted for a moment. "What do you mean?"

Faro bent and hid his face, and from the strangled sounds that came from him, she had a strong suspicion he was choking down laughter. She could not imagine what was so funny. Ware simply looked at her, with an enigmatic smile on his face, as if he too found something amusing.

"We treat the freedmen as equals," he said gently. "You know this to be true, for you have seen how I treat Faro, and you will see how I treat my own slaves—as servants, but not as inferior to myself. We are their conduit to the world of the Mazonites, as I explained to you earlier. We contract to them for goods and services, then contract in turn to the Mazonites. We also take their goods to the world outside Mazonia, and trade there for them. But the service that I believe Faro is so amused by is that we supply them with— hmm—bed-companions."

Bed-companions? Did he mean? He couldn't have meant—

Some of Xylina's shock must have showed on her face, for Faro looked up briefly, and doubled over again. Evidently he found all this very funny. She blushed, feeling her ears grow hot, her cheeks burning.

"But—" she said, then stopped in embarrassment. She did not know what she wanted to say, but she burned with curiosity as well as embarrassment.

"There are female demons as well as male," Ware pointed out, obliquely. "Succubi as well as incubi. But the main—ah—trade is in simulacra. Creatures made from other living things, that look human, but are not. Created 'living dolls,' if you will, with no souls and no more mind than a rodent. Many of them are made from mice, or other lower creatures. They are created for pleasure, and nothing else. These are—well, let me just say that they are very popular with slaves and freedmen who can not afford foreign women."

Well, that certainly explained some things that Marcus would not tell her about the sounds coming over the wall, from what had once been her mother's house! Xylina flushed even deeper, and decided to change the subject quickly.

"What of the change that this new fragment would

bring?" she asked. "Why are your kind so certain that magic would go to males?"

"Oh, they are hardly certain," Ware replied lightly. "That is simply what most of my kind think the most likely, or so they try to tell themselves. I—my opinions vary from day to day." His tone turned to one of warning. "But no matter what happens, Xylina, you must realize contemporary society will suffer extreme changes, dislocation—without any doubt at all, power will go to some group that does not currently have it. That means that there will be a revolution, and whatever leaders are in charge at that time will be deposed. Probably, they will be killed. That is what happened a millennium ago, when the last change occurred. Of this, none of my kind has any doubts. And when the change occurs, we will vanish from your ken until the chaos is over. It will be a catastrophe that will make every natural disaster, every war, every disruption your people have endured seem tame by comparison."

And Adria *wanted* this shard? Xylina was incredulous. Was she insane?

"Why on earth would the Queen wish to possess this thing?" Xylina asked, aghast at the visions that Ware's words invoked in her all-too-active imagination.

Ware smiled, a smile of deceptive gentleness. Xylina saw the smile, and was reminded of a hawk basking in the sun, who could turn into a deadly killer in the time it took to spot a rabbit in the grass. "Ah, but Adria does not know the stone's true nature," he said, a feral gleam in the back of his ever-changing eyes. "She knows only what she has been told: that when properly mounted in gold, it enhances the power of its possessor, and keeps the possessor eternally young. She wants that, more than she let you know. She wants it more than anything she has ever wanted before in her life. Physically, at least, she would be immortal—if she could keep a rival from killing her over it. Anyone who knew she had such a thing would of course want it herself. On the other hand, with her already formidable powers

enhanced, Adria would be the single most powerful conjurer in the history of Mazonia. It would be very difficult to
challenge her."

"And of course, you had nothing to do with her learning
this," Faro put in, his voice dense with irony. "The fact that
all those restrictions on demon-kind would be gone if this
change of yours takes place would have nothing to do with
Adria learning of the shard."

Ware contrived to look innocent. "I? Why should I have
told her these things? Of course, an ambitious person of my
kind *would* have every reason to let this information slip, if
he already had an extensive network among the freedmen.
Although you are correct; the vows to serve and obey the
Queen and the other laws we must obey would no longer
be in effect if there was no longer a Mazonite government."

"Hmm." Xylina grimaced a little. She did not in the least
believe his innocent ploy. As he had pointed out, one had to
be very careful when dealing with demons, who had centuries in which to learn the ways of bypassing oaths.
Nothing Ware said could be taken at absolute face value.
Perhaps he had told Adria nothing directly—but he could
have brought a document to her attention, or something of
the sort. He could even have planted such a document
where he knew she would find it.

She did not particularly like those repeated references to
the fact that the laws governing the demons' behavior
would no longer bind them when the change took place.
And what if the change gave the *demons* all power of
magic? All of humanity could wind up being their slaves!

"I don't suppose this is true," she said, "this tale of
immortal youth—"

"Ah, but it is," Ware replied, his eyes gleaming.
"Remember, dear Xylina, we may not lie to the Queen. It is
entirely true. It is simply not the entire truth."

Xylina tried to think what was wrong with this—there
must be something that Ware had not yet told them. "But if
that tale is true, the realm is in no real danger. She can

simply keep the shard forever, and never take it to the main crystal. In fact, she would not want it out of her possession for even a moment! What on earth could ever induce her to take the shard to the greater crystal?"

But something in Ware's sly and anticipatory expression told her that she had not heard the entire story. Her guess that he still had something to tell them was right. And he was waiting for her to ask.

"All right," Xylina said, finally. "How would or could this shard be brought to the great crystal against the Queen's wish and will?"

Ware smiled again, showing the sharp tips of his teeth. "Because the shard is a subtle thing, as is the parent crystal," he told them. "It has a will of its own. It slowly corrupts its wearer to its will. While it would take something like a hundred years for the shard to wholly subvert its wearer, it does not actually need to wholly subvert someone to get her to do what it wills, as I am sure you realize." Once again, his eyes went strange and full of otherness. She shivered, looking into them. "When it prevails, the person wearing it is compelled to take it to the larger crystal so that it can be merged with the great stone. Once it prevails, the bearer will make up some reason why she wishes to do what the stone wants. It is possible that Adria will convince herself that if a small shard of the crystal is a good thing to have, the greater parent crystal would be better. So you see now, the shard will inevitably prevail, if it has a bearer."

"So unless it is kept hidden away from people so that no one can mount and wear it, the shard will have its will," Xylina said, after a long moment. "There is nothing that can be done that will stop that."

"Quite true. And the present order has endured for so long only because the fragment *has* been hidden," Ware said, his eyes slowly returning to normal. "But the end of the era is in sight. The Queen discovered the existence of the shard, and now she knows where it is, and she means to have it. She desires eternal youth, immortality, and enhanced power—and I think that even if she knew the whole truth, she would convince herself that *she* could withstand the will of the shard."

He looked carefully into Xylina's face, as if he was reading her mind from her expression. "Do not think that you will stop her from this by simply not fetching the stone for her, Xylina. She will merely send someone else, as she has been sending others all along—Guards, adventurers, fortune-seekers. She has had power for so many years that she has become corrupted by it, able to convince herself that what she wants will be good for her people as a whole. And having succumbed to one sort of corruption, she is ripe to be corrupted by another. She will have the shard, and when she does, she will soon have to merge it. She will persuade herself that the will of the shard is her will, and go to find the parent crystal. And when she does—"

Silence. Then Faro spoke. "It will be the end of their world," he said, his voice like the thunder presaging a storm.

Xylina stretched, slipped off clothing she had not, until this evening, considered shabby, and stepped into a simmering white-marble cauldron of hot, soothing water.

At last she was alone. Now she could review recent events and perhaps come to terms with them.

After much discussion, Ware had brought them both to his villa, and housed them in luxury Xylina could not have imagined enjoying a day before. He pointed out that there was no point in keeping the hired guards—Faro could complete the training of his current crop of students anywhere—and if Adria changed her mind, they would be much more secure with his slaves to guard them. And, he added rather pathetically, "Since I must be with you at all times, it would be much more comfortable to be housed in my villa, than in your home." He added hastily, "It is a very good home, Xylina, but it is not what I have grown used to. It will be a bit crowded, I think."

Faro laughed, and even Xylina had to agree that her modest dwelling could not compete in luxury with Ware's villa. So they traversed the city and entered the massive gates—

And Ware showed them the true extent of his wealth.

Within moments, Xylina gave up trying to imagine how much wealth was represented there, and simply enjoyed it all.

True to his word, Ware had not made any advances toward Xylina, although Faro watched him in much the manner of a dog scenting someone suspicious. Instead, Ware treated them to a fine dinner, served as they reclined on fine upholstered couches in his sumptuous, rose-silk-paneled dining room. As he had told Xylina, he treated Faro as an equal, and he treated his own slaves with a courtesy normally shown only by one citizen to another. His slaves were all uniformly good-looking, with graceful bodies. They served Ware and his guests without a sound, though with no sign of the kind of cowed subservience Xylina had seen in other slaves of their type.

She could not identify half of what they were served, but everything she tried was so savory that her own attempts at cooking seemed like childish scrawls compared to Faro's writing. She made a comment, and Ware smiled.

"I also train cooks," was all he said, but the slave serving him at that moment smiled.

When they finished, Ware bid them good night, then had one of his silent, handsome slaves show them to their chambers.

They had a suite of three rooms, the whole larger than her entire house. There were two chambers set up for sleeping, with a private bath that led into both rooms. In order to reach the second of the bedrooms, one had to pass through the first. There was clothing laid out for them, apparel with which Xylina wished she could have found fault. But though the fabric of her waiting outfit was luxurious, the cut was just as severe and modest as she could have required. That was when her own clothing seemed suddenly shabby. She was just vain enough to enjoy looking attractive, and the rich blue silk of this raiment was her favorite color.

She and Faro exchanged a glance; he shrugged, and gestured at the bathroom. "If you would like a bath, little mistress, I can ring for a slave, or I can draw the bath myself."

She really didn't want to don the new clothing until she had bathed—and it had been a long and tiring day. The more she thought about it, the better she liked the idea, and she nodded.

The white marble bathroom was larger than her rear garden, and the tub deep enough to swim in. The large bath was already full of hot water, and steam rose from it in wispy plumes. There was a smaller bath designed for washing in, which Faro filled with hot water for her; the larger bath was meant to soak away muscle aches and relax one's mind. While Faro busied himself with it, she took a look around. There had been a variety of scented soaps and bath oils laid ready for her, and in a cedar cabinet she found a selection of thick, fluffy towels and robes. There was even a silver pitcher of cold water and a half-dozen goblets. Water beaded up on the side of the pitcher, fogging the bright gleam of the metal, but she had no doubt that it was real silver.

Faro left her alone, after he promised her with a smile that he would take advantage of the room himself once she was done. She stepped into the smaller tub, and added an herbal extract to the water; the fresh scent cleared her head. The bath in her home was a good place in which to think, but it was functional, not beautiful, and it was just barely large enough for a good soak. She reveled in the sweetly-scented soap, giving her hair a good wash that left it smelling faintly of violets, and rinsed herself off. She bound up her hair, then took her place in the large bath. There were places built into it suitable for reclining, and that was what she did, with hot water up to her chin, and her head pillowed on a folded towel.

The white marble chamber, full of steam, seemed dreamlike; as if she floated beneath a huge cloud, cradled in the warm hand of a lake. The only sound was the occasional *plink* of a drop of water into the bath.

She half closed her eyes, still gathering her impressions and memories of the day. Day? It seemed like a month—too much had happened today. The wild horse that was her life had carried her into truly unknown country.

It seemed too late for second thoughts—and yet, she could not help but have them. She appreciated how readily a person might be corrupted by such luxury, and knew that it was part of Ware's campaign to win her favor. But she was not one to forget her ultimate values, or to yield to mere convenience. She was here because her situation required it. She might enjoy it, but it was business, and she would give it up when it was appropriate to do so.

Her real concern was of a larger nature. True, she had agreed to this task of Adria's, but in the light of all she had learned, could she truly go through with this? Would she not be betraying her people, and everything she had ever learned of honor?

No. She had to. She was committed. She must attempt to fetch this stone for the Queen. She had given her word, and her word must be good, or she had no honor.

And at the same time, it seemed to her that she was trading *her* well-being, her release from the threat of exile or prison, for the wholesale destruction of her entire world. Ware's words had left no doubt in her mind that the destruction would come, and within her own lifetime.

If that was all there was to it, simply saving herself at the expense of the women of the realm—then that would be a selfish thing to do. If only she could tell the Queen—if only she could make her realize that what she was asking for was death—

But Ware had made it clear that Adria was already too

influenced by the promise of the shard to believe anything Xylina told her. The Queen would never give credence to the notion that the promise of the shard was false. If, indeed, Ware permitted her to tell Queen Adria. It was very clear to Xylina that Ware was more in control of events than he had ever allowed anyone to guess. Perhaps all the demons were.

That was a thought as fascinating as a hooded hissing serpent. Were the demons controlling affairs, yet allowing the women of Mazonia to think that *they* were in control?

Xylina was horribly confused; she felt as if she were compromising her honor—yet she had given her sworn word. How could she preserve her honor by violating her word? How could she keep her word without violating her honor?

She closed her eyes, and let sweat trickle down her face, emptying her mind in the hopes that an answer would come to her. She was no longer in control of anything but her own actions, and that only insofar as they affected only herself and Faro. That much was quite clear. Between them, the Queen and Ware governed her destiny, her actions. She had no choice in that. So in a way, *they* were the ones responsible, weren't they?

No, that was no answer, either. It was casuistry.

She could only do her best to keep her honor and follow whatever runaway course they set for her.

Faro moved a little in the outer room; she heard him stirring in his chair, then turning a page in one of the books Ware had placed in their chambers. Faro had been eager to get to those books; she fancied he missed the reading that he would have done as a scribe. She had often wished she had more books for him to read, but she simply could not afford them. There were so many things she wished she could have done for him. He deserved better. Marcus had deserved better. And that brought another, and very odd, thought to her mind.

Suppose that the change that would come, though

drastic, would be beneficial to everyone? The past few hours had brought changes to her thoughts as well as to her life. She was able to look at circumstances in an entirely different light. What right, after all, did the Mazonites have to keep the men enslaved? Only the "right" of custom. Of power, stemming from the magic. Faro, and Marcus before him, had been very good to her. They had served as parents to her; they protected her—

It was more than that; she owed Faro her very life. If it had not been for him, she would have succeeded in destroying herself. Faro had shown her the reason to continue living. If circumstances had been different, if she could have, she would have freed both Marcus and Faro. Faro she could not free, by law, and Marcus had not lived long enough to be freed.

Both deserved a better lot than they had, under the Mazonite government. Neither would ever have it. The best she could do for Faro, if he ever changed his mind and chose freedom over whatever rewards she could give him, would be to take him to the border, give him gold, and tell him to run. He would then be on his own, in a strange land, among people who by all accounts were barbarians.

Would it be so bad, then, for a change to bring a betterment in the lot of men?

She shook her head, finally, sending drops of sweat into the bath. These things were too deep, too complicated for her. She could go on only as she had been, and hope that, whatever happened, she could make the right choices.

Chapter 10

Xylina looked back along the dusty, sun-drenched track, at the long string of men and pack-animals behind her. She herself rode a mule at the head of the string, a mule being the only animal she felt she could trust herself on, since she had not ridden since her mother died. Her beast was a tall, gentle, gray-white, with a shaggy coat and a patient nature. While a mule was not exactly a prancing charger, it would not bolt with her, and if danger threatened, it would keep its head. That was far more than she could count on from a horse. Or so Ware had told her when she had been given her choice of mounts from the Queen's stable. She was inclined to believe him. He had not once misled her, either in the kinds of supplies he had advised her to take, or the route he advised her to follow. And he had nothing to gain and no real reason to mislead her, which was the final reason to trust him. He wanted her love as well as her body, and he knew that deceit could never win the former.

Faro and Ware also rode; Faro was on a mule, a big-boned rangy black beast with brown rings around its eyes. Very odd he looked, too, perched uncomfortably on its back. Ware rode the kind of spirited horse she, as the expedition leader, would have been riding, had she followed the Queen's suggestions. And, without a doubt, if she had, she would have been thrown a dozen times in the first day. Yes, she looked a little silly on a mule, but she would have looked even sillier falling over her horse's tail, or black and blue from spills. She had too much sense to ride something like that when she did not really know how to ride. But she couldn't help but look enviously at the demon out

193

of the corner of her eye. He looked supremely comfortable and elegant on his graceful beast; the horse was a rich chestnut, and he wore brown riding-leathers to match it. This was not a beast out of the Queen's stable, but rather, out of his own. Another indication of his wealth.

The three of them headed up the column of armed men. Amazingly, Adria had granted the entire expedition permission to bear arms within the borders of Mazonia. Xylina had wondered about that; it seemed very strange to allow so many men to carry weapons, with only herself to command them.

But perhaps Adria had a rival for this crystal, one that she had not seen fit to warn Xylina about. If that were the case—well, such a threat had not materialized during the last month. Perhaps a show of force had been more than enough to keep such a rival from attempting to turn the expedition into a failure before it started.

As Ware had told her, all the servants and guards were men, and all were personally bound to the Queen's service. Xylina had appointed Ware as her advisor, and Faro as her chief of staff—telling the former wryly that since she was going to be burdened with him anyway, he might as well make himself useful.

There were two dozen guards, three servants, and three carts bearing supplies, driven by the servants, plus themselves. As she had gone over the supplies they would need, Xylina had been able to point out that there were things they would not need to take with them. Tents, for instance; blankets and bedding, soap, most clothing for herself, in short, anything she could conjure. Ware assured her that conjuring would work for some considerable distance outside Mazonia. They would not need firewood or oil for lamps. They would not need replacement axles for the wagons, or foul-weather capes. Thus, they were able to eliminate some of the bulkiest and heaviest things and replace them with more food for themselves and the mules and Ware's horse, more weaponry, and medical supplies.

She hoped that they would not need the latter.

While they journeyed through Mazonia, they did not need to use many of their supplies. She was able to purchase fresh food wherever they stopped. But once they reached the border, there was no telling what they might meet.

The men seemed tame enough. They responded immediately to her orders, and to Faro's. She had asked him to spend a great deal of his time with them, if he could, to get to know what they were like. She did not think that Queen Adria had planted a traitor amidst them, but it was possible that one or more of them was unreliable.

At least they looked as if they knew how to use those weapons they carried, although as yet that had not been put to the test. So many of the men that Faro had trained had been totally ignorant of how to defend even themselves. Many had been favored house-slaves, or even husbands and concubines, and they had never needed to think about weaponry. They needed only to keep themselves attractive, raise the children properly, and tend to the duties they were assigned within the household. Faro had often said, in disgust, that it was a good thing his pupils had women to protect them, or they would have been helpless against any kind of assault. This did not appear to be the case with Adria's guards.

There were also several dogs, who would be useful on guard duty, and to sniff out devious trails, and perhaps in hunting. They were well trained, and did not run around getting in the way.

It took Xylina a while to realize that there was something odd about the three servants. Finally she broached the matter to Ware. "Those servants—they don't urinate. They never go to the sanitary trench with the soldiers."

Ware smiled. "They are normal for their gender. They prefer to use the trench privately, as the men do when they defecate."

"Their gender?" she asked blankly.

"They are female. I thought you understood."

"Female! The Queen sent other women along?"

"Not Mazonites. These are from what we call the Animal Kingdom, tolerated here in much the manner we demons are, because they serve a need that it might otherwise be inconvenient to accommodate."

Realization dawned. "Like the stripes!"

"Like the stripes," he agreed. "But less obviously different, in the body."

"Different?"

"Let me introduce you." He whistled, surprising her. In a moment one of the servants made an appearance in the tent. Now it was apparent that under the loose-fitting clothing was the body of a fairly well-endowed woman. "Pattée, show Mistress Xylina your paw," he said.

The woman put one hand to the other and pulled off her glove. There was a — paw. It looked like the appendage of a dog, with stubby claws and thick underlying pads.

Ware glanced at Xylina. "Do you wish to see more? Her feet are similarly configured. It is done magically in infancy, among her people. Some have bird appendages, or goat hooves. It varies. But their torsos are normal by your definition, and the men don't seem to mind."

"No," Xylina said, taken aback. "No more."

"Pattée, cover and return to your business," Ware told the woman, and she did so without a word. "They can't speak," he explained. "Only with animal sounds. This is the way women are expected to be, in that culture."

"It's appalling!"

He shrugged. "By your definition. They do, however, made excellent sexual company for the soldiers. Such women are standard equipment on missions such as this. Your proper course is to ignore them. Certainly they will not cause you any trouble."

Xylina swallowed uncomfortably. "I'll ignore them," she agreed.

As for the men themselves, while Xylina had not gotten

overly friendly with any of them, she had been able, through Faro, to learn quite a bit about some of them.

Most were "surplus" men—too rough and too plain to be desirable as husbands, not graceful or clever enough to learn the skills of entertainers, household servants, or craftsmen. That left them only one possible use: as common laborers or as guards. Faro had told her that these men were only too happy to be spared the lot of the common laborer—men who worked from dawn to dusk, and rarely lived beyond the age of forty.

But of the remainder, there were some surprises. Three of them were what Faro slightingly referred to as "used" men—those who had somehow displeased their mistress-wives. They had not had any skills beyond the ordinary—tending the household and the children. No one wanted them as husbands or even harem-slaves, since they were beyond the young and nubile age. Wanting to be rid of them, their mistress-wives had deeded them to the Queen; the Queen, in her turn, had ascertained that they had a certain talent with weaponry, and so had them trained as guardsmen.

"Somewhat the way you were," she said softly.

He nodded agreement. "They were not angry in the way I was, so were not relegated to the arena. But they do resemble me in having exploitable resources."

And there were two young and remarkably handsome men who hoped by their bravery on this expedition to catch the Queen's attention and be added to her harem—or even given supreme status as her husband. Queen Adria had not yet elevated any of her harem slaves to that position, and the young men of the harem were constantly hoping that she might choose one of them. These two had hit upon the notion that since bravery and strength were the prime Mazonite virtues, the Queen might well prefer a brave and strong man to sire her daughters, as well as a handsome one.

As the expedition traveled across the breadth of Mazonia,

Xylina became aware that these two men sought Faro out at every opportunity for long, serious discussions. Finally her curiosity got the better of her, and she asked him why they kept dragging Faro off to consult with him. Neither of these men was a sub-leader, and there should be no reason why they would want to speak so closely with him so very often.

He gave her one of those darkly inscrutable looks from beneath lowered eyebrows. "I'm not certain that you wish to know, little mistress," he said.

She frowned a little. "Whatever is going on among the guards, I think I should know about it," she insisted. "Especially if there is any likelihood that it could signal troubles among the men."

Faro had sighed. "They wanted my advice," he said, with great reluctance.

"Advice about what?" she persisted.

"Ah—" To her immense surprise, he flushed, profoundly embarrassed. She had seldom seen him so discomfited before. "Ah—you are a very brave, very highly regarded Mazonite, little mistress," he said, looking steadfastly at his feet. "They, ah—they wanted my advice on how I, ah—attracted you. Since they feel the Queen's tastes are likely to be similar, you see."

"Attracted me?" she had replied. "But—" Then some of the sly comments she had heard from the Queen's Guard, directed toward her, but about Faro and the other men of the expedition, suddenly came flooding back. And at that moment, although she had not realized what those remarks had meant at the time, she suddenly understood them.

"Oh," she said faintly. Now she put all the pieces together, and she felt just as embarrassed as Faro. It was assumed, of course, that she and Faro were enjoying the same relationship that Elibet and Marcus had; that Xylina would eventually declare him to be her husband, or at least, the head of her harem. *She* could no more have thought of Faro in that way than she could have thought of her mule— but they didn't know that, and certainly the men of the expedition and those few Mazonites who were her friends, like Lycia, must have assumed the liaison. She wasn't sure if she should be annoyed or if it mattered at all. In fact, she slept completely alone, as she always had, with Faro lying across the threshold. But the fact that he always slept in her tent must have strengthened the assumption.

"Was there anything else?" she asked, since something in Faro's expression told her she had not yet heard all of it.

He coughed, and his flush deepened. "Ah—yes," he had admitted. "They—ah—wanted to know if *they* could—ah—catch your eye. They told me it would not matter since they were not yet harem slaves, and that if the Queen was willing to release them after this, you might—ah—choose them for your own harem—ah— based on the—ah—sample."

Now it was her turn to stare at her feet. That was a natural question of course; even if she and Faro *had* been together, he would have no right to deny her if she chose to take one or more men to her bed. It was, in fact, often the case; few Mazonites could afford a harem, and an expedition like this one would offer a chance at variety they might not otherwise enjoy. On a mission like this one, undoubtably, the leader could take any man she chose to "play" with, and there could be no assumption of commitment. It was the sort of thing that happened, she supposed, without regard to whether the men liked it. That, or so Lycia had hinted to her, was one of the perquisites of such a mission. She hadn't understood the hints at the time, about the "appetite of a younger woman," and the "greater variety available." She had honestly thought Lycia was referring to *food.*

"And what did you tell them?" she asked Faro, unsure whether she really wanted to hear the answer.

But he smiled, as she looked up again to face his eyes. "I told them that you are a very serious and disciplined leader, and that you will allow nothing to interfere with the discipline of the troupe."

That was a good answer, for indeed, if she chose to amuse herself with any of the men, regardless whether she actually played favorites after that, it would be assumed that she was doing so. That would be very bad for discipline, and she was glad that Faro had thought of the response, for she truly was not interested in any of the men in that way.

"Thank you," was all she said.

Faro smiled. "You have been similarly supportive of my situation," he reminded her.

That was early in the expedition, while they were within a week of the capital. After marching for more than a moon, they came to the border of Mazonia. The terrain turned from lush fields and farms, to huge tracts of grazing-land supporting vast herds of sheep, goats, and cattle, and then to land supporting hardly more than the occasional jackalope. Near her home, the landscape was of rolling, wooded hills and well-watered valleys; it had gradually gotten drier, the landscape flatter, and the population sparser. They had not seen another person for the past two days.

They had been subsisting on their own provisions and whatever they could glean from the countryside for several days, for the landscape was barren of farms or settlements here, bare even of the great cattle and sheep ranches that took up as much land as a dozen of the farms Xylina was used to.

The land was flat for the most part, but rutted with shallow canyons and dotted with occasional tall, barren ridges, orange-red hills whose sides had been eroded even as the sides of those canyons had been, etched with deep grooves by wind or water. A scrubby grass and a tough, aromatic shrub were all that grew here, except where there was water. There, trees and other vegetation flourished, proving that the land was not barren if it had water. But there was very little water here, and Xylina decreed that they must fill their waterskins and barrels at every occasion, saving that real water for drinking, and using conjured water for bathing and washing. She considered herself fortunate that the summer had been cool so far; this land would have been unbearable in the scorching heat of a high summer. As it was, she conjured additional water at every halt, letting the men use it to wash the dust from their faces, and to cool their overheated bodies. The dry air evaporated it so quickly that within moments of sluicing it over their heads, their hair and tunics were already dry. They also used it to rinse away the taste of the flat, stale, real water they drank from their waterskins, pouring it into their mouths after they had drunk their fill. She could have conjured other things—wine, for instance—but she thought it might be prudent not to give them anything intoxicating. In heat like this, they were very likely to get drunk or sick much more quickly. In any event, they seemed grateful enough for just the sweet water.

She called a halt at just about midday, and let the men rest while she peered at the map and tried to reckon their location. Ware walked his horse up alongside her mule as she was staring at the horizon, and pointed a helpful finger.

"There," he said. "You see that flat-topped hill? On the map, it is called 'The Anvil,' and it sits exactly astride the border here."

"I don't see anything that looks like a boundary," she said doubtfully, straining her eyes toward the horizon. She had expected fences, or a wall, and border guards. There was nothing but cloudless blue sky and red earth.

Ware shrugged gracefully. "Nor will you," he replied. "There is only a low fence of sticks and rocks to mark it. As you can see, there is nothing hereabouts to guard—so the border is only a convenience, recognized by both sides as the place that marks the region where men are subservient, and where they are not. And, not coincidentally, the place where Mazonite conjuration ceases to be the only magic humans possess. Across that border, other rules prevail. Your magic will still be as strong, but there will be other kinds that are just as strong."

She rolled the map, and put it carefully away in the case. "Then what stops men from escaping over it?" she asked.

Ware gave her a sardonic stare. "Really," he said, finally, as his horse stirred restively beneath him. "Xylina, can you in your wildest imaginings picture very many men who had the strength, resources and fortitude to cross the territory *we* have over the past two days? Alone? With no provisions? And with more of the same awaiting him on the other side? And why would such a man want to endure such privations?"

"But I had thought that there were men waiting beyond the borders for the runaways——" she began.

Ware laughed, softly. "Oh, there are those waiting for runaways here. Tiny tribes of nomadic horse-warriors, who are only too pleased to capture these strays and add them to their *own* slave-strings. No, Xylina, men who escape this way soon find themselves wishing that they had stayed at home, for if they experienced hardship at the hands of their mistresses, what they find at the hands of these Pacha horse-warriors is near to torture."

Nomadic horse-warriors. No one had warned her about those. She looked back at her little train, and wondered how formidable it would look to barbarian raiders. Were twenty-four men enough? Did they look like hardened fighters? And they were afoot; they could not escape mounted men by running. For a moment, she wavered, and fear crept into her heart.

Ware was continuing to eye her, with a wry smile on his lips. "They will find *you* just as tempting a prize, my dear," he said softly. "Any of the Pacha chieftains would be pleased to have you in his tent—properly leg-shackled, of course. Your beauty is rare among the Mazonites; among the Pacha you would shine like a moon-flower among chickweed. A chieftain would claim you as his pleasure-slave immediately."

Her head jerked up, and she looked down her nose at him indignantly. "And *you* would do well to remember who is the mistress here, *demon,*" she snapped. "No unwashed barbarian is going to touch me and live to tell his nomadic kin!"

With that, she gave the signal to Faro to move out, and urged her mule to the head of the column, ignoring Ware's rich chuckle as he guided his horse in behind hers.

She was in the process of conjuring the camp defenses when the first of the Pacha appeared over the horizon.

She had taken into consideration the fact that they were horse-fighters when she built the defenses. The first defense was a tangle of razor-sharp wire all around the camp, waist-high, and too wide (she hoped) for a horse to jump. Immediately behind it was a stretch of pointed metal stakes, slanted outward, no more than a hand's-breadth apart. No horse was going to care to approach that! And if for some reason their attackers passed both those barriers successfully, there was an inner defense, a shallow ditch filled with oil, that could be lit to create a final barricade of smoke and flame. Ware assured her gravely that no horse could be persuaded to jump into fire.

For the camp itself, she had conjured silk and very long, flexible poles, which could be bent over to form a dome-shape, the silk stretched over all and pegged to the ground with stakes. The men had already obtained water from a nearby creek, and she had conjured water for washing, fuel for the fire, and oil for lamps and torches. As the sun neared the horizon, the men had been divided into work-parties; some to set up the tents, some to help the cook with the dinner and fire, some to light lanterns and torches, the rest with other camp-chores.

She looked up from her conjurations, alerted, perhaps, by a hint of movement where none had been the moment before, and saw the Pacha watching her. They were lined up on a low ridge, sitting easily on their horses, as if they were on couches.

She had never seen anything like them before; even the attempts by entertainers to ape "barbarians" paled before these men in their wild magnificence. She wondered what kind of magic *they* had, or if they had any at all.

They rode small, rangy horses, hardly bigger than ponies, but whose manes and tails streamed nearly to the ground. The horses' manes and tails were braided with beads, strips of wildly colored cloth and ribbons, and feathers. The beasts themselves were painted with markings in red, yellow, black and white—spots, circles about the eyes, arrows, and lightning zigzags. They had nothing on their backs in the way of saddles, only bright red and blue blankets, and a simple loop of rawhide rope around the nose seemed to serve their riders for reins and bridle both.

Their riders were naked to the waist, wearing only the simplest of breechcloths of red and blue cloth, their bodies and faces painted with the same symbols as their horses. Around their necks they wore a tangle of myriad necklaces made of bright beads, bones, teeth, and claws. Their hair was as long and wild as their horses', worked into hundreds of tiny braids, each one ending in a bead or a bone. Xylina wondered how they had come up upon her so silently, for they should have rattled like an entertainer's sistrum. They boasted long, braided moustaches as well. Hair and skin was the same brick-red as the raw red earth of this place. Without the breechcloths, or with one of plainer stuff, one of these warriors would blend into the landscape so well that he could creep right up to the boundary of the camp without being seen.

In their hands they bore long lances, topped with wicked points of black, shiny serrated flint that gleamed with reflected sunlight. She could well imagine the kind of damage those lances could do, for the many "teeth" on each lance-head were made to break off in a wound. These lances were cruel weapons, designed to mutilate if they did not kill. There were quivers of smaller, obsidian-tipped throwing-spears at each rider's knee, and on their backs they bore bows and quivers bristling with white-fletched arrows.

Determined not to show that she had been unnerved by their sudden appearance, Xylina completed her conjurations, and then stood with arms crossed, waiting for them to make a move.

At length, after a long period of exchanged impassive stares, during which the entire camp became aware of the Pacha presence, some imperceptible signal passed among them, and they nudged their horses with their bare heels and moved toward the barricade as one.

The men of the camp dropped whatever they had been doing, and moved to stand behind Xlyina at the ready. Ware came up beside her on her right and Faro on her left, and they watched with her, as the entire cavalcade made its leisurely way toward her first barrier. They did not move their ponies out of an ambling walk.

Then again, why should they? The Mazonite party obviously wasn't going anywhere.

"I don't suppose they speak Mazonite," she said, doubtfully. "Do they?"

"Hardly," Ware replied dryly. "These are warriors. It is beneath them to speak your language, for their own is so clearly superior. However, I speak theirs."

"As do I," Faro interjected, with a glance that was not quite a glare at the demon. "It was part of my training as a scribe to learn the languages of the nations around Mazonia. I have not had the benefit of speaking with a native, but I would imagine I can at least understand them, and make myself understood."

Ware said nothing, although this was clearly a warning from Faro that if the demon intended any trickery, he had best give the notion up for the present. Xylina almost smiled, for if the situation had not been so tense, it would have been funny. Faro was determined to protect her from Ware's treachery.

As the riders neared, she saw something that astonished her. Some of the riders had small, but well-rounded *breasts*, the nipples painted with concentric rings! There was no doubt of it, and this was not the kind of deformity that came when a man was neutered. Unless the men were terribly deformed at birth, or were some kind of hermaphrodite, there were women riding as warriors among them!

"Are those women?" she whispered to Ware. "These warriors—do they have women among them?"

He glanced at her for a fleeting second, before returning his attention to the oncoming riders. The setting sun at their backs gilded the entire landscape in rose-gold, lighting red riders and red horses on a red ground against a deep purple sky. The glints of sun on the obsidian points looked like flashes of scarlet fire.

"Of course they are women," he replied. "The Pacha encourage their maidens to ride as warriors, to prove their worth as bearers of future warriors. The strongest and most valiant maidens have the widest choice of suitors. Of course, once a woman bears a child, she must care for her children first, and her days of riding out with the warriors and hunters are over. Still, the women with children provide the main guards for the Pacha encampments, and it would be a foolhardy brigand who would think to make of a camp an easy target, for they continue to practice assiduously all of their lives."

"These are not brigands?" she asked, doubtfully.

"You are in their realm, Xylina," he reminded her. "They are no bandits; they are warriors guarding their land."

Once again, Xylina was forced to revise her preconceptions. She knew he was correct.

"But do not think that because they have women as equals among the warriors, that if they captured you, they would ever use you as other than a pleasure-slave. Foreign women are chattel," Ware continued, "captured Mazonites in particular. Just as foreign men are chattel. All foreigners are dogs; the only difference between a foreign man and a foreign woman is that the woman is likely to be prettier than a man, and a woman can breed children for more slaves. Keep that in mind. The Pacha respect strength, and nothing else; there is a treaty between Mazonia and the Pacha tribes, and you must prove yourself strong enough that they cannot violate that treaty."

So she must demonstrate to them that she was strong, clever, and too difficult a proposition to warrant attacking. Xylina crossed her arms over her chest, and took an aggressive stance. The Pacha halted their ponies just outside the perimeter of the camp. She was quite certain that they had gauged the strength of her defenses, the wire, the stakes, the oil, and the armed men beyond, but they paid no obvious attention to them, staring across the three barriers at her and her entourage.

Finally one spoke, a tangle of liquid syllables.

"He is the leader, or so he says," Ware translated. "There is no telling if that is true; the Pacha sometimes lie about which of them is in charge, to deflect the enemy's attention from the true leader. He wishes to know who the leader of this camp is."

"He knows, of course," Faro added, with a flash of annoyance at Ware. "He knows we've come out of Mazonia, so the only possible leader would be you. But he wants to see if we are going to lie to him. My studies tell me that lying to them is not a good idea, unless it is a lie they can't verify."

Since the idea had occurred to her that she could say that Ware or Faro was the leader, it was a good thing that Faro had added that. She stepped forward one pace, and nodded at the leader of the Pacha, but said nothing. He must know she could not speak his tongue—perhaps it would increase her status to have these translators.

The warrior spoke again.

"He wants to know why we're here and what we want," Faro said quickly, before Ware could translate. "He says the Mazonites have a treaty with his people, as Ware told you, and he wants to know if we're breaking it by raiding on Pacha land."

"What does he mean by raiding?" she asked, thinking that she had better get a more exact translation before committing herself.

Faro asked the question, and was rewarded with another spill of words. "Raiding means hunting for slaves or horses," he replied. "Raiding means stealing from the Pacha the things that belong to the Pacha and to their land."

Again, she pondered the question. "Ask him if the treaty permits hunting only for food as we travel across Pacha land, taking no more than we can eat, and using all that we take."

This time Ware did the translating, as Faro tried to remember the words for Xylina's question. The Pacha responded immediately.

"Hunting for food is permitted by the treaty," Ware said. "But he warns you that if his scouts find the bloated carcasses of animals killed only for horns, teeth, or hide, he will bring down the wrath of his gods upon us for wanton spoilage of his brothers. And it is considered good manners if you leave the hides, bones, horns, and teeth behind where we have camped, for the warriors to retrieve and take back to their people. In that way you prove that you are not a trophy-hunter."

Xylina thought long and carefully before dictating her reply. "Tell him that we are only crossing his land, as permitted by the treaty, that we are not raiding or hunting for trophies, and that I will kill with my own hand any man who destroys one of his brothers for the sake of horn or hide. And to prove that, I will leave the hides and so forth behind at each of our camps."

When Ware translated that, there were slow smiles from the Pacha, smiles quickly covered. She could not tell if those were smiles of pleasure, disbelief, or cynicism. Suppose that they considered her to be a fool for agreeing so readily, instead of rejecting their strictures with contempt?

She also could not tell if there really *was* a treaty that was so detailed, or if this was something the Pacha had made up to lull her into a false sense of security—that the moment she or one of her men killed a jackalope, they would descend on her. Nor, despite Ware's assurance that the Pacha did not speak her tongue, was she sure that one among them was not fluent in Mazonite. She could afford to take nothing for granted—so she could not say things to Ware or Faro where the Pacha might overhear.

But the Pacha chieftain was speaking again. This time Faro translated. "He wishes to join us for a reaffirmation of the treaty," Faro said. "And he adds that he is very fond of Mazonite wine. I gather this is the Pacha idea of a subtle hint."

The tiny germ of an idea crystalized, and she smiled broadly. "Tell them that the Pacha, our fellow warriors, are welcome within our encampment," she said, spreading her arms wide. "Tell him that we will drink to brotherhood in something better than Mazonite wine. Tell him there will be a feast in their honor, and *magic* wine, which will leave no sour stomachs and aching heads in the morning."

Ware looked at her as if he doubted her sanity, but obligingly translated. She, in turn, dispelled her conjured barriers at just that point, and the Pacha ponies picked their way across, with dainty steps. As soon as all the ponies had crossed, she re-created those barriers. If the Pacha felt unease at suddenly being imprisoned behind her defenses, they gave no sign of it.

She left Ware in charge of seeing the ponies picketed and the warriors settled, left Faro in charge of setting up the camp for a celebration, and went to the slave who served them as cook. "I need the tubs we bathe and do the wash in," she told him, as he stared past her shoulder at the wild Pacha perching themselves cross-legged around the fire of conjured wood. "I will conjure meat for these barbarians; it will do them no harm to eat a single conjured meal, and it will save our provisions. And, frankly, it will taste better than anything we have with us. I will also conjure you sweet stuff and flour for cakes; if I guess rightly, they will be very fond of desserts and the like. Barbarians often have little access to sweets. You must make as much sweet cake or cookies as you can while they are eating the meat. And I will conjure wine as well—only see to it that none of our men drink anything but water."

"You intend to poison the wine, mistress?" the cook asked, his eyes round with alarm. "You mean to slay them while they are our guests?"

She shook her head. "No, not at all. Two dozen bodies would be very hard to explain to the other barbarians. No, I am simply going to see that they get very, very drunk, and I want our men to stay very, very sober. I want the Pacha to sleep so deeply that when we leave in the morning, they will not even stir."

The cook smiled tentatively at that, and sent one of the men off for the washtubs. While he fetched the two tubs, she set about conjuring great slabs of meat-like stuff, only a thumb's-breadth thick, as wide as a palm, and as long as her arm—food that could cook quickly over a spit. She did not think that the barbarians would be very likely to care how well-done it was, but she concentrated as hard as she could to make certain it was savory. At the longing looks of the men, who were loathe to subsist on dried-beef stew when this tasty stuff was sizzling over the flames, she gave permission for them to eat of it as well, provided they ate first of the real food. They understood why; it was folly to depend on conjured food for sustenance.

When the tubs arrived, she conjured them full to the brim, creating a sweet red wine, full of sugars and stronger than the strongest brandy she had ever drunk herself. These she had carried to the warriors at the fireside, along with whatever was at hand to use as flasks and cups.

By now, the torches and lamps were all lit, and Ware had settled in the midst of the Pacha, making some long speech. Faro joined her as the first of the tubs was carried to the waiting barbarians.

"He's prating about brotherhood and the sacred earth," Faro said, as she shifted her concentration to create the ingredients required for sweet sugar-cookies. "He's been using the biggest words he knows, and describing you as a 'valiant hawk of the wild Mazonites,' and 'a wily she-cat, who wins as much by guile as by strength,' but 'one who values honor and oaths more than meat and drink.' It's one of those long-winded speeches the politicians make. They just might appoint him chieftain when he's done, if he's not careful."

She chuckled, as the Pacha lost their interest in Ware's speech when the tubs of wine appeared. The sweet aroma told them this was something special, and they had no patience for speeches when fabulous drink like this awaited them. They snatched cups and bowls, and gathered around the tub with exclamations of delight and wonder, dipping out containers full.

But they waited until Ware had dipped one as well, and had drunk it to the dregs, before the chieftain took his first sip. Xylina wasn't certain whether this was protocol or caution. Perhaps both.

The Pacha warrior exclaimed something that set the others to laughing—and all the rest drank their first cups off as quickly as Ware had downed his. Xylina had to give them credit for strong constitutions; *she* would not have been able to drink the "wine" so quickly.

"What did he say?" Xylina demanded.

Faro grinned. "Waugh! That is no wine! It is honey-fire! It kicks like an unbroken stallion!"

She sighed with relief. "Good. I hoped they'd like over-sweet wine. Although at the rate that they are drinking, I may test my abilities to the limit to conjure up enough to keep up with them!"

"Your abilities are quite impressive already," he murmured. "And getting stronger, I think. The Queen's warriors are taking note, as is Ware."

She realized that between the defenses and the food, she

had done more than ever before. She *was* getting better with the constant practice of each night's camping. She might do well to try to mask the extent of her conjurations, so that no one would know what her limits were. It could make a difference, if an enemy should try to wait for her magic exhaustion before striking.

The first of the slabs of meat arrived then, and the Pacha set to, eating only with their fingers and their knives, wiping their greasy hands on their chests and hair with gusto. Evidently Xylina's efforts met with their approval, for they stuffed the boneless "meat" into their mouths as fast as they could chew. They reminded her of hawks eating—happy hawks, for the air filled with their easy laughter. Ware looked relaxed, and even Faro seemed pleased with the way things were going. The empty tub came back to her and she filled it again, then left the camp-kitchen to the cook and joined the others at the fireside.

The Pacha were definitely happy, now, each taking his turn to stop eating and drinking long enough to sing a song. Like their language, their music was surprisingly melodious; they sang without accompaniment other than the drumming of hands on thighs. The firelight shone on their glistening faces and chests, their bright black eyes snapping with pleasure as they ate and drank, dipping their bowls and cups into the tubs of wine. This time, when the tubs emptied, Xylina stood up and conjured them full again before their very eyes, making them exclaim with wonder as the wisps of crimson fog solidified between her hands and turned into a stream of crimson wine that filled the metal tubs. Evidently they saw little of magic, less of conjuration. That comforted her; at least she would not be confronted with alien magic quite yet.

Faro translated as much of their singing as he understood; mostly it seemed to be songs of each warrior's personal prowess, or that of his or her ancestor's. There was no differentiation between the male and female warriors; they ate and drank and slapped one another on the back in rough camaraderie, but made no kind of sexual advances toward one another. Xylina had already warned her men that they must treat these barbarians as one would a momentarily quiescent wild beast: with care, and with respect. Even if they had been thinking that a drunken Pacha maiden might welcome one of them, they should dismiss that thought completely. And since the Pacha kept all their weapons well to their hands, her men were only too happy to obey her.

When the sweet cakes and cookies came out, the Pacha were overjoyed. As she had expected, they did not see sweet things very often, and the cakes were a high delicacy for them. Of course, in the afternoon, when they woke up, they would do so with empty bellies—but one night of conjured debauchery would do them no harm, and she doubted that they would know that the food had vanished from their stomachs in a way they were not used to. It would have been a cruel way to treat men and women who were starving—but the Pacha were clearly in excellent shape, and one conjured meal would make no difference to them.

By now, they were very, very drunk; one or two were unable to hold up their cups, and sat staring stupidly at the fire, blinking owl-eyes at the flames, with their cups dangling dripping from limp fingers. The rest had gotten to the stage of happy carousal, where everything was funny, and there was nothing wrong with the world. She conjured more wine, then thick, blanket-like swaths of fabric for each of them, which she had Faro put unobtrusively near to their hands. As she had thought, they mistook the blankets for their own, which were probably still with the ponies, and gathered the fabric about their shoulders against the growing chill of the desert night.

One by one, they drank their last cups, clutched their blankets a little closer, and dropped off into drunken slumber. At last, the entire circle of barbarians lay snoring, cups and bowls dropped from uncaring hands, spilling conjured wine into the sand.

She directed two of the defter men to pick up the cups and move the tubs, spilling out what was left of the wine onto the ground. She conjured water to wash the last of it away. She was weary, and she did not want to dispel the wine left in the tubs only to make the mistake of dispelling all of it and leaving her "guests" sober. She had done a hard job of conjuring, and did not trust her control at this point.

Finally the last of their property was picked up, leaving the Pacha, the ponies picketed nearby, the sole occupants of the fire-circle. And the fire itself was dying down; she did not want to risk an ember popping out and waking anyone, so she did not conjure any more fuel to feed it. Instead, she signaled Ware and Faro to leave their "guests" and follow her to their tent, where bowls of real stew awaited them.

Faro let out his breath as they fastened the flap behind them. "Were you doing what I think you were doing?" he asked. "Getting them drunk enough that they'll still be sleeping like the dead when we leave in the morning? That was better than any notion I had."

She nodded, and reached for her stew. She was absolutely exhausted, and the stew had never tasted so good before. "I have no idea what their capacity for strong drink is, but as the leader said, that was no wine I gave them. It was at least as strong as the best Mazonite brandy, possibly stronger. I wanted to be certain that they slept through our departure."

Ware took his own bowl and smiled ironically. "I nearly gagged on the first swallow," he said. "It is well that my self-control is as good as it is. And it is good that you thought to make that potion as strong as you did; the Pacha drink a strange concoction of fermented cactus that can easily double as varnish-remover. I have only drunk it once, and I can testify that it is a terrible and powerful drink. I do not think that mere wine would have sufficed for your plan."

"I have one guard just on the barbarians all night," she

told them both, blinking sore and weary eyes. "The rest will be watching to make certain that their brothers and sisters do not move upon us in the night." She yawned hugely. "That is all that I could think to do. Oh, and I have done my best to make those conjurations as strong as I can. I do not know how long they will last, beyond tomorrow night. If luck is with us, our friends may not awaken until two mornings from now!"

Ware chuckled, and Faro beamed at her with brotherly approval. "Very well, little mistress," the slave said, warmly. "Let us then take care of the rest of the night, while you take your well-earned slumber."

"Thank you," she told them both, with a weary smile for each. "I hoped I could count on you."

And with that, she swallowed the last of her meal, and retired to her pallet just beyond the billowing curtain that separated the dome into front and rear halves. And she was so very tired that she did not even remember lying down upon it—nor did she even think to regret she had left herself too tired to conjure a hot bath.

The Pacha were still snoring in the morning, and not even the braying of the mules was enough to awaken them. Xylina worried about them, after a moment; if they did, indeed, sleep away the whole day and night, they would be lying unprotected out in the desert heat and sun, and it was possible that they could come to harm.

Finally she made up her mind. Her conjurations lasted at least one full day and night; by tomorrow morning, they would surely be awake. She conjured water and fodder for their ponies, then surrounded warriors and ponies with a stockade of conjured thorny branches. Last of all, she conjured the materials to erect one of the dome tents over the warriors. If their own people came looking for them, they would see that the Pacha were protected within shelter and a stockade. If anything else was attracted, the stockade should protect them long enough for the noise to wake them. She was sorry to have left the ponies with only conjured food and drink, but she did not see that she could leave them any of her own.

The tent she made the same red-orange of the earth, so that it did not stand out so much from its surroundings. And when she looked back at it, she saw with gratification that the only thing she truly noticed was the pony herd.

"Those are nasty beasts the Pacha ride," Faro commented, as she turned to face the road ahead. "They bit any of our men who came too close. I'd say those barbarians are as safe in that stockade as they would be in their own camp."

"I hope so," she replied. "Because I have the feeling that we would be in as much trouble from *allowing* them to come to harm as from harming them ourselves."

"True," Ware agreed. "When they wake they will appreciate the fact that we stole none of their equipment and raped none of their women. We have given them an excellent carousal without harming them, though it will be obvious that we could have killed them had we chosen to. They will realize that we made fools of them, but in a benign manner. That makes a difference."

She sent two of the men out to hunt parallel to the road, hoping to stretch their supplies a bit. She cautioned them about trophy-hunting, and after their close view of the Pacha last night, it seemed to her that they took her warning to heart.

They camped that night with no incident, and without sighting more than a few birds in the air and the occasional jackalope. Those loping, long-eared beasts were about the size of their dogs, and were good eating; both hunters managed to bag a pair apiece to add to the stew. Fresh meat made it far more flavorful and nutritious. Xylina was fairly certain that even this desert country had plants that were edible—after all, hadn't Ware told her of the Pacha's cactus-drink?—but without knowing what they were, she was loathe to experiment.

That night passed without incident, and with no sign of

anything but the howling of wild dogs off in the distance. When Xylina made her last circuit of the camp, she saw only the posted guards and one of the female servants going into the soldiers' quarters. Those women tended to sleep by day, evidently being kept busy at night. Once she had awakened from sleep, hearing something by her tent entrance, only to realize that Pattée was quietly visiting Faro. Xylina was almost envious. It was a signal of her gradual accommodation to the realities of this type of mission.

In the morning, they packed up quickly; the air had gotten progressively hotter as they had traveled the prior day. They wanted to get out of this area as quickly as they could, traveling as much in the cooler hours of the morning as possible. She had already told the men she planned to stop at midday for a prolonged rest, and since the moon was full, she planned to travel past sunset.

But as they halted for their midday rest and meal, a line of dust heading in their direction signaled that they would not be alone for long.

By the time she had conjured shelters from the sun, it was possible to make out a troop of riders under that dust. It did not take a great deal of imagination to deduce who and what the riders were.

This time the Pacha wore red and yellow breechcloths, their ponies sported red and yellow blankets, and the painted markings were crude bear-tracks, parallel lines, and a glyph that looked like a child's depiction of a flying bird.

The warriors rode up casually, with huge grins upon their faces, and with none of the wariness that had marked the first group. Their number was almost double that of the first warrior-band. The leader hailed the camp immediately, and Faro translated, grinning more and more widely with each word.

"These are the Bear Tribe of the Pacha," he said. "Their cousins, the Thunder Tribe, are the ones we left sleeping.

Evidently word of our hospitality has traveled faster than we did—these warriors are here to 'celebrate our brotherhood, just as you feasted our kin.' And from what he says, the rest of the tribes all along the track are expecting the same."

"No—" she said, trying not to moan. "Oh, no—"

"I am afraid so, Xylina," Ware replied, with a hint of mockery. "You are going to be exercising your conjuration powers to the fullest, I fear. These tribes take hospitality very seriously."

"He also says that in gratitude for the feasting, all the 'civilized tribes'—whatever that means—will make certain that we are not molested by anything other than thunderstorms." Faro cocked his head to one side. "All things considered, it sounds like a bargain to me. You simply conjure enough meat to stuff these barbarians full, enough wine to drown them, and we pass through their land with no enemies but sun and rain."

"You aren't the one doing the conjuration," she replied, but secretly she was pleased. Faro was right; it was a bargain. Tribute was better than combat.

Now she needed only to worry about what lay beyond the next border—and whether she could continue to conjure sufficient wine for an ever-increasing number of thirsty Pacha. If practice really could expand her magic ability, she would soon be formidable indeed.

• Chapter 11

The numbers of Pacha never increased to the point beyond Xylina's ability to conjure, but she often went to her rest feeling strained to her limits. She had little time to get to know the men she commanded, and less time to learn anything about Ware. The strategy of feasting and entertaining the barbarian horse-folk never failed to work, however; not once during their crossing of the Pacha lands did the nomads ever seem the least unfriendly. Rather, each new tribe greeted them with the same enthusiasm as the last. It occurred to her that waking up alone and without hangovers after a night of feasting was as convenient for them as it was for the Mazonite party, because they did not have to make any exchange gifts.

Faro still slept near her, and she was glad of that. But she was feeling increasingly alone. She caught herself wondering what it would be like to spend the night with a man. To wake and find him beside her. To be the object of his passion. Even a demon. She knew that if she asked Ware to join her, he would gladly do so.

No! She had sworn to pay him in silver if not in gold, and she intended to hold true to that. This mission was really a third way to pay him, doing a service for the Queen. Once that service was done, Xylina would be free not only of her monetary debt, but of the dread harassment that had ruined her family. She knew her proper course.

Still, she almost wished she could put on paw-mittens and pretend to be from the Animal Kingdom, just for one hour. Just to see what it was like. Just in case she was missing anything. But of course that was impossible.

Ware, however, was possible.

She banished that thought and focused on sleep. Faro was right: she had more important concerns than such foolishness.

A new challenge was waiting for them on the other side of the great red-earth wilderness. Ware confessed that he was not familiar with the peoples beyond Pacha lands, although he thought he would probably know their tongue, since he was a student of languages. The Pacha themselves were no more help than the demon. At first, when asked about those who dwelled on their border, they could only shrug and say, "We do not know these people." Then, as the expedition drew nearer to the border, the tribes would say, "They close themselves behind their thorn-wall, they do not travel, they do not trade, we do not go there. We call them the Hates-All-People."

Not a lot of information, and it was difficult to tell if the Pacha had ever really *tried* to make contact with this new nation. Nor was it certain what some of their primitive descriptions of the "Hates-All-People" meant. Xylina had been certain from the moment that she heard those words that the reference to a "thorn-wall" was the barbarians' attempt to describe the kind of fortified border she had expected on the Mazonite side of the Pacha lands. Certainly a border-wall with spikes to prevent climbing would answer the description of a "thorn-wall." But when at last they approached this "thorn-wall," she saw for herself that the Pacha had not been descriptive, but literal.

The Thorn-Wall began as a shadow on the horizon, a gray mist that neither she nor those with her could see over or past. Xylina stared at it in puzzlement as they continued their journey, for it would not resolve itself into anything more substantial, even though they drew nearer to it with every footfall. It was something like a dark gray fog-bank looming up ahead of them, yet it could not be fog, for it did not move or dissipate despite the heat of the sun or the movement of the wind. It did, however, seem to grow taller;

she had first judged it to be about twenty or thirty cubits in height, but the nearer they approached it, the taller it seemed. She felt a stirring of cold fear in her throat as she took in how large it was—how could anyone build something so very *tall?* It must have taken hundreds of years to complete it!

Then, finally, as her eyes were struggling to make sense of this senseless, formless structure, Faro cursed. "By the gods! Those red savages were *right!* It *is* a wall of thorns! Who are these people, to use plants to guard their borders for them?"

She blinked, and suddenly what had been making no sense to her eyes became clear. The "structure" was no structure at all, but a massive hedge of thorny branches, so tightly interwoven that it must be pitch-black a few paces deep within. What her puzzled eyes had taken for tendrils of mist were in reality twining branches.

The road led up to a hole in this hedge, and there seemed to be no viable alternate routes. If they were to pass into the next realm, it must be via this passageway or none at all. There was no other way through, not that she could see, and to leave the road was to court death from lack of water. The Thorn-Wall stretched from horizon to horizon; it was either go on, or go back—or, she suddenly realized, try to make a home among the Pacha.

That might not be too terrible, really. She could certainly keep them happy with nightly drinking-bouts and occasional feasts of magic meat! But she knew, really, that such a thing was not possible—not without losing whatever small honor she still possessed. She must go on; the Pacha had not said that these people were hostile, only that they avoided contact. They could be friendly; they could simply be frightened of the Pacha. People who hid behind a wall of thorns could be gentle and unwarlike.

She tried not to show her trepidation as the column approached the Thorn-Wall; she could well imagine why the Pacha had never bothered to attempt to traverse the tunnel leading into the heart of the Wall. To them, worshipers of the sun as she had learned them to be, it would have been a descent into a nightmare-hell of their worst fears, to dive down into this dark hole with only the hope of light on the other side. Their tales of the afterlife for evil-doers depicted a dark and unending void. Surely this tunnel must seem a tunnel to that terrible afterlife to them.

She halted the men just outside of the passageway, and considered it, and the Wall. The Wall itself seemed to be composed of millions of plants rather than just one; each one reaching upward to the sun, tangled with its neighbors until there was no saying where one began and the next ended. The branches ranged from limbs the thickness of a man to twigs slimmer than her little finger; the thorns from fearsome projections as long as a horse to mere threads. All ended in points that were probably as sharp as they looked; she did not care to test them herself. They could be envenomed; she had no way of knowing. The branches were covered with tiny round leaves, a dusty gray-green in color, thick and waxy, and about as large as her thumb. That was what had given the mist-like quality to the Wall when they were still some distance from it.

She stared upwards at the Thorn-Wall, deep in thought, trying to imagine who or what had grown this prodigy. For surely nothing like this could have occurred without a controlling mind behind it! It was too deliberate, too regular, and too purposeful to have simply sprung into being accidentally. She saw no signs of pruning or other shaping within the tunnel, and yet it was as regular as if it had been cut by an exacting hand. Someone must have control over these plants. And besides, the Pacha had spoken of people on the other side of the Wall.

She peered into the darkness of the tunnel, shading her eyes with her hand, but saw nothing. No sign of the other end at all. They probably have some kind of gate or guard on the other side, she thought, considering how impossible it would be to climb to the top of the thing, much less climb over it. There was no sign of light, as though the tunnel came to a dead-end, but a gate closed across the other end would account for that. She did not want to consider the idea that it did not go all the way through.

And yet she must.

If it did not go through—why would there be a road here? They couldn't completely close themselves off. No, there must be a portal on the other side; this road was made by someone or something. And it went beneath the thorns. So that was where they had to follow. There were other possibilities; that the "road" was no road at all, and that the tunnel was the work of the plants in order to trap prey within. But others must have come here; the bolder of the Pacha must have dared this road. They did not have reports of folk being devoured by the plants, or of vanishing, never to return. She must trust in that.

Finally, she conjured oil and ordered the lanterns brought out and lit. If they must travel under this monstrous thing, at least it need not be in darkness. She sent the lanterns down the line, one to every two men. They seemed glad of her foresight; she was just grateful that conjured oil burned as readily as "real" oil.

A few cubits into the tunnel, and it was as black as a starless night—and quite surprisingly cold. Not cold enough to freeze, but certainly as chilly as the nights hereabouts became. And damp, as well: a kind of clamminess that clung to the skin and penetrated her clothing. She had ordered one of the men to walk in front of her with a lantern, and his little circle of light illuminated bare, dark earth, of a dark brown that was nearly black, utterly unlike the soil outside. The light cast upward from his lantern shone on a densely interwoven mat of gray-green branches and thorns, as tightly intertwined as any basket she had ever seen. And still no sign of the marks of pruning. The air, besides being chilly and damp, smelled like the earth in a cellar: dank and redolent with mildew.

The men and even the beasts became strangely silent.

She had no wish to break that oppressive silence with so much as a whisper. She had the uncanny and uneasy feeling that to do so would be to call down unwelcome attentions on all of them. From time to time, she thought perhaps she heard rustlings out there just beyond that mat of thorns, or whisperings from the darkness ahead of them and behind them. But she did not want to halt the column and call for silence. She did not want to *know* that she heard these things.

There seemed no end to this tunnel, and no way of judging how long they had been inside it. With no light of day to tell, it could have been mere moments, or hours. She kept herself from looking back at the bright circle of light behind her for as long as she could. After all, what was behind her did not matter, really.

When she looked back at last, she could no longer see the end of the tunnel. She fought down panic at that; it occurred to her that it might have grown closed the moment they passed it—

No. No, she couldn't think that. There was no evidence that these plants could grow that quickly. And it wouldn't matter if they could; she could always conjure oil and burn them free, or conjure great slabs of stone to crush the branches at the entrance. There were a hundred things she could do. So long as she did not panic. No, probably they had been curving off to the right or the left, and the end of the tunnel was hidden behind that curve. There was no easy way to tell if the tunnel curved from within it.

The tunnel itself remained the same size, which was reassuring—tall enough for a tall woman to ride a tall horse, carrying a banner, and still have a cubit to spare above the tip of the banner, and wide enough for three horses to walk side-by-side with comfortable space between them and between the sides of the outermost and the walls. There was certainly enough room for her men and wagons to pass along it. And interestingly enough, the horses gave no signs of fear or restiveness.

Perhaps they had no concern about vegetation, which was what this was.

Nothing changed. They rode on and on, and nothing changed; there was only the endless tunnel before them, the same tunnel behind them. Finally, when she was beginning to wonder in despair if there was no land, no people, only an unending thorny growth over the length and breadth of this county, there seemed to be a change in the texture of the darkness just ahead of them.

She narrowed her eyes against the darkness, and leaned forward, trying to see beyond the little circle of light ahead of her. A moment later, and she was certain of the change ahead. And that was when she noticed that the tunnel itself was beginning to widen, opening up like a great funnel.

Finally, after being beneath the hedge long enough that she was chilled to the bone and longing for a bit of sun and warmth, they came to the end: a huge, bark-covered slab, with a round, door-like aperture in it, without visible hinges or any way to swing it forward or back to open it.

Before she could direct her man to knock on that door, it opened, and a single, slender figure stepped through to face them fearlessly.

That figure was as strange as the hedge; it was dressed in a bright blue, form-fitting garment of something shiny and flexible, a fabric that moved with it as easily as a skin. "It," she thought, because she could not put a sex to the person; there was no sign of external genitalia, neither breasts nor penis, and in *that* garment the existence of either would have been quite obvious. There did not even seem to be nipples on the chest, only flawless skin. The face was as smooth as a prepubescent child's, with no sign of beard or other facial hair, but the hair upon its head, of a white-gold in color, was as long and luxuriant as Xylina's own. Its eyes were a bright, unnatural blue, and its skin was a dark brown, as dark as the earth beneath this hedge. It did not seem to have a weapon, but she did not take that as being evidence that it was weaponless. For one thing, it could very well have formidable, and unknown, magic. And probably did. The very arrogant posture was a challenge, a dare to attack and face the consequences. She did not intend to try and call the creature's bluff.

It looked over Xylina and her expedition with a cool, calculating gaze, and a complete lack of expression. After staring at the slaves for a long moment, its gaze returned to her, and there its attention remained. "Ah," it said after a pause, in a high, fluting voice. "A Mazonite. A Mazonite warrior and her entourage of slaves. And one other. A demon, it would seem."

To Xylina's surprise, it spoke *her* tongue, with no discernible accent or inflection. She wondered where and how the creature had learned the language.

"Yes," she said simply, deciding in that very breath to keep the real task of their expedition a secret. "We are sent by Queen Adria, and our mission lies beyond your borders. May we pass your land? This is all we ask, that you not hinder our passage."

The creature continued to gaze at her, as she attempted to keep her face as expressionless as the one it showed her. "You passed the Pacha without incident?" it asked, finally. "You spilled no blood, murdered none of the savages?"

"We passed peaceably. The Pacha tribes have declared themselves our brothers," Xylina replied, making no attempt to elaborate on that statement. Perhaps this would be enough. She really didn't want to lie to this creature. It might have ways of detecting such a lie. She could not guess how it might react if it knew that she was lying. But she was also dubious about the impression the truth would make.

The creature burst into peals of bell-like laughter; Xylina fought down her resentment, for it was making no effort to conceal the fact that it was laughing at her. "Fitting!" it crowed at last. "Oh, fitting! One barbarian declares himself to be brother to the next! Pledging eternal peace like a pair of children promising to be best of friends forever!" And it resumed laughing.

Xylina stared at her mule's ears, and told herself that if this creature called the Mazonites "barbarians," it probably had good reason to. *She* was petitioning to cross *its* land. There was no point in getting it angry with her. There was even less point in getting angry with it. Nothing she could say or do would change its opinion of her civilization or supposed barbarity.

Get it angry, and it might make them go all the way back through that tunnel again, she chided herself, and suppressed a shiver. No, it was worth bearing with a little laughter, to avoid *that*. At least the creature wasn't actively hostile; it was not rejecting their request to travel out of hand.

Finally the creature composed itself. "What is your mission?" it asked. "If it is to seek out lands for conquest, you have come to the wrong place. We could shut the door here, and let the Thorn-Wall grow up, and you could throw your pitiful conjurations against it for the next thousand years with no effect. Our science is beyond your meager magic; we can eliminate you without risking so much as a patch of skin. So tell me now: what is it you come here for?"

Interestingly, it made no mention whether it could tell if they were speaking the truth. It seemed to Xylina that if she were in its place, and she had that power, she would make a point of it. Still, this creature hardly seemed human, and she could not make assumptions about how it would think. She had already made clear that they were only passing through, and it refused to credit that truth. What would it accept?

"We are here for trade," Ware said. "As you know, the Mazonites are skilled in many things, but only lately have they looked beyond their borders for things other than conquest. The Queen and my people are looking out for new opportunities for trade, for my own kind are skilled at such things. Obviously, it is no use to them to expand the boundaries of Mazonia beyond the place where women's conjuration reigns supreme. It is therefore much more logical to expand by commerce rather than conflict. The Queen has heard of lands of great wealth and civilization beyond the Pacha territories, and she has sent us to find the truth of the matter. It is logical to send one of her subjects to discover this, rather than depending upon the tales of travelers and foreign traders."

The creature turned its strange blue eyes upon him with seeming approval. Xylina noted Ware's emphasis on the word "logical" and wondered if this had some meaning for the creature. "It is," it agreed. "You show a firm grasp of reality. Perhaps you are not as barbarous as you once were, you Mazonites. Well, come. You may travel through our land, and see what you will, and when you come again, perhaps you will have some trinkets we think worth trading for. We, of course, will have much that you will want. Some of it we may be willing to trade."

Such arrogance! Xylina forcefully reminded herself that it was better to deal with an arrogant person than a savvy one, because the advantage was with the realist. She quelled her ire. It was possible that the creature was trying to make her angry, so that *it* would have the advantage.

"Thank you," Ware said gravely.

"Before you enter our land, I must search your belongings," the creature continued. "In particular, I must see what you carry in your wagons."

That was hardly an unreasonable request. Xylina had heard that many lands required a search at the border. She nodded acquiescence, and waited patiently while the creature rummaged through their goods.

But it paid no attention to the weapons, the gold, or even the souvenirs the men had picked up from the Pacha. What it *did* pay close attention to was the kitchen-stuff. Finally, when it was through, Xylina asked it what on earth it had been looking for.

Its face hardened for a moment. "Plants," it said in a dire voice. As if "plants" were carriers of some deadly peril.

Xylina simply blinked, and said nothing. Plants? This

creature was afraid of plants? Surely this was some kind of joke!

The creature touched the door behind it, and the shaggy brown bark moved—but now Xylina saw that rather than swinging open as a door in an ordinary wall might, the wood actually receded, irising open large enough to permit the wagons to move through. She urged her mule out into the sunlight beyond, and it was eager to go.

On the other side of the Thorn-Wall, she saw that the branches on this side, besides sporting thorns and little leaves, were ablaze with palm-sized, three-lobed, flat, vermilion flowers. What she had taken for a slab of wood seemed to be a huge, flat trunk of some other kind of plant, grown athwart the entrance to the Thorn-Wall, its thornless branches mingling in apparent symbiosis with the thorny ones. The brown bark of its vining tendrils twined among the gray of the Thorn-Wall, and it, too, nourished palm-sized, trumpet-shaped flowers, of a deep cerulean. It was an unexpectedly lovely sight, and it took her breath away. The air here within this place was perfumed with scents she could not name, all of them mingling to form a heady, delicious aroma. The sun shone down, but without the punishing heat of the desert on the other side of the wall. The heat felt wonderful after the dark and cold of the tunnel.

She turned to look about her, and could hardly believe her eyes. On the other side of this growth, there was arid near-desert. But here—here there was a veritable jungle of vegetation of every sort, most of which she could not put any kind of name to beyond that of "tree," "flower," or "bush."

Huge silvery trees reached for the sky, smooth barked, and branchless for hundreds of cubits, then branching out with mushroom-shaped growth at their very tops; the leaves were a golden-green, and formed a lovely dome-shape above trunks so perfectly smooth that they could have been created on a lathe. Beneath these trees grew clusters of smaller trees. Some resembled the oaks and ashes and poplars that she was familiar with. Others were strange things that dangled sausage-like brownish-green growths on long vines beneath their branches, or grew huge, red and yellow fruits the size of both her hands. There were even trees that seemed to have very little foliage at all, but consisted mostly of trunks with small twiggy growths at the top, covered with tiny emerald leaves and white flowers.

Among all these were trees that were stranger yet. Akin to the plant that barred the entrance to the Thorn-Wall, these were round rather than flat, with enormous, barrel-like trunks and slender, flower-covered, viny branches. Those trunks were so huge that they were larger than Xylina's house in girth, and reached twenty or thirty cubits tall or more. These trees were riddled with holes—

Holes which had been fitted with glass windows, and beaded curtains; holes which sported balconies of twisted, polished vines, and stairs which spiraled down the sides of the parent trunk.

Were these—*houses?* It seemed as if they were, yet how could they have been formed from the flesh of still-living trees?

Even as she gaped at them, a smaller version of the creature guarding the entrance spilled out of one of the doors, ran laughing down the staircase, its pallid hair flying like a flag, and ran off into the undergrowth. It sported a kind of skintight singlet of brilliant scarlet and violet-pink.

The creature that had met them emerged from the door behind the last wagon, and stroked the bark. The portal irised closed again. "Simply follow the road," it said, with evident indifference. "We are educated beings. Most of us speak either your tongue, Pacha, or both; many languages are part of our learning from childhood. You can not become lost, for if you do not take any turnings, this road will lead you to the portal in the Thorn-Wall on the other side of our land. If you wish to purchase food, ask along the

way. If you wish to make a camp, you may do so at any clearing linked to the road."

It started to turn away, then turned back, as if it had suddenly thought of something. "We permit nothing to be
killed," it said, sternly. "Do not presume to cut wood for
your fires, nor take what you think to be game for your
meals. I can see by your clothing and equippage that you
are still barbarous enough to kill for the feeding of your
bodies; we do not do so here."

Then it turned its back upon them, and walked away
before Xylina could think of anything to say. In a moment,
the foliage beside the road had closed about it, hiding it
from view.

Ware looked at her out of the corner of his eyes as she
stared after the creature, rather taken aback. She had
feared many things; it seemed that the worst these creatures could be bothered to greet them with was contempt.

Ware seemed to feel the same astonishment and resentment. "So friendly," he drawled, in a voice heavy with irony.
"Do you know, I believe I prefer the Pacha."

She managed a smile; Faro chuckled.

"For once, demon," the slave said, "I believe I agree with
you."

Before they had traveled a league, Xylina had grown
heartily weary of being the object of so much unpleasant
attention. The inhabitants of this place—which, she had
learned, was called "Sylva"—seemed to treat her and her
expedition as a kind of circus-cavalcade of freaks, when
they were not regarding them as if they were some kind of
unreasoning beasts.

The inhabitants, dressed in a myriad of odd, brightly-
colored costumes that displayed their sexlessly beautiful
bodies as if they were pleasure-slaves, gathered curiously
beside the road as they made their way along it.
Everywhere the result was the same, the natives pointing
and making comments in their own tongue, which was a
sing-song affair that reminded her of the chanting of

priestesses. And from the laughter that most of those comments elicited, she was fairly certain that none of them were flattering.

The men were just as uncomfortable under this scrutiny as she was; the column drew close together, as if to minimize the amount of time anyone would have to spend under those critical blue eyes.

Every one of the inhabitants looked like every other; even the children were no more than miniature copies of the adults. Xylina had the uncanny feeling that she was traveling through a land of cast-clay dolls: beings as sexless and identical as the cheap toys sold for boy-children in the marketplaces of Mazonia. As she continued to pass these creatures, she became aware of something else as well— none of these beings showed any signs of aging. Their faces were all unlined and placid; their hair the same white-gold, with no threads of gray. That unnerved her further; were these creatures immortal?

It was difficult to tell time with so much of the sky covered by branches, but the hints of deepening shadows gave her the notion that it might be time to call a halt. Accordingly, she began to watch for one of the clearings the first Sylvan had told her of.

She soon found one: it seemed to have a well with a hand-pump and a long trough for water beneath the elaborate spout. That was something of a relief; at least there would be real water for drinking and cooking, and they would not need to use the stale stuff in their water-casks.

She directed the expedition to begin making camp, and took her mule off to one side to picket it for the night. Ware joined her, and for once she welcomed the demon's company. He seemed far more human than any of these creatures.

While they were unsaddling, one of the Sylvans, its mask-like face actually creased with a faint frown, approached them with a hint of aggression in its posture.

"What are you doing with these poor, gentle beasts?" the Sylvan demanded. "Why are you torturing them like this? What gives you the right to treat them like slaves, exploit and abuse them?"

Since Xylina's mule was cropping the grass with every evidence of content, she could not for a moment imagine what the creature was talking about. And as for rights—an animal could not reason, and had no responsibilities, so how could it have rights? Didn't having rights also mean that you had to take on responsibilities too?

"I'm afraid I don't understand you," she said carefully. "Could you be a bit more specific?"

"Why are you forcing these helpless creatures to bear you on their backs?" the Sylvan asked angrily. "Why are you forcing them to pull your wagons?"

Xylina blinked at it. "They're horses," she said finally, as if speaking to a child. "They're mules. I feed and care for them; they earn that by serving me. It's their job."

That seemed to enrage the Sylvan further. "You are not content with enslaving your own kind, but you must torture and oppress even the poor animals, who are utterly helpless to resist you! They can not escape your unwelcome attentions, they can do nothing to protect their freedom! You oppress them, and they must bear with whatever you choose!" it exclaimed, putting one hand protectively on the shoulder of Ware's stallion. "I demand that you—"

What the Sylvan was about to demand, Xylina never discovered, for at that moment, Ware's horse, a high-tempered beast who did not suffer the hand of anyone but his master upon him, reacted. With a squeal of rage he whipped his head about on his long flexible neck, and sank his huge white teeth into the Sylvan's shoulder.

The Sylvan screamed and jerked free, its clothing torn and bloody, its shoulder lacerated. It fell into Xylina's mule, who laid his ears back and with a joyous look on its face, kicked with all his might.

The Sylvan flew through the air and landed in an

undignified heap several cubits away. A dozen or so of its fellows gathered about it, and helped it, weeping, to its feet. Surrounded by horrified Sylvans, it limped off into the darkness.

Ware looked at Xylina with suppressed laughter in his eyes. "I suppose we should punish the beasts, but—"

"Oh no," she replied, strangling her own mirth. "No, that would only confirm our barbarous natures in their eyes. After all, the poor, helpless beasts cannot defend themselves against us."

Ware turned his attention back to unsaddling his horse, but his shaking shoulders told Xylina that he was silently laughing.

They finished picketing their animals, and went to fetch the mules from the wagons. Faro brought his own mule to the picket-line, and was accosted halfway there by yet another Sylvan. Xylina was near enough to overhear every word it said.

It looked at his riding-breeches, boots, and light leather armor with disdain, standing directly in his path so that he could not avoid a confrontation with it. "Murderer!" it said. "Do you know how many poor, helpless animals died so that you might flaunt their skins on your back?"

Xylina saw Faro's face go blank; he looked very stupid at that moment, and she knew from experience that he was about to respond with something as scathing as possible.

Then he smiled; Xylina recognized that smile. It was the same one with which he had greeted his attackers in the street. That seemed a lifetime ago! "As a matter of fact," he replied jovially, "I do. I killed them all myself. It was great fun. Would you step out of my path, or would you care to become a tunic?"

The Sylvan's mouth worked silently for a moment, as it tried to deal with Faro's reply. As it stood there, face twisted with distress, the slave reached forward and lightly pinched a fold of the skin of its arm between his thumb and forefinger.

"You'd make a very nice tunic," he said helpfully. "Gloves, too, I think. Although I doubt you'd put up enough of a fight to make it entertaining. Still, my mule has acquired a taste for man-flesh since I've had him—and you look soft and sweet. I think you'd please him."

That was too much for the Sylvan, who fled in terror.

They were not disturbed for the rest of the evening.

Ware had plans for this evening that he preferred Xylina not know about. He waited until Xylina had set up the camp, using her magic to create a barrier-wall between her people and the prying eyes of the Sylvans. He knew why she was doing this, although she had said nothing to him or to Faro. It was not for protection, so much as to preserve some semblance of privacy, and he heartily agreed with her. In all his experience, he had never encountered people quite like these, and he feared that they were impolite and impolitic enough to march directly into the encampment for more of their lectures, if they were not held out by a physical barrier.

He wanted to discover a few things about these people on his own, and thought that he might best do so if he could get away from the rest of the party.

He watched patiently until darkness, then used his ability to dematerialize to pass the barrier that Xylina had created around the camp. When he emerged on the other side, he found that he was alone. Evidently the Sylvans' passion for freeing helpless creatures and confronting the murderers of animals did not outlast being confronted with an unyielding and unresponsive barrier.

Although they had been told not to leave the road, Ware decided that a look around this strange place was in order. The more information he had to bring back to Xylina, the more valuable he would be to her. And he wanted passionately to be of value to her. If she came to value him, she would be open to more intimate feelings in time. Already, she trusted him in some small things—and he had managed to make her share moments of humor with him as well. In a way, he blessed the road that had brought them all here, for in comparison to these Sylvans, he looked positively human.

There was a pathway leading from the road, lit by a succession of dimly-glowing blossoms of some night-blooming plant. It had occurred to him, as soon as he saw the sort of life these people led, why they had considered plants to be contraband. They evidently manipulated plants in a variety of sophisticated ways, until they served every purpose possible. Foreign plants might carry disease that could wipe out entire species of the plants the Sylvans had come to depend on. What would they do, for instance, if their house-trees began to die? Live in tents? He wondered what the trees were like inside, how they were grown. It was true that the only living part of a tree was just beneath the bark, and that birds often lived inside cavities in hollowed-out trees, but how could people do so?

He spotted one of the house-trees just off to the side of the path, and on impulse, took cover among the shadows. He saw two of the Sylvans leaving it, going down the twisted vines that served as a staircase. They walked hand-in-hand down the path away from him. Now it was the time to satisfy his curiosity, while the owners of this tree were away.

He waited, making certain that he would not be seen, then instead of climbing up the usual way, he simply passed through the rough bark-wall of the tree.

The notion of living inside a tree had seemed romantic: living so closely with nature, at one with the world. But once inside this peculiar dwelling, he found it was something other than romantic.

The floor was soft and pulpy, far from level, rather unpleasant to walk on. The rooms were dark, cramped and oddly shaped, with little space for furniture. In fact, there was little in the way of furniture: mostly large pillows for seating, and larger ones for sleeping. There seemed no place to prepare food or store it; perhaps they ate communally. Clothing was hung in a small room, from a rod wedged across the middle of it. He could find no bathing room, and the room for elimination was a simple primitive jakes, no more sophisticated than a poor Mazonite's outhouse. There was a peculiar smell, both sharp and damp, and it appeared from the marks on the walls about the windows that they were not entirely weather-tight.

So much for romance.

Ware passed back out of the house, and followed in the wake of the two owners. In a moment, a smell of cooking wafted on the breeze from ahead of him, confirming at least one of his guesses, that these Sylvans ate communally.

A glow of light warned him that he was about to encounter the Sylvans again. He slowed his steps, hoping to see something of the strange creatures before they saw him. Perhaps he could pick one a little more sympathetic than the last few to pose his questions to.

The path dead-ended in a sizable clearing, with an outdoor kitchen set up in the midst of it. Large pots simmered over carefully tended fires, and Sylvans both adult and child walked or sat in groups. They were talking and eating from bowls containing what he assumed to be a soup or stew of some kind. No one noticed him, there in the shadows at the entrance, and he took his time looking the Sylvans over.

He could not tell if any of these people had been privy to the unpleasant encounters earlier, but looking closely, he finally saw something he had seen on no other face thus far—the slight signs of aging. It was on one of the Sylvans sitting and eating nearby, and the only one who seemed to be doing so alone. It had faint wrinkles around its mouth, crow's-feet at the corners of its eyes, and its hair had a few streaks of coarser white amid the silken silvery blond.

Ware approached the creature cautiously; it looked in his direction as he neared. "Ah," it said. "You are one of the barbarian strangers, are you not?" It seemed unconscious of its rudeness. "Have you any questions? I am the oldest Sylvan here, and I should be able to answer anything you care to know."

As Ware approached and took a seat at its side, the creature said something to one of its fellows about "getting the barbarian proper food." He understood the creature only imperfectly, since it spoke so quickly its words blurred together. As the second Sylvan went off towards the cooking pots, the first turned his attention back to Ware. "I am Sharras," it said. "What would you like to know?"

Ware hesitated for a moment, but the creature's opening line gave him an opportunity he could not pass by. "You say you are the oldest Sylvan here," he replied, "And yet it is true that you all seem incredibly young and vital—how is it you remain that way?"

"Proper nutrition," the Sylvan said, proudly. "We consume nothing of animal nature. To consume such things is to degrade the flesh; we consume nothing that is not pure."

Ware took a glance into the bowl of soup that had been brought to him: nothing but vegetables, with cubes of something white. Politely, he ate a bite; it seemed harmless, but nothing to be excited about, and the white stuff was virtually tasteless. "I am sure," he replied politely. "But how old are you?"

"Oh, a little above forty years," Sharras replied. Ware concealed his surprise. From the Sylvan's words and attitude, he had assumed that the creature was much older, well over a hundred. It appeared that this "proper nutrition" was no better at retarding the effects of aging than any other regimen.

Still, it could not be doubted that the creature was in excellent physical shape; the diet surely contributed to that.

"I find it difficult to tell your males from the females," Ware continued diffidently. "I know this may seem blind of me, but—"

"There are no males and females," Sharras interrupted.

Ware gave him an incredulous look.

"There are no males and females," Sharras insisted. "This is a society of complete equality, and there can be no equality where there are two separated sexes. We are all both male and female, and life-partners take turns in bearing the children. Only in this way can there be complete equality in all things. Life-partners wishing to bear children must wait until there have been two deaths in our land; then they both become gravid, and bear their offspring at the same time. This makes all things equal."

"So you *are* mortal," Ware exclaimed without thinking.

Sharras made a face, but said nothing. "All of our people are changed by our science, so that all are equally beautiful," he continued. "In this way, too, we achieve complete equality. There is no ugliness, and when the signs of age become too obvious, the Sylvan will retire from the world. I am about to do just that," it concluded proudly.

"Retire?" Ware said, carefully. "Do you mean—die?"

"Die? Great Forest, no!" Sharras laughed, as if Ware were some kind of idiot for even suggesting such a thing. "Do you understand nothing I have said? We take no lives, not even in defense. No, I will simply join the rest who are aged, in a special community, surrounded by a wall of roses, where we will clothe the signs of age with pleasant masks and costumes, where we will live the remainder of our lives with nothing but leisure to fill our days. And when the final time comes, I will be taken to a place where I shall fast and be given special herbs, so that I may meet rebirth with a tranquil spirit."

Where it would be closed off so that none of its kindred would have to look upon the terrifying reality of age and death, Ware thought in disgust. And where it would be drugged and starved so that it would die more quickly, so that someone else could have a child.

The masks and costumes would disguise the fact that the population of these little communities changed so quickly; no one who did not know the secret would guess. But Ware had centuries of observing humans and their nature, and changed as these people were, they still were human, and there was very little they could do that would surprise him.

Disgust him, yes. Surprise him, hardly.

"You have answered all my queries most gracefully, Sharras," he said, putting aside his stew and standing up. "And I thank you for your time and trouble. Now I must go, before my companions miss me."

He turned and walked quickly away, slipping into the shadows at the entrance to the clearing, and keeping to them as only a demon could, becoming the next thing to invisible. Sometimes he was tempted to enter Xylina's sleeping chamber this way, just to gaze on her as she slept. But he did not; he was not looking for illicit temptation, but for a relationship meaningful beyond the comprehension of most human beings. So he had to be patient. He did believe that he was making progress; Xylina no longer looked on him with disgust, and indeed seemed to be coming to respect him. In time she could come to him of her own accord.

Then, of course, he would have to tell her the rest of the truth. That well might destroy the relationship. So, much as he desired her now, he was not eager to rush the matter. This tacit relationship might be the best they were to have.

When he passed through the stone walls that Xylina had erected around the camp, he found the Mazonite in her tent, discussing the Sylvans with her slave. They both looked up at his slight cough, and Xylina waved him inside.

"I assume you've been out of the camp," she said, "since no one could find you in it. Did you learn anything, skulking about?"

Was there an edge to that query? Or was she genuinely concerned for him? Perhaps both. She was so lovely even in her incidental ways! "Some," he replied, and described his conversation with Sharras in detail—then added his own guesses.

Xylina made a face. "And these people call *us*

barbarous!" she said with contempt. "Well, I will give orders to the men to take no notice of them, and to answer no provocations. I think the best way to deal with Sylvans who choose to harass us is to ignore them."

"That is probably a good idea," Ware said thoughtfully. "They may have sanctions against the taking of lives, but I would not care to find myself being drugged and 'educated' so as to see the error of my barbarous ways."

"My thought precisely," Xylina replied. "They are slippery, these Sylvans; they say one thing and mean twenty others. I think they have very little idea of honor, and I would put nothing past them. We have provisions enough to carry us across their land; I think we should eat nothing of theirs, and drink nothing but water, and have as little to do with them as may be. I do not trust them." She looked directly into Ware's eyes for the first time since the journey began. "In fact, compared to them, you are a model of honor and humanity, demon. I had far rather trust my safety with you and your word. If you can slip off every night and learn more, I would appreciate the effort."

Ware's heart exulted, although he kept his face as impassive as any Sylvan's. "I will do my best to help you, Xylina," he replied gravely. "You know this is true: I will give you every effort I can."

"Yes," she said, suddenly and unexpectedly, with a shy smile that lit her eyes. "Yes, I do. Thank you, Ware. You are proving a better and truer friend than I had given you credit for."

He bowed a little in recognition of the praise, and his heart leapt again.

She had called him "friend."

Soon, perhaps, she would be ready to call him more than that.

• Chapter 12

At last it was over: they had passed through the land of the Sylvans without any mishap. The guardian of this "door" dilated the orifice to let them out across the border, making no attempt to conceal his contempt of them. The men marched through quickly, making no effort to conceal their relief at being on their way out of Sylva. Xylina rode her mule into the Thorn-Wall tunnel with a feeling that she and her men had narrowly escaped. It had been very difficult for the men to hold their tongues in the face of ridicule and harassment on the part of the Sylvans. She suspected that only the fact that the Sylvans tended to concentrate their harassment on her, as the mistress, ignoring the slaves for the most part, had kept serious incidents from occurring. She had been able to keep her temper only by following Faro's example, playing to the Sylvans' expectations and exceeding them, ridiculing them in turn. She had not known she was capable of that. But then, there were a great many things she had not known she was capable of.

The past week of crossing Sylva had taught her many things about herself and about the men, but the most profound was something that simply could not be put into words. It was a feeling, and she experienced it once again as she looked at her guards and servants.

Kinship. That was the closest she could come to it. These men, slaves though they were, and utter strangers a few short weeks ago, felt as close to her as if they had all been born of the same mother and raised together. They were, together, a tiny enclave of "home" among strangers, speaking the same language, following the same customs. Even the three paw-footed women; they had been some time in Mazonite service, and identified with the group. So far, unified, the members of this mission had survived encounters with the surprisingly friendly barbarians, and with these arrogant creatures so completely unlike anything she had ever seen that they might as well have been created from the plants they were so fond of. She and her men and servants were far more alike than any of them were like the Sylvans.

In fact, although she hated to admit it, the Sylvans frightened her, and she was very glad to be out of their reach. She didn't understand them, and doubted that anyone not born among them could. Ware had spoken with them and spied upon them every night that they were within the Thornenclosure, and nothing he told her brought her any closer to understanding them. In fact, at this point she wasn't even certain that she wanted to understand them; if she began to do that, she might start to act like them. No, she would far rather turn barbarian and go to live with the Pacha than even think of turning Sylvan.

On the other hand, Ware didn't seem to understand a great deal about them, either, other than simple things, like the obsession with absolute equality. "It can be an admirable goal, Xylina, so long as people realize that an absolute goal can never be reached," he told her, trying to explain why the Sylvans changed their very bodies so that there were neither males nor females among them. There were stories of shape-changers, were-creatures, that were told to Mazonite children—even *that* she could understand. She could see why someone would want to have the power of a bear, the grace of a panther, but not this.

Ware continued, trying to find words that would make it clear to her. He seemed to want her understanding, in an almost flattering way. And—she found herself being flattered, though she resisted it. "There are no absolutes; there never can be," he said. "When people like the Sylvans refuse to accept that, though—"

"That is when they begin to twist things," she had finished, finally getting a glimmering of what he was trying to tell her. He nodded.

Still, she could not understand what really drove these people, and she doubted that even Ware could explain them. "These people frighten *me*," he continued. "I think I know why the demons have never tried to make any kind of contacts among them. They are so sure of their superiority; people like that can resort to force to 'convert' you, if persuasion does not work. They are so passionate about what they believe in, that there is no room for anyone else's beliefs." His eyes had swirled with a confusion of colors that mirrored an internal distress. "I tell you, Xylina, there is no creature more dangerous than a fanatic. You must either join them or escape them, for they will bury you. Reason does not enter into their thinking."

She did not ask what *his* reasoning was, but the idea that the placid-seeming Sylvans frightened a being as powerful as a demon was disturbing in itself. She did not understand what he meant about fanatics, but she tucked the words away to think about later, in the darkness of the night. Instead of allowing her blank mind to fill with fantasies of a demon lover, perhaps.

"Your people have far more in common with my kind than we whom you call 'demons' do with these Sylvans," he continued. "Never mind that the ancestors of the Sylvans were humans like you. Believe me, my dear, we are far more like you than we are like them."

In that, she had to agree with him. When Ware had first revealed his identity, all she had noticed was how strange, how alien he was. She had not been able to read his emotions; she was not even certain that he possessed anything she would recognize as an emotion. But now—now she could read him as easily as Faro, and now she trusted him. And he was far more "human," if such a word could apply to him, than these Sylvans were. That bothered her, oddly.

The "door" irised shut behind the last of her men. "I am

glad to be gone from this place," Ware said, from just behind her, echoing her thoughts.

"I hope we can find some other way through, or around," Xylina sighed. "I do not like those Sylvans, and I would not willingly put myself in their hands again. Not unless I commanded the kind of power that would make their numbers trivial. If I meet them again, I would wish it to be with them as my petitioners, and not the other way around."

She moved to the head of the cavalcade, as the men waited for her to assume her position in the lead. It felt right and good to be there, and without all the critical eyes of the Sylvans upon her, she felt more confident than she had in several days. Confident enough to face whatever unknown dangers lay outside this passage.

The Sylvans, though for the most part professing ignorance of the lands that lay on this side of their country, had told Ware that this region was one full of wild magic. It was hazardous to cross, so they said, and Ware's memories of the last time he was here agreed with that.

As if in answer to her thought of him, Ware rode up to take his place at her side. Since their first night in Sylva, Faro had begun to ride at the back of the cavalcade, telling Xylina that he trusted in the demon's honor enough to believe that Ware would not deliberately bring them into danger. In fact, he and Ware were getting along much better than she would have believed; something about Ware's dry sense of humor appealed to Faro's own. Now Faro took his mule to the rear, behind the wagons, and Ware held his stallion to a pace that matched Xylina's mule.

"What are we likely to meet with?" she asked, as the lantern-bearer walking in the front of the column illuminated the way ahead. "Can we expect trouble the moment we break out of the tunnel—or even before?"

"I wish I could tell you, Xylina," Ware said, his face fixed in that calm mask that she now knew meant that he was thinking furiously. "This region changes from year to year, and it has been a long time since any of my people were here. I can tell you only generalities. That the place is dangerous and treacherous. There are illusions here which cover the reality of the land. You may see a terrible beast which proves to be only an illusion—you may see it a moment later, may even believe that it is the same beast as before and you find that it is not an illusion, but a beast which will kill half your men. Illusions of water can conceal desert, and illusions of solid ground can conceal chasms. There are monstrous creatures here, and sometimes the very fabric of nature seems to have been warped and changed beyond recognition."

"You don't sound very comforting," Xylina said, wryly. She might have taken some alarm at his words—except that Ware had known all along that they would be coming to this region, and he had said all along that with his help, Xylina could survive this. She and her men had learned to work together; the men had learned to work with Ware instead of staring at him and expecting him to transform into something hellish for no particular reason.

"I suppose I don't sound comforting." Ware actually smiled a little—a warm smile, and the most genuine that Xylina had ever seen on his face. She smiled back, feeling a pleasant rush of corresponding warmth as she did so. "I am trying to err on the side of caution; where we are about to step, nothing can be taken for granted, and there is no such thing as taking too much care."

He had changed, she decided. He was no longer stalking her. He was—a friend. Maybe he had finally given up the notion of possessing her, and was going to settle for friendship instead. But strangely enough, that idea didn't seem to comfort her as much as it should have.

Ware continued, interrupting her thoughts. "The one thing that you can always be sure of is that the illusions *always* fade for at least a little, and that the cycles of change are no more and no less than one day and night in length. That, or so I was told, is due entirely to the effect of the crystal shard in the heart of the land; the cycle is a limit it imposes on the chaos of the wild magic here. So if we study the hazards carefully, we should be able to weave our way through them."

"If they give us time to study them," she pointed out. "Does anyone actually *live* out there?"

"Oh yes," he told her. "Yes, humans and other things. There are even likely to be some that will be friendly to us."

"And just as likely to want to kill us." She nodded, actually with a little satisfaction. *This* was something a Mazonite could understand: foes that fenced with weapons, not words, and situations where it was simply "kill or be killed." The sophistry of the Sylvans had confused her; right at the moment, she would prefer a raging beast that charged straight at her.

But she was careful not to say that aloud. Something warned her that to do so might be calling down misfortune on herself and her party. An old saying was, "be careful what you ask for, because you might get it." That was the last thing she wanted. Thus far, care and thought had kept her little band intact. She would like it if she could continue to do so. She had killed, herself, and had seen many dead men since she attained her citizenship—but never ones that she knew personally. There was a difference; she had learned that over the course of this journey, too.

Ware was right: a little precaution wasn't going to hurt anything—and whatever lay ahead of them, *it* might not be as reticent about entering the Thorn-Wall tunnel as the Pacha had been. It would be best to prepare for trouble coming to meet them.

"Keep your weapons at hand, men," she warned, speaking over her shoulder. "We don't know what is ahead of us. The Sylvans wouldn't say, and whatever it is, it just might think that this tunnel makes a perfect site for a nest."

There was a rustling and a clatter that told her that weapons were being loosened in their sheaths, and quivers were being uncovered.

Good. She stared ahead into the darkness beyond the

moving spot of light, and called the lantern-bearer in until he was walking just in front of her mule's nose. She noticed that he was now walking with his sword in the hand not burdened with the lantern. "If you see something charging you, throw the lantern at it and get behind me," she told him. "You should be safer behind us. Ware's stallion is battle-trained, and my mule is at least accustomed to reacting to defend himself."

"Like he did with that critter he kicked into the treetops?" the man—Ladan, that was his name—answered, with an uncertain grin directed back at her. "Yes, mistress, if that's what you want me to do. But I am a fighter; I am trained—"

"It's what I want you to do," she assured him. "If there is a monster, it may be nothing you are prepared or even able to fight against. By throwing the lantern at it, and getting out of its way, you may buy us time. That is the best thing you can do, and since you are trained, I am sure you can manage to hit it squarely with the lantern. I hope a face full of hot oil will make it stop long enough for me to conjure a rock wall between it and us."

Then she laughed. "And nothing at all may happen. After all, remember how the Pacha avoided the tunnel on their side. Probably the creatures here will do the same." Still, caution was best. Whatever a group was prepared for, never happened. Or so it was claimed.

Nothing leapt on them in the dark, nor was there anything lying in wait at the mouth of the tunnel. Xylina counted her blessings, and gathered her men into a defensive position around the tunnel entrance, while she and Ware surveyed the lay of the land.

Under a cloudless blue sky, the sun shown down upon them with a great deal less heat than she would have expected. An odd kind of mist rose in the distance: a mist, or a heat-haze. She could not really make out anything that was more than a couple of leagues away. There could

have been mountains out there, or oceans, or nothing at
all.

Directly before them was a large expanse of white sand,
sloping slightly downward. To either side, this empty sand
began at the foot of the Thorn-Wall, and continued for
some five or six hundred cubits before the signs of life
began. They stood on a rock shelf that extended into the
sand from the tunnel entrance, like a kind of stage.

To Xylina, this empty stretch was all she could have
asked for. Nothing could approach them without being
seen. The only drawback was that they could be seen as
well, by anything watching for prey. On the other side of
this open stretch was a brownish-black area that was
covered in sand with rocks heaving up out of it, and
dotted with odd and twisted growths, all in a rainbow of
colors.

"Does this look familiar?" she asked the demon. It would
be a good thing if Ware only knew what to expect here.

Ware eyed the stretch dubiously. "No," he replied. "And
do not be deceived by this apparent emptiness. Remember
what I told you about illusions. There could be creatures
creeping up on us at this very moment."

She glanced at the shimmering sand with alarm. That
had never occurred to her—but an illusion of emptiness
would be just as much an illusion as the vision of a
monster.

"The trick is that they cannot eliminate all signs of their
passing," Ware continued hastily, and the men looked
about them and formed a defensive square, without needing to be told to do so. "We would hear them, or see their
tracks on the sand. Or if they were buried beneath the sand,
we would see the sand itself moving—"

"Like that?" One of the men exclaimed, and pointed off
to the right.

Instantly they all followed his pointing finger. There, in
the middle distance, the sand was pushed up in a growing
ridge, approaching them with the speed of a trotting horse,

as if there were some kind of giant mole burrowing beneath it. A mole as large as one of the wagons, from the size of the mound being created.

Xylina felt her breath stopping in her throat, and the men swayed back an involuntary pace, closing their square.

It—whatever it was—was coming toward them, but not directly; unless it changed its course, it would pass about halfway between them and the place where the rocks and strange, multi-colored growths began.

"What is it?" Xylina whispered.

"I don't know," Ware replied, also in a whisper, "but it may be sensitive to vibrations. Don't move—and keep the animals from stamping their feet, if you can."

Somehow the animals seemed to realize the need for quiet; the entire expedition froze in place, and not even the mules lifted a hoof. The creature beneath the sand continued on its way, lifting the sand between them and the rest of the world, then passing on, and out of sight. The sand slowly subsided in its wake, until it lay flat again, as if it had never been disturbed.

Xylina breathed a sigh of relief, and the men relaxed. All but Faro, who peered off after the creature with a frown. He was the first to speak.

"We still have to cross that open stretch," Faro pointed out. "There may be more of those things—whatever they are. Or that one might come back."

True enough. Xylina nodded, and closed her eyes for a moment, thinking. They had to cross it—but not necessarily on the sand.

She opened her eyes again, and examined the stretch of empty sand between them and the rocks. It would be folly to cross on the sand—but there was no reason to. Not while her powers were strong.

She had seen no weakening of them, despite the distance from Mazonia. Ware said that all magics worked equally well here. Well, now was the time to test that. She pursed her lips thoughtfully, gathered her powers about her—and raised her hands to conjure.

The mists of her powers gathered out over the sand, taking shape, solidifying in place. Gray mist, which formed into gray stone, heavy and substantial. First, she created pillars of stone in pairs, rising up from the sand, pillars that were much wider at the bottom than at the flat tops. Once she had those in place, she conjured a single slab of material, curving up over the sand, supported by the pillars, running from just below their feet to the other side of the sandy expanse.

The men murmured to one another as the mist rolled up and over the tops of the pillars, leaving the bridge in its wake. She made the surface rough, so that the feet of men and beasts would not slip on it. For safety's sake, she made the material, which was neither wood nor metal nor stone, but an amalgam of all three that only conjuration could produce, strong enough to bear the weight of all of them at once.

Then she looked at them all, and nodded once. She needed to give them no other orders. Faro pointed to the men nearest the end of the bridge, and waved at the other side.

Two of the men ran lightly up and over the conjured bridge, and took their places at the other end, bows out, and arrows nocked and ready. They might have rehearsed this a thousand times, so quickly did they obey Faro's silent commands.

"Wagons next," said Faro. The men parted, giving the wagons enough room to pass between them, and the drivers snapped their reins over the mules' backs, rolling out onto the surface of Xylina's creation. The mules obeyed—but slowly. They did not entirely trust this bridge, and went forward only after they had tried each foothold carefully.

Xylina kept watch to the right for any more telltale burrows in the sand; Ware watched to the left. Faro urged the men on in hoarse whispers, as if he feared that the sand-creature might hear a shout. She held her breath, for she was not as confident of her conjuration as she tried to appear. Her creation might not stand if one of these unknown creatures burrowed beneath a support, or even struck one.

The sun beat down upon them without mercy; there was no shade, here on this side of the Thorn-Wall. The air was so dry she had not noticed the heat at first—now it was obvious that they would not have been able to stay here for very long without serious damage from the heat. Already Xylina felt sweat trickling down her back, and beading up on her upper lip; she licked her lips and tasted salt-crystals. In just that short a period of time, the sweat had evaporated, leaving behind the salt. They would need real water, and lots of it, if the rest of this strange region was as dry and hot as this part.

She glanced back from time to time, keeping track of the expedition's progress. The first wagon made it across her bridge without incident; as it reached the end, the second was in the middle of the bridge, and the third just beginning the journey. She couldn't help wondering about the noise of their progress. Every hoofbeat echoed hollowly upon the material of the bridge, and how far would the sound travel? Could a creature that lived under the earth hear things above it? Would the vibration travel down the stone and into the sand?

The second wagon reached its goal, and at that moment the third was halfway there. Nervous now, Xylina waved orders to the men to begin the climb; she and Faro and Ware would bring up the rear. Obediently, and nervously, they began to trot up the slope of her creation, crowding behind the wagon. But the slope was steep; they had to fight their way up it, just as the mules had.

The wheels of the third wagon had touched the earth on the other side, when one of the men on the top of the bridge cried out wordlessly and pointed in the direction the unknown creature had gone. Whatever he was pointing at had frightened him witless; he was white and shaking. Xylina looked, but saw nothing.

That didn't matter. Xylina did not need to know what he was pointing to: it was trouble and it was probably one of the sand-creatures. A moment later, before she even had a chance to react, she saw the mounding earth approaching, and at a much faster speed than it had come the first time. The sand-creature, or one like it, knew they were here, and was coming for them.

With a curse, she urged her mule onto the bridge; it scrabbled up onto the slope with clattering hooves, its ears laid back, but perfectly willing to move. Faro's was right behind her, and Ware's stallion ahead of her. The men scrambled to get off the bridge and out of the way.

Ware shouted to the drivers to take the wagons deeper into the rock- and growth-covered landscape on the other side. "Move those wagons out of here!" he called, his voice somehow amplified and carrying above the sounds of panicked shouting, mules braying, and running feet. "We don't know how far in it can go!"

Now there was no order to their retreat; it was something of a panicked rout. The drivers whipped up the mules, who were not loathe to move; they rolled their eyes and brayed, but threw themselves into the harness to haul the wagons over the smaller rocks and deeper into what Xylina hoped was a safe zone.

If the different color of sand meant that the sand-creature could not come there, they would be safe. If not—

First they had to get off the bridge! For the moment, that was all that mattered; Xylina's mule strained beneath her, sweat streaming down its sides, panting with exertion. The men on foot scrambled over the opposite side of the bridge and down onto the rocks, just as the three riders crested the top of her creation. Xylina dared a glance to the side, and her heart nearly stopped when she saw how near the mounding sand was.

She laid her whip along the mule's withers, heedless of how

he got to the other side so long as he did so. "It's coming!" she screamed to the other two. "I think it's going to ram—"

The mule slipped, his haunches slinging sideways—but he sensed the nearness of danger, and did not stop for a second. They were nearly off the bridge, their mounts scrambling for a free space among the fleeing men. And at that precise moment, whatever it was beneath them reared up.

Something as white and glistening as the sand rose nearly the height of the bridge; sand poured from it in a cascade, and the dogs in the last wagon shrieked as if they had been disemboweled. The white shape, still clothed in sand, rammed into the middle pillars of the bridge.

She never really saw what it was or anything other than that vague white shape: only flying sand and something huge. But there was no doubt of the result.

The bridge shuddered, sending all the support pillars tumbling with an avalanche-roar, and then fell over sideways. The crash nearly deafened them all, and the dogs howled again, yet were too panic-stricken to flee the shelter of the wagon. As they cowered behind a bale of supplies, another cresting wave of sand reared up and fell down over the toppled bridge, and engulfed it. There was a grinding noise, and the sand where it had been churned wildly in a kind of whirlpool.

Xylina's mule had fallen to its knees, and she had been thrown against the saddlebow, knocking the breath out of her. She somehow managed to stay in the saddle; she was afraid that the mule might freeze in terror, but it wanted no part of whatever was underneath that churning maelstrom, and it staggered to its feet without any undue urging on her part. It bolted to the hoped-for safety of the wagons, in company with every other member of the expedition. By the time Xylina reached the wagons and dared to look behind her, the last pillars and the ends of the bridge were sinking into the sand, as if they were being pulled down by something beneath the surface.

But whatever it was did not venture into the area of the black sand and rocks.

When they were certain it was not going to follow them, they were able to collect their scattered wits and breath. With a feeling of awe and amazement, they watched while it finished the work of demolishing the bridge, then turned and churned off back the way it had come.

The new zone seemed free of hazard, and extended for some distance. The mist remained, however, obscuring whatever lay beyond this zone. Although Xylina and Faro strained eyes and ears, and Ware made whatever arcane efforts were possible for demons, they were unable to detect any invisible threats. That left only the visible ones, and there did not seem to be anything large enough here to count as such. What life moved and crawled through here was all small. There might be snakes, scorpions, or some kind of equivalent, but there was little cover to hide them, and they should, by all rights, be easy to avoid.

This place looked rather like an odd rock-garden, in fact, and not like anything natural at all. It was full of strangely shaped boulders, collections of stones, and rock formations, none of which looked as if they belonged here, or matched the brown-black sand beneath them. These stones were of so many different kinds of rock that Xylina could not imagine how they had all come to be here. Some even looked as if they had been freshly chiseled from an alabaster cave: huge icicle-formations of stone, gleaming pale and wet in the sunlight, thrusting upwards from their soft beds of dark sand.

The stones were bewildering shades of color, everything from the red-orange of the Pacha country to the black of obsidian flows. There were huge boulders of green marble beside rough slabs of blue-gray slate; broken sandstone tumbles, water-smoothed quartz, and monoliths of granite. Schist and gneiss, porous limestone and chunks of coquina.

And yet their variety paled beside that of the strange growths that flourished among them.

Nothing stood taller than Xylina's waist, but she had never seen plants like these, not even in Sylva. At least the things growing in Sylva *looked* like plants. Most of these didn't even come close.

There were lacy red fans spread out to face the sun, and low green mounds with a structure so like that of a brain that she had to look twice to be certain that it was nothing of the sort. There were sticklike trees with no leaves at all, and a bright purple color. There were bristly growths, covered in thick needles, in every shade of pink and yellow imaginable. Mosses and lichens in rainbow hues clung to the sides of rocks and sprouted from cracks and niches. A wide grass with wavy leaves grew wherever there was shade, and a yellow-green plant that looked exactly like a deer's antlers grew in the sun between the rocks. Other plants, rosettes of fat, waxy leaves, or long swordlike, thick stalks, sprouted at the bases of boulders.

Among these rocks and growths crawled creatures like slugs, only these were slugs the size of a hand and covered with ruffled membranes of bright red and acid yellow. The slugs shared their domain with brilliant golden, webless spiders with fat hairy legs and bodies like saucers, and with attenuated blue stick-insects as long as Xylina's forearm, that stalked about with an unsteady and uncertain gait. There were also armored creatures that Xylina could not assign a species to: eight-legged plates with eyes on stalks, something that looked like a rabbit with a mounded and articulated coat of armor covering its back in place of a fur coat, and things that looked like upside-down cups with four little feet. There were plenty of ordinary insects, too — or at least, Xylina thought they were ordinary, until she swatted a fly and saw that it had no head that she could find, no eyes and no mouth. There was nothing larger than a rabbit; nothing that looked big enough to be a hazard to the party.

She, Faro, and Ware traded glances as the party got back into their accustomed marching order. Ware shrugged, and Faro shook his head. It seemed fairly obvious that neither of them knew what to make of this place. Well, neither did she.

She looked back at the smooth sand where the bridge had been. There was no going back, that was for certain. Not that she had ever expected that choice.

With a resigned sigh, she gave the order to move forward.

The sun continued to shine down upon them, but now the mist that rose ahead of them seemed to be hazing the sun over as well. It was not quite so hot, and the light had a kind of shifting quality, as if there were ghostly shadows passing overhead constantly. That made Xylina uneasy, but when nothing came of these odd shades, she ignored them. The going was a lot harder than it looked; the wagons were not built for this kind of uneven ground, and there were places beneath the sand where wagon-wheels lodged without warning. Often, they had to stop and lift a wheel over a particular obstacle. She tried to gauge their progress, and finally guessed that by the time they reached the place where the mist began and the terrain changed again, it would be near nightfall.

So far, only the land itself seemed to be fighting them, she thought, wondering if this was luring her into a feeling of relative safety that was in no way justified. Still, this was enough. They couldn't go more than three lengths without getting stuck.

But her suspicion proved to be correct. It was at one of these halts, as the men struggled to pry one of the wagon-wheels from between two rocks where it had gotten stuck, that the seemingly harmless landscape revealed another of its perils.

This was the first time they had come so near one of the purple stick-trees, for Xylina had simply not cared for the look of them. Once again, the men heaved at the wagon to get it out of a crevice between two boulders, and as the wheel finally broke free, one of the men scrambled back to within a few paces of the thing.

Xylina did not even see a movement; one moment the man was laughing and joking with his fellows, and the next, he was screaming in agony. A long purple tentacle coming from the top of the "tree" tried to drag him into the grasp of several more emerging from the ends of the branches.

The man who had been caught was clearly in terrible pain, and not just screaming from fear. The other slaves were equally divided between running to his rescue and backing away. The tentacle was wrapped several times around the man's waist and arm, trapping his sword against his body. The men going to his rescue eyed the other tentacles, eagerly waving, as if the tree was hoping they would come within reach. One dashed forward to slash at the tentacle dragging the captive in, but his sword simply bounced off, leaving the tentacle unharmed.

Xylina did not even stop to think—she simply acted.

Before the man had been dragged more than a cubit, she conjured a huge slab of stone right beside the "tree"—a slab she had created purposely off-balance. The moment she released her magic, it toppled over onto the "tree," crushing it.

The tentacle released the slave instantly, dropping off of him like so much limp, wet rope—but he collapsed where he was, moaning in pain, unable to move. The rest of the men now gathered around him, until Faro called them to alert, with sharp orders.

"Let the mistress tend to him!" he snapped. "Hellfire! This would be a perfect time to pick us all off! Get your rears back to duty!"

As Xylina jumped from her mule and went to see to the hapless victim, his eyes rolled up into his head, and he passed out. As she knelt beside him, she saw that where the tentacle had been there were red marks, where the skin was blistered and peeling back, as if he had been burned by a length of wire rope heated red-hot and wrapped around him.

Ware was there beside her as she examined the slave. His pupils were contracted to pinpoints, and he showed no sign of consciousness; his breathing was irregular, and so was his heartbeat. The demon took the man's arm in his hands and examined it minutely, then pointed to a series of regular red dots in the center of the "burned" stripes.

"Puncture-marks," Ware said succinctly. "He has been injected with some kind of poison."

Xylina looked at him for further advice, but he could only shake his head. Clearly, he knew nothing more than that. There was no way of knowing what, if anything, might be the antidote.

"Put him on the wagon," Xylina ordered the three wagon-drivers, wishing there was something else she could do. But without knowing the poison or its effects, there really was nothing else. He would either live or die as the poison and his own strength dictated. She recognized him as Kyle, one of the discarded husbands, and sighed. This seemed a sad end for one who had once been some woman's pampered favorite. "Make him as comfortable as you can; wash his wounds with clear water, and bandage him with soft cloths and the burn-salve."

The drivers hastened to do her bidding, and poor Kyle was soon cushioned among the bags of grain and the men's personal belongings, moaning occasionally in pain as the lurching of the wagon jostled him. Pattée appeared, tending to him, and that seemed to help.

The rest of the men gave the purple trees a wide berth thereafter.

Despite their best efforts, Kyle died before they could reach the next territory. That left her with a problem. Xylina was not certain what to do about the body. Custom dictated that a mere slave need only be left for scavengers, but somehow she felt that was hardly right. The men watched her closely, as if waiting for her to make some kind of error—and she sensed that the "error" would be in dumping Kyle and his belongings on the ground for beasts and birds to quarrel over. Finally she told the men who were about to remove the body to wrap it in some hastily conjured material and move it from the property-wagon to the weapons-wagon.

"We will give him proper—ah—treatment when we halt," she said, at their inquiring looks. The looks of question turned, she thought, to looks of approval before the slaves turned to their sad task. She conjured enough material to shroud him in a cocoon that made him look less like a body and more like a parcel. That quelled some of her own unease. She had not known much about Kyle, and yet she was indirectly the cause of his death—and that made her feel rather guilty, although she did not know why.

They halted at the very edge of the "rock-garden," in a relatively smooth place, completely free of the purple trees. The mist had retreated at this point, and it was possible to see the landscape beyond, the new territory they would face in the morning. This was a kind of forest, but a forest of huge leaves, as if kale or spinach had decided to grow as tall as an oak. Nothing more could be seen but the plants, and that itself was hardly comforting. Anything could be hiding in there—and probably was.

Xylina created the kind of rock-slab enclosure she had used in Sylva to protect their privacy, but this time she took care to make it proof against as many things as she could imagine. With luck, this would be enough for the night. She left one slab out, so that the others could bring the body of Kyle outside the stockade. She did not look at the grass-forest; there was no point in courting trouble before it came calling.

"Does anyone know how to—deal with this?" she asked instead, awkwardly, uncertain what to do next. She had no idea what the burial customs of the slaves were; she didn't think any Mazonite knew. Finally one of the handsome and ambitious young ones, Hazard, stepped forward.

"I do, mistress," he said submissively, keeping his eyes down. "I have—dealt with our dead before. If you like, I can lead the others in tending to Kyle. If you will grant us permission."

"Is there anything you would like me to do or supply?" she asked, feeling uncomfortable and helpless.

"Yes!" he replied, raising his eyes for a moment in surprise, then dropping them quickly. "It is our custom to burn our dead, with their possessions. There does not look to be anything much here to burn. If you would be kind enough to conjure a pyre—"

That was something of a relief—to have some way to contribute. It was something she definitely could do. Quickly she gathered her magic about her, selected a clear spot, and built a pyre of oil-soaked, fragrant shingles. It was the work of a few moments. She watched the fighters soberly as they lay the cloth-wrapped body atop it, together with the bag of Kyle's own goods. The sunset to her right painted the sky with spectacular streaks of red and yellow, making it seem as if the pyre was already ablaze.

She stood a little apart, but Faro took a place in the silent circle of men that gathered around the pyre. For a long moment no one spoke, and there was no real sound from the strange landscape about them, except for the slight sighing of the breeze which lifted her hair and cooled her brow.

"Kyle was a good man," Hazard said into the waiting silence. "He always did his duty, and shared every labor. He deserved—" There was a hasty glance at Xylina and a pause. "He deserved a fine life, but he found a terrible death instead. If the gods are listening—" and here Hazard made a strange gesture, a kind of circle upon his chest, inscribed with a forefinger, a gesture copied by all the others, even Faro "—let them hear me. He liked the Pacha, and they welcomed his songs and stories. Let him be reborn as a Pacha warrior."

"Let him be reborn as a Pacha warrior," the others echoed. "So let it be."

Hazard stepped back from the pyre and nodded at Xylina. That was enough of a signal for her, and she nodded in turn to Ware, who conjured fire.

The pyre ignited immediately, with a *whoosh* of flame. The oil-soaked wood burned with intense heat, and all the men had to step back a pace or two.

They watched for a moment, then turned their backs on the pyre and filed into the encampment. After a moment of staring at the pyre, Xylina did the same, then turned and conjured the last slab of rock to seal them all inside.

• Chapter 13

In the morning, there were vague prints of unidentifiable creatures all around their stockade, and the giant plants were still there, unchanged. The huge leaf garden was still so dense that Xylina could not see more than a cubit or two into it, and was still refusing to disclose its secrets. "I don't like this," Xylina said, frowning at the "spinach-forest" (or whatever it was), as the men packed up their belongings and stowed them in the wagons. "There's no way to tell what's in there. There could be anything, monsters or mansions, or things we can't even recognize."

The men looked tired this morning, as if they had not slept well. Of course the myriad strange noises coming from beyond their rock-stockade could have accounted for that. But she had the feeling that there had been many eyes peering into the darkness last night, thinking about Kyle, tossing restlessly, agonizing over their first casualty. Xylina had not slept well herself; she kept starting up at every shriek or scream, every howl and bark, expecting monsters to come swarming over her rock palisade at any moment. Wondering if there had been anything she could have done to prevent the tragedy. She had wished more than ever for the comfort of close company, and wondered whether Ware was similarly discomfited.

"I agree with you about this place," Faro replied, running a hand through his hair. "I agree entirely. This is the best place for an ambush I've ever seen. I wish there was some way to mow the stuff down."

Ware led his stallion up beside them, the handsome beast picking its way carefully across the stones of the "rock-

garden" territory, his hooves making little clicking sounds
against the rocks and thudding dully into the sand-pockets.

Faro turned to the demon as he got within speaking distance. "I don't suppose you recognize this, do you?" he
asked, without hope. "Have you or any of your people seen
this kind of territory before?"

Ware stared at the forest for a moment, then nodded,
slowly. "Actually, I do recognize this place," he said.
"Although it wasn't here at this spot the last time I passed
this way—it was growing up against the border where the
Sylvan Thorn-Wall is now. If this kind of growth is the
same thing I remember, we should have some warning
before anything attacks us. As I recall, the creatures here
are large and cumbersome, and they make a great deal of
noise." But the longer Ware spoke, the less certain he
sounded.

"But I also remember what you told us yesterday; that
these things can change a lot, even from year to year,"
Xylina replied cautiously. "I don't think we can trust anything, not even old memories, or things that look safe." She
shook her head. "I think we should assume that we can
assume nothing. We should figure that this is nothing like
the place you knew, and go from there."

Ware nodded, agreeing with her; so did Faro. She
turned back to look at the growth. It really did look like
some kind of giant vegetable patch. What kind of menace
could be lurking in there? Giant rabbits?

For a moment that seemed hysterically funny, until she
remembered that when things grew that large, even her-
bivores, they could be just as dangerous as any carnivore.
And an animal that looked like an herbivore might not be
one.

A rabbit the size of an elephant could easily bite the head
off a man. And the fur, proportionally thick, could defend it
against arrows and even spears to some extent. Suddenly
the idea of giant rabbits was no longer so funny.

There appeared to be a road, or the remains of one,

passing into the foliage a little to the right of their camp. That would be the only place the wagons would be able to pass—but a road meant a place where humans had been; if there were any bandits about, they would know that the place for ambush was the road. If there were any predators big enough to take down a man, they might have learned the same thing.

Still, if they were to have the wagons with them there would be little choice. "It looks to me as if we should go in there," she said, pointing. "What do you think the proper order of march should be?"

"Divide the men equally," Faro replied. "Half in front of the wagons, and half behind. Ware to take the foremost position, myself the rearmost, and you in the middle. Ware has some magics that are likely to be useful if we're attacked, and he is an expert marksman on a trained horse. I'm a trained fighter. That takes care of two vulnerable positions."

She raised an eyebrow. "That hardly seems fair," she retorted. "You're putting me—"

"No, I'm not," Faro said, completely seriously. "If there are bandits, they'll strike at the weak middle—or what they think is the weak middle. You'll be guarding the wagons from attack from the side. We won't be able to see a damned thing in that muck. If you take a hit in the middle of the train, Ware and I won't know it until you've already engaged. There's just too much damned green stuff; it's going to block our view. In fact, I'm not certain I would be able to find my way through this garbage without going in circles."

"Which is where I come in," Ware picked up smoothly. He smiled at Xylina. "Faro and I discussed this in Sylva when he pointed out he was just trusting to the road, and had no way of knowing if we were going in the right direction. We have a compass with us, and I know how to use it. We also have other navigational aids, and I can use them, as well. We simply haven't needed them until now, but I knew that eventually we would. So I made certain we had them, and that I could use them."

"Well, that's good, because I can't," Xylina replied, just a little irritated. Why hadn't he mentioned this before? Had he planned all along on trotting this little prize out, taking his bow, and waiting for the applause? She would much rather have had a chance to learn to use these things herself. "And I think you'd better start teaching us. What if you got swallowed by a giant snake or something?"

Ware had the audacity to laugh. She stared at him, a little affronted. "You're quite right," he said, agreeably. "I am not in danger of getting swallowed; I would simply dematerialize and walk out. But I have been remiss; I should have been instructing you and Faro all along. And since I have begun this so late, I think the first lesson should be this very moment."

He removed the compass and the other instruments from his saddlebags, and proceeded to instruct them in the use of all of them. There were instruments to take a direction from the angle of the sun, others to do the same from the stars, and charts and maps of all kinds. Soon she was immersed in calculations and complex geometries. The compass was easy enough, but Xylina despaired at ever mastering the astrolabe and the other complex instruments, although Faro seemed to grasp the way of dealing with them at once.

Finally, she decided that she had learned all that she would for the moment. There were other things she could do that would be more profitable. She left the two of them conferring over readings, content for the moment to leave their navigation in the hands of Faro and the demon. She had another potential situation to deal with.

Yesterday they had experienced their first casualty. Kyle was dead, and there would be no bringing him back. The threat to this expedition was now no longer an abstract notion, but a reality. Men who had been cheerful and cavalier about the danger were not laughing this morning.

Now they knew, viscerally, that they could die, that they could be hurt. Now this was no longer a game, a pleasure trip, an entertaining trek through strange lands.

They had been talking, quietly, of the rewards they expected to enjoy at the end of this quest. She had heard them, and Faro had reported more of the same. Rewards seemed of little import now, when the cost of the attack had been a life. They must be having second and third thoughts by now, after a long and perhaps sleepless night.

Now her position as leader was at its most precarious. The men might be tempted to desert, and she was in no position to try to stop them. She was not part of an army, and she was the only commander this group had. The cost of attempted desertion was death, under normal circumstances. This was not "normal." There was no point in killing a deserter; that would only create bad feelings and resentment, and might even *cause* desertions. Actually, in these circumstances, the terrain might cause the deserters to die anyway. No, she had to somehow make it clear to the men that they were all in this situation together, and that their safety lay in loyalty to one another and trust in her ability to lead them.

She was not entirely certain how to do this—but making Faro into a friend had certainly worked to cement his loyalty. Perhaps it would work with the others. It was time to give over some of those affectations of the Mazonite mistress; time to make it clear that she had the welfare of her men as much in mind as her own—and to make it clear that she took every casualty personally.

She decided to talk with Hazard, the young man who had conducted the funeral service last night. He was already well-disposed towards her, according to Faro; he had hopes of attracting her attention or getting a high commendation from her when they returned. The other men seemed to like him, so with luck they would not see her singling Hazard out as "playing favorites." There was that business of the little ritual he had conducted as well; that implied a certain level of unofficial authority over the others. He would be a good man to start with.

And she must stop thinking of them as "only slaves." They were not "only" anything. They were all the men, all the reinforcements she would have. They were important. She needed them. *They* did not necessarily need her.

The men were packing the wagons and cleaning up the site. As luck would have it, Hazard was the one saddling her mule for her.

Well, that seemed like a good omen, she thought. As if the fates just confirmed her choice. She smiled as she approached him, but he averted his eyes and quickly bowed his head, keeping his eyes down submissively. That was proper slave etiquette, though Faro never averted his eyes from hers, but had always met her gaze squarely. She suddenly found the aversion unnecessary and annoying.

"Hazard, I would like to talk to you," she said, and he glanced up quickly to assess her expression before looking quickly down again. She chuckled; it was forced, but she doubted he could tell that. "Hazard, you don't have to look at your feet when we speak. In fact, I'd really rather you didn't. This place is full of traps and danger, and if there's something coming up behind me to eat us, you won't know if you keep staring at the ground. Since I suspect you'd rather not be eaten, and I know I'd rather not, why don't you dispense with formalities from now on?"

The young man raised his eyes, cautiously, and smiled a little when he saw that she meant what she had said. "That is quite true, Mistress Xylina," he said. "And it is a sensible thing to do, really. So long as I have your permission to be so bold—"

"*Everyone* has my permission, from this moment on," she told him firmly. "I'd much rather that you all be practical. And while we're at it, let's just forget all the other protocols as well, shall we? There's no one out here to see or be offended; there's no one out here to report you for 'insubordinate behavior.' Even if there was, it would be *me* they'd have to report to, and it will be me who will be making a report on you all when this is over. I am not going to be offended if—oh, just as an example—you were to knock me to the ground to keep something from swooping down on me! In fact, I will probably be very grateful. Just behave the way Faro does. That will be the easiest, all the way around."

She wasn't sure how he felt about this; she couldn't read him the way she could read Faro and Ware. But at least he kept his eyes raised, and he didn't seem overtly disturbed at the idea of abandoning "proper" demeanor. Was there a hint of approval? Was there a touch of wary humor? She thought perhaps that there was. She would find out more, in a little while.

"I'm going to be riding the middle today," she said, before he could take his place in the ranks and escape her. "I would like you to stay beside me, and watch the left while I guard the right."

"If you wish, mistress," he said immediately. He couldn't have said anything else, of course. He was the slave; her word was law. Still, she hoped he didn't think her craven for taking the middle position. She didn't want these men to regard her as a coward; that would undermine her authority. Her authority must come from strength and from their admiration, not from custom and habit, or they would not believe in her or obey her orders when they thought their lives were at risk.

But Hazard was about to surprise her. He cast a sideways glance at the "forest," and immediately returned his gaze to her. "There will be no safe position in the column in growth like that, will there, mistress?" he said shrewdly. "I know that if I were a bandit, I would let the foreguard pass and attack the middle. And if I were a monster—well, who can tell what a monster will do? Were you planning on guarding the provision-wagon? If there is an attack to the middle, it will probably come there. The scent of the food in the wagon could draw a predator."

She nodded, slowly, pleased with his quick intelligence. "Yes, I thought so too, and I was planning on riding beside the food-wagon. In fact, why don't you pick two other men to stay right with the wagon along with us? That way we can have one on each corner." She smiled. "I'm sure the driver will appreciate the extra guards."

"Yes, Mistress Xylina," he said, "I will do so at once." And there was no doubt that he looked faintly disappointed. For a moment, she could not imagine why he would be disappointed. As he went off to choose the other two guards, she realized the reason.

He thought he was going to have her all to himself; she felt embarrassed amusement. He thought he was going to have a chance to attract her attention, and perhaps attract more than just her attention. Ah, well. Perhaps it was better to get *that* misunderstanding over with quickly! Such attentions as poor Hazard was hoping for would likely cost her more in respect than it would ever gain. She let him go off by himself, and busied herself with rechecking the saddle on her mule. Better to spare him any discomfit; better to let him think she had not guessed what his hopes and motives had been.

When the group formed up, at the opening under the plants that signaled the beginning of the road through them, she took her place at the right front corner of the provision-wagon, and Hazard took the left. To the rear were two of the older men, career guards who had been trained to fight all of their lives. They were good choices for this position; of all of the men, it was the ones who had seen combat before who had been the least shaken by Kyle's death. One of the men Hazard had chosen was a man called Gurt, the other, a bearded fellow, Jan. The driver of the provision-wagon was Horn, the cook, and he seemed very glad to see them all. He was no kind of fighter, and he had seemed very disturbed after Kyle's death.

With Ware in the lead, the expedition crossed the last of the rock-waste, and plunged into the green gloom of the "forest." Faro had been right; the leaves tended to sway over the primitive road, and the road itself wound around them, so that once the entire train was inside the area, she found she could not see either the front or the rear of the cavalcade.

It was, in fact, quite dark under those leaves after the brilliant and unshaded sunlight of the rock-waste. Xylina was not entirely certain what to make of the plants they traveled beneath. She could not imagine how they remained standing. They were nothing more than a cluster of immensely long leaves, each as wide as her mule, but very narrow in proportion to the length, and standing cubits above her head. The clumps of leaves, six or seven to a cluster, were joined only at their bases. Fat roots plunged from that joining straight into the ground. There seemed to be no support for the plants except for a thick central rib, which hardly seemed strong enough to bear the weight of the enormous leaves. The ground underneath was entirely devoid of growth except for a few pale fungi; it was not possible to see the earth, however, for the remains of dead leaves piled up beneath the plants. Xylina would have been surprised to see anything growing here, actually; there wasn't enough light under these plants to grow much of anything. Even a fern would have had a hard time subsisting here. Odd: this place actually looked as if it had been planted and then left to itself.

The road, or at least the remains of one, continued on under and through the plants. That made it a bit easier for the wagons; the plants didn't seem to care for what was left of the roadway, and did not grow up through it. There was plenty of room for the wagons to pass between them so long as they stayed on the road.

Once they had passed a few lengths into the depths of the forest, it was impossible to see the area that they had just left; Xylina looked back once or twice, and could see nothing, not even the hint of sunlight. They could have been in another world entirely. And there was a whole new set of noises under these trees: creaks and chirps, squeaks and chatterings. Xylina took a certain amount of comfort in the fact that none of these sounds was terribly loud. She hoped this meant that whatever produced them was not terribly big.

Though something didn't have to be large to kill; yesterday had proved that. She must not assume that if something was small, it was harmless. She must not assume anything.

That thought led to another, and questioning Hazard about his burial rite might be a good place to start a dialogue with him. "Hazard?" she said, prompting the young man to jump just a little in startlement. "If you don't mind answering, how did you come to know what to do for Kyle yesterday? I did not wish to simply leave him—but I had never heard that the—the men had special burial customs." She had almost said, "the slaves" and had stopped herself just in time.

He gave her a very strange look, but replied slowly, "I am not surprised, mistress. Few of the Mazonites pay our customs much heed. It was—something I was trained in by my father. These things are passed from father to son, whenever possible. And when they are not, the man who is trained finds a likely boy in the household and trains him. More than one, if the first boy is taken away from the household. In that way, there is one Rite-Holder in every household, so that the proper rites may be observed."

That answer seemed to imply that there was more to this than just a simple rite or two; it seemed to imply an entire religion. She said nothing, however. It seemed to be almost a secret, and she did not wish to make him think she was trying to force his secrets from him. "What do you generally ask to be reborn as?" she asked impulsively. "I mean, you probably never even heard of the Pacha before you all came on this expedition. So what do you usually ask for at home, as a rebirth?"

It was not Hazard who answered, but the cook, who knew her better than the others. "Simple enough, mistress," Horn said, with a crooked grin. "A girl. Which of us would *not* rather be reborn as a girl?"

"Ah." She nodded, and the others seemed relieved that she was not offended. "I can understand that."

Jan snorted, just a little. "Oh, there are some pampered pretties who like their soft lives; they generally ask for the same rebirth as what they enjoyed. But not all of us are born with pretty faces and winning ways. And some of us that are—well, Kyle found out the hard way that a pretty face don't always stay pretty forever. Then—" Jan coughed. "Then, well, life don't stay soft."

That was a good opening for a change of subject. "I was very sorry about Kyle, yesterday," she said, and hoped that she sounded as if she meant it. "I never dreamed those purple things were alive. I wish there had been some way to know what was dangerous. . . ."

She let her voice trail off for a moment, then cleared her throat. "This is a very strange place we are entering. Ware says that it is full of wild magic, and that we should expect nothing and be wary of everything. Well, we just had that proved to us, I suppose. But it is hard to be alert all the time."

"What's a demon doin' with us, mistress?" asked the other man behind her, Gurt. "What's a demon doin' outside of the court? Is the Queen's word gonna hold him out here? I've heard they were pretty nasty customers before the Mazonite Queens made 'em behave. What's to stop him from kicking over the traces now?"

Now that was a very good question, and one she hadn't considered. Not that it mattered, because what Ware wanted was something the Queen's word had nothing to do with. He would not endanger them, because he had sworn his word to her that he would protect them, and she knew, somehow, that he was an honorable creature. She didn't care to announce that Ware also wanted to possess Xylina herself, and knew that any dishonor on his part would immediately destroy any chance of that. But still, she could see how the men might be nervous about the demon. She could only imagine the kinds of stories they'd heard about his kind.

"Ware knows how to find the thing that we're hunting," she said, choosing her words with care. "He knows where it is, and how to get at it. The Queen trusts him, so I suppose her word must hold him even outside Mazonia."

Out of the corner of her eye, she saw that Hazard looked dubious, as if he feared these were not good enough reasons to trust a demon. She thought quickly, trying to find a reason they would believe among all the ones she did not want to tell anyone else. "He also wishes to keep me very safe, because—because I owe him a great deal of gold."

She heard Gurt trying to stifle a chuckle at that, and turned in her saddle to grin at him. "Oh, go ahead and laugh! I don't mind! If it hadn't gotten me in such trouble, this *could* be very funny, and I fully expect one day to be able to laugh at my dilemma myself!" Carefully, she gave the men an edited version of her misfortunes, leaving out the fact that the crown had guaranteed her debt, and leaving out Ware's other "offer" entirely. "So you see, if he's to be repaid in gold or in silver he must keep me safe, and in order to keep *me* safe he will have to do his best to keep *you* safe. That was why the Queen ordered him to come along—but I do think that even if she had not ordered him to come, he would have done so anyway. He would not want me to escape him before his debt was paid."

All of that was entirely true. It simply was not the whole truth.

"Now that's a reason I can understand," Gurt declared roundly. "Everyone knows how the demons feel about good gold. Always after more of it. Trading and selling, training and bargaining with the freedmen—even going outside the kingdom to get it."

"Well, they can't exactly live on air, can they?" Horn demanded. "Even a demon's got to eat! And if he's got to eat, he might as well eat good. They live forever; living forever shackled would be just plain stupid! With their magic and all . . . " He coughed. "Well, it stands to reason they want to live good and they got the means."

Not like us. Horn didn't say it, but Xylina almost heard it. The demons, who looked so human, had all the privileges human men did not. And all because the men had no magic.

"Old Ware's all right," said Jan, who had a deeper voice than the others. "Never has high-and-mighty ways. Never puts up a fuss about not having his fancy house to live in. Puts up with the same things we do. He does—well, he never fusses about our—ah—entertainment."

Hazard again cast a sideways look at her, as if to see whether she understood that oblique reference to the paw women and their purpose—and whether she was offended by it. She simply nodded. "I'm glad to hear that," she said, striving not to blush. "I will never know whether he is doing as the Queen asked him to in that way unless you tell me. You are all doing *your* duty, and you deserve everything you are entitled to. But unless you say something to me about the things I cannot oversee—well, it will be like the little girl who did not speak until her nurse salted her honey-cake—I will have to assume that you do not speak because everything has been fine until now."

Horn grinned at the old joke—or possibly, at her acceptance of the situation. Hazard looked a little embarrassed. She could not see the other two without turning, but she had the feeling that they approved. "Everything is still just fine, Mistress Xylina," Horn said forthrightly. "Hazard or me will tell Faro or you if it ain't."

"Good. In fact," she continued, "if there is something you are entitled to that I have somehow missed, I would like you to tell Faro. If you have any ideas that might bear trying, tell him as well. This is new territory for all of us, and anything that might help us defend ourselves should be tried. I have no prejudice against trying something new, and I can see you are all intelligent men."

She glanced at the two she could see out of the corner of her eye. Horn was nodding with pleased satisfaction;

he had worked with her during the "Pacha entertainments," and she suspected that she had just confirmed the opinion he had formed of her then. Hazard looked quite stunned.

Good. Now they saw her as a person, not just as "the mistress." It was going to be harder to desert a reasonable person than an icon, someone who did not seem quite real to them, someone who did not have their welfare at heart.

"You know, Horn, we must have fed several thousand Pacha back there, and yet I hardly know anything about you," she said, after a moment. "Where did you ever learn to cook so well? I can't imagine how you make dried peas and old leather turn into such wonderful stews."

Horn was only too happy to talk, and she was only too happy to listen. Horn's words, and those of the other three men, gave her a window on their world. Faro had given her a glimpse of that world, but only a glimpse. This was a broader, wider view, not filtered through the educated caution of a scribe. And she suspected that it was a view very few other Mazonites ever had.

She learned how the boys were segregated early in their lives, left to be educated—or not—by other slaves, some not even their fathers. How what happened to these children was largely a matter of chance. If the fates smiled upon them, they remained with their fathers and their families, growing up as part of a household, and given nearly the same education as their favored sisters. Then, when they grew to manhood, they would find themselves noticed by a young woman and bartered off to her as her chosen husband, earning their families an agreed-upon spousal-price. But if the fates were not kind, if they were not part of a small family or the offspring of a "marriage," they would find themselves sent off to a nursery until the age of five, with one slave to simply tend to the needs of thirty small boys and boy-babies. Then they would be appraised and tested, their aptitudes determined—and sent off to be trained. Once trained, at the age of fifteen or thereabouts, they went on the auction-block. There would be little chance for a family or to better their lot. They were, simply, property. No different from a horse or a mule.

And even if the fates were kind at first, that did not mean they would continue to turn a smiling face. Kyle had learned that, being discarded for the sake of a younger, handsomer man. There was another of Kyle's ilk with them, a man called Maric, who marched just behind Ware.

The other men of this expedition were of the second class, the sons of harem slaves with little or no chance at a better fate. They felt, for the most part, that they were at least fortunate that they had not been sold off as common laborers. Such a mind-numbing fate was the worst thing that could happen to a slave. Save, perhaps, being condemned to the arena as a gladiator. All of them looked up to Faro as a survivor of that experience. And she had the feeling that her act of inadvertent mercy in saving him from death had also begun the work of earning their respect.

When they halted at noon for a quick meal, she felt that she had a good start on her goal, to make herself their leader by loyalty rather than by default.

It was in the late afternoon that the first of the monsters appeared.

These were singularly peaceful "monsters," and they seemed to take no notice of the humans on the road below them.

The first of them appeared floating through the leaves, pushing them apart, and gliding between them. The entire caravan froze in place, as the creature's snout appeared above them, shoving the fronds aside. Xylina's heart was in her throat, and the men around her grew pale with fear. The thing was about the size of one of the wagons, patterned in brilliant scarlet and gold chevrons, and shaped roughly like a teardrop. It floated majestically above them, about halfway between them and the tops of the leaves, with no sign of anything supporting it.

And no sign that it noticed them.

As they watched it drifting above them, they held their breaths, hoping that it would continue to ignore them. Its round black eyes remained fixed on the fronds around it, however; it stopped once or twice to nibble off a nodule-like growth on the ribs of one of the leaves, but otherwise paid no attention to anything about it.

After a long wait, it drifted further off into the leaves, and was lost to sight.

Xylina let out her breath, and color returned to the faces around her. After a moment to be sure that the monster was not going to return, the caravan started off again. They had not gone very far, however, when several more of these floating creatures appeared. All were brightly colored, patterned regularly in blue and green, red and yellow, orange and black. They varied in shape from long, pipe-like forms to round, ball-like creatures. They did not seem to have heads as such; their faces were built into one end of their bodies, with their eyes so positioned that they could not look directly at something but could see only what one or the other eye was aimed at. They had no kind of a nose that Xylina could see, and their mouths varied from a slit that could readily have encompassed one of the mules to tiny round holes hardly larger than her fist. None of them paid any attention at all to the figures so far below them.

The troupe had frozen in place again, but they still did not seem to attract the attention of the monsters. The creatures continued to drift lazily above. Several of them, however, were capable of very quick movement. When one of the mules brayed loudly out of sheer nervousness, the three turquoise-blue monsters currently above the road suddenly sprang into startled life and darted into the protection of the leaves so quickly Xylina could not believe it.

After more than a dozen of these monsters had passed by with no incident, Xylina relaxed. She was not surprised when, shortly after that, Ware started the column moving again.

The monsters continued to appear above them, and now that they were in motion, these strange creatures began to pay them a little more attention. It seemed to be completely benign, simply curious attention. The beasts drifted downward to hover over the road for a few moments, twisting to one side or another to peer down at them with a bright eye. After a time, their curiosity seemed to be satisfied, and they moved up and away again.

Perhaps the party did not look edible, Xylina thought. That was encouraging, actually.

More variations appeared: round creatures covered with spines, slender ones with huge, gauzy draperies trailing from them, flat ones with appendages like fans. All of them were brilliantly colored, and all of them showed either simple curiosity or complete indifference to the travelers.

Now Xylina caught sight of something new on the ground on either side of the road. These were enormous black mound-like objects, covered with spines as long as the wagons. At first, she thought that they were some kind of growths, like the spiny objects back in the "rock-garden" area—but then she saw one moving.

It crawled like a snail, although she could see no way for it to do so, unless, perhaps, there were feet of some kind hidden under the bottom spines; the spines waved restlessly in all directions as it crawled, but it did not seem to see them—or, for that matter, to see anything at all. It bumped into the base of one of the plants even as she watched, and lurched its way around the plant by continuing to bump into it, before resuming its journey across open ground.

It finally came to rest just beside the road. Recalling the lesson of the purple "tree," she was very loathe to take her men by it.

Fortunately, that was a decision she did not have to make. One of the yellow and red beasts drifted into view above, and turned to peer down at them. It saw the spine-creature—and its behavior changed completely. It turned from a graceful, gentle beast, to a predatory killer.

It dived down out of the fronds, like a falcon stooping on prey. It attacked the spine-creature aggressively, biting at the spines and snapping them off. In a moment, it had been joined by three more of its kind that appeared as if by magic, and together they attacked the spine-creature without mercy, as it waved its spines at them in a futile gesture of self-defense. Soon they had denuded the entire top of the creature, and were attacking the outer skin of the beast.

Once they had begun that part of their attack, it was soon over. The outer skin was broken, and the three monsters devoured the creature as quickly as a child would eat a sweet fruit, diving down to snatch away mouthfuls of flesh until there was nothing left but an empty shell and the broken spines. Then they transformed again into the peaceful creatures they had been. They rose into the tops of the leaves, and drifted away, sated and replete.

Cautiously, the caravan drew near the remains. It was hard to believe that such a large animal had been reduced to fragments so quickly. Hazard stepped forward to pick up one of the broken spines and hefted it in his hand, a thoughtful look upon his face.

The piece he held was as long as his arm, and ended in a wicked point. It was hollow, and Xylina wondered if a shaft could not be fitted to it, giving them a kind of spear. In the hands of a thinking creature it could be much more effective than it had been on its original owner.

Evidently Hazard had the same notion. "Our own weapons are the only ones of their kind, mistress," he said to Xylina. "It would not be a bad thing if we could use these materials that we have at hand, and save our old weapons as much as we may. These, we could afford to lose, I think. They might make good arrows, or throwing spears."

Xylina nodded. "Let us stop long enough to gather as many of these spines as we can," she told the others, raising her voice so that it carried to the rest of the men. "Put them in the weapons-wagon; we can figure out what we can do with them when we stop for the night. Keep anything that looks useful—and take care with the points. They might be envenomed."

Soon the poor creature had been completely denuded of its ineffective defenses, and the end of the wagon had been heaped with broken and whole spines. Only when they had gathered everything that looked worth salvaging did they move on.

But the attack on the spine-creature served to remind them that they were far more vulnerable than it had been, in many ways. They had been rather cavalier until now, since the floating monsters did not appear hostile. Now they were on the alert; ready in case the benign creatures suddenly decided they *did* look edible.

And that proved to be their salvation.

The plants had begun to thin, but there were other things, neither plant nor animal, but an odd amalgam of both, taking their places. These were mound-like creatures covered with waving tentacles, about the size of the spine-creatures, but rooted to one spot. They seemed delicate, vulnerable, far more helpless than the spine-creatures. The tentacle-creatures were pastel in color rather than the bright colors of the floating monsters, and that reinforced their look of delicacy, but a quick demonstration proved that they were deadly.

One of the spine-creatures bumbled out into the open again, and the brightly colored floating monsters saw it. Several of them dived upon it to begin picking it apart, and one of them ventured too near to one of the tentacle-beasts. In fact, it brushed against two or three of the gently waving arms.

Immediately, the tentacles shot out to touch the monster. That was all they did, but the beast froze; then shuddered as if it had been struck a terrible blow, and uttered a strange, thin cry. At the sound of that cry, the others of its kind fled, leaving behind their prey and their fellow. The spine-creature, left alone, bumbled off into cover. The floating monster seemed trapped by the gently caressing tentacles.

The monster thrashed, strongly at first, but gradually weakening. The tentacles continued to hold it as it writhed, weakly, then stopped moving altogether. The tentacle-beast reached out again with more of its tentacles, and wrapped the silent form in a close embrace, then drew it towards the center of the beast. There it sank into the mass of tentacles, and disappeared. Presumably to be eaten.

Xylina stared at the tentacle-beasts, and tried to measure their proximity to the road by eye. One or two of them were too close for her comfort. The tentacles moved too much; some of them would reach near enough to the road that they could have touched the men or the animals.

"Mistress, I don't think those creatures can actually see anything," Hazard ventured after a moment. "They seem to be as blind as the spiny-beasts. I think that you would probably have to touch one of their limbs before they knew you were there; that would be when they knew to attack."

Faro had urged his mount up beside hers while the young fighter was talking, and he grunted agreement. "That's exactly what I was going to say," he told them both. "They can't see us, and they can't move. So as long as we don't touch those things —"

"Look!" cried Hazard. He pointed at another of the tentacle-beasts. "There is someone in there!"

Xylina blinked, and rubbed her eyes to clear them, then looked again. There *was* something hiding shyly in the tentacles of the beast; her eyes were not deceiving her, nor were Hazard's. "It's not someone," she said, "it's some*thing.*"

It was something about the size of a child, bipedal and upright, and peering out at them with huge green eyes, and covered with golden fur. It hid well within the tentacles, and did not seem to be taking any harm from them. The closest thing she could compare it to was a lemur, for it had very long arms, but that did not seem to keep it from

walking erect. It was surely not human, for it wore no clothing and carried no weapons, and it had a sharply pointed
muzzle like a fox.

"Should we try to capture it, mistress?" one called Barad
asked eagerly. "We could keep it with the dogs! It would
make a fine beast for the Queen's menagerie!"

But Xylina noticed that he looked from the lemur to
Ware and back again, and she suspected that he had other
things in mind than catching it for the menagerie. She had a
vague notion of what he might be thinking of—that this
two-legged beast might be worth considerable as a freak in
a black-market show. Certainly it would be different.

The notion made her uneasy. This creature—it was a
wild thing, and she could imagine how frightened it would
be. Perhaps it was intelligent. That would be worse.

Xylina shook her head. "No," she replied slowly. "No, let
it be. If we disturb the tentacle-beast, it will probably sting
us. How would we capture the lemur without coming to
harm ourselves? The lemur is doing us no harm, and there
is no point in risking ourselves to catch it. We should let it
alone. We don't know how to care for it, even if we could
capture it, and it would probably die if we took it away from
here." Out of the corner of her eye she noticed Ware nodding in approval.

"Let us simply pass these creatures as quietly as we can,"
she continued. "I think if we are very careful, we can get by
them without mishap." She looked down the road, and
frowned a little. "It will be night soon. I would prefer not to
make a camp anywhere near them—and I would like to
find a place to camp with some running water nearby."

The wagons edged past the tentacle-beasts carefully; the
mules sweated with fear, but fortunately did not balk,
though they must have sensed their danger. It did not help
that the tentacles groped constantly; the sightless movement was unnerving at best, and brought danger a mere
finger-length away at worst. It was horrible to remember
that the tentacles *could* stretch, and that if the beast knew a

man or a wagon was there, they would stretch out to give him one of those deadly caresses. And the wagons could not be driven off the roadway; they would sink into the soft ground at the side of the road.

One of the dogs could not bear the waving tentacles, and finally broke the leash holding it in the wagon, fleeing and howling with fear. Unfortunately, its mindless panic sent it blundering right into another of the tentacle beasts, and if there had been any doubt in the mens' minds about whether those tentacles would be effective on *them*, the dog's instant demise cleared that doubt immediately.

The poor beast let out a terrified shriek as the first tentacle brushed it; the dog howled in pain as more tentacles joined the first. Then it gurgled as it thrashed convulsively as the tentacles continued to hold it in that deadly embrace. It died quickly after the last convulsion ended; it was carried into the middle of the tentacle-creature, and vanished as the monster had, into an unseen maw.

None of the men wished to go lemur-hunting after that.

As nightfall approached, they finally came upon a clear spring welling up from a rocky outcropping in a relatively clear spot. The plants had thinned to the point that sunlight reached the ground, and the resultant light allowed other things to flourish among them, things that looked more like the plants and bushes Xylina knew from Mazonia. Some of them bore what looked to be fruits and berries, but in colors and shapes that none of them recognized. Although fresh fruit would have been very welcome, there was nothing that Xylina recognized as edible, and she really did not want to experiment with her men's lives. So instead, she directed them to empty and refill all the water containers, set up her palisade of stones, and ordered Horn to prepare a meal with the dried and preserved provisions, and the conjured stuffs she provided for the purpose of flavorings. It seemed cruel to subject them to bland provender in the sight of what might have been fresh food, when simple conjuration could add to the flavor of their meal.

Their defenses seemed secure, as secure as she could make them. They had held until now. But she was not easy in her mind. They had already seen that some creatures about here could fly—and how could anyone predict what would appear at night? A stone palisade would prove little defense against monsters capable of dropping down out of the air.

For that matter, there was no telling if something capable of climbing the palisade was not out there.

She wondered, as the men set up camp, if she should keep her fears to herself. Perhaps she was being too cautious. It would do no good to agitate the men with her imagined beasts. But on the other hand, it would be stupid not to alert them to the possibilities of attack from above. Not just stupid—insanely suicidal. She had no right to risk their lives because she was afraid she might sound foolish.

So as they gathered to share supper, she also shared her fears for the night. She opened up the possibility of floating and flying carnivores, or creatures large enough to climb over their defenses. She reminded them of the sand-burrower. It did not make for a cheerful meal.

"If any of you have any ideas of how we can defend ourselves from attack from above or below, I would like to hear them," she said when she had finished. "I had thought of creating a metal mesh across the top of the palisade, but the problem with that is that it would be too large to support itself. The only other mesh I made like that needed to cover a much smaller area, and was supported quite evenly on all sides. Besides, some of these beasts have tentacles long and thin enough to reach through such a mesh, unless I made the holes between it very fine, and that would make it even heavier. A metal plate with holes in it might serve, but these monsters might be able to lift it, for I have no way of anchoring it to the stones. And in any case, that much metal would surely attract lightning if we were to have a storm tonight."

Hazard stroked his beardless chin in thought. "If such a construction were to fall, it would surely crush us," he pointed out. "I am not certain that I would like a conjuration of that nature suspended over my head all night long."

"And I am not certain I would, either," Xylina agreed. "That is the problem with such things; I can't fasten them to the rock walls that I have created, and if there is a monster out there large enough to shift it, it will fall on top of us all. If I create pillars in here to help support it, there will be very little room for us to move."

"What about an active defense?" Jan asked. "What if you made a lot of sharp poles thrusting upwards, like the spines on those spine-balls we saw?"

"The spines did not help those creatures much," she pointed out. "And if I planted them that closely together, there would again be no room for us."

"What of a solid wooden roof?" asked Faro.

"Fire," she replied succinctly. "And wood can be broken. Rock and the amalgam I made for the bridge are both heavier than metal. And there is another thing; making our palisade is very tiring for me. I could begin creating a large covering of metal mesh or wood or almost anything, but frankly I am certain I could not finish it."

It cost her something in pride to admit that, and from the surprise on the men's faces, it must have been the first time they had ever heard a Mazonite say that something was beyond her.

"You can create oil, can you not?" Barad asked.

She nodded. "Several barrels' worth, I believe."

"Then let us make torches and have a trench of oil about the inside of the palisade," Barad suggested. "If something seems to be coming over the wall, or attempting to fly down into our camp, we can set fire to the oil. I have never seen a wild beast that would willingly fly or climb into fire."

That seemed the best solution possible, and this was precisely what Xylina did.

As the last of the light died, they set their guards. There

were twenty-nine of them altogether; they set watches of nine, ten, and ten. Ware would command the first watch, Xylina the second, and Faro the third. The rest drew lots for which watch they would take.

The first watch passed without incident, but midway through the second watch, Xylina's fears of an attack from above were realized.

The first watch had noted strange lights that passed overhead, but they did not seem to portend anything, and they did not descend far enough down that anyone could see what they were. Xylina guessed that they might represent some night-flying version of the floating monsters, creatures which carried lights like fireflies, or like the fox-fire found in rotting stumps. They might even be lights like those that floated above swamps: false-lanterns, the Mazonites called them. All about them, the night remained peaceful. Xylina dozed through the first watch, waking from time to time as the men spoke with each other, but there was nothing to suggest that they were in any danger.

The sounds from outside the palisade, which had been suggestive of insects and small animals, suddenly changed midway through the second watch, however. Xylina had patrolled with the rest, listening carefully to the chirps and buzzes of insects, and the rustling noises that could be small animals disturbing foliage. She peered up at the floating lights—red and green and blue, some in patterns, some alone. Nothing threatened, and she began to feel very foolish.

Then the night grew suddenly quiet. Alerted, she strained her ears for some sign of what had come to prowl out there, for surely something had, and had disturbed the night-creatures enough to silence them. But Gurt heard the noises first—scraping sounds, but very loud, as if something was being dragged through the sand outside. As these sounds drew nearer, Xylina felt the hair on the back of her neck rising. Whatever was out there, it was heading for the palisade.

Then Xylina heard more of the sounds, coming from another direction—and Maric heard them as well, from his section of the palisade. The conclusion was inescapable. Whatever was out there, there were many of them, and they were *all* converging on the palisade!

Xylina sent Gurt around to wake the others, and lit her oil-soaked torch, going to stand beneath the wall with her sword in one hand and her torch in the other. Fear sent a chill hand walking down her spine, and her eyes burned with the strain of trying to see what was over the top of the wall. Would the wall stop it, whatever it was? Or could it fly or climb?

The scraping sounds reached the rock wall—and stopped for a moment. She thought then that it was over, that they were safe, but then the sounds resumed—and continued up the wall. Her heart pounded in her ears; her mouth tasted dry, and her knees trembled. Still, she stood her ground, standing at the foot of the palisade, waiting to see what was coming for them. She could not let the men see how frightened she was—or they might lose their own courage. She *must* hold fast, or they would not be able to. But she followed the sounds up the wall with her eyes— and so she was the first to see the new monsters as soon as they topped the rock of the palisade.

Something like a talon hooked over the edge of the rock; a second appeared beside the first, then the edge of something huge and saucer-like heaved up into the light from the torch. It was shiny, and there were many legs attached to it; a pair of faceted eyes, glittering like some malignant jewel, looked down at her in the torchlight. Beneath the eyes were sickle-shaped mandibles, sharp and as long as her arm, serrated on the inner edges. Another moment passed, and a second creature hauled itself up to stand on the palisade beside the first. More followed, until the rock walls were ringed with them.

The first thing she thought of was that they were some kind of horrid giant spider. But their limbs were armored, and besides those terrible mandibles that clicked menacingly, each of the monsters was armed with two huge pinchers, as large as Faro's torso, that they held just in front of their mouths. They were each as large as two horses put together; they glared down at her, their eyes reflecting a hundred tiny flames in the light from her torch, and one of them made a move to descend the wall, groping down for a foothold in the stone.

She acted before she thought, on pure reflex. She plunged her torch into the oil-filled trench, and leapt backwards as the flames exploded upward, licking hungrily at the wall.

The flames were not the only things roaring; the monsters let out angry sounds of their own as the flames lashed out toward them. Most of them retreated backwards, down the way they had come—but a few of the largest gathered their legs under themselves, and sprang at her, at the men, landing in the camp on the other side of the flaming barrier.

Afterwards, she could not recall anything clearly; only a horrible confusion of claws and blades clashing together, of Faro dousing one of the things with oil and setting it afire, so that it scuttled madly about the encampment, shrieking. Fire and reflected flame, screams of men and monsters—at one point she found herself fighting back-to-back with Gurt, Horn, and Barad, sweat pouring down her face and stinging her eyes, her body shaking with fear and fighting-frenzy. She conjured weapons for those who had lost theirs, calling up anything that happened to spring to mind—torches, staves of metal, fistfulls of fabric to cast over the eyes of the monsters to blind them for a precious moment. Someone called an alarm as the flames in the trench died; she conjured more oil to keep the trench burning. Faro backed three of the things into a corner, catching them between himself and the flames; she sprinted to his side and conjured more slabs of rock to topple onto the monsters to break their armored legs. Jan fell and one of the beasts grabbed his leg, trying to drag him away. She left the fighting circle to dash in and sever the joint of the claw holding him, then stood over him until two of the others came to drag him to cover. In the next instant, Barad was taken and torn apart by two of the beasts, then devoured before their eyes, the creatures stuffing still-twitching limbs into their greedy maws.

Ware took advantage of their preoccupation with feeding to slay them both, stabbing them with long poles topped with spines, up through their mouths. Horrid black ichor spurted from their mouths as they backed into the flames from the trench.

There was no time—no time—

In the next moment, she came between Gurt and another of the beasts, forcing it away from him, hacking at it with an arm that felt leaden and burned with fatigue. Ware got this one as well, tossing a swath of oil-soaked fabric over it from the rear and letting her back it into the fire from the trench so that it went up like the others, screaming and waving its pinchers in the air.

Faro seemed to be everywhere, stabbing at the crea- 'ures' eyes with improvised spears made of spines and ten -poles, snatching up an abandoned bow and shooting out their eyes. All of the fighting was lit with the hellish glare of the oil-fire, making it seem as if they fought demon-creatures in a nightmare.

Finally, just when she thought that she could not swing her blade again, she looked up in a momentary respite, after killing yet another of the beasts by hacking its legs off then stabbing it through the eyes—

—to see that the sky was turning lighter, and that the only creatures left within the palisade were all dead. It was over.

They had won.

• Chapter 14

Xylina wiped a grimy hand across her brow, feeling grit mix with the sweat, and surveyed the rest of her exhausted crew. They would take what sleep they could, when morning drove the armored spiders away—but first they needed to drag the remains of the dead monsters out of their camp, and to dispose of their own dead. Altogether, they had managed to slay over twenty of the creatures; it was hard to tell exactly how many there had been, because so many of them had been burned. There were five more men gone now: four of the fighters and one of the three servants. Miraculously, all of the animals had survived the attack; she was still not certain how. Ware said that at one point he had seen the mules in a defensive circle with his stallion; that was all he could tell her.

It took them several hours to hitch the mules to the charred and dismembered bodies and drag them out of the gap Xylina created in the palisade. Sadly, the disposition of their own dead took far less time. They piled the bodies—or, more aptly, what was left of the bodies— onto an improvised pyre, and poured the last of the oil over them, while Hazard spoke the words in a voice harsh from smoke and shouting. Then Ware ignited the pyre, and they returned to the camp while the flames still burned. Xylina had just enough energy left to create another palisade stone—and she had to hold onto the tent-stake lest she collapse when she finished. Fortunately, both Faro and Ware were so tired that neither of them seemed to notice.

They slept the sleep of the utterly exhausted until noon,

291

when the heat woke them. Xylina dispelled the palisade and tents, while the men broke down the camp.

They were following the road again within the hour, pushing the mules to put as much distance between them and where they had been attacked as they could. Between sunrise, which was when they had left the hacked-up bits of spider outside the palisade, and noon, which was when she had dissipated the stone, scavengers had already reduced the dead monsters to bits of tough armor and scattered claws.

They did their best to put as many leagues between them and the spiders as possible. Ware confided that he hoped they would come within another magic zone soon, but as night fell, and the land about them had not changed in any significant way, Xylina and the demon had to admit defeat. They had not escaped the danger region. Tonight there would likely be another such attack, and they were just as ill-prepared to meet it as the first time.

They were forced to halt in a place where the tentacle creatures were particularly thick on the ground, and that was not encouraging, either. It was very difficult to find a large enough space free of them to make any size camp at all. But that was not the worst of it.

When Xylina steeled herself to conjure another stone palisade, she realized that her efforts of last night, and perhaps lack of sleep, had seriously depleted her resources. This was a new experience for her; she must have overextended herself, magically, and would have to wait a few days for recovery. She could not conjure stone to give them protection. Even her efforts at conjuring oil for a trench were frighteningly difficult, and she very nearly fainted after the second barrelful.

Ware approached. "You are magically exhausted," he murmured. "Faro and I hoped this would not be the case. We shall have to cover for you, lest the men think they lack protection."

So she had not fooled Ware or Faro. "Think?" she asked wanly.

Ware caught Faro's eye, and nodded. He approached as if just thinking of something. "Mistress," he said, loudly enough to be heard throughout, "it occurs to me that we have been depending too much on your magic. Last night we thought the stone and oil was sufficient, so we were caught by surprise when they weren't. We should assume more of the burden of defense ourselves, keeping your powers in reserve for ugly surprises."

The other men paused, then slowly nodded. They weren't lazy, and they wanted to survive. Last night had been brutal, but perhaps it would be better if Xylina used her magic only when their efforts failed. Faro directed them in the preparation of earthworks and wooden stakes, keeping them busy. "Build as close to the tentacles as you can," he said. "So that any intruders will brush them before reaching us." There was a mutter of almost humorous agreement.

Nevertheless, Xylina had to try to do her part. She decided that it was best to begin with the oil, rather than the palisade, for when she gathered her power, she felt disoriented and dizzy. The next barrel filled sluggishly, the oil flowing from a point between her hands much more slowly than she was used to—and it was not that the magic power was not available. She sensed the power waiting for her to call upon it—but *she* was the one lacking. She felt as if she had begun a long run directly after a marathon swim: her "muscles" were tired, and could not direct the power as she was used to. And the more she tried, the harder it became to control.

"Do not push yourself too hard," Ware said. "I have seen this before, on rare occasion. Too much exertion interferes with the recovery process."

She smiled at him, grateful for the understanding. At that moment she wanted to kiss him. An aspect of herself pondered that with bemusement: she was so fatigued that she was attracted to a demon. But she kept working.

As she finished the following barrel, she had a moment

of disorientation—and then her sight went gray around the edges, her knees gave, and she swayed where she stood.

Ware caught her before she fell, and lowered her gently to the ground. There she sat, surrounded by the worried and frightened faces of her men, wondering if she had doomed them all. What was she going to do? They couldn't possibly survive another attack of the spiders without some kind of protection to keep *some* of the creatures out. The oil she had conjured would scarcely last an hour in a trench, and she was not certain that she could conjure more at this point.

Now it was not possible to conceal the fact that her magic was low. She saw recognition passing through the group. Yet there seemed to be as much sympathy as fear. They were concerned for her almost more than for themselves. She appreciated that tacit support. Some other group might have chosen that moment to rebel, realizing that the magic of the mistress could no longer stop them. But her efforts to treat them like human beings were now being rewarded; they were treating *her* like a human being. And so this moment of her devastation was, in its subtle way, also her success.

Ware looked around. "I had hoped this would not occur yet," he said to the group. "Mistress Xylina was doing so well. The problem is that though Mazonite magic works beyond Mazonia, it fades with distance. Thus her resources are not what they were before, or what they will be when we return. She will have to do less conjuring for now, so that her strength is not depleted."

Of course that was it! If Mazonite conjuration were strong everywhere, the other cultures would not have been able to maintain their independence. Xylina found that reassuring; she was not really weakening. It was part of the problem of far traveling. At least the men understood, now, and so did she.

But it was still her responsibility to protect this group. What could she do, without strong conjuration?

Outside the circle of concerned faces, she caught sight of other curious onlookers. The last sunlight gleamed on the huge emerald eyes of the lemurs, who peered at these invaders of their realm with unblinking gazes. This was the nearest she had ever seen them before. Perhaps the fact that they were all standing quietly had reassured the shy beasts. They had come to the very edge of the tentacle-beasts, and stood just within that charmed circle, watching the naked strangers avidly.

Charmed circle—the lemurs were weaponless, far more helpless than the intruders. Yet they were certainly surviving the night, with no palisades and no weapons. Could the tentacle beasts be protecting them?

"Ware, Faro," Xylina said urgently, as the latter brought her a cup of cool water and the former helped her to stand. "Look at the lemurs! They have no defenses, no weapons, no shells to protect them! *They* manage to avoid the spiders—could we do the same?"

"By hiding within the tentacle-beasts?" Ware asked, quickly seeing what she meant. "We could, if we could avoid the poison, or whatever it is that the beasts produce to kill with. I can't see any other way that the lemurs could be avoiding those spiders."

"I think their fur must protect them from the poison," she said thoughtfully. "The dog that died had such short hair it could not possibly have protected him; in fact, there was no fur to speak of on his belly or his paws. But look at the lemurs! Look, how thick their fur is, and how it covers every part of them, right up to the eyes, even the palms of their hands and the soles of their feet—"

"Then we should kill them and skin their fur, and wrap ourselves in it—" began Horn. But she shook her head, for that was no answer, and something in her rebelled at killing the gentle-seeming beasts.

"No, no, that won't serve," she told him. "Even if we were to kill the poor things, how would we retrieve the bodies? The bodies would certainly fall well within the

reach of the tentacles. And I don't think we have time to
kill and skin enough of them to cover us all. No, I have a
better idea. Get all the clothing, every bit of it you all have,
and armor as well—"

"Ah!" Faro cried, seeing what she was getting at. "You
mean us to wrap up in our own clothing, to protect ourselves that way." He led the men and servants to the supply
wagons, and shortly every one of them was muffled in every
stitch of clothing he owned, turning them into motley
bundles, looking like nothing so much as overstuffed dolls,
stiff-limbed and awkward. But that would not matter, so
long as they were protected.

Xylina surveyed them critically. "Not enough," she
declared finally. "But this, I still have strength for."

And she began to conjure, producing length after length
of thick, insulating fabric. Fabric was the very first thing she
had learned to conjure, when she was small. Fabric took
the very least of her own energies to produce.

It was hideous stuff; her weakness did not permit her to
produce anything fine or attractive. The dull brown color
and coarse "weave" said more about her state of exhaustion
than she suspected any of them guessed. Not since her
power of conjuration had first come to her had she created
anything this crude. Any Mazonite worth her citizenship
would laugh at this stuff; it was worse than bad, and the only
thing it had to recommend it was the fact that she knew
that, like silk, it was an insulator and probably proof against
most contact poisons. Wrap a man in enough of this, and it
would be as good as the lemurs' thick fur.

Crude it might be. But she could spin it out of the air in
quantity, and spin she did. It was almost therapeutic,
reverting to this primitive conjuration. Soon there was
enough to muffle every man to the eyebrows in a thick
cocoon of fabric, and all the animals as well.

The animals had worried her, until Ware came up with a
solution. As the stories she had heard had hinted, the
demons *did* have a kind of mesmerizing power. Ware used

that one of his abilities on the animals, sending them into a trance in which they were three-quarters asleep and completely without fear.

One of the dogs was their test subject; they wrapped it in its swaddling-cloths of conjured fabric, laid it in one of the wagons, and backed the wagon carefully into the midst of one of the biggest tentacle-beasts.

The tentacles groped softly over the wagon, feeling each cranny and crevice blindly. As Xylina held her breath and the men watched with mingled fear and hope, the tentacles moved over the bundled body of the dog.

The dog slept on, oblivious. The tentacles completed their exploration of this new thing that had invaded, then the beast went back to waving them aimlessly in the air. The beast accepted the dog and wagon as it would a rock—or a lemur.

Hazard shouted with tired joy, and the rest joined him in a weak cheer.

"All right," Faro said, as if this were routine. "Let's get the wagons and the animals into the protection of these bigger beasts. Then get yourselves under cover—no more than three to a beast. We can't be sure how effective they are going to be. Hurry it up, now, the sun is setting! Those spiders are likely to be here any moment. If any of you are afraid, let Ware put you in a trance as well; that way you will not tear loose your protection, or be tempted to flee where the spiders may find you."

The men didn't need much urging. Ware put the rest of the dogs and the mules and his horse under his trances. The dogs he placed in the wagon beside the first. The mules and horse he led in himself, and got them to lie down. Then he layered yet more fabric over them as the tentacles groped him and animal with complete impartiality. He left them sleeping and looking like bundles of discarded laundry.

Then it was the turn of the rest. Walking stiffly in their swathings, each of them picked a tentacle beast and moved carefully into its groping embrace. The only exceptions

were the three or four men who confessed to being too terrified of the tentacle beasts to remain awake. Those, Ware
led in as he had the horse. He got them sitting and then
entranced. He left them lying on their sides and snoring
happily, oblivious to the tentacles waving over their heads.

Xylina was sweating, and not from the heat of her wrappings, as she inched her way toward her chosen beast. She
was afraid, too—but she felt that she could not confess it
and retain the respect of the men. This was, perhaps, the
hardest thing she had ever done. Not even facing Faro in
the arena had taken this much nerve.

She paused, just inside the reach of the beast, and waited
for it to kill her. But the tentacles passed over her, touching
her with surprising gentleness, and finally leaving her
alone. She remained where she was for a moment, gathering her nerve, but every heartbeat that passed with the
beast leaving her in peace gave her a little more of her
courage back. At length she made her way as far in as she
could, finally finding a place where the tentacles seemed to
meet. She lowered herself stiffly down on the ground
beside the base of the beast, with her legs stuck out in front
of her, like a doll. She was weary beyond words, and she
knew that the men must be just as exhausted. Now they
must wait and see if their guess was correct—that the
spiders would avoid these beasts, and so leave the party
unmolested.

She found that she could see through thin sections of the
fabric. She maneuvered to get the best view.

The sunset was glorious, a kaleidoscope of reds and
oranges, with swaths of purple near the zenith. The light,
fresh breeze that sprang up as it vanished cooled her under
all her coverings. She wondered when the first of the
spiders would appear. Perversely, she did not want to wait.
She would rather know if they were going to be safe, and
know it immediately.

Movement at her side made her turn, expecting an
attack of some other animal. But it was nothing of the kind.

One of the little golden-furred lemurs approached her cautiously, pushing aside the tentacles with its furred palms. She sensed that if she made any kind of sudden movement, she would frighten it, so she remained completely quiet. It seemed fascinated by her; its huge green eyes were fixed on hers, and the careful grace with which it moved rather surprised her. She had not expected the creatures to be so lithe.

It sidled up to her, and reached out to touch her wrappings, then snatched its hand back quickly, all the while watching her face. When she did not move, and only reacted by making soothing and encouraging nonsense sounds, it ventured another touch. Finally it came to squat beside her, examining her wrappings minutely, but taking extraordinary care not to dislodge them. She was impressed by its intelligence, for obviously it had made the connection between the wrappings and the fact that the tentacles had not harmed her.

"Yes," she told it softly. "Yes, that's right, little creature. I want only to share your home for the night, if you do not mind. I do not want to hurt you, or frighten you. If you will let me stay, I will do nothing to make you unhappy."

The lemur seemed encouraged by this, and settled down at her side, blinking sleepily as the stars came out. After a few moments, she watched it tuck its head down between its knees, and wrap its long arms around its ankles—then the faint sound of snoring told her that it had, without a doubt, gone to sleep, curled in a cat-like ball of fur.

She continued to watch for the spiders, but the confidence the lemur had shown gave her a great deal more heart. She could not imagine the shy and delicate creature dozing off like that, unless it knew it was completely safe.

The mystery of the floating lights was solved, at least; once the sun set, the lights began to appear, but soon descended to within a few cubits of the ground. The owners of the lights were, indeed, a nocturnal cousin of the floating beasts of the day. These were, perhaps, more fantastic in form; they had huge mouths, many of them, or no mouths at all, and long, trailing tendrils beneath them. Some did not even seem to have a head, for they had no mouths or eyes. In fact they looked like a more tenuous version of the tentacle-beasts, with a glowing spot in the very center of them.

Finally, after watching until her eyes ached, she saw the first of the spiders appear, clambering out to hunt beneath the light of the full moon.

It climbed out of the heart of one of the spinach-like plants—and she shuddered as she realized just how close they had been to the horrid monsters all along. And yet—there had been none of the spiders in the heart of the spinach-forest. Did they live only here? Or did competition within the forest preclude their reaching this fantastic size? There was no way of knowing, really. She was just grateful that none of her party had ever disturbed one of the plants during the day.

The spider stalked directly to one of the tentacle-beasts, the one, she thought, that held Faro, and stood just outside of the reach of the tentacles, its mandibles clacking together angrily. It seemed to know that he was there, and it wanted him. But it would not brave the tentacles to get him. At that, her heart rose. She had been right! The spiders were afraid of the tentacle-beasts.

It was joined by another—then more—but they would not venture near enough to the tentacle-beasts to come within reach of the deadly caresses. For now, they seemed to be concentrating on Faro's beast. It occurred to her that perhaps he was moving about, taunting and testing them, taking the danger on himself to prove whether the tentacle-beasts were the safe harbor they hoped.

"Fah! You'd just love to eat me, wouldn't you, ugly!" Faro's voice said cheerfully from somewhere near the center of the beast. "Well, why don't you come in and get me? I've even got a couple of friends here for your dessert!" He made a rude noise, and the spiders danced in rage.

"Faro?" she called, and the spiders swung their attention away, looking for the source of her voice. "Are you doing all right? Don't tease them too much! If you get them too angry, they might rush you!"

"I'm right and tight, little mistress!" he called back, with a laugh. "I don't think you need to worry; I don't think there's anything that could tempt the ugly things into coming within reach of these beasts—you should see the tentacles on this side, waving as if there's a high wind. I think the beasts can sense when there's a spider around, and they are hungry for spider!"

Well, *that* was certainly comforting! She relaxed a bit more.

"There's a couple of those lemur creatures in here with me," Faro continued. "Cute little things, and they keep trying to offer me fruit or something."

"Don't take it, Faro," Ware said, from somewhere off to Xylina's right. "You don't know what it is. What is fine for them might poison you; we know nothing about this land and what is in it."

"I'd figured that," Faro replied. "I just take it for a minute, then give it back, and that makes them happy." He raised his voice. "Men! I think we've proved we dare to sleep tonight! How about a roll-call before we do?"

One by one the men called out their names, all but the ones already sleeping. All of them were fine, and more than Faro and Xylina seemed to be sharing their accommodations with lemurs. They seemed to be charmed by the golden-furred animals, who had not molested them or interfered with them in any way. Now Xylina was glad that she had discouraged killing or capturing the gentle beasts.

She turned her attention to the weird wilderness about them, and was gladder than ever that they had found this strange sort of shelter. More creatures than just the spiders were appearing to prowl the night under the full moon. There were long things with too many legs to count, covered in jointed armor that shone under the moonlight.

There were some things like giant scorpions the size of ponies in faceted shells that glittered like gemstones. Beetles even bigger than the spiders scuttled across the sand like huge moving hills. But all of these alarming monsters avoided the proximity of the tentacle-beasts, and at last even the spiders gave up waiting for the humans to emerge.

The floating animals descended again, and now she saw the reason for the trailing tentacles and huge mouths. Many a battle took place under the moon, as the tentacles snared a giant insect and the floating creature carried its prey up into the sky. Many a beetle was attracted to the light on the nose of a beast, only to be snatched by the huge, toothy mouth. Even the spiders were not immune; Xylina silently cheered on the floating animals as they seized unwary or too-slow spiders and carried them off.

When the last of the arachnids had prowled away, their claw-tips making that dragging sound she had noticed last night, she looked over at her lemur-companion. It was still sound asleep, and her eyelids were getting so heavy she thought that she might as well follow its example.

"Good night, little one," she said, reaching out to stroke its fur as it had stroked her wrappings. Then, curling up in a ball in the sand, and covering her eyes to protect them from groping tentacles, she let her exhaustion overcome her.

She woke at dawn, as the huge insects of the night before were retreating into their hiding places. And this was when she saw how the lemurs earned their safe homes.

Her companion of the night was already awake, and looking alertly about. It was watching the insects, measuringly, although she could not for a moment imagine why.

Then, after a moment, a much smaller spider came ambling by; a spider just a little larger than her mule in the body, although with the legs added it seemed much bigger. The lemur suddenly darted out of cover, before she could do more than cry out in alarm. Why was it doing this? It had no weapons—the spider could move incredibly quickly, as she had learned only too well yesterday. The poor lemur would be devoured before her very eyes!

The spider spotted the potential prey immediately; mandibles clicking in excitement, it turned and ran straight for the lemur. The golden-furred beast paused a moment while Xylina caught her breath; then, at the last possible instant, turned and ran for the safety of the tentacle-beast.

It stayed just barely out of reach of the spider, which redoubled its efforts to catch this tantalizing prey, scuttling across the sand as fast as it could run. And after a few moments, Xylina realized that the lemur was *deliberately* lagging, to stay out of reach, but only *just* out of reach, of the spider.

The lemur ran straight back to the shelter of its home. The spider, so intent on the prey that was so *very* near, ignored its danger until it was too late.

The lemur made a strange, shrilling sound—and the tentacle-beast was galvanized.

Xylina ducked as the tentacles lashed out over her head like so many whips. They extended farther than she had guessed, and struck the spider in hundreds of places. The armor protected it everywhere but its eyes and the vulnerable joints, but with so many tentacles lashing out at it, there was no way it could avoid being struck in those places, again and again.

The lemur cowered within the shelter of the beast; the tentacles receded, quieted, and went back to their normal aimless waving. On the sand outside, the spider writhed in its death-throes, mandibles clashing, mouth drooling, legs waving in the air uncontrollably. The tentacle-beast had struck with good effect.

Finally the spider made its last shudder, and lay still.

The lemur got up, cautiously, and sidled up to the dead spider. It tossed a pebble or two at it—perhaps to see if it was really dead—but when it failed to react, the lemur rose and loped boldly over to it.

Then, while Xylina watched in astonishment, the lemur

seized one leg and began tugging the dead spider towards its chosen beast.

But the spider was too heavy for the lemur. It gave up after a moment, and looked directly at her.

It couldn't want her to help—could it?

Evidently that was exactly what the lemur wanted, for when she did not move, it came over to her, reached down for her hand, and tugged at her, impatiently.

Well—why not? The lemur had accepted her as a friend with surprising readiness, perhaps on the assumption that she was merely another species of tentacle-beast residents. All of them would have this in common, earning their keep. It behooved her to play the expected role.

She obediently rose and took one leg while the lemur took another. It was not easy, moving in the stiff bundle of wrappings, but it could be done. And after all, she had shared the shelter; it only seemed right that she pay for that shelter. Together, she and the lemur brought the spider within tentacle-touching distance.

It took a moment for one of the aimlessly groping tentacles to connect with the dead spider, but the moment the beast had done so, every tentacle on that side of the beast lashed out, seized on the spider and began dragging it in towards the center of the beast. At that point, the lemur let go, and so did Xylina. The tentacle-beast quickly conveyed the dead spider to its hidden mouth.

Content now, the lemur turned its back on Xylina and retreated into the waving arms on the other side of the beast, and was soon lost to sight.

And she, in her turn, moved out of the reach of the beast to gather her men together. It had been a surprisingly good night.

They spent four more nights this way, sharing the shelter of the tentacle-beasts with the gentle lemurs. Two or three of the boldest men even imitated the lemurs, luring spiders and other predators into reach of the tentacle beasts. The men could not imitate the lemurs' shrill warning to their hosts that "dinner was coming," but they didn't need to; the lemurs themselves saw what they were doing and galvanized their hosts into the appropriate action. Xylina marveled over their reckless courage; they treated it as a game, as if they could not believe in their own vulnerability. Faro pointed out to her that it was all the younger men, and not the ones with any real experience. "They haven't yet learned they aren't immortal," he said wryly. "No matter what they've seen, the fact that they've survived so far makes them certain that the fates and luck are with them."

The more time Xylina spent with her men, learning all about them and their lives, the less able she was to justify her position as "mistress" over her "slaves." What had she done to deserve it, after all? She'd had no more training or schooling than they had; in Faro's case, she'd had less. She was younger than most of them. And what had they done to deserve *their* fate? That they were not female and full citizens was only an accident of birth. It was not fair. . . .

She spent the next long night, alone but for a drowsing beast, thinking about these things before she fell asleep. There was nothing she had done on this quest that any of the men could not have done, save only a bit of conjuration. How could something like that give her the right to life and death over, not only these men, but any man in Mazonite hands? The word of a single citizen could send any man to the arena unless his mistress protested. Men could not hold property, carry weapons without a permit, defend themselves, or contradict the will of a citizen. Except, of course, within the Freedman's Quarter, and among other men. She could not speak for all men, of course; surely there were lazy slaves, and stupid, and men who needed the firm hand of a mistress to rule them, lest they get themselves into trouble. But the men of this mission deserved better.

She would free them if she could, she thought, as she looked back over her shoulder at them, marching stolidly into the unknown. But these men were not hers to free.

They belonged to the Queen, and several of them felt a very powerful sense of loyalty to their royal mistress. So, in a sense, did Xylina. She "belonged" to Adria, at least until the mission had been fulfilled, and her loyalty had been ensured by her own oaths. And by her honor. That above all must drive her forward. She could afford to indulge her doubts only after the mission was fulfilled.

There seemed no end to this particular realm; no mist-wall appeared on the horizon, and Xylina wondered if they were ever going to find their way across this perilous place. But land began to change a little on the third night, the plants and creatures becoming larger and fewer; the third night in this realm, the tentacle-beasts no longer outnum-bered the party. They had to share the protection of the house-sized creatures, and somehow Xylina wound up paired with the mules, Ware, and his stallion.

As night fell, she found that she was not in the least sleepy. The inevitable lemurs snored quietly nearby, but the continuing silence between herself and Ware began to feel very strained. Finally she decided to break it.

"Have you ever seen anything like the creatures here before, Ware?" she asked into the darkness.

"Both yes and no," the incubus replied, softly. "Yes, because I *have* seen beasts with these powers, and of this nature, but no, because the creatures I saw were no larger than the palm of your hand at best. And there was nothing magical about them, nor were they as deadly, except to things their own size."

She made a noncommittal sound, trying to think of a way to continue the conversation. Ware found one for her.

"It is very strange, how magic works across the many realms," he said, as the nocturnal versions of the floating beasts drifted into view. She wondered how the lights were made. It was quite remarkable how often the land-creatures were lured into striking range by those fascinating lights. "I have seen a number of realms, over the years. Including my own, for I am not a native of Mazonia, you know."

"No," she replied. "No, I had no idea—*are* there demons who are native to my kingdom?" The idea of a demon calling himself a "native" seemed absurd, but where else would they have come from? Had she ever heard where demons came from? If she had, she could not recall; they had simply been part of Mazonia, to be dealt with, but carefully, for they were dangerous. They were allowed most of the freedoms and privileges of a citizen, in exchange for the oaths they swore to the Queen, and that summed up all she had ever known about them, until crossing wits with Ware.

"No, I was born—yes, dear Xylina, we *are* born—in one of these places of wild magic. Most of us were, in fact—and most of us had no idea what our own nature was, until something revealed it to us. There have not been any demons born since the kingdom of Mazonia was founded, though. Perhaps the change that made your kingdom and conjuration possible ended the conditions that permitted the creation of my kind." He fell silent for a long time, but Xylina had the feeling that it was because he was thinking. "I know that I have told you that in many ways, we are not different from your kind, but I have not told you why we feel this way."

"That is true," she admitted. "And I thought you were mad to say something like that—that is, until we met the Sylvans."

"Ah, the Sylvans." He chuckled for a moment. "No, that is not what I meant. You see, most of us had at one point every reason to believe that we *were* of your kind. Humans born in the realms of wild magic can have so many things odd about them—everything from extra fingers to extra heads, and powers ranging from conjuration to wingless flight. There seemed no reason in my case to think that I was any different from the humans about me. I thought only that I had a particular talent for dematerialization and for entrancing. No one told me that these were things associated with demon-kind; perhaps no one knew. I thought I was no different from the rest of the folk I knew."

He fell silent again, and Xylina asked the obvious question. "How did you find out differently?"

"Ah," came the reply, "I fell in love, you see."

There was such a bitter sorrow in those few words that Xylina would have left it there. This was the first time Ware had allowed the conversation to drift into the area of the personal. She was not certain she wished to hear or know more. But Ware seemed now determined to continue.

"I fell in love with a human woman—and my nature became—obvious. I was appalled. Horrified. It was a very difficult time for me." He took a deep breath, and let it out in a sigh. She wanted to ask what he meant, but she felt she dared not. Let him reveal what he chose, she decided. If she overstepped the bounds, he might never tell her anything again.

She did not question why she wanted to know these things about him; it was more than simple, or even perverse, curiosity. It was almost as if she *had* to know.

"I am not a light-minded creature, Xylina," he said, after a moment. "I am not a philanderer. That was why it was so difficult for me. I honestly had not thought about this for a very long time, you know—it was a very painful period, and I often choose to forget it. But I was true to her for as long as she lived—"

"But you outlived her," Xylina was moved to say.

"By more years than you can reckon. I had not thought to find another woman like her." He chuckled dryly. "Then, as I gained in experience, I realized that like every first love, mine was somewhat callow. I would not care for her, if I met her today—though I cared for her deeply then. So then I thought that I would never encounter a woman who could match my somewhat demanding tastes. And for many, many years, I did not. I do not engage in liaisons for amusement, and so I remained without liaisons of any kind. Then, of course . . . "

He said nothing more, but Xylina knew him well enough

by now to fill in what he did not say. He was as honor-bound in his way as she was in hers. He had certain rules—"playing the game," he called it—and he would not violate those rules for any reason.

What this confession meant, then, was that he was telling her something she had not even dreamed of. He had been in love with this unknown woman; presumably she had loved him in turn, never mind that he was a demon. He had said that he was not light of mind or heart, that he did not have affairs simply to assuage his lusts.

It followed, therefore, that not only did he desire Xylina, he was actually in love with her. Not the kind of "love" that a Mazonite male could offer to his mistress, a fawning kind of lap-dog emotion, but something astounding, the love of an equal for an equal.

She did not know what to say, and sat bundled up in her wrappings, trying to find some way to turn the conversation to something more comfortable.

In the end, it was Ware who did just that, telling her tales from his wanderings that almost made her forget what he had revealed. He had a knack for storytelling, and it did not hurt that his experiences of other times and places were fascinating. But when he stopped, out of courtesy, to let her sleep, she found her thoughts going back to his startling revelation.

And she fell asleep wondering just what she was going to do about it.

Finally, the mist-barrier in the distance signaled that they were about to reach a new region, and Xylina put all her speculations aside for the moment. As eager as she was to get out of this realm of giant insects and killing plants, she was reluctant to face a new set of dangers. Yet she had no choice—for the shard lay ahead.

But for once, when the expedition crossed the border, Ware gave a brief exclamation of mingled pleasure and apprehension. Xylina looked at him askance, for there was nothing in this stark landscape to give cause for such an exclamation.

"This is territory that I know," he said. "In fact—it is the same place where I was born. It has moved, of course; I did not expect to find it here—but I think we can be certain that it is the same."

Xylina wondered what it was that made him so certain; Ware himself had said that realms that looked familiar would often have changed in ways both unexpected and deadly. Still, she was not going to argue with him just now.

The land immediately in front of them was a hilly grassland, with never a sign of trees or bushes. The grasses were waist-high, and rippled in a brisk wind, green and silvery-gray. Yellow-gold, white, and pink flowers dotted the sea of grass, and closer to the ground many herbacious plants filled in among the tall, slender grass stems. There was nothing in sight but grass for as far as Xylina could see, but she did not trust her eyes. In land like this, entire villages could be hidden in a fold between the hills, and they would not know one was there until they stumbled on it.

That was, in essence, exactly what Ware told them. "The magic in this realm is confined to the people and their domesticated beasts, and not the plants or the wild things. There is much conflict in this realm; virtually every tiny enclave of humans is at war with every other enclave, and they trust outsiders no more than they would trust their familiar enemies. We are as much at peril here as we were among the beasts behind us. More."

Xylina nodded, slowly. "So, we must trust no one, and nothing, is that it?"

Ware nodded his agreement, and she sighed. "Well then—which way are we to go?"

Faro consulted the instruments that Ware had entrusted to him, and pointed off into the entirely trackless grassland. Xylina considered the lack of roads, and the supplies that they had left.

"Can the wagons go through this?" she asked Horn.

He considered the grass. "I think so," he replied. "Don't hold me to it, though. That stuff might get tangled up in the axles, and if we have to cut the wagons loose every couple of cubits, we might as well not have them."

"All right. Men," she said, projecting her voice so that it would carry to the rear of the column, "we're going to try taking the wagons across this, but if they can't make it through, we will have to leave them. If that happens, we will load all the beasts with as much as they can carry, and ourselves as well. Faro, Ware and I will march with you, in that case. But for now, we will try to keep them with us."

There were nods, and expressions of relief among the men. Xylina did not blame them; she was not looking forward to walking, with or without a pack.

There seemed nothing else to say, so without another word, Xylina led them off, her mule pushing through the grass as if he were swimming.

He reined in his horse. "I think we have had enough," he said finally, thoughtfully, and it might read as if he means his aide, and if we have to pull the wagons loose every several miles, we might as well put the effort—" He let the subject vanish with a shrug, but his gesture . . .

• Chapter 15

The wagons made slow progress through the tall grass, but it was progress, and Xylina saw no reason to abandon them yet. Nothing interfered with them during the day except omnipresent clouds of stinging insects. But Xylina thought she saw shiny glints of something, like gleams of metal, on the horizon now and again. That could have been nothing more than the sun shining on a bit of water—or it could have been a reflection off armor or weapons. There was no way of telling, really. Ware had a distance-viewer, but it was useless here, for something in the air kept distant things hazy and indistinct. Whatever it was that made those glints of sunlight kept its distance—or else they passed it by.

Faro said once that the creatures that were circling over them like curious vultures were like no birds *he* had ever seen. Sunlight glinted from them, too, as if they wore some bright bits of metal about them, or were even metallic constructs themselves. Still, there was nothing to be made of any of that; Ware had told them that the people here would be hostile, and it made sense that they would keep a watch for intruders. Creatures of the air would make good spies for such a purpose. Xylina hoped that her party appeared too small for a threat but too large to trifle with.

Night came slowly, here; the sun descended through a golden haze, and the enormous clouds on the horizon turned red, yellow-orange, and gilded as it sank behind them. There was no particular place that seemed better than any other for a camp, so Xylina arbitrarily chose a hill and decreed that they would stop for the night. They trampled the grass flat for a camping-place, and Xylina conjured a huge, flat stone to put the cook-fire on, a stone covering an area as large as her tent. Horn, who had been on many a campaign before, cautioned her about setting fire to the grass accidentally. He swore that such a wildfire was as dangerous as any enemy, and Xylina was prepared to take his word about it. The stone was his suggestion, and it seemed a good one to her.

She conjured the tent-materials, and while the men assembled the camp, she debated setting up a stone palisade as she had done before. Her magic power had returned during the respite of the tentacle plants and now seemed stronger than ever, but she remained cautious. The lessons of the spiders had shown her that such a "defense" was not necessarily the best idea. While it was true that such a palisade would protect them from some things, the spider-creatures had already shown that such a defensive ring was not proof against creatures that could climb or fly over it. Only luck, and her forethought in creating the fire-ring inside the palisade, had kept them from being trapped in there, and had enabled them to trap some of the spiders in turn and keep the others at bay. And if they were confined within a high stone ring, they would not be able to see what was coming up upon them from the grasslands in the night. They could, in fact, wake to find themselves surrounded.

Ware cautioned against such a defense; when Faro came to see what they were discussing, he argued for it. Finally, she decided to compromise.

She set up a ring of stones with gaps in them, gaps at which she stationed a guard for the watch. If an entire army came marching up to confront them, she would have time to conjure stones to fill those gaps. And if something that was able to pass over or through the stones attacked them, they would at least not be trapped inside their own protections. This would be no harder to guard than any other perimeter, and it had the added advantage of requiring only four guards on any one watch.

The air felt overly warm, heavy, and thick. Every little exertion made her sweat uncomfortably. Her temples began to throb, but she saw no point in complaining. She conjured wood for the fire, torches, and oil for the lamps as usual, but by the time full dark fell, she was suffering from an inexplicable headache, and one which no amount of headache-powder would cure. Although since they had first hosted the Pacha she had made a point of taking meals with the men and sharing their camaraderie, tonight she excused herself, ate sparingly, and took to her bed. When Faro came to see how she was, the pain was sufficient to ask him to substitute someone for her on night-watch.

This was unusual enough to prompt Faro to return several times to find out how she was doing, and for Horn to appear with a special sweet posset and a solicitous inquiry on behalf of the men. Finally Ware arrived, as she endured a throbbing in the front of her face that nauseated her, and asked if he could help.

"Only if you can magic away this pain," she said crossly, the dull ache making her short of temper. "I am afraid to take any more drugs for it—if something attacks us, I dare not have my senses blunted, and pain-drugs often interfere with conjuration. But if I do not, I am not certain I could hold my concentration long enough to be effective. I can't imagine what has caused this. I do not feel feverish or ill, and I have not eaten anything that the rest have not also eaten."

"I cannot magic it away," he replied, keeping his voice soft and soothing, for which she was grateful, "but perhaps I can entrance you so that you may sleep. I can make certain that the trance is a light one, and any disturbance in the camp will awaken you. I can if you will trust me, that is. I should not blame you if you did not. I know the Mazonites claim that an incubus can do whatever he wills with an entranced victim, and I would not be offended if, in the present circumstances, you would rather not take the chance that I might exceed the bounds I promised."

It was the sad resignation in his voice that decided her in his favor as much as anything else. That, and the fact that she knew now that he was far more honorable than many of the Mazonites who told those tales about dishonorable demons. "Of course I trust you," she replied, the pain making her voice sharper than she had intended. "You are honorable, Ware; you made me certain promises, and you will not violate them. If I know nothing else about you, I know that, for a certainty, as certain as the sun will rise."

"Well, at least the sun is beyond the vagaries of wild magic," he replied, some of the humor coming back into his voice. "And I do not think anything is likely to change that at any time soon. Well then, if you will permit me—you must look deeply into my eyes, and try to relax."

She nodded, and fixed her eyes on his. The flame of the lamp he had brought with him reflected a metallic scarlet in the center of his pupils; the many colors of the irises seemed to swirl, and swirling, pull her whirlpool-like into those orbs—further, deeper, away from her body, until the pain was nothing, a thing remote and far from her and no longer a part of her. She relaxed further; now that the ache in her head was no longer the center of her thoughts and she emptied her mind as the soft voice told her, and in a moment, there were no thoughts at all to distract her.

She woke all at once in a spasm of pure terror, her heart pounding and her ears echoing. She was so very overcome with fear that there was no room for anything rational, only animal fear and paralysis in the darkness.

A heartbeat later she knew what had awakened her—as a lightning-bolt lashed down somewhere near the camp and thunder flattened her to her bed. The first one must have hit right on top of the camp—

One moment, the air was still; the next, a blast of cold wind slammed into the wall of the tent, bringing with it the storm. A torrential rain lashed at the tent-walls, and lightning flashed so constantly that there was no true darkness. Thunder, wind, and rain pounded the tent and the ground made it impossible to hear anything clearly.

The fabric of the tent billowed and writhed in the intermittent light, and the poles threatened to pull out of the ground at any moment. Wind caught the tent-flap and ripped it open, sending in a torrent of rain. Quickly, she seized some of the non-conjured pieces of her wardrobe, pulled them on, and ran outside.

She dashed into the worst storm she had experienced; the worst she had ever heard of. Rain drenched her to the skin the moment she left the tent—and then the tent-poles *did* pull loose, and tent and contents went flying out into the darkness. The tent itself caught on one of the stones, and wrapped around it; she couldn't see what happened to the rest. Hail struck her painfully, and she shielded her head with her hands, as stones fell all about her, seeming to jump up from the grass in the uncertain light. Lightning lashed down nearby again, striking one of the conjured stone walls. Thunder stuck her with a physical shock, just as something hit her from behind, sending her down face-first into the soaked grass.

There was a man clinging to her knees; he crawled up beside her to shout at her. "Stay down!" Hazard bellowed into her ear. "Lightning hits whatever is above the ground! Two have already been killed!" Lightning and thunder punctuated his words; she saw no reason to argue with him.

"What's happening? Where's Faro?" she shouted back, over the howling of the wind. "Where is Ware? How long has this been going on?"

"It just started! It caught us all off-guard, and everything is completely confused! Ware is trancing the animals—the ones he caught before they spooked and ran," Hazard yelled. "Faro is trying to find all the men still alive and bring them to one place so you can conjure a shelter over us!"

That was the best idea she had heard yet. As hailstones continued to pelt them both painfully, she followed Hazard in a crawl across the grass that led them to the huge stone that had held the cook-fire. The fire was out; the very logs gone, washed or blown away. Now it held a huddle of miserable humans, their eyes wide, their hair and clothing plastered to their skins. She could not count them; the lightning made counting uncertain. There were not as many as there should be; that was all she knew.

"This only started a few moments ago," Hazard shouted, as she took her place among them. "One moment everything was fine, then this storm blew in out of nowhere! The tents went flying, lightning hit Lisle and Stef and killed them where they stood, the livestock panicked—Ware went after the mules and his horse, and Faro has been collecting us here—half of us were already asleep, and the first thing we knew was that we were being half-drowned and bombarded with hailstones."

Well, that explained why no one had tried to awaken her; they hadn't had time. Their experience matched hers.

Right now what they all needed most was a shelter that would stand against the wind and rain. And the lightning. She closed her eyes for a moment, gathered her concentration, and began to conjure.

She was afraid to construct anything too tall; it would be a target for lightning. What they needed was fairly basic, a shelter that wouldn't blow away—

Wait a moment; she remembered something. Lightning went to metal; that was why they made fighters take off their armor in a lightning-storm. If she could create a tall metal pole out *there*—maybe she could get the lightning to hit something besides people.

Quickly she switched her focus, concentrating on the tallest stone in the ring, and creating a thick, heavy rod of metal projecting up from the top of it. She had to work quickly, for she was not certain what the effect on her would be if lightning stuck her creation while she was still conjuring it. So what she made was quite crude, but it did not need to be anything but functional. And it needed to be able to withstand multiple lightning-strikes, for she had the feeling that after this storm was over she would discover it more than half melted away by the power of those bolts.

It was one of the fastest bits of conjuration she had ever performed. And she finished just in time, for no sooner had she pulled her concentration away from her creation, than it became the target for every lightning-bolt for furlongs around. Now they truly did have their very own source of light, as lightning lashed the top of the stone and thunder became a continuous roar. So many bolts struck the stone-slab that it crackled with energy. Their hair stood on end despite being plastered down by the rain, and little blue lightning-snakes and sulfur-yellow balls ran down the stone and into the ground. The air was sharp with the scent of ozone. The men stared in fascination as she turned her attention to getting them some shelter.

Something basic, she told herself. Four—no, eight supports. Heavy stone would be best, something the wind could not pull up or push over. She built eight square, squat pillars of stone, wider at the bottom than the top, and just a little taller than the tallest of the men. Then the roof—a slab of heavy wood, as thick as her waist. Nothing to attract an errant bolt of lightning that was not obeying the laws of nature.

She built a wall only on the side the wind was coming from—another heavy slab of wood. She was afraid to try to put up any more walls; it would be too easy for the wind to topple them. She had no way of bracing them, other than by their own weight.

Shortly after she completed that wall, Faro came dashing in at a bent-over run and cursing under his breath, followed by Horn who was cursing quite audibly; from the other side of the compound Ware ran in under the shelter as well, with the lead-ropes of his stallion and three of the mules in his hands. The animals rolled their eyes in terror every time a bolt struck nearby, and they were pathetically eager to get in out of the rain. Xylina noticed one thing with a sinking heart. None of the three were the two riding-beasts; she and Faro would either have to ride in the wagons or walk unless the two riding-mules turned up. The heavy odor of wet equine filled her nose, but the mules and the horse were warm, and unlike a fire, they were not going to blow out. The wet humans and animals crowded together into the minimal shelter, and Xylina reached for Ware's arm, to bring him near enough for her to ask him for advice—

This storm could not be natural. Was this why she had the headache? Was that a harbinger of the storm? She remembered how her mother used to get headaches before storms. She had a dozen questions to ask Ware, but she never touched him, for at that moment, one of the men screamed, a sound so shrill with terror that it carried even over the pounding of the thunder.

All eyes went to him, blanched and wild-eyed, then followed where he pointed.

What they saw was more terrifying than any of the monsters they had thus far encountered. As if the storm, not content with blasting them with lightning, had decided to grow tentacles to seize them, a dozen groping, black funnels eeled their way across the grassland towards them, moving impossibly against the wind. They towered into the lightning-lit sky, hundreds of cubits tall, larger than anything, living or not, that Xylina could remember. As they drew closer, Xylina made out the shapes of entire trees flying weightlessly around the funnels, trees that had been torn out by the roots and sucked up into the sky.

Even as Xylina gasped, frozen in her place with fear and uncertainty, one of the funnels moved straight towards them, as if it had eyes and could see them cowering there.

Utter panic ensued. The horse and the mules broke away from Ware's hold and dashed madly out into the storm. Several of the men cried out in inarticulate horror and ran out as mindlessly as the animals. Xylina could only stand and stare as the funnel moved closer.

Faro and Ware simultaneously threw her to the ground and threw themselves down beside her. She had just enough wit to curl into a ball and try to protect her head and neck with her hands. Then there was no more time—for the whirlwind was upon them, roaring like a waterfall, shrieking like a legion of the damned, howling like a hundred thousand mindless monsters—

—and the world came apart.

It seemed to take forever, and it was over in moments. When the thing had passed on its inexorable way, there was nothing left standing of any of Xylina's conjurations. The stones of the palisade were flattened—those that were still *there*. As for the rest, the whirlwind had picked them up and danced them about, then carried them off, somewhere. The shelter she had conjured so hastily was completely gone, and only the flat hearth-stone remained of the encampment.

Xylina, Ware, and Faro prized themselves off the rock, and stared about in the flickering lightning—and even Ware seemed completely dumbfounded. Horn and Hazard remained clinging to the rock, unable to move or even open their eyes. Xylina sat up slowly, the rain plastering her hair to her head and back, and tried to put together a single coherent thought. Faro simply sat and shook like a bush in a high wind. Ware tried several times to say something, then shrugged, and gave up. Finally, he managed a single word: "Light." She knew what he meant, of course, and after several tries she succeeded in conjuring a glowstone large enough to guide any other survivors toward them. Of the men, less than half returned, soaked and shaken to the core, plodding back through the soaked and flattened grass to what little was left of the encampment, shreds and shards and the occasional recognizable object.

Somehow she, Faro, Ware, Horn, and Hazard had managed to cling to the stone while the whirlwind sucked up rock and wood and reduced them to splinters. As if the storm were satisfied, the whirlwinds moved off into the distance, the wind and lightning died, and even the rain faded away to little more than a drizzle. When she stopped shaking, Xylina's first thought was to give her men some kind of comfort, so she created another shelter and made a bonfire beneath it for Ware to light. The five of them sat huddled about it in thick swaths of conjured fabric, joined by others, staggering in one at a time. One of them, Xylina was relieved to see, was Pattée, sadly bedraggled but whole. Xylina put her arm around the woman and conjured warm material to surround them both. Theoretically one was a member of the ruling elite and the other a foreign whore who couldn't conjure; those had become meaningless distinctions.

Gradually, all those men that could, returned. When the roll was taken, they were down to a total of eleven, including Ware, Xylina, and Faro. Horn and Hazard survived; the other five were all fighters—Tron, Steel, and Jerig of the experienced men, and Pol and Ren of the men that had not had any previous campaigning. Even those three experienced campaigners were shaken to the bone by what they had just lived through. Tron had actually seen one of the others sucked up off his feet into the maw of the whirlwind, and hurled into the sky, screaming helplessly. He could only speak about what he had seen in broken fragments, augmented by gestures. "Never seen nothin' like it," he mumbled, over and over. "Not never . . ."

"First that terrible headache, then this," Pattée murmured.

So she had felt it too, while the men had not. That suggested that something strange had happened, but Xylina wasn't sure what to make of it.

They sat about the fire, glumly, and no flame or blanket could warm the chill in their hearts. Xylina was too numbed even for tears, and Faro still shook with tremors that came and went and had nothing to do with the cold. Finally, after long silence, Ware spoke.

"That was no natural storm."

He *knew* this place; somehow he must have recognized something about the whirlwinds that none of the others could have guessed. Xylina and the men looked at him expectantly, and waited for him to continue.

Ware stared off into the darkness, and his face was frozen into a cold mask that made Xylina shiver. "That was a mage-storm," he said at last. "It was created by a weather-wizard. There is only one tribe here that practices such magic. The Julamites know we are here; they somehow thought we were challenging them, and this was their answer."

He paused for a moment, and then turned to Xylina, his face now full of sorrow. "I did not know there was a weather-wizard this powerful in existence," he said to her, with mournful desperation. "If I had known, I would have warned you. I thought the worst the Julamites could produce would be lightning—I thought we would have plenty of warning of their storms. I never thought they would deign to bother with an expedition as small as ours."

The men stared at him, expressions of accusation beginning to form on their faces. But Ware was more than apologetic; he took the responsibility for what had happened on himself. The sorrow in his voice, and the despair in his eyes, were as moving as anything she had ever heard, and she felt impelled to answer them.

"How could you have known? And even if you had known, what could we have done about it?" she asked, softly, trying to keep her own fear and borderline hysteria out of her own voice. "No one could run away from something like *that!* And nothing I built could have withstood it! If these Julamites were determined to slay us with their storm, I fear that there was nothing we could have done to prevent what happened. I know of no conjurer who could match that kind of power, not even Queen Adria."

Accusations died unspoken, and slowly the men nodded

a grudging agreement. Ware shook his head slightly, but said nothing—only his own bleak face told her that he did not consider himself to be any less at fault. She felt a strange pity for him; he was so alone among them, and he was so accustomed to being the authority, that this failure to anticipate disaster must come doubly hard to him.

He turned his gaze from the darkness to the flickering fire. "If the Julamites are this strong, I must assume that the other tribes of this land have become just as strong," he said, finally. "The only good news I can offer is that I do not think we will be troubled by another mage-storm. It takes particular conditions to enable a weather-wizard to turn an ordinary storm into a mage-storm, and it is very draining on the wizard himself. And I know the Julamites cannot have more than one weather-wizard of such strength; they are an ambitious people, and a powerful wizard would not permit any rivals."

Like the Queen, Xylina thought, but did not say aloud.

"Then what can we expect?" Faro asked after a moment. He cast a glance past Ware's shoulder at the east. "You said yourself these people are all likely to be hostile. It's almost dawn; surely we're in for some other surprises." Faro seemed to be recovering his strength and his wits, and Xylina was grateful. She had hated to see him sitting there, trembling.

"I wish I could tell you," Ware replied helplessly, shrugging. "I am sorry, but since I was last here a few months ago, many things have changed that I did not expect to change. For that matter, I did not expect to find this realm *here;* it was much farther to the east when last I traveled. There are a score of tribes in this realm, and all of them have different wild magics. I know I saw the ur-birds of the Lgondians above us yesterday, but I do not know whether they will attack us, or whether their masters will. If the Julamites are so strong—have the other tribes become weaker, or stronger? I simply do not know!"

"Well, give us a starting point at least!" Faro snapped.

"Give us a plan! We can change the plan, if need be, but at least we will have one. You are the only one who knows anything about this place."

Ware opened his mouth as if to retort angrily—then closed it. He nodded slowly. "I apologize," he said. "You are right. We must do something other than sit here on a rock. We will have to try to travel stealthily—and Xylina will have to conjure everything we need, from this moment on, save for food and drink. We must try to be unobtrusive, unchallenging, and if the fates are with us, the tribes may think us too weak to bother with. That is the only way that we will succeed in passing through here, now that our company is so decimated."

"Eh, well," Horn replied at last, with a glance around him, "at least we won't be carrying heavy packs."

That elicited a laugh—a strained one, but it was at least genuine. Xylina felt a little of the tension leave her. Things were bad—but they were not yet dead.

When there was enough light so that it was possible to see effectively, Faro sent the men out to try and find whatever might have been left of their supplies and weapons. That was when they discovered some of the fantastic things the whirlwinds had done. A straw was found driven into the wood of the ruined wagon-frame like a nail. A single wild-bird egg scarcely larger than Xylina's thumbnail was found balanced on top of one of the toppled palisade-stones. One of the swords was discovered twisted into a bizarre knot-like shape.

Xylina scoured the grass, looking for anything that seemed out of place, for often only a corner of something protruded out from under the mat of rain-flattened grasses. She found scraps of fabric, bits of wood, and a few metal arrowheads and spear points, but that was all. After a few hours, her eyes ached from peering into the grasses, and squinting against too-bright sunlight. She returned to the rest with a pocket full of metal and a few ragged bits of cloth that was not of her conjuration.

When they all gathered again at mid-morning, there was not much good news. Some few of the food supplies had been found: a bag of grain, some journey-bread, and some dried peas; also enough of the weaponry that each of them could be armed after a fashion. The wagons were wrecked and there wasn't a piece larger than a hand anywhere; the livestock were gone beyond even Ware's ability to hunt. Only one of the mules and two of the missing men were ever found dead; as for the rest—Xylina did not care even to hazard a guess.

Horn butchered the poor mule as well as he could with nothing more than his belt-knife, and strung as many ragged strips of meat as he could over conjured fires to smoke-dry. They conferred together over a strange and haphazard meal of soaked journey-bread and roast mule about what, exactly, Xylina could conjure that would be effective as weaponry. She could not produce a sword, of course—but she could manage a pointed rod of metal enough like a spear to make no difference. Finished bows and arrows were impossible, but she discovered through trial and error that she could produce a tapered and flexible stave that Faro could notch, something strong enough to serve as bowstring, and thin dowels that worked well as arrow-shafts. That, together with the arrowheads she had gleaned, gave them each two real arrows—and when Faro sharpened the dowels they, too, served as cruder arrows. Slings, of course, were easy; a length of leather-like substance and a couple of thongs, and every man was armed. There were few stones suitable, but she could conjure with no problems the kind of leaden shot that made a good slinger so effective—all she had to do was concentrate on making *small* bits of "lead" and the conjured metal appeared in rounded globules. She could still create their shelters and defenses each night, albeit more slowly than before, and the fuel for the fires to warm them and cook their food. Water could be a problem; they only had three waterskins among them, and unless they found water each night, they might run short fairly quickly. Food itself would quickly grow to be a problem unless they could find good hunting on the way; the food they had found and scavenged would not last that long, divided among so many.

But there was no hope of turning back. Not only would that be an admission of defeat, but it might not even be possible at this point. None of the men said anything about giving up—and Xylina had the feeling that they knew as well as she did that the road behind them was as hazardous as that ahead. She did not think they would be able to survive the country of the tentacle-beasts as poorly armed as they were now. Assuming that when they turned back, they actually *found* that country there! It was entirely possible that the border itself would now reveal an entirely new and deadly realm, for Ware had not expected to find this realm *here*, and that meant that the boundaries were changing more frequently than he had thought. More than that, Ware knew the country here, and that should help them.

At roughly noon, they set off again, this time afoot. Ware scouted ahead, seemingly indefatigable, covering the ground with a tireless stride that Xylina could not help but envy. She had gotten used to riding; she had thought she was inured to the hardships of this trek, but to her chagrin, she found herself coping with aching legs, and cramps in unexpected places, by the time they made their first halt.

Fortunately for her aching legs, their progress was slowed by the need to hunt. Of the three experienced campaigners, Tron and Jerig were the best with slings, and so they ranged to either side of the rest, hoping to bag something scared up by the passage of the larger group.

By the third halt—at a tiny stream, which gave them all a chance to slake their thirst—the hunters still had come up empty-handed. "You know," Horn said to her at one halt, "if we have to, we can always eat them hoppers. Bugs ain't bad toasted, and there sure are a lot of 'em."

Xylina gave him a sideways look, uncertain if he was trying to make a joke. His expression convinced her he was serious. He *was* an experienced cook, and he did know the secrets of surviving on campaign, where supplies might be captured or destroyed by the enemy. But that was one trick she had never heard of.

The "hoppers" were thumb-sized insects, shaped like the tiny leaf-hoppers of Mazonia, but much larger. They had been scaring these creatures up all along the trek, dozens of them with every step, and until this moment Xylina had not considered them as a food-source. She probably would not have considered Horn's proposition seriously, except that she knew from personal experience that there were a great many things that one would eat if one became hungry enough. There had been several times when she had made cakes of flour full of weevils, and told herself that if the weevils were eating her flour, she might as well eat them. She had certainly come to no harm from the experience.

The hoppers *were* convenient, and they seemed easy to catch, but they were very small. It would take a lot of them to make up a meal—and while they seemed easy to catch now, if the group hoped to make a supper of them, it might prove a lot more difficult than it looked to scoop up enough of them. And while they were catching bugs, they would not be making any progress. All things considered, unless they were starting to starve, it would probably take far more time to catch a meal of hoppers than it was worth devoting to catching them.

She wondered briefly if there were any other resources in this grassland that she had overlooked. She was, after all, a child of the city, and unused to scavenging her own food. There did not appear to be any edible grasses here; no seed-heads, at any rate, and she was relatively certain that if Ware knew some of the plants could be eaten, he would say something. Perhaps they should do some experimenting with boiling the roots of the grasses, or trying the stems of larger plants. On the other hand, she had no idea what was poisonous and what was safe.

Besides, the time to gather such things would be when they halted for the night.

Still—Horn's observation proved to her that this was not a hopeless trek into nowhere. The men were thinking— and more importantly, were standing by her. If they were going to desert her, this would have been the time, because they were no longer amidst the dangerous spiders and tentacles. There was always the possibility that one of these foreign tribes would take them in, and they would be free. But they were still here, still standing by the quest.

And none of them had made any move to be rid of her— or to suggest that she was not acting as she should. That had always been a fear of hers; she was the one female with authority among the many males, and conjuration alone was not enough against such overwhelming odds. Not when she slept, or when her guard was down. Faro was hers, of course, and Ware, but there could have been dissidents. There might even have been some agents for the Queen among them; it no longer mattered. They were a unit, and they believed in her.

She nodded at Horn, feeling her spirits rise for the first time since the storm, and turned to the others. "What do you think?" she asked. "Should we stop now and hunt bugs, or go on, and hope we get something larger?"

"Well," Tron said slowly, with a hint of a smile beginning on his otherwise stern face, "reckon if a man be hungry enough, he can eat 'bout anything." The smile broadened. "Recall eatin' m'shoes once. Reckon toasted hoppers be better nor that. But I'd rather we waited till a bit 'fore sunset afore we tried hoppers or shoes."

The rest burst out into relieved laughter, and Xylina joined them. She was right: they were going to stand by her. The quest was still possible to complete. It was going to work. By all the ancestors, it was going to work!

The fates were with them, and the hunters eventually brought down enough for all. At about sunset, they found another small stream, and there they made a camp. Since before the storm, she had still been the one who conjured materials for tents and fires, things did not look appreciably different, and that in itself made the men feel better. They still had Pattée, and that certainly made them feel better. This time, though, she made the tents low, and grass-colored; when the camp was set up, the tents blended somewhat into the landscape. She also made the material thick, so that lights from glowstones would not shine through them. And to compensate for the hardships they were enduring, she took particular pains with their bedding.

The end result was that the men who were not on watch-duty went to their beds in a reasonably cheerful frame of mind, and that in turn cheered Xylina. When Ware rejoined them, she wished that she could give him some of her own lighter spirits, for although he had found nothing to cause alarm, he was still obviously depressed over his imagined "failure" of last night. He sat with her and Faro in her tent after a dinner of some kind of game-bird—she was secretly relieved they had not needed to resort to hoppers, at least not yet—supposedly to report on what he had found, but in actuality, to sit in unhappy silence.

Despite what the men thought, he did not actually have to eat human-style food, although he did usually make a polite gesture with conjured food. But tonight he was not even making that much effort.

Finally Faro, tired of the continued silence, left them to take his own turn on guard-duty. Ware remained sunk in depression, and her heart ached for him; never had he seemed so human as now. As she watched him, waiting for him to speak, he suddenly turned his head so that she was looking straight into his eyes, and she recalled with a shock how warm and firm his body had felt last night, huddled next to her, how gentle and graceful his hands were as they had touched her brow. And at that moment, she became aware that not only was he now a friend, not only was he no longer an alien monster to her, but the stirrings in her body told her that he was the most desirable male she had ever known.

And that thought did not bring with it the feeling of appalled repulsion that she had expected. In fact, it only made her body ache more in a way that had nothing to do with pity. It occurred to her that he might have entranced her into this very thought—and she dismissed the notion immediately. It was not his way. He was as honorable and honor-bound as she, and his desire for her had been hedged around with some very specific promises. He wanted her of her own free will—and being entranced would mean that her will was not free.

So what had suddenly made her realize how attractive he was? She knew the answer to that as well. It was simple enough. For the first time since she had met him, he was vulnerable. And he was strong enough and confident enough to show her that vulnerability, and to hope that as a friend she would try to give him the comfort of her friendship. It was his momentary weakness that made her aware of his constant strength.

It took a brave person to admit to being afraid; it took a strong person to admit weakness. It took both to show these things to someone else.

Yet, though he might for the moment be vulnerable, he was still in every way her equal: intelligent, clever, erudite. A gentle being, and as bound by honor as she. Every bit a warrior in his way as she was in hers. That, she sensed now, was the reason why she had felt no attraction to any Mazonite man, not even her friend and confidant Faro, nor the handsome and youthful Hazard. She could not respect a man who could only be her inferior and not her equal partner—and every male raised in Mazonia would be, somewhere in the back of his mind, conditioned as a slave. There was no help for it; they were as controlled by their upbringing as she was. Even Faro, for all that he hated other Mazonites, was conditioned to obey them. His protectiveness of her was an outgrowth of that very obedience—"Mistress is unhappy, and I must make her happy." He was probably not even aware of the fact, but now that Xylina had a chance to get to know a male who was *not* so conditioned, it was obvious to her.

Her friendship was not cheaply bought—her love was not to be bought at all. Her friendship came only when it was reciprocated, but friendship did not make the demands that love did. Now she knew that she could only love a male whom she could also respect. She could only love a male who would respect her—because of herself, and not from training. And she had come, all unknowing, to love Ware. The knowledge came as a shock, as sudden and as earthshaking as seeing the ground open up beneath her.

He looked away again, and the expression on his face did not change. So she had not betrayed her sudden insight by a shift in her own expression. Things could go on just as they were—if she chose. He would never know how she felt. She could fulfill the quest, claim the Queen's reward, and be free of him and his desires. She would have her honor, keep her vow intact.

For what? a little voice deep within asked her, sarcastically. This mission might never succeed. Even if it did, what would she have earned? A bare existence, for the best that would have happened was that she would have repaid her debt. She would have all the struggle to do over again. Even if she did well, what would she have? A lifetime of continuing to placate the Queen, of trying to soothe her suspicions—and every time she succeeded in something, the Queen would be certain that she was trying to challenge her. But worst of all, it would be a lifetime spent alone. Any children she had would be conceived in lovelessness, and only for the sake of having a child. She could never bear to marry . . .

But if she followed her heart and gave herself to Ware? This would make her unclean, ineligible for leadership. Surely the Queen had spies among the men, perhaps even all of them were spies; such a liaison could not be kept secret forever. She could never challenge the Queen for the position of Mazonite leader. Yet it was a leadership she had never coveted, and still did not want. She had not even enjoyed "leading" these few slaves—and losing so many! Making decisions for every Mazonite would be sheer misery. Better a lifetime with the male she cared for—and who cared as much for her. The male who valued honor—

Honor. How could she keep her honor and yet pay Ware in the coin he desired most—a payment she now desired ardently to give him?

The voice returned, but this time without the sarcasm. *Wait a moment. What was it he said about the way that demons think? How a vow can be read in many ways, and still be valid? Surely I can use that*—

She turned her head a little to stare into the fire, lest her eyes betray her, and her heavy braid fell over her shoulder to gleam golden in the firelight.

Golden hair . . . hair, the symbol among her people of the essence of a person. Hence the superstitions about cursing through a lock of hair—and the custom among some of the women of leaving their hair at the altars of the goddesses, symbolically offering themselves as well. In the marriage ceremony, a lock of hair from the Mazonite and her chosen consort were braided together, and to divorce him, she had simply to unbraid the marriage-lock and cast his hair in the hearth-fire. Xylina's hair was the same color as—

She paused, taken by an awesome realization.

She closed her eyes for a moment, and asked herself if this was, truly, what she desired. She searched not only her heart, but her soul and her mind for the answer—her body was already informing her in no uncertain terms what *it* wanted, and she was grateful that females did not show their desires as openly as males. For at this moment, Ware was very far from thinking of the reason that had brought him on this quest. If she let the moment pass, there might never be another.

She would not let it pass.

Carefully, she gathered her hair in her hands, loosing it from the braid, and draping it across her palms; a heavy golden skein that represented all she was, as golden as the gold she had pledged him. Ware continued to stare into the fire, oblivious to her or anything else around him.

"Ware—" she said, startling him; the first time she had ever been able to do that! He jumped a little, and turned his gaze upon her, blankly. She held out her double-handful of hair to him.

"I pay thee in gold," she said softly.

His eyes widened as he realized what she was offering; her hair, herself. Just as he had wanted, planned for, schemed to achieve.

His reaction, however, was not what she had expected.

"Oh, Xylina—" he said, and made an abortive move towards her. But then, unaccountably, he held himself back. "Xylina—I can not accept this," he said, myriad emotions warring on his face. "I can not—"

Conflicting emotions beset her as well. Dismay, annoyance, even a touch of anger. What, was she no longer good enough for him? What was wrong with her—or with him? "Why?" she demanded. "What has changed? What has happened that I am no longer what you desire?"

"Circumstances—oh, Xylina, I desire you, love you still, never, ever doubt that! But—" he laughed weakly, and raised a graceful hand to rub his temple "—this is not precisely the best time—"

She started to protest; he held up a hand. "Wait, please, let me explain. You have heard that there are two of demon-kind, the incubus which is the male, and the succubus which is the female, correct?"

She nodded, wondering impatiently what that could have to do with anything.

He coughed, and his face twisted a little. "There is no delicate way to put this. What if I were to tell you that there is only *one* of demon-kind, that each demon is both incubus and succubus?"

What? How could that be? It ran right across all the laws of nature! But did the laws of nature apply to a demon, a creature who himself had told her he was born in this realm of wild magic? "I would say that you are insane, except that I know you are not," she said flatly, beginning to think that she was not going to like what he was about to tell her.

"That is the nature of demon-kind," he said gently. "That we are male *and* female, incubus *and* succubus. But never at the same time. And that which triggers—forces—the change from one to the other, is—the act of love."

Her eyes widened as she took that in, and realized what he meant. "You mean that if you were to share love with me, you would become a female?" she exclaimed incredulously. This was too strange for horror; she could only gape at him.

He nodded, sadly. "I would not be able to prevent it. That is what revealed my nature, so long ago. I joined with my lover—and awoke a woman. It was something of a shock to me—and my lover was not exactly pleased, either."

She shook her head. There were too many things that she had witnessed already for her to think this was impossible—or even particularly terrible. Except in what it meant for her.

If he joined with her—but how did he become male again?—oh. Of course.

"I can imagine that she was not happy," Xylina said, with wry and sad irony. "But if you were to love a man in your female form—you would go back to being male?"

"Until I shared love with you again, yes," Ware said. "But—Xylina, it is not that simple."

She sighed. "Somehow, I had the feeling that it would not be. I think I can guess the rest. You must have a mate that you love as a female, even as you have one that you love as a male." Her mind accepted that as logical although her heart rebelled. "There is a certain unpleasant symmetry to that."

He nodded, as unhappy as she. "You understand it exactly, Xylina. My commitment to a male must be as my commitment to you: lifelong. There is no one in this party with whom I would be willing to make that commitment. Not even Faro, who is an admirable fellow, but is not to my taste, I fear. Simple, casual liaisons, which are so common among your kind, are impossible for me. Unless I sought out . . . " He shook his head. "No, it will not do. We must wait, Xylina. We must wait until we are back in lands that are not so uncanny, and you and I must find a slave who suits our natures, who can fit this pattern that we must have."

She was beginning to put all of the pieces together, and she was beginning to reassess the entire situation. Bad enough that she would have to share him once—but it was obvious from what he had been saying that she would have to share him *all her life* with a man. She would have to send him to that man's bed every time she shared love with him. Every single time . . .

Ware was continuing, even as she was beginning to see the whole of the pattern. "I cannot accept what you have offered here and now, don't you see? It would be very difficult to explain the sudden appearance of a woman and the sudden disappearance of Ware. Even if I dematerialized and traveled with you in that state, it still would not explain the absence of Ware." He leaned forward, and took both her hands in his. "This is a great secret, Xylina. Not even the Queen is aware of our double nature. I am trusting you with it, and I am about to trust you with more. Another secret which only the demons know—each demon and two others."

Two others. Of course. That long-ago lover he spoke of, and the male lover he did not mention.

"The man whom I choose must be utterly faithful—as you must, Xylina. There is a terrible price to be paid if either of you is not, and the one who pays it is myself." He stared deeply into her eyes, and his had gone as dark as the black night outside. "If either of you is unfaithful to me, I will perish. It is that simple. I am immortal—unless and until I am betrayed in love. That is one reason why you made me fall in love with you, Xylina. Your honor is a part of you. It *is* you; I think that you would rather die than break it. I can trust you with my life—and if we share this bond, I will be doing just that."

She nodded, slowly. This was the most dangerous secret that anyone had ever trusted to her.

"The Queen does not know this about our nature either," he added. "If she did—"

"It would be a terrible weapon to hold over you, and one I won't give her," Xylina told him fiercely. "No matter what happens between us, she will never know this."

His eyes warmed, just the slightest bit. "I know, for I know you. There is only one other recently. . . ." His eyes grew thoughtful for a moment, then he shook his head. "Never mind. It does not matter. Xylina, I honor your offer as I honor you, and I will ask you for no commitment. You must make your decision in full knowledge of all that it will mean, because a casual fling will destroy far more than just our relationship."

She swallowed with difficulty. "I can see that," she said awkwardly.

A heavy silence lay between them. "I had intended to tell you this long before you came to this point," he said at last, with a shy and painful smile. "I had honestly thought I would be able to tell when you were attracted to me. Evidently I am not as good at reading you as I had thought I was."

She hid her confusion by rebraiding her hair, concentrating all her attention on that homely task. "I take it that this is the same quandary you came to when you first discovered your—true nature."

She heard him sigh, but kept her attention centered on the thick strands of hair in her hands.

"In a word, yes," he said finally. "And I was fortunate, in the end, because my lover had a friend that she loved as dearly as a brother—and only as a brother—who was attracted as deeply to me in my female form as she was in my male form. And the fates were kind to all of us. If Faro were—perhaps as he must have been before he was sent to the arena—" He sighed again. "Or perhaps not. I call myself 'Wara' in my female shape, and the person that Wara loves must be as unique and special as the person Ware loves—and Faro is simply too filled with hate and bitterness toward women for him to love any woman, and Wara must be *loved*, Xylina."

She nodded; her mind understood. Perhaps at some point, her heart might, too.

"And there is an added complication." He coughed with that inflection that she now knew was embarrassment, and Xylina looked up from her task. "Again, there is no delicate way to put this. A demon is, in and of itself, sterile. But—" He reddened, and she felt her eyes widen in surprise, for never had she seen him *flush* with embarrassment before. This must be something very hard for him to say. "But—once we found—this man—you would be likely to bear children. For what he—gave to me—I would in turn be giving to you. And that is another reason why Faro is—not suitable. I do not think that you would care to bear his children."

It took her a moment to put *that* together as well, but when she did, she flushed even redder than he, and looked away from him in confusion. He rose.

"I think perhaps it is time for me to go," he said, hurriedly. "Good night, Xylina. I—please think on all these things, and take your time. This decision is one that should not be made until you are very, very certain of how you feel."

He did not even leave by the door; he dematerialized and wafted through the wall, as if to emphasize how very inhuman he was. Human considerations simply would not apply to him.

She sat staring into her little fire, braiding and unbraiding her hair. Her mind was in turmoil; her emotions

so confused that she could not even begin to untangle
them. She did not think that there was any way that she
would get any sleep this night.

It was just as well that this day's journey had left her so
physically exhausted—for in the end, her body decided for
her. She did not even remember falling asleep—until she
woke the next morning, her half-braided hair still in her
hands.

Her gold, which she had proffered—and which had not
been accepted. Not quite.

• Chapter 16

Xylina wrestled with her thoughts and her doubts all the next day, and the day after. Ware did not approach her once in all that time, except in Faro's company. In that, he showed extraordinary sensitivity, for she was able to keep up a calm front with him when there were others present, but she might not have been able to do so had he approached her alone. The men did not seem to notice her preoccupation, or if they did, perhaps they put it down to the fact that she was tired from purely physical exertion. Pattée, too, found the walking fatiguing, so that it was easy for the men to dismiss Xylina's distraction as that. It helped that the terrain they crossed required little in the way of thought, and that the men had no real need of leadership at the moment, for all her attention was focused inward.

No one spoke to her unless it was absolutely necessary, a precaution urged by Ware, who feared that voices would carry for some distance out on these plains. She could have been completely alone, out in the sea of grass, and the "solitude" helped her concentration. Nothing threatened them, and there was nothing much to distract her, so she was able to examine everything as dispassionately as was possible under the circumstances. And although it was difficult to set her emotions aside and try to consider every aspect to the situation, she had long practice in reducing a problem to its component parts and dealing with them one at a time. That discipline helped her here, as well.

So much time for concentration enabled her to set her thoughts and strengthen her resolve before she approached

Ware a second time. She made certain that she had weighed all her options, and there were many. She did not want him to be able to say that she had not considered every possible aspect and complication before she decided on a course of action.

For after all, whatever decision she made, it would be for life.

One possibility was simply to go on as before. She might even be able to say with complete justification that her debt had been discharged; she had, after all, offered Ware what he wanted. That he had not accepted had no real bearing on the situation as read that way. She could be considered legally free of the debt, since he had not immediately accepted her offer—although she would not herself, in all honor, consider herself free. Still, there were those who *would.*

But the fact was that she could pretend that none of this had happened—that she had not even made her offer. She could complete this quest and discharge her debt with true gold, just as she had always planned. And she would be free of him, and of this disturbing emotion of love.

Well, no. She would never really be free of it. She would always want him, and knowing that he wanted her would be sheerest torture. She could never really spend the rest of her life alone. Not now.

The next alternative was to wait, as he said, until they got back to Mazonia and he could hunt for a suitable male. If they waited until they returned home, and together they could scour the slave-markets, looking for someone with a compatible personality. . . .

But that did not seem practical. It *did* seem very, very cold-blooded; as if they were looking for a pet dog, or a nice goose to roast. So what else was there?

He had made some hints, once or twice, that there might be a man he had already considered for such a—liaison. Perhaps he did not realize that he had let such a thing slip, but Xylina had heard the tone of his voice, and she had a shrewd notion what it meant. After all, although Ware was male, he must have had a great deal of experience in knowing what "Wara" would find attractive; really, in many ways, these things would be the same for either of his aspects, incubus or succubus. In some ways he might *always* be looking for potential mates, on the chance that he would be able to find a matching pair.

And unless she was greatly mistaken, Ware had said that he not only was born in this region, but that he continued to visit. Putting two and two together was no great feat . . . the man surely existed, and must be alive and living in this very realm.

And that was what finally decided her. As Ware was no doubt already aware, the chance of finding a "matching male" for Xylina was very slim. The chances of finding two such were much smaller. Why take a chance that there *might* be another of sufficient intelligence and independence?

She decided at that moment that if such a man already existed, Ware must go to see if he could persuade that man to join them. Or rather—Wara must. That night, she made some pretense of bringing him something as he stood his watch, and once they were out of earshot of the other men, she put her proposal to him. Or rather, her supposition that this mysterious "perfect" male existed and was in this very realm.

She walked alongside him under the stars, keeping her voice pitched low so that it would not carry. The night air was cool, and insects sang in the grasses all around them. It would be a perfect night to share their love for the first time—if what she had guessed proved to be the truth. "The other night, you kept starting to say something about a—a man for Wara, and stopped before you got very far," she said, feeling her skin turning so hot she was surprised she didn't glow like a fire-coal. Now that she had come to this point, she was rather surprised at how embarrassed she felt about it all. "What was it that you didn't say? Is there a man you were thinking of somewhere out here? In this realm? I know you said before that you were born here and that you visited here fairly often; it seemed to me that if you were here a great deal you might have found this—this man who is a match for your succubus side."

He did not reply for a long moment, but when he did, his voice was full of surprise. "Just when I think that I know all there is about you, Xylina, you amaze me again. I had not thought I had revealed that. Either I am far more transparent than I had thought, or you are more observant. On the whole, I am inclined to think it is the latter."

"Well?" she persisted, now feeling her very ears afire. "Is there such a man? And is he within reasonable distance of us? Would he consent to join us?"

Another long silence, while off in the distance some sort of dog-pack howled at the full moon above them. It was a very mournful sound, and it made the hair on the back of her neck rise.

"Yes, there is someone who might be suitable," he said at last. "I have known him for several years, and he knows what I am, and my dual nature. People in this realm are more familiar with what a demon is, and what their natures are. He is a close friend, or as close a friend as a demon may have and not be a lover. And I think he may have considered this kind of a liaison himself, with me. The last time I saw him, he said something that was half in jest and half in earnest—that while he loved me as a dear male friend, he could love me better as a female friend, and he would not be loathe to do so."

Xylina digested that for a moment. "That sounds promising," she ventured. "In fact, that sounds better than I had thought. Is he far from here? Could you reach him by foot-travel?"

"Several days' journey and all in the wrong direction," Ware said ruefully. "Although I will grant you that I can probably dematerialize and steal some kind of mount before I have to go too far afoot. But there are other considerations. For one thing, I have not seen him for over a year. Many things could have changed in his life. He could have changed his mind. He could have found a mortal he loved and married. He could even have died; this is a violent realm, and that is quite likely, in fact. He was not the oldest son, but the oldest might have died, forcing him to consider the family before he considers his own desires."

"But if none of these have happened—what prevents you from offering him what you offered me?" she replied, stiffly. It was very difficult for her even to say the words, yet she did not want Ware to know that. She did not want to share him. She knew that. But if sharing him was the only way she could have him, then she would.

"Nothing," Ware admitted. "Nothing. Only . . ."

"Then go and *find* him, Ware!" she said, keeping herself from shouting by an act of great self-discipline. "Go and find him and bring him back here! Why should we wait forever to find a male, when there is one that you already want right here? That makes no sense at all!"

"I will have to first love you," he warned. "I will have to make the change, then go to him in female form, or he might not believe the offer is genuine. It will take time— even if I dematerialize, I cannot fly, I must move as any ordinary being can, even if I can steal a mount—it would still be better to wait until we have returned home, and we can look in the slave markets together. Such a male would be subservient to you, and a male from this realm never would be. You might not find him to your liking, even though he is to mine."

But now she burned with a deeper emotion than embarrassment. "No," she said firmly. "I may die tomorrow—or the next day, or on the way back. Perhaps you are immortal, but I am not, and I do not wish to waste a single hour. And I *do* wish to have your love before another hour is over! Share love with me now, and go and find this man of yours—"

"Thesius," Ware interjected. "His name is Thesius. And he is very, very like you." He smiled. "Just as stubborn and willful."

"This *Thesius* of yours, then." She raised her head and

looked at him, challengingly. If he was going to call her "stubborn" and "willful," he was going to find out just *how* stubborn she really was! "If *you* have not changed your mind, then I will be in my tent. And Faro will not be there; I will send him elsewhere, so you need not fear betraying our secret even to him."

Without waiting for a reply, she turned and walked back to her tent, her back stiff, and her neck aching with the tension she tried not to show. He said nothing; she reached the circle of the camp and eventually the door of her tent without knowing whether he would come to her.

But she unbraided her hair, conjured jasmine scent and soft, silken sheets, and waited for him by the light of a single glowstone, aching with need and anticipation. She felt as tight as a bowstring, and jumped at every little sound, thinking that he had come. Half the time she burned for him, certain that he was going to arrive at any moment, and half the time she was quite sure that he was not going to come at all.

But in the end, he appeared with no sound whatsoever, materializing just as he had in her tiny office so many months ago. He was simply there, standing beside her bed of soft pillowy shapes and silken sheets, staring down at her with his own need naked in his eyes. Very discreet of him, she thought absently. And then, as he sank down beside her, there was no room for thought at all.

Xylina woke as the sun peeked over the horizon, and the first birds began to sing out in the grasslands. The red light of dawn was not what woke her; it was the stirring of the body in the bed beside her. But as was her habit since beginning this quest, she woke instantly, and so he—no, *she*—was not able to slip out without her knowing. In fact, *she* had not even awakened when Xylina herself woke.

Her eyes widened with amazement, as the lovely eyes opened and looked deeply into hers from beneath a tangled tumble of shoulder-length black hair.

"So," said a gentle, husky soprano voice, a voice with just a hint of chagrin in it, "you have caught me in my other guise. I had not intended for you to see this just yet."

It was quite obvious why Ware had not even bothered to mention the possibility of assuming a masculine disguise when discussing how his alternate form must vanish. Tales of women posing as men to infiltrate the enemy were legion among the Mazonites, but this woman could never pull such a ruse off with any kind of success—not unless the men in question were blind and never touched her. There would be no way in which Wara could be disguised as a man. She was, in every way, a dark, exotic copy of Xylina; full-breasted, small-waisted, with long, slender legs, a sinuous curve of spine and hip, and a graceful neck that could bring only the adjective "swan-like" to mind. If Xylina had not known that this was Ware, she would never have guessed it—although she would have assumed that Wara was some kind of relative. If demons had relatives. The eyes remained the same, the strange, wine-red eyes with their golden flecks—looking at her with wry amusement from a feminized version of Ware's face. But no amount of binding or padding was going to make the succubus look like Ware.

"So I see," Xylina replied, and chuckled a little, despite her disappointment at discovering that some miracle had not saved them from their plight. "You are really quite pretty as a girl. Although the Mazonites would *not* approve of the way you look, I fear."

"No more than they approve of you, Xylina," Wara said, tossing her hair back, and smiling. "You and I could have been born sisters; we are certainly a match in looks." She laughed as if at some secret joke, and then let Xylina in on it. "If circumstances were different, and we were not in such haste—or if you were not the woman I love, but some friend—I could wish that you and I could stay this way for at least a little time. We could cut quite a figure among the swains of the Lgondian city-state, for instance." Her eyes twinkled with flirtatious amusement. "It would be great sport, and a kind I think you might enjoy, once you got used to it. In fact, we would, between the two of us, break every male heart in the city."

"Well I, for one, am glad we are not going to remain in this awkward set of circumstances," Xylina replied with a touch of acidity. "After last night, and sharing my bed with you, I have to say that I prefer to see Wara as *little* as possible!"

Wara tossed her head back and laughed throatily, and Xylina found herself oddly liking the demon all the more for being *female*. It was, as Wara had said, rather like having an unexpected sister—she had sometimes wished for such a sister, in the long-gone days of her childhood. Wara was as attractive in her own way as Ware was. In fact, she could not imagine how any mere male could resist the succubus.

But she would rather have Ware, she thought stubbornly. No matter how attractive Wara was, she wanted and needed Ware. And the sooner he returned, the better pleased she would be.

"I can understand that completely," Wara replied, "and I sympathize. So, I suspect that I had better go, before you either murder me with impatience, or Faro comes to see who is whispering to you in your tent."

Xylina nodded, and impulsively leaned over to kiss Wara. "Return to me quickly," she said, blushing.

Wara nodded, then winked. "And *male*," she said, before she faded out.

And once again, Xylina was alone.

She told the others that Ware was scouting ahead; she was not certain that they believed her when she made up some tale about his going in dematerialized form to try to find some kind of help for them among people he knew here, but they seemed to accept his absence as unquestioningly as they had his presence, and that was all that mattered. So long as no one suspected what had really happened, it did not matter what the men thought of Ware's absence. Even if they suspected that he had deserted, his return would eventually disabuse them of that notion.

She felt horribly alone and uncertain once he was gone, although she did her best not to show it. For the first time she was without Ware's advice, and she had not realized until that moment how much she had come to depend on that advice. It was something she was going to have to adapt to, and quickly.

But more, much more than she had come to depend on his advice, she realized she had come to depend on his company. That was far harder to adapt to. The men were useless when it came to conversation; they might well be very intelligent and have varied interests, but they clearly felt inhibited in her presence. Faro was no substitute, for his conversation was limited when it came to discussing anything having to do with the Mazonites. He hated them so much that there was nothing he could find that was admirable about them.

And that was a pity, for although the Mazonites had many faults, they also had many virtues, particularly when it came to martial matters. Ware had been able to advise her on how best to handle the men—who were, after all, trained in the Mazonite-army way of doing things when it came to any kind of organized defenses and moving in hostile territory. As one of the men had once said, dryly, there were three ways of doing things: "the right way, the wrong way, and the army way." When Ware had advised her to deviate from the things that were ingrained in their thinking, he had also been able to give her the best way to explain the situation to them in terms that they would understand and agree with. Faro, who had not had Mazonite military training at all, could not. His training had been for the arena, a rather different matter. Arena fighters were always single, trusting no one. She had found that, on the whole, it was better to explain things to the men and then give them their orders; it made it seem as if she was being something other than arbitrary. Perhaps that would not have worked in the army, but this was not the army, and she was not a trained commander.

Still, she managed to muddle through, finding ways to explain why they were camping in low areas rather than on the high ground, and why it was best for the scouts to keep below the level of the grass when checking over the top of a ridge. She made some mistakes—but they managed to pass an entire week, and come out of the grasslands into more wooded country.

They also managed to avoid some obvious trouble— three separate sets of armed men, all looking for something. Xylina did not want to take the chance that these hunters might be hunting for her and her men.

They were all strange in one way or another. One of the sets was mounted on horses, one on bizarre lizard-like creatures, and one set of men rode on wheeled carts that propelled themselves across the grasslands by some kind of magic. It was the third set she feared the most, for she could not tell what kind of weapons they bore—they carried things that might have been crossbows and spears, but were of no make she recognized. Perhaps only Ware would have known what such weaponry could do, but she was not going to find out the hard way.

Her nights were tortured, filled with longing; her body ached with needs newly-discovered. And deep in the lonely darkness, she found herself wondering if Ware was ever going to return. Perhaps he had deserted. Perhaps this Thesius had found a mate—and had offered Ware a place in that household. Perhaps he had found a woman among Thesius's people who suited him better than Xylina. After all, his first mate had been from these folk.

Finally they made their first camp under cover of trees. And it was there that Ware found them.

She was tending to the dinner, under the direction of Horn, when she heard the sentry challenge someone and heard a longed-for, heartbreakingly familiar voice

answering. She managed to keep from revealing everything that had happened between them by *not*
impulsively jumping to her feet and flinging herself at
him. That would have been incredibly stupid as well as
obvious. Just at the moment, although she didn't particularly care that the Queen might find out about all
this, she had another consideration. This was something
that had occurred to her in one of the few moments that
she was certain Ware would return. If the men discovered that she was a demon-lover, they might refuse to
follow her. That would not only doom the expedition, it
would doom her as well, unless this Thesius, if Ware
returned with him, could be persuaded to bring her to
his people.

So she waited until Horn's exclamation of greeting told
her that Ware was in sight before looking up with a smile
she hoped would not be read too clearly by any of the men.
It was a smile of welcome, warm and happy, but not too
warm, and not too promising. Ware and his escort came
threading their way out of the shadows beneath the trees,
and into the circle of light from the fire.

Ware looked—as he always looked, with the sole exception that he was dressed in better clothing than he had worn
since the mage-storm. Even at the worst of times, he had
never seemed tired or stressed for very long. But there was
one surprise. He was leading a string of seven horses, each
of them with a pack up behind the saddle. Beside him was
another man, a stranger, who led seven more. Was this—?

"Xylina, this is my old friend Thesius," Ware said carefully. Carefully enough that she knew, instantly, that she was
expected to read between the lines. "Everything was *exactly* as I had hoped, and he agreed to help us, and to come
with us to guide us, all the way home if need be."

The man moved further into the light—and Xylina bit
her lip. He was nothing like a Mazonite male. Now she realized why Ware had thought she might have trouble with
that particular concept. There was nothing subservient

about him; he gazed at her directly and proudly, exactly as another Mazonite would have, and she knew that he was going to judge her as a peer, and not as a mistress.

She stood up, slowly, very conscious of the fact that her hair was coming undone, that she was sweaty from the long walk and had not had a chance to bathe, that her nails had dirt under them, and that there was soot on the side of her nose from the fire. The stranger was more than immaculately well-groomed and impeccably, though strangely, attired—he was physically perfect.

He was as blond as she, with large, gray eyes, a chiseled face, and a slender but muscular build, like that of a dancer or runner. From his clothing and the jewels on the hilt of his sword and ornamenting his collar, he was wealthy as well. He watched her, measuringly, and she flushed. Her automatic reaction, which she stifled, was to punish him for insolence. Never in her life had a mere man looked at her that way. But this was no "mere" man, it was a free man, and therein lay the difference. Not a freedman; that was another distinction that had suddenly become critical. This was something she was going to have to keep in mind.

She pulled herself up to her full height, and looked him straight in the eye. "I am the leader of this expedition," she said proudly, matching him glance for glance. "Thank you for agreeing to help us."

He replied in some unknown tongue; Ware translated for both of them. "Thesius says to tell you that he was pleased to be able to aid his old friend in whatever way possible."

I can well imagine, she thought, unable to suppress a twinge of jealousy. Obviously, they had already shared love, since Ware was *Ware,* and not *Wara.* It occurred to her also that this Thesius could pass for her very own brother; they shared the same hair-color, the same body-type, and given Ware's exacting standards, he was probably well-spoken and well-educated. He might even be of some kind of noble birth.

Had Ware chosen her because she looked like Thesius? she wondered. Was he amused by the fact that they could be siblings? Was it really Thesius he had wanted all along, and was she only the means to get this man?

"We don't have a great deal, as I am sure Ware has told you," she said, trying to cover her uncomfortable thoughts as well as she could. "The mage-storm destroyed most of our supplies, but you are welcome to share our poor meal."

Ware translated, and again the man spoke. "He is simply saying what I was going to tell you," Ware said. "That he has brought mounts and supplies for us, and that he thanks you for your ready hospitality. He also—ah—says that he brought some gifts especially for you, clothing and things, and that if you would like to make use of them . . . " Ware's voice trailed off, somewhat embarrassed. "He's trying to be kind, Xylina. He is not intending to insult you, but you do look as if—"

"As if I've been walking across the hills for several days without a bath or a change of clothing; thank you, Ware, I was quite aware of that," she replied sharply, then took a deep breath and softened her tone, although she could not bring herself to apologize. "Tell him that I appreciate his generosity and that I would be *very* glad to get out of these things and into something clean."

The man smiled when Ware translated, and Ware dropped his eyes, though from embarrassment or amusement, Xylina could not say. "Thesius says that your things are on the last horse in his string, and that someone of my age and experience should have found a more graceful way of telling you of his gifts."

"You can tell him that I agree!" she snapped, considerably irritated now as well as embarrassed—but she also went straight to the indicated horse and availed herself of the clean clothing she found in its pack. It was not, as she had feared, a completely impractical dress—some kind of fancy, long-skirted robe unsuitable for travel or fighting. It was, in fact, a slightly feminized version of the trousers and shirt that Thesius himself wore, right down to the jeweled collar-studs.

Now they really would look like brother and sister, she thought, with dismay. But she took the clothing anyway, and leaving Horn in charge of the meal, went off to conjure herself soap and water to make herself presentable.

When she returned, the others had already started the meal without her. To her continued chagrin, Thesius fit comfortably in with the rest of the men, despite a lack of common language. When she rejoined them, taking her place as unobtrusively as possible, she could not help but notice an exchange of glances between Ware and Thesius, glances that said more than words. And although she put on a cheerful face, her resentment—and yes, jealousy— smoldered just below the surface.

That resentment and jealousy did not abate as they drew nearer their goal, aided considerably by the horses that Thesius had brought with him. Whenever she looked at Thesius, instead of remembering what she and Ware had shared the night before, she kept recalling that Wara had risen immediately from *her* bed and gone to *him*. She kept wondering how much Ware cared for *her*, and how much he cared because she looked like Thesius. She knew that he had to do it, because Wara could not afford to show her face by day, but her emotion refused to be reconciled. Whenever he left her bed, she tortured herself with doubts; whenever he came back she felt guilty about doubting him. She tried to drown both emotions in passion, and did not succeed. One night, after persuading him to return when he had made the change back to male, she sent him shuttling back and forth for half the night—and it did not help that Thesius seemed perfectly capable of keeping up with her in this undeclared contest.

Faro had it all figured out, of course, and one of the few things helping her to keep a civil "public" face on all of this was his tacit protection of all three of them from discovery. When she asked him how he had known, he simply shrugged; she could only assume that Ware must have told him about the changing—and that in itself was a cause for resentment, since Ware seemed to be trusting *everyone* with this "secret nature" of his, and yet he had not trusted her until she forced the revelation out of him.

Things could not have gone on in this way much longer—but the fates had some other surprise in store for them: one that made such trivialities superfluous.

The woodlands gave way to a flat country, hot and humid, covered with scrub plants and bordered on one side by a salt sea of some kind with a flat, soft sand beach. There was not a great deal of shade, and all the vegetation was bent in a perpetual slant away from the coast. Xylina did not like the look of this country; aside from the fact that it was the most boring place she'd yet seen, it was too open, and there were no good places for defense. There weren't even hills to vary the countryside, they were plagued by swarms of biting insects which made the horses miserable, and the sticky heat made all of them irritable.

The insects were particularly hard on the horses, and nothing seemed to keep them off. Xylina tried to conjure repulsive oil, but it repulsed the horses more than the flies. As a result, they were paying more attention to their restive mounts and the fetid heat than to keeping quiet and to "blending" with their surroundings—and that was when an entirely new enemy struck.

A huge metallic-black creature, droning like some kind of giant insect, swooped down out of the sun straight at their column. As the thing plunged down to within a wagon's length of Xylina, she saw that it had a rider that was guiding its motions. It actually did them no harm—

But it spooked the horses, who began to rear and shy, their eyes rolling wildly.

The men and Pattée were unused to riding, and lost all

control of the beasts. The monster rose into the sky again, turned, and came back for a second pass. That was when the horses panicked completely, and bolted, bucking and kicking.

Xylina, Faro, Ware, and Thesius managed to keep their horses running in the same direction, but the same was not true of the rest. Most of the men were thrown immediately; some clung to the backs of animals that ran blindly for whatever direction the monster was *not*.

Xylina clung to the reins and saddle of her horse, trying, not to stop it, but to keep it going in the same direction as Ware's—and fortunately, Faro was doing the same. She looked back over her shoulder just once—and that was when she realized that the best thing she could do would be to *keep* her frightened animal running.

For the monster in the air was herding those horses that still had men riding them; herding them towards the beach, where they would quickly tire, trying to gallop in the surf and soft sand. And as for the men who had been thrown— there were strangers dressed in brown uniforms, armed, and helmeted, who were rounding them up and making them prisoners. There were many more of these strangers than there were of Xylina's men, and she realized that the most she could hope for would be to escape without being captured herself.

Thesius looked back as well, and he must have made the same conclusion, for he suddenly began urging his horse to greater speed, and took over the lead from Ware. Since he seemed to know where he was going, Xylina tried to get her horse to follow his. It was quite willing, and she concentrated on clinging to her saddle.

The strangers who were taking the others prisoner did not seem inclined to follow. They disappeared into the distance, and the bushes and scrubby trees intervened.

The horses galloped until their flanks streamed foamy sweat and their breath came in huge, painful gasps. Thesius pulled his horse up to a walk; the rest slowed completely on their own. He spoke quickly and quietly to Ware, pointing in the direction of the mist that signaled a change in realms that lay just on the horizon, and Ware nodded, then turned to Xylina.

"Thesius recognized those soldiers; they are slavers, and they are not likely to follow us this far, for they are only concerned with gathering as many slaves as they can with as little effort as possible. They will be satisfied with the men and horses that they have captured, and let us escape."

Xylina pushed her sodden hair back from her forehead. She was nearly as tired as her poor horse, for it had taken all her strength to stay with him on the wild ride. "I am about to say something that might sound very callous—" she replied, hesitantly. "Are these people known for mistreatment of those they take?"

Ware questioned Thesius, who only shook his head. Xylina sighed. "Then I see no point in risking ourselves to free the men, since they are merely going from one set of mistresses to another."

Faro looked troubled. "You're not going to try to help them?"

She turned to him, hoping that he would understand this. "Faro, I am very sorry, but there are many more of those slave-catchers than there are of us—and I am not certain that my diminished ability to conjure is going to make that much of a difference in a case like this."

Faro shrugged. "Maybe you have a valid point, little mistress. The men might even be better off; who knows? They are certainly used to being enslaved."

Thesius listened avidly as Ware translated all this for him in an undertone, and he nodded vigorously when Faro concluded. He gabbled something else; Ware managed a dry chuckle.

"He said that most of them will likely be recruited to take slaves themselves, since they are versed in the use of arms—or they will become caravan guards for the slave-takers. Even Pattée evidently has skills they will value. So really, their roles are likely to take a reversal for the better, since they will find themselves to be the masters over women taken as slaves."

Xylina gave Thesius a black look for that little remark, but said nothing about it. Instead she asked Ware, "What was that he said when he pointed to the next realm?"

"That this is where the crystal shard is, and that the slavers will not follow us in there." Ware did not elaborate on that, and Xylina wondered if there had been more said than Ware had mentioned.

"Then let us go there as quickly as we can," Xylina said flatly.

Ware gave her a measuring look, and Thesius said something. This time Ware translated without being asked.

"He wants to know if you are certain that you wish to continue."

She gave that question sober consideration, as the sun burned down on them, and the horses plodded onward towards the border. The thought crossed her mind—as it had many times—that the Queen had certainly set herself up in a situation in which Adria could not lose and Xylina could not "win." Ware had told her, many times, that Xylina was the only Mazonite likely to make this mission a success; the Queen wanted this shard desperately, for it was her path, not only to immortality, but to immortal youth and to undefeatable power. If Xylina brought it back, the Queen would have all those things, and Xylina would no longer be any kind of threat.

And if Xylina died in the attempt, she would still be no threat. The Queen simply had to send her out, and wait, like a spider in her web. This mission was a stroke of genius, for the purposes of the Queen.

Even if Xylina turned back at any point, the Queen would win—since Xylina would still owe her debt to Ware, and the crown guarantee of that debt was contingent on Xylina's return *with the shard*. Xylina would face the same threats as before she left—give in to Ware (which would take her out of the running for the throne), go into debtor's prison, or face exile. One of those options had already been fulfilled.

And now, there was really no way in which Xylina could possibly retreat. With all of her men and resources gone but Faro, Ware, and Thesius, it would be suicide to recross all that dangerous territory. It might not even be the same: deadly new lands might have take the place of those they had struggled through. Only one thing would make return possible: if Xylina possessed the shard, for its possession would magnify her own powers.

So, hopeless as the situation looked, she might as well go on. It was certainly no more hopeless than going back.

"Yes," she said flatly. "Let us go on."

As they crossed the misty border, the land changed abruptly, as it nearly always did. This time the sea remained, but instead of a land as flat as the back of her hand, hot, and oppressively humid, the countryside became mountainous, washed with a brisk, cool breeze, and with high cliffs facing the sea. The drop in temperature and humidity made her spirits rise, and the clouds of stinging flies that had bitten them and their horses with blithe impartiality deserted them. The tired horses raised their heads, and exhibited a little more energy. Faro looked less dour. Even the air, scented with pine, seemed livelier.

The horses were on another road: this time, a kind of well-defined track through the mountains. By the time they were ready to stop for the night, Ware looked about and told her that they were within striking distance of the shard—for once again, a realm had changed since a member of their party had last visited it. This time, the border between the realms had moved closer to the area where the shard was being kept.

Thesius located a cave for them to use as a shelter, rather than having Xylina conjure tents. He and Ware both seemed anxious that she not perform her conjurations so near the shard, and she was inclined to go along with that. It might well be that the inhabitants of this realm had some way of knowing when magic was being practiced, and there was no point in warning them. She hoped that prohibition would not be needed when actually taking the shard, or she would be in serious trouble.

All of them retained some of their journey-food; Xylina had suggested that they divide it up among all the men rather than keeping it together with Horn, and now she was glad she had done so. If Horn had kept the food, they would now be spending a very hungry night.

So they built a conventional fire, with wood that Faro and Thesius gathered, and settled down to eat and confer. A vent at the back of the cave drew off the smoke from their fire, and the cave screened it from outside eyes, so they were relatively safe and quite cozy.

"Now," Ware said, after their initial hunger-pangs had been satisfied. "Here is what I know. The people who guard the crystal are quite well aware of its nature, and they also know that eventually the Mazonites will desire it. They are determined to guard it, for they fear correctly that possession of the shard will make the Mazonites more powerful. They fear that if your Queen has it, she will use its powers to enlarge the borders of Mazonia, by extending the area in which the magics that prevail are Mazonite conjuration and those used by demons."

Xylina nodded; Thesius did, too. That made her wonder if the young man understood more of her language than he had let on. Still, that did not matter at the moment—

Except that she was very glad that she had not *said* many of the things that had been on the tip of her tongue. At best, he would have formed a very unflattering opinion of her. At worst, she would have looked like a jealous fool.

"They keep it under heavy guard in a cave—not too surprising, since the folk this realm live in caves, and their philosophy is to make as little mark on the land as may be." Ware shrugged as she gave him an incredulous look. "This is their way; I do not pick quarrels with other folks' philosophies. Here is the problem: I can not take the shard, for it can only be handled by a mortal. Thesius and Faro may not touch it, for it will kill a man—recall that it 'wants' to be taken to the great crystal in Mazonia, and the only way for it to get there is to be taken by a woman."

Xylina nodded. "I remember that. So this magic has a kind of intelligence. Well, that means that I am the only person who can actually retrieve it. But since these people must know this, I would assume that they will be specifically watching for a woman, which will make it very hard for me to approach it."

Ware and Thesius both indicated agreement; Thesius looked pleased. "We can do reconnaissance, though, we men," Faro spoke up from the other side of the fire where he was arranging a pallet made of pine boughs for himself. "As men, we would be under no suspicion."

"That was my thought exactly," Ware said. "Two of us should go—two should remain. Xylina will have to remain, of course—"

"And I will stay with her," Faro replied. But Ware shook his head.

"No, for Thesius has been here before, and they might recognize him," Ware said, by way of explanation. "You are a stranger, and if they recognize me as a demon, they will *know* that I am no threat to the shard. And, to be brutally frank, Faro, you are a much better fighter than Thesius. If there is some kind of incident, you are more likely to be able to fight your way free than Thesius will."

Xylina cast a startled glance at the young man, who grimaced, then shrugged. Apparently this was true.

Now that she thought about it, she realized that she never had seen him use that sword he carried. "If that is the case, then I am afraid Ware is right," she said to Faro. "You are one of the best fighters I have ever seen, and I rather doubt that I am likely to get into any great trouble, hidden away in a cave while you two go off to scout the territory."

Faro flushed with pleasure at her praise. "If that is your will," was all he said, but she felt that he thought she had made the right decision.

"How long will this take?" she asked, assuming that it would be less than a day.

"A week, perhaps a little more," Ware replied with an offhand gesture. "Less than nothing compared to all the time it took to get here."

A week? More? Xylina hid her dismay, since she had already agreed to the plan, but she was considerably less than pleased. A week all alone with this—this man. A week *without* Ware.

On the other hand, if *she* was to be without Ware's company, so was *he*. Suddenly the prospect was not totally without its charms.

"Very well," she said. Then, with a meaningful look at Ware, she added, "In that case, we had best go to bed—and get some rest."

Faro rolled his eyes up heavenward, and Thesius did not—quite—hide a smirk. Ware only sighed.

It was quite a lively night.

As birds first greeted the dawn light, Faro and Ware set off on their journey. Thesius and Xylina watched them go, side by side, yet quite, quite separate. Finally, long after they were out of sight, she turned back into the cave. She was not looking forward to a week spent in this man's company: a *silent* week, since he could not even converse with her.

But then Thesius surprised her. "I have—" he began from behind her, and she whirled to face him, eyes wide with shock. He stood silhouetted against the light for a moment, then came down to the cave floor beside her.

"You can speak my—?" she asked, not completely pleased with this development.

"I have," he said carefully, "been learning. Your tongue, with the help of Wara."

I'll just bet you have, she thought cynically, and yet she could not help but be a little curious about him. After all, they were both Ware's lovers—and they knew nothing about each other. They had both made a lifelong commitment to their beloved, which meant to each other as well. It would be too much—far too much!—to say they were friends; still—

"I suppose we really ought to start talking," she said aloud, with a lifted brow. "Since I am going to have you around for the rest of my life."

He stiffened a little at her slightly imperious tone. "The opposite, I would have said. That I must learn to tolerate you. Not easy, that."

It was her turn to stiffen with resentment. Not easy to tolerate *her?* How dared he?

But the next moment, she realized precisely how he dared. He was not a slave. He was under no rules of behavior. They were complete equals.

And she did not like it at all.

But she was going to have to get used to it.

She sighed and shook her head. "Then we can begin by sharing the chores," she said aloud. "You know this place, and I do not. *You* find things to eat. *I* find wood."

He frowned. "Stronger, I—" he objected.

"You are physically stronger; I am magically stronger," she countered. "Since when does that have anything to do with collecting wood for a fire? There's no point in dragging entire trees in here!"

He looked rebellious, but nodded, grudgingly. She picked up a strap to carry the wood with, and left, without waiting to see what he would do.

When she returned, he was not there—which meant, she supposed, that he must be out looking for edibles or hunting. She made several trips—by now she had a good idea of how much wood a fire could burn over the course of a day and a night, and she was not minded to give him an opportunity to scoff if the wood ran out before daybreak. It was a pity that she could not risk conjuring wood—but it was far better to be safe. At least this was giving her conjuration an extended rest, which was a relief after the extremely heavy use of her magic during their journey.

When she thought she had gathered enough and a little to spare, she paused for a drink of clear water from the stream outside the cave, and to take a rest. She had pushed herself considerably, physically, working much harder at the wood-gathering than she really had needed to.

Because she was, by the fates, going to impress that independent, imperious creature, she realized. Against his will, if she had to! Huh. He would probably return with a handful of inedible mushrooms and a mess of weeds, and think he should be praised.

But when he did come back, shortly after noon, it was with the saddlebags from both their horses bulging at the seams. When he disgorged their contents, she had to admit to being impressed.

He had found edible tree-seeds, a double-handful of hard, tart berries, fresh watercress, some shelf-like fungi that smelled so delicious that her mouth watered, and four fat, ugly roots that he promised—via a few words and pantomime—would be very tasty when roasted in the ashes of the fire. She was almost ashamed to hand him the last of the hard journey-bread for lunch, although he did raise a surprised eyebrow at the amount of wood she had collected.

"Horses now," he said firmly, when they had gnawed their way through the rock-like biscuits. She sighed, but agreed.

They had stabled the horses in the rear of the cave, and that meant that the horses had left what horses always produced. Faro had gone to the trouble of dumping dry leaves and pine needles back there, which at least would make it easier to clean up. But still . . .

"Share horses?" she asked, more than half expecting an argument, and an insistence that she should be the one to do the cleaning. But, with a shrug of resignation, he nodded.

Together they cleaned the stabling area and left more of the bedding material for the horses to stand in. She started to haul the used bedding just out of smelling-range, but he shook his head, and gestured her to follow him. Admittedly curious, she did so—and found that he was dumping it all in another, smaller cave nearby. After a moment of thought, she saw that this made sense; if they threw the used bedding down the cave mouth, it would not be out in the open to attract insects and advertise their presence.

He indicated that he wished to water the horses while she pulled up grass to feed them. And while the former task seemed a great deal easier than the latter—

She didn't know anything about the stupid beasts, she admitted to herself. He did. If they over-gorged themselves on water or tried to drown themselves, she wouldn't know what to do. So she agreed without an argument, which seemed to surprise him.

After that, they had nothing to do except improve their rather primitive beds and cook their dinner. Since he seemed to know what to do about food, she let him deal with the latter while she made up the former with something a bit softer than branches.

But long before true night fell, the tasks ran out and they found themselves facing each other over the fire, with no idea of what to say.

By now, Xylina's initial resentment had become a certain grudging fascination. One thing was sure: Thesius was a handsome young man, and on looks alone, she could see why Ware—Wara—had chosen him. But his actions this day had proven that there was something more there than mere looks, and now she was curious. She knew that the demon would not have chosen an ordinary man, any more than he had chosen an ordinary woman. Appearance was only part of it.

"What are you?" she asked. And at his puzzled frown,

she elaborated. "What do you do in your home? What is your family?"

His expression of confusion faded, and he actually smiled slightly. "My family rulers are," he said—which confirmed her suspicion. He was a prince, or something similar. She nodded, and encouraged him to go on.

By the time they were both tired and ready to sleep, she had learned a hundred times as much about him as she had already known—which, admittedly, was not a great deal. His family was of some kind of nobility or landowners; they were certainly very wealthy, and commanded what must have been a small kingdom of traders. This, of course, was how Ware had come to know him, since the demons were great traders themselves. Thesius was, however, a very junior child—she was a little confused as to how junior, but got the impression that there were more than a dozen siblings ahead of him, and a half-dozen younger than he. As a result, his "share" of the family wealth was fairly small, and his aspirations to power minimal. She gathered that he had welcomed Wara's proposition, because he truly loved Ware as a friend, so it was easy to make that love into something physical for Wara. Also because this would give him an opportunity to escape a stultifying and increasingly boring life at home. The fourteen horses he had brought with him were, in fact, his "dowry." He was used to wealth, but it was not *his* wealth.

She let him know (feeling a little cynical) that if they did make it back to Mazonia, he would not lack for wealth, since Ware was quite rich in his own right. But somewhat to her surprise, he made it quite clear that it did not matter. That he would have been perfectly willing to share a cave with Wara.

She thought that she surprised him a time or two, as he in his turn questioned her. For one thing, he was startled to learn that her origins, at least, were in a family almost as privileged as his own. For another, he was amazed to find out how well educated she was. She got the impression that he had thought she was little better than a peasant, and that Ware had chosen her mainly because she was so physically beautiful and intelligent, though unlettered.

He expressed sympathy, which seemed to be quite genuine, when she revealed that her mother was dead. She expressed envy, which *was* genuine, when he told her about his parents, and that the family was very much like the ideal of Mazonite families, save only that authority and responsibility were shared between father and mother.

By then, they were both exhausted, and ready for sleep; it seemed a positive note to end on, and Xylina, at least, retired to her much-more-comfortable bed feeling as if she might actually be able to live with this man without wanting to kill him once a day.

By the second day, she began to see some of what Ware saw in the man; by the third, she had acknowledged that their similarities went more than skin-deep. They were not only similar in looks and intelligence, they were similar in status and attitude. By the time she went to sleep on the night of the third day, she and Thesius were friends.

So things remained on the succeeding days; Thesius' command of the Mazonite tongue improved out of all recognition, and she actually began to learn his odd language. That opened the way to further communications, and she picked up something about his land as she taught him about Mazonia. Both of them assumed that Mazonia would be the end of their journey; it was, after all, Ware's home. It made sense to go there, rather than somewhere else.

She could certainly see why Thesius had been so eager to leave his home. The passions that drove his family, for increased trade and increased territory, were things she had seen in successful Mazonites and had never understood. And the customs! The Mazonites had at least one positive thing going for them, even Thesius agreed: they tried to keep pomp and senseless, ancient customs to a minimum. But Thesius' people made a fetish of ceremony.

He had confessed to a feeling of profound relief when he rode out of the tiny kingdom of Copera, and she could not blame him. Every moment of his time had been hedged about with some custom or other—most of which had no real meaning any more.

When he woke, he must immediately rise and go to the window to recite a child's rhyme to the rising sun. Then he would be given a "breakfast" consisting of a single slice of bread, a spoonful of jam, and a sprig of herb. He must fold the bread in half, crosswise, and eat it from one of the two longer points, then take the herb sprig and leave it precisely in the middle of the plate. Then recite yet another verse.

For every action of the day, there was a verse. For putting on clothing, for taking it off. For eating and for drinking. For greeting and departing. For seeing sunny weather or clouds. Food must be eaten in a certain order, clothing donned in a certain order, the body bathed in a certain order. Floors must always be swept from right to left. And so on, until the verses of retirement and sleep.

The customs of the court were even worse.

"I could never live there," she declared. He nodded in complete agreement.

"We are more slaves to our customs than you women have ever made your men," he replied, and she had to agree with him.

Finally, she made him a pledge: one that she had never expected to make to any man. That there would be neither mistress nor slave within the walls of their home. They would have to play the game for the sake of peace outside those walls, but it would be a game. And never, outside those walls, would she use the game to hurt or humiliate *any* man, much less the men that she knew and cared for.

She had changed; she knew that now. Men had never

been faceless automata to her, but now she could see them as human and as equal as she herself was. She would never be able to go back to thinking of them as something less.

But then, something unexpected happened. From understanding why Thesius was desirable to Wara, she progressed until she became attracted to him.

Then she found him more than merely attractive. Of course she concealed her feeling, knowing it to be illicit. But it tormented her at night, in much the way her longing for Ware had, before she had finally capitulated.

The week passed, and still Ware and Faro did not return. A week and a day. The attraction was stronger than ever. She found herself watching him covertly, thinking about that dancer's body. Wondering if he was as skilled in using that body as Ware was. She caught herself getting careless when it was her turn to wash, taking longer than she should, so that he might return on schedule and catch an accidental glimpse of her torso. Would she impress him as much as Wara had? She condemned herself, for she had never been a tease, but in the boredom her fancy ran rampant.

She found herself facing another question: what if Ware and Faro had been captured or killed? What if she and Thesius were on their own?

As the days stretched on, coming nearer to two weeks than one, she finally voiced that fear.

And Thesius was forced to admit that he, too, had been thinking of just that, and suffering shameful feelings. And she caught him watching her, covertly, with speculation in his eyes.

What had been a long, anxiety-filled day became worse. Just about sunset, the weather turned. A high, cold wind came up, bringing with it clouds and rain. By the time the last light had left the sky, the rain had turned to sleet—and their clothing and few blankets were totally inadequate.

They layered on item after item, and still the cold

penetrated to make them shiver, The wind kept stealing the heat from the fire, blowing straight into the cave and carrying the heat away through the vent that had been taking the smoke. They sat across from one another, shivering miserably, as the bitter cold penetrated into their bones.

She wanted to conjure warm blankets, but Thesius was clearly terrified that this would pinpoint their location to the enemy. "They always watch near the border," he said. "*Always.*" So she shivered until she began to feel sick.

Finally Thesius looked across the fire into her eyes, and gestured. "There is no point in this," he said. "If we are together, we may as well share these blankets and the heat of our bodies, such as it is."

That made perfect sense, and at that moment, all she could think of was the prospect of getting warm. The very memory of warmth felt years away. She made her way around the fire, and joined him, adding her coverings to his, and clasping her body against his.

The difference was immediate. Warmth pooled between them; she relaxed and closed her eyes, feeling it ease the aches and tension from the cold.

For a long, long time, all she was aware of was the warmth, the blessed, blessed warmth. But then Thesius's arms tightened involuntarily around her, and she was aware of a different kind of warmth entirely. They were clothed, but that could so readily change. They were already so close, and there was such heat between them.

Her eyes flew open, and met his. There was no mistaking the need, and the passion, in his face.

It would be so easy . . . so very easy. They shared so much, had so much in common—

"Maybe—just one kiss," she whispered.

"That couldn't do any harm," he agreed huskily.

Their faces slowly came together. They were so similar, in their backgrounds and their passion.

And they were both human. Ware would not even be able to protest, for Ware would be no more. . . .

It was that which brought her to her senses, and she saw that he must have remembered the same thing at the same moment. Their lips, almost touching, halted. She shook her head, gently, and he nodded. They both knew that if the kiss did not destroy the demon, what would surely follow it would.

They remained chastely cradled in each other's arms for the rest of the night, sharing no more than physical warmth. Finally, after a long, long, time, the wind died, and they slept.

Xylina dreamed she was Wara, clasping Thesius and exciting him to such a pitch of excitement that all of his willpower was crushed by his need. But even in her dream she had caution, and she woke—to find him waking similarly. "I thought you were—" he said, agonized, shuddering.

"I know." She turned her face away and pretended to ignore the desire she knew he suffered. Only in that manner could she suppress her own.

In the morning neither of them spoke about their near-catastrophe, but it was on Xylina's mind and she knew it must be on Thesius's. The air was still brisk and chill, but Xylina generated her warmth with exercise. That exercise also took some of the edge off her desire, although it did not remove it. Only the knowledge of how nearly they had murdered Ware did that.

While she was hauling in more firewood, she heard a hail, and looked up to see Ware and Faro—at last!—approaching up the trail to their cave. They looked tired, but satisfied.

Thesius was nowhere in sight, and Xylina did not want to wait for him. She dropped her firewood and ran, as fast as she could, all the way down the trail to the two returning explorers.

Ware dismounted, giving his horse's reins to Faro, and met her embrace with one of his own, caressing her comfortingly, as if he understood all her conflicting emotions. She did not weep, but she was very near tears.

"Come," he said gently, after a long, long time. "We were not gone all that long—"

"Oh, Ware," Xylina cried, half in laughter, and half in hysteria, "you will never know how glad I am to see you! It has been—the fear, the cold—"

She could not continue, but he seemed to understand everything she could not say.

"But you were true to me, both of you," he whispered comfortingly in her ear, "because otherwise I would not be here."

She could not tell him that this was exactly what she meant, but when she finally pulled away a little and looked into his eyes, she saw that he already knew.

He had known the risk he was taking, and he had trusted them both: trusted their honor, and their strength of spirit. Trusted them more than they had trusted themselves.

Chapter 17

That night, the three of them shared a sleeping-place, with Ware between the two humans. And oddly, now that the temptation had been weathered, Xylina found that she no longer desired Thesius—and when he glanced at her, she no longer saw that mirroring desire in his face. He felt, instead, like the brother he resembled, and for the first time in her life, she felt complete—for now she had everything, a friend in Faro, a brother in Thesius, and a beloved in the form of Ware.

For the first time, she made love to Ware with Thesius lying naked beside them. When she finished, she lay without jealousy as Wara made love to Thesius. She had accepted the new reality, though it was alien to anything she could have believed before this excursion. She didn't even feel guilty. This was love of a different kind, but nevertheless love, all the greater for the understanding it required.

Her contentment was short-lived, but only because there was still a task ahead for all of them.

The next morning they saddled all four horses and moved out, leaving everything they no longer needed in the cave. With luck, they would be back for it, but if not, there was nothing there that they could not do without, and the less burden the horses carried the more speed they could make.

Ware had discovered an additional entrance to the shard-cave that the guardians did not consider to be as important as the main entrance. It was above the main entrance in the valley, in an area covered with goat-tracks. It led to a place where water had eaten a way down into the main cavern; a place that actually caused the lower caverns to flood on occasion. Granted, it was a very *small* entrance, and one that the average Mazonite could never squeeze through—but Xylina was small enough that *she* could get in. For once in her life, her small size was going to prove an advantage!

By the time they reached the cave and its guarded environs, their plan was as solid as any plan could be, considering how many variables were involved.

Xylina, Thesius, and Ware lay hidden just outside the valley of the cave. They were near enough to the entrance so that they could reach it quickly, but just outside the guards' usual perimeter. False dawn was just beginning, and the guards were at their most relaxed. No one truly expected an attempt on the shard in broad daylight, so the guards on the day-watch were not particularly alert. In fact, they often played at games of chance to wile away the hours—and that figured very largely in the plan.

Faro returned just as the sun crept above the horizon, a bundle of fabric under his arm. He passed it silently to Ware, who quickly donned it. It was one of the crystal-guards' uniforms; Xylina did not ask Faro how he had obtained one, and from whom. She was just grateful that there was no blood on it.

Even though Xylina would be entering the cave by a different route, someone would need to distract the guards at the main entrance, in case they heard a noise in the cave and became alarmed. Since Ware could not be harmed by any weapon, he was the logical choice for the role of "distraction." He would pretend to be a new guard, and would introduce the other guards to an entirely new game of chance, a very noisy one, and one that was both exciting and required a great deal of concentration. Faro had learned this game from the Pacha, and he had tutored the demon in it at every possible halt until Ware was as expert as any non-Pacha could be. To give him an initial stake for the game—and to whet the guards' appetite for it—Xylina had taken the risk of conjuring a small pouch of silver and gold nuggets. Ware would soon lose many of those; greed would make the guards want them all.

Ware fastened up the uniform tunic and tied the pouch to his belt. With a wink, he strode boldly up the valley to the entrance. Now it was time to wait again.

Finally, at mid-morning, excited shouts and cheers echoed up the valley toward their hiding-place. Ware had succeeded in his distraction, and it was time to go.

They slipped up the valley, then climbed the cliff above the main entrance to find the secondary way in. The ascent was not difficult—in fact, there was even a path there. The problem was not access, but the three guards that waited at the tiny slit in the cliff-face that led down to the main cave.

She needed a second distraction, but this one was easier to come by. Faro took one handful of gold nuggets—this time, though, they were dirty, loaded with quartz, and in general, looked very much as if they had just broken off of a larger mass. Xylina took a handful, and Thesius took the third handful. They climbed above the trail to the second entrance, and located the three little goat-tracks Faro and Ware had found. They scattered their nuggets all along these paths, until they reached the point where all three trails met. There, Xylina worked a little more conjuration, creating a false front to the cliff-face of quartz ribboned with veins of gold. It would take men with proper tools several days to chip the gold free—and those men below had no such thing. But she had no doubt they would try.

Then they returned down the goat-trails and concealed themselves in three separate places near and above where the guards would pass.

Xylina waited, as the others were waiting, and as the guard passed below her position, dropped the last of her nuggets so that it bounced down the side of the mountain and onto the trail just in front of the man, as if it had been naturally dislodged at just that moment.

The gold caught the light perfectly, and the guard leaned over to see what it was.

She could not see his face from here, but his whole form stiffened. He snatched up the nugget, and looked around furtively, then looked up.

She could easily see him, but he could not see her through the screening of the gorse bushes. She waited, and shortly she heard him ascending the goat-trail, on a furtive, silent hunt for more nuggets. With luck, the other two would be doing the same. If Faro and Thesius got the opportunity, they would knock the guards out, but only Faro had the skill and strength to carry such a move off without one of them calling a warning. Her plan called for Faro to dispose of his own guard; the other two would then presumably meet at the cliff face, and either quarrel over the gold, or reach some kind of conclusion, and each would greedily try and remove more than his fellow. In either case, there would be no further interference from the guards.

She dropped down to the trail and sought out the entrance to the upper cave.

It was less of an entrance than an exaggerated slit in the rock. Only the fact that Ware had been here before and that it was guarded left her inclined to trust that it led to the lower caves. She squeezed herself inside—literally—with no more space between her face and the rock-face than the thickness of a piece of paper, and rock pressing into her back.

Of all the things she had needed to do, this was the worst. It was dark, darker than the blackest, overcast night. She barely had room to take a breath—in fact, in order to make any progress at all, she had to exhale, inch forward, then stop to take another breath. She was very glad that her tunic was of leather, or she would have been leaving skin behind on the rock-face by now.

Several times she had to stop and fight back panic, telling herself that Ware had already been here, and that the passage did get wider eventually. All she had to do was to go a little further—just a little further—

Suddenly, she broke free of the rocky embrace, and tumbled into a larger chamber. She landed on her hands and knees, and quickly sat down to take several lung-filling, free breaths.

Now she took a chance and conjured a glowstone to light her way. The chamber in which she sat was a small one, but quite spacious compared with the passage.

At the end of the chamber opposite the passageway was a large hole in the floor of the cave. This, Ware had told her, led down to the guard-chamber just outside the one holding the crystal shard itself. It resembled a steep rabbit-hole, but it was large enough to take several people her size, slanting downward when she crawled over to it to look. Ware said that it looked to him as if it had been made by the passage of a great deal of water down that hole over the course of many centuries, water that had since found another outlet. But there were marks in this upper chamber that indicated more recent flooding, and he had learned that from time to time a sudden storm might send water into that passage even these days. That would flood the lower cavern, and the guards would retreat to the valley, waiting for the full day it took the caverns to drain. She saw nothing down below, not even a light; the slanting passage and the distance it had to cross in order to reach the guard-chamber made certain of that. But if she listened, carefully, she could hear the guards talking.

She would have to risk one more conjuration, and hope that no one detected it. So far, no one had; Ware had thought that the shard itself might mask such magic-workings. She hoped he was right. Because this was going to be something more than a few nuggets of gold or silver.

She conjured water.

Floods of it, torrents of it. She sent it rushing down

the passageway to the guard-chamber, filling the entire passageway with her conjured flood, creating a river of water that she sent pouring down on the heads of the unsuspecting guards. Who would, of course, assume that the upper chamber had flooded again, and abandon their posts for the length of time it usually took for the water to drain.

When she thought she had conjured enough water to fill the lower chamber completely, she stopped. Then, steeling herself, she took the glowstone in one hand and edged over to the passageway, sat down on the edge, and pushed off.

She slid, as if the sides had been greased. This was as exciting as the trip through the outer passage had been harrowing. The smooth walls of the water-tunnel slid by her; as Ware had instructed, she put out her feet now and again to brake her speed, but for the most part, she simply thrilled in the feeling of near-flight. As a small child she had slid down mud-slick banks on the family estate; this was to that feeling as her first primitive conjurations were to what she could do now!

Finally, and without warning, the slide ended. She had just enough time to gulp in a breath, before she plunged feet-first into her own conjured water. In a single heartbeat, she was several feet under the surface, glowstone in one hand, the other flailing away at nothing.

In the next moment, she had banished it, and she stood, completely dry, in the midst of the guard-chamber. She was alone.

Now there remained only the crystal.

She was almost disappointed when she spied it. The thing looked just like a piece of glass. But of course that was what it was: a glassy fragment of a much larger crystal. A shard. *The* shard. It was set into a holder in the wall, and she wondered why. But then it occurred to her that the guards would want to see it to know it was still there; if it had been locked into a box, it could have been stolen and no one would know until some later routine check.

Her immediate inclination was to take the crystal from its setting, and flee. But that would set off traps. Surely these people had traps. If she had been guarding this stone, *she* would have set traps!

She did not think that she would be able to conjure a copy of the crystal, either—at least not in time to get it into the holder without setting off the traps. Without a doubt, these people had planned for a Mazonite conjuror to attempt to take the shard, and would have acted accordingly.

Ware had not been able to give her any advice here. He had not been able to get near enough the chamber holding the crystal to see how it was held. The attempt would have caused him harm.

Xylina came close to the wall and stared at the holder, taking a good look at it. How could she remove the shard without setting off traps and alarms? As transparent as the shard was, it was fairly easy to see the rods set into the holder, pressed against the crystal itself. And it was easy to see how the slightest movement of the shard would move the rods. No, these people had planned very carefully for a Mazonite conjuror—

But suddenly she saw her solution, and smiled. For they had planned for the kind of conjuror that Adria was: one who concentrated on major effects. Adria would have either snatched the crystal and attempted to insert a duplicate, or smashed the holder.

There was another way. For as she stared at the shard, she felt its magic ambience. It reached out to her, touching her mind, making it more clever, and it touched her heart, making her desire it with a passion as strong as she had ever desired a man. It touched her power, and suddenly she knew what she could do. And the crystal itself would help her.

Lightly she touched one finger to the shard, closed her eyes, and concentrated. Creating—vapor. Water vapor. Forcing water into every tiny crack and crevice of the holder until it was completely saturated. And then, with a twist of thought unlike any she had done before—

She turned it to ice.

Water, she had learned in her lessons from Marcus, expanded when it was frozen. Everything else contracted. In a moment, she had chilled the area down to where her breath made clouds in the air; the ice itself was as hard as steel.

In the past she had been able to conjure many substances, but they were normally of ambient temperature. Metal would not be hot or cold, water would seem cool but be the temperature of the surrounding air. One exception was ice: that was by its nature cold, so conjured that way. Otherwise it would have appeared as a puddle of water. But to actually, magically, change the temperature of an existing object or substance—that was a power hitherto reserved to the demons. Now, by virtue of the shard, it was hers. So she could heat water—or freeze it. She could do what no other Mazonite could, and what therefore the defenders of the shard had not anticipated. It had outsmarted them.

The frozen ice held the rods in place while she carefully extracted the shard from the holder, and continued to hold them while she conjured a perfect replica in its place.

Tucking the shard inside her tunic, she returned to the outer chamber, conjured a ladder of stone to the hole in the ceiling, then continued conjuring and dissipating stone steps before and behind her, until she had reached the chamber above.

Then it was another squeeze through the passageway to the outer world—and a joyful, but silent reunion with Faro and Thesius, before the three of them made their escape into the mountains and the rally-point with Ware.

Only one thing disappointed her: she did not know how long that conjured replica would last. It had, after all, been produced with the aid of the shard itself. It might last only the day; it might last for weeks, months, or even years.

But eventually, it would dissipate on its own.

And she truly regretted the fact that she would not be there to see what happened when it did!

"Xylina, why are you stopping?" Faro asked, as Xylina reined in her horse at the edge of the Pacha realm. Their trek across it had been a near mirror of their original trip, although with fewer people, and instead of the Pacha visiting their camps, they had traded conjured wine and feasts for Pacha hospitality. The Pacha had been thrilled with the bargain, and nearly every chieftain that had hosted them had begged them to stay.

She did not answer at once; instead, she stared at the bleak, and yet beautiful landscape. Finally, she spoke.

"Gentlemen—do you still like the Pacha? Do you think you could live here?" Perhaps it was the effect of the shard, which she now wore in a conjured gold locket, so that it enhanced her while not harming Ware or the men. But perhaps it was instead the time she'd had to think on the way back—to reflect on exactly where her loyalty should lie, and the effect on the Mazonites when the shard came into Adria's hands.

Ware urged his mount to take the few steps needed to bring it beside hers. "You are not going to take the crystal to Adria, are you," he said quietly, making it more of a statement than a question.

She shook her head. "No matter what I do, if the shard goes to the Queen, it will change my realm and my people, and for the worse. Adria will become a terrible tyrant, and no one will be able to stop her. Eventually, the shard will force Adria to bring it to the main stone, and that will be the end of everything I have known."

Faro's brow wrinkled for a moment. "You did make a vow—" he reminded her.

She smiled. "I am learning to think like a demon, my friend. I made a vow to retrieve the shard. I did *not* vow to give it to Adria."

Thesius shook his head as she turned to see his reaction. "You can't take it back to where it was. That would be stupid *and* suicidal!"

She sighed, and her horse stirred restively under her. "No. I can't take it back, I can't simply 'lose' it, for some poor fool will be drawn to it and in her ignorance take it to the main stone. I must keep it, and attempt to use it as little as possible. And if I am going to keep it—I must stay out of Mazonia." She looked searchingly at all of them. "This is an exile, you know—"

"Not for me," Thesius protested. "You can't be exiled from somewhere you've never been! The Pacha are plenty interesting enough to keep me busy for a long time!"

"Nor for me," Faro said. "This isn't exile—"

"No, my dearest friend," she told him, with a warm smile. "For you, it is freedom. You may stay with me if you wish, or go if you wish—"

"I'll stay," he said firmly. "Someone has to keep you out of trouble."

That left only Ware, but as he slipped his hand wordlessly into hers, she knew what his answer was. She squeezed the hand, the unhumanly graceful, beloved hand, for a long moment—

Then turned her horse and led them all back to the last Pacha village they had visited.

There was only one thing remaining.

To wait for the Queen's answer to this betrayal.

The answer was not long in coming.

"What?" Adria shrieked, rising from her throne like an enraged cat.

The Pacha agent, still in her leather and paints, repeated her news, although she shrank back a little from the Queen's rage. "Xylina has obtained the stone you wished, but has evidently decided to retain it for herself. She has had it set in gold and wears it about her neck. She has taken up residence with the Sandfox Clan of the Pacha. They are building a home for her and her retinue. There are three men with her: the demon, her personal slave, and another man who looks like her brother."

Adria's anger cooled as swiftly as it had heated, but it did not leave her. Instead, it turned to something colder and more purposeful. She sank back down onto her throne, and considered the matter carefully, dismissing the spy with an absent wave of her hand.

She had hoped that the naive child would bring the shard directly to her, but the demon must have revealed what it was and what its powers were to her, and greed had overcome her. This was unsurprising, really; it was what Adria herself would have done if their positions were reversed.

But there were only three with the girl. The Pacha would not protect her against the Queen's wrath. They had a treaty, after all; they would abide by that treaty. There was only one thing to be done: to go and take the shard from the girl by force.

Adria summoned her majordomo and ordered him to bring Xantippe to the private audience chamber. When the old warrior appeared, Adria studied her for a long time before speaking.

"You once commanded one of the armies, did you not?" she asked.

Xantippe nodded, brusquely. "It was before your reign, my Queen," the older woman replied, "but yes, I did. My record will show that I was a very successful commander."

"Good," Adria replied, leaning forward. "Now—how would you like to participate in both the downfall of Xylina and the destruction of her slave Faro?"

Xantippe's eyes widened slightly, and she smiled.

Less than a day later, two armies marched out of the capital. The first, smaller and faster than the second, and composed entirely of veterans, was commanded by Xantippe, and was intended to cut Xylina's path of escape across

Pacha lands. The second, composed mostly of newly-recruited slaves, was commanded by Queen Adria herself. This was the army that Xylina was intended to see.

The other, she was not meant to see until it was too late.

"I'm sorry, Xylina; I should have guessed she would do something like that—" Thesius was babbling; this was the fifth or sixth time that he had repeated his apology, but the second of Adria's forces had come as a terrible surprise to all of them. Xylina could not blame him for babbling. The jaws of the trap had closed on them, before they even realized that it *was* a trap.

Adria had done exactly what Xylina had expected—in part. She had brought an army across the border, and had come straight for Xylina, presumably to claim the crystal. Xylina had thrown dozens of traps, pitfalls, and dangers into the army's path; Adria had simply used her men to clear her way, marching forward sometimes literally over the bodies of her slaves. The Mazonite Guards with the army had ensured that no man who tried to desert survived the attempt—so the poor slaves had the choice of a probable death, or a certain one.

All four of them were exhausted by their work on defenses; they had not changed their clothing in days, or eaten except whatever they could snatch on the fly. But Xylina was the weariest, for upon her had fallen the burden of conjuration. She had been aided by the shard, but the time and effort still were hers. It had not helped that Ware had insisted on training her in a special way, to learn to better control the new power the shard gave her to affect temperature. So that she could not only freeze water, but heat it to boiling, or heat other substances to the burning point. She understood his logic, for the ability of temperature conjuration was potentially an enormous asset. But the constant practicing was wearing, and she wished he had been willing to let it wait until she didn't have so much else to do.

Xylina had been sickened by the wholesale slaughter; so much so that she had not thought to look for some other trick of Adria's until it was too late. Now their only route of escape was closed—and Adria and the remnants of her army were closing quickly.

There must be something she could do, she thought in desperation. There had to be some other way out of this trap! If only she could challenge the Queen to single-combat . . .

"Xylina," Ware said urgently, recalling her to her surroundings and the tiny rock-walled room in which the four of them sat, "you must challenge the Queen. It is the only way."

"How can I?" she wailed, despairing. "This is not Mazonia! She is not bound by the rules with a traitor and an oath-breaker! She need not—"

"But you have something she wants, little mistress," Faro pointed out, shrewdly and unexpectedly. "You have the shard. Send to her by the Pacha, and tell her that you will destroy it unless—"

"Unless she agrees to meet me! Of course!" Xylina's despair turned again to hope, and she jumped out of her simple wooden chair to hug Faro around the neck. He blushed, but grinned. Thesius had already run out of the room to fetch one of their Pacha "allies," who were willing to act as messengers and sometimes scouts so long as such duty did not directly involve them in combat.

But no sooner had the messenger been dispatched than Xylina's mood deflated. "I will not need to—" she said to Ware, pleadingly. "Will I? I do not think I could bear to—"

He sighed. "You do realize, beloved, that this is the shard's first effect upon you? That it makes itself so precious to you that you cannot bear the thought of destroying it?"

She nodded, sadly. She *did* know that, and her intellect rebelled at being so controlled—and yet, controlled it was, and she could no more smash the shard than destroy Ware.

But the demon moved to stand behind her, and put his hands on her shoulders, massaging the tense muscles of her neck and shoulders gently. "Do not worry, beloved. The Queen is more influenced by her desire for the shard than you are. She will think only that you are serious, and seeing yourself lost, your cause in ruins, and yourself about to be killed, that you will be willing to take the shard with you. She will believe your bluff, and she will not know that it is a bluff. You will see."

Before half the morning had passed, the messenger had returned, and all was as Ware had foretold. The Queen had agreed to meet Xylina in a traditional Mazonite challenge. She had even proposed the conditions, all of which both Ware and Xylina agreed were reasonable. With one addition.

They were to meet at noon, in an isolated area of Xylina's choosing. All men and Mazonites were to stand out of bow-shot range of the site. Xylina was to be permitted to booby-trap the area, so long as she led the Queen inside herself, thus ensuring the safe way in. They were to meet nude, so as to ensure that neither carried in physical weaponry, and the crystal was to be placed on a stone in the middle of the ground, to be taken by the survivor. Other than that—there were to be no rules. Just one modification, concerning the crystal, to make that aspect fair.

"You are younger and stronger, since this journeying has hardened you, beloved," Ware said, when they had read the proposal through. "But do not underestimate Adria. She is cunning and vicious, and she has survived many of these challenges."

Xylina took a deep breath, and looked into his eyes. It had finally come to this—a challenge that she did not want, for power she did not wish to have; something she had tried to avoid and which had, in the end, come for her.

And yet—the reward would be something Adria had never known, and would never understand.

"I have to survive only one, beloved," she told him. "And believe me, I do intend to survive that one."

* * *

The burning sun beat down upon the two women: two combatants, who were the very antithesis of each other. Xylina, small, slender, long-waisted and high breasted, with her blond hair streaming down to her waist—and Adria, lean, whip-cord-tough, no more figure than a boy, and with her dark hair cut aggressively short. And yet Adria, who was by far the more experienced and tougher-looking, already showed some slight discomfort—perhaps from the exposure to the sun. Xylina, clothed only in her signature banner of hair, seemed completely serene and at ease— perhaps because she had been the plaything of the elements for some time now, and had gotten used to them.

Between them lay the crystal, on a flat rock in the center of the makeshift arena. Xylina had insisted on that one change in the challenge-rules; the crystal lay beneath a pair of transparent domes of near-unbreakable adamant. She had created one, Adria had created the other. Any force great enough to smash the domes would also smash the crystal. Neither of the combatants would be able get at the crystal unless the other was dead, for at death, all conjurations dissolved.

Adria had not liked that rule, although she had agreed to it, and her glance kept straying to the glinting gold-and-crystal shape of the protected shard. Perhaps she hoped to trick Xylina into dissolving her conjuration so that the Queen could grab the shard and use it to win. Or to lure Xylina away from it, to where she could be ambushed or driven away. In a day her conjuration would dissolve anyway, and then the Queen could get the shard. Ware had warned Xylina that if the Queen found any way to get the shard without finishing the combat, she would. "Kill her," he had cautioned. "No mercy, no hesitation. Just kill her, as quickly as you can. Nothing else." Faro and Thesius had nodded agreement.

So Xylina did not look at the shard. She kept her attention

fixed firmly on the distant figure of Xantippe. When the old warrior dropped the banner she held, the combat would begin. Only Adria knew what Adria would do first, although it was a fair bet that it would be a sudden and overwhelming attack. One of the reasons that Adria had been so successful in these challenges was that she never did the same thing twice, so there was no way to anticipate her. Every combat she had undertaken had begun differently.

Xylina hoped that her own first move would take the Queen off-guard.

The banner dropped.

An enormous block of stone appeared just above where Xylina was standing, and crashed down into the ground, smashing everything beneath it to powder.

But Xylina was no longer there.

She had created a tiny springboard just in front of herself, and had used it to catapult herself through the air, landing well out of range of the stone, and—most importantly—right next to the domes protecting the shard.

Now she could use the domes as a kind of shield, and unless Adria wanted to risk smashing the crystal, she could not use any more weapons like that block of stone. If she dispelled her own dome, Xylina would be able to get her hands on the crystal, thus greatly increasing her own power.

Adria's scream of rage told Xylina that this first ploy, at least, was a success. Now Xylina took her second move, while Adria was still off-balance. It was the essence of simplicity: she copied the Queen's first move.

A block of stone the same size as the one Adria had made appeared over the Queen's head. And stayed there—for the Queen had conjured several stout metal posts to support its weight. A standard defense for a standard attack.

So the first round was done. There were no turns in such combat, but the action did tend to fall into segments as one attacked and the other countered. A woman who did not counter would soon be dead.

There was more than the usual significance to this round,

however. The Queen had tried to finish the battle swiftly, and had failed. Conjuration was limited; a woman's magic grew progressively fatigued, until finally she was unable to conjure any more. The victor in past battles between ranking women had generally been the one whose power of conjuration outlasted that of her opponent. Xylina suspected that the Queen had gambled most of her power on the first ploy, hoping not to have to follow up. She also suspected that her own power of conjuration was now significantly greater than the Queen's, because of her practice in the wilderness. Xylina could conjure a second block the mass of the first; she doubted that the Queen could.

But at the moment this didn't matter, because there was no way to drop such a block on the Queen. The stout posts would support both, leaving the Queen unscathed. Defense in such cases was usually cheaper than attack. So the massive conjurations were over—unless Xylina could somehow force the Queen out of her impromptu shelter where she would be vulnerable to another block. She wanted to save her power until the Queen thought she was safe from it. So for now Xylina planned to limit herself to diminishingly smaller conjurations, as if she were weakening, hoping to make the Queen overconfident.

The Queen conjured a spiked metal ball that she hurled at Xylina. Xylina, wary of what else might be coming, stepped aside while conjuring her own matching spiked ball. Sure enough, the Queen's second ball came at her, and she was unable to dodge it. So she conjured her own second ball in the path of the Queen's. The two collided in air and dropped to the ground as Xylina threw hers at the Queen. The Queen stepped behind a post, and the ball missed. But Adria looked wary; she saw how readily Xylina was matching her, and she didn't want to try something that would hurt her when the response came. Xylina was, in effect, teaching her manners.

This was proceeding into early stalemate. Xylina didn't trust that. She knew she could not afford to stand around while the Queen figured out something more deadly. But she wanted to force the Queen to use up her power of conjuration. The very best thing that she could do would be to make Adria so angry that she would stop thinking and merely react.

And the way to do that would be to attack Adria with a weapon that Adria was not expecting, and by her very nature, would not ever expect.

She must make Adria look ridiculous.

While the Queen was still trying to change her plans to include Xylina's use of the domes as a shield, Xylina concentrated and conjured something of her own above the Queen's head. Directly above, and so near that Adria would not react by creating anything to shield herself from what was about to drop over her. For the Queen had left Xylina an opening, inadvertently, by remaining under the propped-up block of stone.

And since this was one of the simpler things Xylina could have conjured, it appeared instantly. On top of the block. Then Xylina dissolved the block, for it was hers. Before Adria even knew that Xylina was launching an attack, she had been buried waist deep in a very large, and very fragrant, pile of manure that lost its support just above her head and fell on her.

And to add insult to injury, Xylina topped it off with a brief rain of overripe vegetables.

Of course the Queen reflexively conjured a small shielding tower, so that the material did not land on her head. Such fighting reflexes made it difficult to score directly with barbs or acid, which was why Xylina hadn't tried them. But the stuff did pile up around her, and enough of it slopped in around her body to achieve good effect.

There was shocked and startled silence. And then, from the sidelines where the slaves of the army watched—and smelled—came the unmistakable sound of laughter. No one had expected such a joke in such a serious contest, which made it twice as funny.

Just one man laughed, and slightly hysterical at first—but that one was joined by another, and another, until the whole army was laughing, and the voices of the Mazonite officers trying to restore order were drowned in the sound.

Adria's face turned red, then white, then red again; this time an apoplectic-looking purple-red that betokened exactly what Xylina had hoped for. Complete loss of self-control and concentration. Xylina had gambled that the Queen was fatigued by her conjurations and the tension of the occasion, and prone to overreaction, especially to the ridiculous and insulting. Stressed-out, she felt the laughter of her own troops like a physical attack.

Adria's next attack showed just how far she had fallen from that self-control; she began manifesting and throwing metal lances, one after the other. If the domes had not been in the way these could have been deadly, but now mostly clattered harmlessly off the adamant. This was basic, unsophisticated conjuration, worthy of a girl's first arena demonstration—as had been the case with Xylina. It was almost beneath the notice of an experienced Mazonite.

Xylina's reply was a deluge of water that washed away the manure, and left Adria's legs dripping wet. She looked almost as ridiculous as before. The men roared again with helpless laughter, which was redoubled when Xylina dropped an enormous sponge and recognizable bar of soap in front of her. Mazonia had never seen combat like this!

But Xylina's purpose was not humorous at all. Her life was on the line, and she knew how dangerous the Queen remained. Adria had attacked once from above and once directly; she would probably come up next from below. Xylina could use that if she did.

Xylina was prepared when lances of rock thrust up from the sand; she had already created a table-like shield just beneath her feet, and the thrust of the rock spires carried her up into the air so that she could jump from the table to the top of the domes. Before Adria had a chance to react to so obvious a target, Xylina turned the water about her to ice, making the Queen slip and fall when she flinched back, then sent shards of ice lancing upwards in mimicry of Adria's rock-spires. Now Ware's insistence that she practice with temperature conjuration was paying off; the Queen had not been prepared for this. Indeed, Adria probably didn't yet realize exactly what was happening.

Adria dodged out of the way, slipping ridiculously and causing the men to laugh until tears ran down their faces. She was really losing it—if this weren't a ruse. Then when Xylina continued to create the razor-sharp ice-spires, the Queen angrily countered with a great pile of cotton batting to protect her from them. This would both shield her from their points and soak up the water as they melted. She was evidently nonplused, realizing that Xylina's power was greater than anticipated; she had not expected to be forced into a defensive mode.

"Spin it!" someone called, laughing.

"No," Faro called. *"Burn* it!"

His voice was like a light illuminating the arena. Yes—she could make it burn.

This was just what Xylina had been waiting for. Adria had made a critical error. She had surrounded herself with flammable material. She didn't know what Xylina could do with it. And of course Xylina would not have been able to conjure flammable material around the Queen and ignite it; it had been all she could do to keep Adria at bay. She had to work on one thing at a time. But now that she had her opening, it was time to pounce.

Xylina got to work. She lay down on the dome, getting as close to the shard as possible, and felt its power radiating out to her. She concentrated as hard as she could, heating the Queen's cotton. It was hard at this distance, but her recent practice had made it possible. She drew from the shard and conjured a tiny spot of heat.

"Giving up, child?" Adria called mockingly. She thought Xylina was lying on the dome from exhaustion. She had no inkling what was in the offing.

It better light soon, though, because the Queen was getting ready to return to the attack. An ominous fog was forming over Xylina. She focused with all her might—and saw a tiny wisp of smoke just behind Adria.

Then there was a puff of flame. She had done it! The batting was burning!

The Queen turned, smelling the smoke. "What—?"

Xylina wasted no time. She knew that the Queen would banish her cotton in a moment, leaving nothing to burn. She had to pounce while she had the flame. So she conjured more fluid.

This time, what Xylina doused the Queen with was not water. It was naptha. And she followed it with oil.

The Queen, and everything around her, exploded into flames. They leaped up throughout the area as the oil flowed. It was impossible for Adria to run out of the fire fast enough—not with her oil-soaked legs already burning. There was so much oil that it fueled a fire that reached far into the sky, an inferno. Much more than the Queen must have thought Xylina was capable of conjuring at this stage. So she had been caught by surprise, thinking her opponent no stronger than herself.

Xylina slid down off the domes to cower behind the adamant as the fireball blasted everything in the vicinity. The Queen's scream of agony echoed in her ears, and went on for a long and terrible time; she covered both her ears with her hands, and still it echoed in her very soul, until she feared that the echo of it would never leave her, and she would hear it in her dreams for the rest of her life.

Finally she could not bear it any longer. She conjured one last time; another block of stone identical to Adria's first attack, a stone which she dropped on the burning Queen, extinguishing blaze, scream, and the last pitiful remnants of Adria's life.

Complete silence descended upon the field of combat, and in that silence, Xylina dissolved the sole remaining dome of adamant and claimed the shard. Then there came a low exclamation of amazement, as the watchers realized that Xylina had actually conjured almost *three times* as much mass as the Queen had. Xylina herself hadn't realized how much, until she paused to ponder. Maybe the mere nearness of the shard had enhanced her power in that respect too. What awful power lay in that little bit of glass! Yet she could not fear it; she loved it, despite her knowledge that it was really doing its will, not hers. It would inevitably corrupt her, and she would be an absolute fool to believe she could resist it indefinitely. But she had to—for as long as she could.

She looked out over the armies—which now technically belonged to her. She could become Queen of the Mazonites by right of battle. While her association with the demon made her technically ineligible, she could now change that law by fiat. The victor made the law, ultimately. But of course she wouldn't. That would be early corruption. She could return to her own land, *and* she could keep the shard. There was nothing that she could not do, but this was all she *would* do.

Though she was far from those assembled armies, there was one emotion she read clearly in every pair of eyes, slave or Mazonite.

Fear.

The new Queen of the Mazonites tasted her power, and found it a bitter drink. She looked out over her troops, and she said only three sentences into the waiting and frightened silence.

"I will not be Queen. Go home. All of you, go home."

Then she turned and walked wearily back to the comfort of the three who loved her.

The little rock-walled room was very crowded with five people in it. "My Queen—" Xantippe said, awkwardly. Xylina interrupted her with a shake of her head. She was bone-weary, and wearing the plainest tunic and trousers she owned, simply to try to show Xantippe by her very clothing that she had no intention of taking power.

"I told you, I am *not* your Queen. I am not anybody's Queen. Do I have to go all over this again?" She sipped cold water to ease a throat raw from weeping. And she was not certain for whom she had wept more—the Queen, the hundreds of slaves slaughtered in this stupid battle, or herself. "Or do you finally understand?"

"I do not understand, but I know what you want," Xantippe replied, dubiously. "You want someone else to be Queen; you do not care whom, so long as the new Queen leaves you in peace. You even suggested me! You do not want power. You will sign a treaty with the new Queen that pledges you will remain in Pacha lands and attempt to keep this stone you wear from dragging you off to the main crystal—and in return, you wish some trade with the demons, all of Ware's property and gold to be accessible to him so that he may build you and Thesius an estate here, and sanctuary for any slaves that escape and make it this far. I do not understand this, but I think that we can pledge it."

"Good." Xylina sighed, and leaned back in her seat, which was now of fine leather and strong velvet. The only spoils of war she had accepted were the Queen's traveling properties—a luxurious tent and all appointments—and those slaves who wished to remain in Pacha lands and join one of the tribes. She could not grant that wish of her ten dead men—but she could grant it to others. "Xantippe, I wish only to preserve my land and its way of life for as long as I am able. The shard is dangerous. I will not be able to do this forever. Ware tells me that eventually this shard will cause me to turn against you, and on that day, when I cross the border of Mazonia, you must consider me an enemy. But that will be long after you are dead, and probably long after every other Mazonite in this army is dead. For now—just leave us in peace. We will not trouble you, and we will not permit the freed slaves to trouble you."

Her eyes flashed for a moment, and Xantippe stepped

back a pace. "And remember always, that if you will not grant this as a wish—it will come as a demand that I can enforce. The shard gives me enormous power. Do not force me to use it."

"Yes my Qu—yes, Xylina." Xantippe could not bow, but she did salute smartly, before turning and leaving. Xylina turned to Ware and Thesius.

"Well?" she asked.

"If you are asking me whether you made the right decision, I cannot tell you," Ware replied, truthfully. "If you are asking me if you made an honorable decision—I would say yes."

"I would agree," Thesius seconded, dropping a fraternal kiss on her forehead. "Now—I must see to all those slaves who have been newly emancipated. It is not easy learning to be a free man. Faro would be the first to tell you that, and he is the farthest along of any of them."

The handsome blond clapped Ware on the shoulders, and took himself out, leaving Xylina and the demon alone.

"Was it worth it, beloved?" the incubus asked, his face mirroring a concern he had not shown the two men. "I know how everything since the challenge has troubled your soul. It was I who urged you to all of this in the first place. If I had not done this, entrapped you, gotten you involved—"

"I would have ended my life a bitter and hateful woman, just like Adria," Xylina interrupted, taking his hand and kissing it. "If not long since ignominiously dead. And with your help—we have given my people some warning, and perhaps some time to adjust to what will inevitably come. Perhaps this time when the change comes, it may come without terrible cost, death and chaos. And no matter what happens—"

She took his hand in hers, and looked deeply into his eyes, smiling for the first time in many days.

"We will meet it together."

• AUTHORS' NOTES

Mercedes Lackey

For biographers, I was born in Chicago, June 24, 1950. My father was the Chief Computer Programmer, Systems' Design and Systems' Analyst for first Sinclair Oil then Arco, nearly from the moment there was such a thing as a commercial computer. I have a Bachelor of Science in Biology with a specialization in ethology from Purdue University; I was for many years a computer programmer on the cutting edge of airline reservations programming, and I am firmly a technophile.

My husband Larry Dixon and I live in a lovely, heavily wooded area in Northeast Oklahoma, with rising hills and wonderful views. We keep our home acres and two ponds as wild as possible. We are wildlife rehabilitators specializing in raptors and the corvidae, and apprentice falconers. Larry is my "first editor" on everything I do. We feel privileged to have a "partnership," not only with each other, but with our editors. We believe that the editor and the writer work most successfully when they work together, and we enjoy our editors not only as wise counselors and advisors, but as friends.

Other than that, we are very private people, and while we don't feel we are creating High Art, we hope we are creating enjoyable writing, and we prefer to let our work speak for itself.

Piers Anthony

I too live in the forest; in fact I live on a tree farm whose pine trees I hope will not be harvested in my lifetime, and whose natural trees will never be cut at all. I am an ardent environmentalist, and in this way I am protecting my bit of the wilderness. We have deer, gopher tortoises, piliated woodpeckers, armadillos, and many other wild creatures, some of whom are becoming unconscionably rare elsewhere. And yes, we have raptors too; large owls and hawks nest near our house and forage in our yard, not seeming too shy; the young will snooze on branches outside our windows. We love it. The outside of our house gets messy with spider webs and wasp nests, because we leave everything alone that leaves us alone. Perhaps my favorites are the dragonflies, green, blue, brown, red, yellow, and two-tone, who will on occasion perch on an upraised hand. They hover marvelously, always wanting to know what I'm doing outside.

But this is about collaboration. Collaborations come in many varieties, and I've done twenty. There is no standard way; each is its own type. Overall, I believe this is my 99th book, so collaborations represent about one fifth my total, and I'm still learning from them.

This particular one was like an arranged marriage. Collaboration, it has been said, has the problems of wedlock, without the benefits. That's why most writers avoid it. But sometimes the vagaries of situation can force such a merger. In effect I went to Jim Baen of Baen Books and said, "Here's my notion, but I don't have time to do it myself; can you find me someone to write it?" He checked his prospects and found Mercedes (Misty) Lackey. "But I'm too busy too!" she surely protested. But he had an answer: "You're the best possible writer for a notion such as this. I wouldn't give it to just anyone." So she reconsidered,

and concluded that she would have to make time. Thus it
came to be. No, I never met Misty; remember what I said
above about no benefits? My daughter Penny did, however, at a convention, so there was a tenuous connection.
Daughters are marvelous creatures. I can't think why
anyone would want to have sons. So Misty wrote it, and
then I went over her text. This was no rubber stamp effort;
anything with my name on it must meet my standards. I did
a complete job of copy-editing and spot revisions and addi-
tions, exactly as I do for my own drafts, polishing the novel
to my satisfaction and expanding it by ten thousand words.
Those who are conversant with Misty's writing and mine
will see aspects of both here, just as both of our ideas are
represented. Thus I did the top and bottom of it, the sum-
mary and the revision. Picture a sandwich: I'm the two
slices of bread. Most of the nourishment is in the center,
but without the bread it wouldn't exist.

This particular notion had a considerable history. It
started in 1979, as an offshoot of my earlier research in the
Arabian Nights Tales for another novel. I'm a Nights fan; I
have several multi-volume editions. In one of those tales a
highborn woman incurred a debt, and the man to whom
she owed it suggested that there were ways other than
monetary to expiate it. She caught his meaning perfectly,
and declared—ah, yes, I see you understand. Thus the title
and heroine of this novel. The project had a thirteen-year
history as I considered doing it for another publisher. But
by the time I had figured out how to organize it, my
relations with that publisher had soured, and I had gotten
caught up in so many projects that I was writing and selling
more than half a million words of fiction a year and still
barely keeping up. Thus the compromise, and this is the
result.

Naturally, as I reviewed it, fate stepped in. My belief in
the supernatural is nonexistent; I write fantasy, I don't
believe it. This may be why supernatural occurrences keep
pestering me. In this case, just as I was reviewing the scene

in which Xylina contemplates suicide, I received a letter from a young woman who was doing the same. Her name was Julie, and she had a cross that she wore continuously, day and night, her most precious possession. She enclosed that cross, and it sits by my computer as I type this. By that token I knew that she was near the end. Yes, I'm doing my best to persuade her to take back her cross, but the issue is undecided at the time of this writing. I researched to ascertain what type it is, and concluded that it is of the general description known as pattée: that is, widening in the arms, in the manner of paws. Pattée means paw-like. And so I added a character in honor of that cross—a character who did not die. I hope. Further research satisfied me that the cross is actually of another description, clechée, meaning like an ancient key, but I decided to let Pattée the character be. There are limits.

Those who wish to order any of my books or newsletter "troll free" may call 1-800 HI PIERS. No, I'm not the one who answers that phone, but messages do reach me eventually.

There Are Elves Out There

An excerpt from

Mercedes Lackey
Larry Dixon

The main bay was eerily quiet. There were no screams of grinders, no buzz of technical talk or rapping of wrenches. There was no whine of test engines on dynos coming through the walls. Instead, there was a dull-bladed tension amid all the machinery, generated by the humans and the Sidhe gathered there.

Tannim laid the envelope on the rear deck of the only fully-operated GTP car that Fairgrove had built to date, the one that Donal had spent his waking hours building, and Conal had spent track-testing. He'd designed it for beauty and power in equal measure, and had given its key to Conal, its elected driver, in the same brother's-gift ceremony used to present an elvensteed. Conal now sat on its sculpted door, and absently traced a slender finger along an air intake, glowering at the envelope.

Tannim finished his magical tests, and asked for a knife. An even dozen were offered, but Dottie's Leatherman was accepted. Keighvin stood a little apart from the group, hand on his short knife. His eyes glittered with suppressed anger, and he appeared less human than usual, Tannim noticed. Something was bound to break soon.

Tannim folded out the knifeblade, slit the envelope open, and then unfolded the Leatherman's pliers. With them he withdrew six Polaroids of Tania and two others, unconscious, each bound at the wrists and neck. Their silver chains were held by some-*things* from the Realm of the Unseleighe—inside a limo. And, out of focus through the limo's windows, was a stretch of flat tarmac, and large buildings—

Tannim dropped the Leatherman, his fingers gone numb. It clattered twice before wedging into the cockpit's fresh-air vent. Keighvin took one startled step forward, then halted as the magical alarms at Fairgrove's perimeter flared around them all. Tannim's hand went into a jacket pocket, and he threw down the letter from the P.I. He saw Conal pick up the photographs, blanch, then snatch the letter up.

Tannim had already turned by then, and was sprinting for the office door, and the parking lot beyond.

Behind him, he could hear startled questions directed at him, but all he could answer before disappearing into the offices was "Airport!" His bad leg was slowing him down, and screamed at him like a sharp rock grinding into his bones. There was some kind of attack beginning, but he had no time for that.

Have to get to the airport, have to save Tania

from Vidal Dhu, the bastard, the son of a bitch, the—

Tannim rounded a corner and banged his left knee into a file cabinet. He went down hard, hands instinctively clutching at his over-damaged leg. His eyes swam with a private galaxy of red stars, and he struggled while his eyes refocused.

Son of a bitch son of a bitch son of a bitch. . . .

Behind him he heard the sounds of a war-party, and above it all, the banshee wail of a high-performance engine. He pulled himself up, holding the bleeding knee, and limp-ran towards the parking lot, to the Mustang, and Thunder Road.

Vidal Dhu stood in full armor before the gates of Fairgrove, laughing, lashing out with levin-bolts to set off its alarms. It was easy for Vidal to imagine what must be going on inside—easy to picture that smug, orphaned witling Keighvin Silverhair barking orders to weak mortals, marshaling them to fight. Let him rally them, Vidal thought—it will do him no good. None at all. He may have won before, but ultimately, the mortals will have damned him.

It has been so many centuries, Silverhair. I swore I'd kill your entire lineage, and I shall. I shall!

Vidal prepared to open the gate to Underhill. Through that gate all the Court would watch as Keighvin was destroyed—Aurilia's plan be hanged! Vidal's blood sang with triumph—he had driven Silverhair into a winless position at last! And when he accepted the Challenge, before the whole Court, none of his human-world tricks would benefit him—theirs would be a purely magical combat, one Sidhe to another.

To the death.

* * *

Keighvin Silverhair recognized the scent of the magic at Fairgrove's gates—he had smelled it for centuries. It reeked of obsession and fear, hatred and lust. It was born of pain inflicted without consideration of repercussions. It was the magic of one who had stalked innocents and stolen their last breaths.

He recognized, too, the rhythm that was being beaten against the walls of Fairgrove.

So be it, murderer. I will suffer your stench no more.

"They will expect us to dither and delay; the sooner we act, the more likely it is that we will catch them unprepared. They do not know how well we work together."

Around him, the humans and Sidhe of his home sprang into action, taking up arms with such speed he'd have thought them possessed. Conal had thrown down the letter after reading it, and barked, "Hangar 2A at Savannah Regional; they've got children as hostages!" The doors of the bay began rolling open, and outside, elvensteeds stamped and reared, eyes glowing, anxious for battle. Conal looked to him, then, for orders.

Keighvin met his eyes for one long moment, and said, "Go, Conal. I shall deal with our attacker for the last time. If naught else, the barrier at the gates can act as a trap to hold him until we can deal with him as he deserves." He did not add what he was thinking—that he only hoped it would hold Vidal. The Unseleighe was a strong mage; he might escape even a trap laid with death metal, if he were clever enough. Then, with the swiftness of a falcon, he was astride his elvensteed Rosaleen Dhu, headed for the perimeter of Fairgrove.

He was out there, all right, and had begun laying a spell outside the fences, like a snare. Perhaps in his sickening arrogance he'd forgotten that Keighvin could see such things. Perhaps in his insanity, he no longer cared.

Rosaleen tore across the grounds as fast as a stroke of lightning, and cleared the fence in a soaring leap. She landed a few yards from the laughing, mad Vidal Dhu, on the roadside, with him between Keighvin and the gates. He stopped lashing his mocking bolts at the gates of Fairgrove and turned to face Keighvin.

"So, you've come to face me alone, at last? No walls or mortals to hide behind, as usual, coward? So sad that you've chosen *now* to change, within minutes of your death, traitor."

"Vidal Dhu," Keighvin said, trying to sound unimpressed despite the heat of his blood, "if you wish to duel me, I shall accept. But before I accept, you must release the children you hold."

The Unseleighe laughed bitterly. "It's your concern for these mortals that raised you that have *made* you a traitor, boy. Those children do not matter." Vidal lifted his lip in a sneer as Keighvin struggled to maintain his composure. "Oh, I will do more than duel you, Silverhair. I wish to Challenge you before the Court, and kill you as they watch."

That was what Keighvin had noted—it was the initial layout of a Gate to the High Court Underhill. Vidal was serious about this Challenge—already the Court would be assembling to judge the battle. Keighvin sat atop Rosaleen, who snorted and stamped, enraged by the other's tauntings. Vidal's pitted face twisted in a maniacal smirk.

"How long must I wait for you to show courage, witling?"

Keighvin's mind swam for a moment, before he remembered the full protocols of a formal Challenge. It had been so long since he'd even seen one. . . .

Once accepted, the Gate activates, and all the Court watches as the two battle with blade and magic. Only one leaves the field; the Court is bound to slay anyone who runs. So it had always been. Vidal would not Challenge unless he were confident of winning, and Keighvin was still tired from the last battle—which Vidal had not even been at. . . .

But Vidal must die. That much Keighvin knew.

From Born to Run *by Mercedes Lackey & Larry Dixon.*

*   *   *

Watch for more from the SERRAted Edge:
Wheels of Fire by Mercedes Lackey & Mark Shepherd

When the Bough Breaks by Mercedes Lackey & Holly Lisle

HIGH FANTASY
Bardic Voices: The Lark & The Wren
Rune could be one of the greatest bards of her world, but the daughter of a tavern wench can't get much in the way of formal training. So one night she goes up to play for the Ghost of Skull Hill. She'll either fiddle till dawn to prove her skill as a bard—or die trying....

The Robin and the Kestrel: Bardic Voices II
After the affairs recounted in *The Lark and The Wren*, Robin, a gypsy lass and bard, and Kestrel, semi-fugitive heir to a throne he does not want, have married their fortunes together and travel the open road, seeking their happiness where they may find it. This is their story. It is also the story of the Ghost of Skull Hill. Together, the Robin, the Kestrel, and the Ghost will foil a plot to drive all music forever from the land....

Bardic Choices: A Cast of Corbies with Josepha Sherman

If I Pay Thee Not in Gold with Piers Anthony
A new hardcover quest fantasy, co-written by the creator of the "Xanth" series. A marvelous adult fantasy that examines the war between the sexes and the ethics of desire! Watch out for bad puns!

BARD'S TALE
Based on the bestselling computer game, *The Bard's Tale.*℗
Castle of Deception with Josepha Sherman
Fortress of Frost and Fire with Ru Emerson
Prison of Souls with Mark Shepherd

Also by Mercedes Lackey:
Reap the Whirlwind with C.J. Cherryh
Part of the Sword of Knowledge series.

The Ship Who Searched with Anne McCaffrey
The Ship Who Sang is not alone!

Wing Commander: Freedom Flight with Ellen Guon
Based on the bestselling computer game, *Wing Commander.*℗

Join the Mercedes Lackey national fan club! For information send an SASE (business-size) to Queen's Own, P.O. Box 43143, Upper Montclair, NJ 07043.

THE SHIP WHO SANG IS NOT ALONE!

Anne McCaffrey, with Margaret Ball, Mercedes Lackey, and S.M. Stirling, explores the universe she created with her ground-breaking novel, *The Ship Who Sang*.

ELIZABETH MOON

THE DEED OF PAKSENARRION

Anne McCaffrey on Elizabeth Moon:

"She's a damn fine writer. The Deed of Pak-senarrion is fascinating. I'd use her book for research if I ever need a woman warrior. I know how they train now. We need more like this."

By the Compton Crook Award winning author of the Best First Novel of the Year